Novels by Charles Mercer

PACIFIC

Charles Mercer

SIMON AND SCHUSTER
NEW YORK

Copyright © 1981 by Charles Mercer
All rights reserved
including the right of reproduction
in whole or in part in any form
Published by Simon and Schuster
A Division of Gulf & Western Corporation
Simon & Schuster Building
Rockefeller Center
1230 Avenue of the Americas
New York, New York 10020

Manufactured in the United States of America

1   3   5   7   9   10   8   6   4   2

Library of Congress Cataloging in Publication Data

Mercer, Charles E
Pacific.
1. World War, 1939–1945—Fiction. I. Title.
PS3563.E73P3   813′.54   80-22418

ISBN 0-671-25587-8

To three who believed:
Alma Mercer
Mitch Douglas
Fred Hills

The history of a soldier's wound beguiles the pain of it.
——*Tristram Shandy*

1

In the early hours of December 7, 1941, it was my lot to be headquarters company duty officer at Hickam Field in Hawaii. Like most military chores, mine was dull. There was no guard to post; because of vague warnings from Washington of possible attack, the airplanes parked on the strips were under the watch of special Infantry details. All I had to do was account for the drunks who stumbled back from the pleasures of Honolulu.

The enlisted man assigned to be charge of quarters with me was a neatly uniformed young soldier of average size with a fiery thatch of red hair and green cat's eyes. When he reported to me in the company office after Saturday night chow, he threw a snappy salute and said, "Private First Class Andrew Jackson Jack happy to report to Lieutenant Boswick."

I responded with a sloppy three-fingered Boy Scout salute and told him, "Let's try to preserve some integrity around here. You are reporting, but you're not happy about it."

"Sir, I *am* happy to be here. My name, as I said, is Andrew Jackson Jack. Friends call me Red. It's a pleasure to be on duty with you, Lieutenant Boswick. I hear you're not just a photographer—you're an artist."

Disappointed in him, I said, "Just sit out there at the sergeant's desk and answer the phone calls, Private Jack. I'll sit in here and read my book. You don't have to kiss my ass."

He shrugged it off. "Have you applied for pilot training, sir?" Of course not; I was scared to death of flying. He was persistent: "But why be in the Army Air Corps, Lieutenant, if you don't want to be a pilot?"

"Being in the Air Corps prevents you from being in the Infantry."

He was not a jerk; he expressed intelligent horror of the Infantry. His failing was an adolescent wish to be a pilot.

"Think," I told him, "if you're capable of it. In this peacetime army a pilot faces a shorter life than an infantryman."

He was not worried about life-span. He was obsessed with becoming a pilot and railed against the injustice of the Army's requiring one to have at least two years of college education in order to qualify for flight school. An early peacetime draftee, he had a high school education and had been employed as an auto mechanic. A good rating in his IQ test had helped him realize his wish for Air Corps duty.

"I've had my application in for gunnery school almost a year," he said, "but nothing ever happens about it. I just float from motor pool to motor pool." He became accusatory. "*You* could become a pilot, Lieutenant Boswick. *You* have a commission. *You* have been to college."

Young though I was, I knew how badly educated I was. My father had forced me to go to a southern military college where we learned nothing but bad habits. At the end of my sentence there, I had "got a girl in trouble," as they used to say. My father had seen my second lieutenant's reserve commission as a means of spiriting me out of the trouble zone into active duty in Hawaii. My assignment to the Air Corps was sheer chance. Years of military prep schools and college had given me a loathing of the military life. Being the world's worst soldier, I was put in public relations. There, for the past several months, I had been indulging my interest in photography.

"Why are you frothing on like this?" I asked Red Jack.

He looked at me; he liked to affect the hard expression of a Dawn Patrol fighter pilot. "Frankly, Lieutenant, I'm trying to draw my case to the attention of higher authority."

"Your *case?*"

"My case for going to flight school, never mind gunnery school. Isn't this a democracy? I defy you, sir, to find anybody on this base who knows more about motors and mechanical things than I do. I'm twenty-two and getting older every day. I hear the General thinks a lot of you. Maybe I can interest you in my case, then maybe you can interest the General."

"A word of advice, Private Jack. You'll be a lot happier in the Army if the General never hears of you."

"He's really that bad? I heard he was pretty bad, but—"

"Please!" I glanced around, as if somebody might hear us. "The phone is ringing, Private Jack."

Our General really was that bad. Invariably he distorted truth; his life had become a game of dodging reality. I'd managed to get along with him—a short, stout man of mercurial temperament—by making him look tall and lean in my photos, transforming him from a chinless wonder into a sternly jowled warrior. (The trick was to shoot *up* at him.) He was so fond of my photography that he loaned me out to acquaintances as if I were a slave available for a day's labor. ("I'll loan you Boswick. He'll take pictures of your daughter's wedding you'll never forget. Have to charge you for films and developing of course. Can't cheat the Army, you know.") A favor for a friend of the General's was my coming assignment at 5 A.M. on Sunday morning when another officer would relieve me from my all-night duty. Meanwhile, I tried to grab a few hours shuteye on our temporary cots in the office.

About 1 A.M., Red and I were awakened by a wild-eyed enlisted man yelling, "There's a hooker loose in D Barracks!"

I thought he must be a hallucinating drunk. No prostitute could possibly get past the guards on *this* base to solicit the inmates. Nevertheless, I sent Red to investigate. Then, before I could doze off again, the phone rang.

"Boz!" It was my friend Ira Goldman, the General's staff sergeant. "I'm in the General's office. He can't sleep, so he won't let me sleep either. I've been taking dictation. Some nut just called him saying a prostitute is soliciting in the barracks. Put him in a tizzy. He's coming to see you about it and I'll be with him. Be careful, old buddy."

Our brigadier general had enslaved both Goldman and me. Goldman had graduated from Yale *summa cum laude* with a degree in engineering, then begun work for his master's before being drafted. In a typical Army misunderstanding it was believed he had a law degree rather than one in engineering. The General, deciding he wanted to add a kind of legal secretary to his staff, shared the misunderstanding that Goldman was a lawyer. In their first interview Goldman had tried to set him straight, but the General—like nearly everybody—heard only what he wanted to. He wanted Goldman to be a lawyer and to have this brilliant lawyer on his personal staff, so Goldman did his best to oblige and act like a lawyer.

Goldman's warning that the General was coming annoyed more than alarmed me. The General's worst failing was an inability to decide what was trivial, what important. Personally, I thought it trivial that a whore might have shown the enterprise to practice her profession for a night in headquarters company. Why should a brigadier general trot around trying to interfere?

I had just got my shoes on when the phone rang again. It was Red, shouting above a babble of voices and phonograph music: "Lieutenant, I'm in First Sergeant Yaromski's room on the second floor of D Barracks. He's gone to town. But nearly everybody else is here. The report is true. We have her cornered. I mean she's got us cornered."

"Get her out of there! Stop that noise! The General's on his way!"

"She won't leave till she has a drink!" Red yelled back. "Nobody here's got a bottle. She's high already, but wants more."

"Pipe down the noise and douse the lights. Then zip back here and pick up a bottle. Hurry!"

Although I was not an efficient officer, I could be practical: I knew in which file cabinet drawer the company commander hid a bottle. Just as I took it from the drawer, Goldman raised his voice outside in warning. I barely had time to thrust the bottle into a wastebasket before the General strode in, booming, "Boswick, are you running some kind of damn whorehouse here?"

Goldman, trying to divert the General, paused in the doorway and looked back. "Sir, what a great view of all your fighter planes lined up under the searchlights."

"Sure is, Goldman. Should have Boswick snap a picture of 'em."

Red galloped in, crying, "Lieutenant, gimme the bottle!"

"Bottle?" the General demanded. Red drew himself up and saluted twice, but the General paid him no attention. "What's this about a bottle, Boswick?"

"Sir, it's what we call 'bottleships for the war' games the men like to play when off duty."

I thought I displayed some cleverness, but Goldman—tall, dark, intense—winced at my remark and glowered at me. Still trying to divert the General, he said, "May I ask a question, sir? With your planes all packed together out there, don't they make a perfect target for incendiary attack?"

"No." The General went outside to gaze at his airplanes, giving me the chance to snatch the bottle out of the wastebasket and give it to Red, who tucked it under an arm and ran off like a football player bound for the goal line. "See, Goldman," the General went on, "the planes are out in the open and patrolled by guards so they're safe from saboteurs.''

"Yes sir, but I'm thinking about air attack."

The General's small eyes appeared to bulge. "Just where would these enemy planes be coming from?"

"From enemy carriers," Goldman said. "Put yourself in the place of the Japanese."

"By God, Goldman, that's a downright unpatriotic remark."

"All right, sir," Goldman continued patiently, "then put *me* in the place of the Japanese. If I were they and wanted all those industrial riches of Southeast Asia as badly as they seem to, I might launch simultaneous attacks by carriers against us here and in the Philippines. And I'd do it early on a Sunday morning like this when everybody is asleep or hung over."

The General made a hooting sound. "Do they teach you asinine ideas like that at Harvard Law School? Now let's get on to something practical. Has a whore somehow infiltrated the base and got into headquarters company? This is real trouble. I can't imagine a worse stain on my record. The first one I want to question is Sergeant Yaromski. I don't trust that man. He used to be in the Infantry. Pimping would come natural to him. We'll go to his quarters and take him by surprise. Maybe catch him in the act, eh?"

I spoke quickly: "Yaromski's out on pass, sir. Thought I heard yelling in A Barracks. Will check. No need to trouble you, General."

"No trouble," he said. "Can't sleep anyway. If I catch a whore, I'll court-martial the whole barracks. Come along, Goldman."

As they went toward A Barracks, I dashed to D and up the stairs. The voices had stilled; the music, sounding louder than ever, came from Yaromski's phonograph. ". . . pretty girl is like a melody . . ." blared through the walls. I flung open the door and stopped dead.

A pretty, chestnut-haired young woman was dancing slowly on Yaromski's big table while holding a glass of our captain's booze. A score of men crowded into the room and gaped at her as she let her skirt fall, revealing red briefs and shapely legs. Her eyes were glazed, and her fixed smile and radiant expression recalled every woman who ever danced and stripped in an American burlesque house, and every man who ever watched. Red, having forgotten he was in charge of quarters, stared along with everyone else as she began to unbutton her blouse.

Recovering from my surprise, I turned off the phonograph. The men groaned and cried out in protest. "The General is on the way," I announced. "I'll have to take the name of everybody who isn't out of this room in ten seconds." They fled, like a thundering herd.

The woman smiled at me. "Lookit the pretty second lieutenant." She had the flat tone of the American midlands. "Lieutenant, you want the two-buck job, or the five, or the eight?"

"All I want is to get you out of here before the General comes in and sends you to jail."

"If'n I go to jail," she said, "I'll take along the ten men in this barracks that already had me. And him." She pointed at Red, the only man remaining in the room with me. "The redhead here is the pimp that sneaked me in."

"Hey! I never . . . ," Red Jack responded angrily, but he had more cause to be frightened than angry, for the General was irrational enough to believe whatever she said and hang him.

"Get down off that table and the hell out of here," I told her.

Her grin turned wicked. "I scream real good. Wanna hear me?"

"Boswick!" The General's voice reverberated through the barracks. *"Where the hell are you, Boswick?"* Now the area had fallen dead silent and the last lights except ours were suddenly extinguished.

I leaned out the window. "Just checking, sir." My voice sounded shrill and squeaky. "All present or accounted for in D Barracks, General."

"Tell you what, honey pot," the woman said to me, "fill this here glass an' fill that one. You drink that an' I'll drink this. If'n you finish before me, I'll go real quiet. But if'n I finish first, I'll go back to work in this here barracks."

Having little choice, I decided to believe her. The glasses belonging to Yaromski held about eight ounces; the captain's bottle contained 96-proof bourbon. I considered myself a capable drinker, though not a suicidal one. But with the General bearing down upon us, I told Red to fill the glasses to the brim.

He said, "It'll kill you, Lieutenant. Don't do it."

I turned to the woman. "Sister, take that glass in your hand, and when Red says, 'Drink,' pour it down the hatch."

I gulped the bourbon like water; it blazed a trail of fire from my tongue to the pit of my stomach. I slammed my glass on the table where the woman still stood, drinking and gasping. The effects of the drink on me were almost as instantaneous as cyanide: the room began to tilt and turn around me. I heard the woman uttering a hoarse, gagging sound. She staggered across the table, which had been set close to the open window. Dropping her unfinished glass of whiskey, she leaned out the window—to vomit, I thought.

Instead, she began to flap her arms like a heron in a Southern marsh on a spring morning. A girl with such pretty legs and tail deserved to fly if she wanted to, I thought.

"Ladybug, ladybug, fly away home," I called to her drunkenly. "Your house is on fire an' your children will burn."

She looked around at me almost wistfully. "*Whut* did you say, pretty boy?"

"I said . . ." I could not remember what I had said. "Well, if a girl wants to fly, she has the right to."

"Right!" she cried. "I fly!" Then, waving her arms, she toppled out the window.

"Jesus Christ, Lieutenant Boswick, she just killed herself! How we going to explain this?"

"She forgot her bag." I tossed it out the window after her. "And her shoes." I tossed them. "She should have put her skirt on." I threw it, too, as the room spun faster around me.

Red bolted for the stairs, and I went after him. Part way down the flight I tripped and fell to the bottom. The sound of my tumble was thunderous, but I felt nothing. Red picked me up, and I lurched outside after him to view the body of the dead woman sprawled on the ground.

"Poor child." I felt close to tears. "She's a beautiful thing."

In the distance I dimly heard the General bellow, "*Boswick!*"

"I would have loved to have the chance to love her," I said to Red. "There's not enough love left for anybody any more."

The body stirred, and I knelt beside her. "Are you in pain?" My eyes filled with tears. "Lie still, dear, we'll send for an ambulance."

She sat up slowly and said, "Lousy lieutenant son of a bitch pushin' me out the window. You screw as good as you drink?" Then she got to her feet, fumbled into her skirt and shoes, picked up her bag, and disappeared into the darkness.

"Did this," I asked Red, "really happen?"

"Yes sir, Lieutenant Boswick, it really did. She's gone. She just got up and walked away. Now let's get you to your cot. I'll explain you fell down the stairs and have a concussion."

What seemed to be much later in my life, as I lay on the office cot,

I heard the General's heavy voice: "Concussion or no concussion, Boswick has to take off at five hundred hours. Make sure he does, Private. Drive him yourself if necessary."

Then Goldman's voice: "Shouldn't we have the dispensary send somebody to check him over?"

"Pointless," the General said. "Everybody at the dispensary is drunk at this hour. At least we know that was a false report about a whore on the loose in the company area."

"Yes," Goldman said, "we can sleep in peace, General. No hooker invaded us this morning."

When Red awakened me at 4:45 A.M., I had a ghastly headache. With his aid I got my shoes on and swallowed the aspirin and black coffee he brought me. A grumbling lieutenant arrived to perform as duty officer, and when the sedan came from the motor pool, Red decided to take over as driver. It was the act of a true friend, and I felt much in need of one just then.

Red loaded my photographic equipment into the car and asked where we were going.

"To Pearl Harbor," I told him, slumping in the seat. "I'm on another lend-lease job for some Navy captain. Friend of the General, who wants to borrow me." I sighed.

"What for?"

"I think I'm supposed to take pictures of the guard making morning colors aboard some battleship. *Nevada,* that's it."

"Why so early?"

"Has to be done on Sunday morning so I won't interfere with important naval functions."

It was a beautiful dawning over the green sugarcane fields of Oahu as Red and I were passed onto the Pearl Harbor base. We boarded a launch which started us across the blue bay toward the *Nevada* while a red sun rising over the Tantalus Mountains revealed the might and splendor of the United States Pacific Fleet: seventy combat ships and twenty-four other vessels which serviced them.

In the midst of this armada, anchored well out of the main channel, was the largest, most beautiful private yacht I had ever seen. Red exclaimed at its beauty: "Holy shit—white as an angel and dripping minks and jewels! What's *that* doing here?"

A launch crewman cursed it and its owner, one Ivory Spence. "Son of a bitch sailed in yesterday. Some absent-minded jerk opened the boom to let him come right in. Spence says he's here to protest the

Navy's preparations for war. And the fucking brass is such a bunch of cowards they don't throw him out because he's supposed to be the world's richest man.''

Ivory Spence was one of the dozen richest men in the world and certainly the most publicized of living pacifists. He had inherited a fortune in Texas oil that had been metastasized around the world. Then, at forty-two, he suddenly denounced his money as ill-gotten gain; but he did not give it back because, he said, he could not decide whom to give it back to. After divorcing his third wife, he proclaimed himself a pacifist, a recovered alcoholic, a Baptist, a vegetarian, a celibate, and a passionate sailor determined to win every ocean race he could.

''There's the son of a bitch now,'' the sailor said. The helmsman turned our launch off course to pass the stern of the yacht, *Dove of Peace,* so that they could thumb their noses at the unhappy-looking man dressed in white who lounged in the fantail and refused to acknowledge our existence.

Some of the battleships were moored in pairs along the shore of Ford Island, but the *Nevada* was by herself at the northern end of the row. There was no hitch in the arrangements. We climbed the ladder of the old, gray battleship, Red lugging my stuff. An ensign greeted me, explained the Navy ritual of making morning colors, and granted me the freedom of the ship. He was the Officer of the Deck on that obscure Sunday morning watch, and he looked much too young to become a hero.

I found a good angle, loaded my camera, and figured out a second position. The band ever ready—even early on Sunday morning—blared a ruffle and flourish. Through my sight I found the face of a young drummer: tired, bored, as hung-over as I.

The men stood rigidly at attention while the band struck up ''The Star-Spangled Banner.'' Suddenly I was distracted by something strange astern. Planes were flying in low—too low. Probably those redneck Army pilots buzzing us again.

It was then that I saw the white wakes of torpedoes. And over on Battleship Row, there rose a heavy *crump—crump—crump.* The big dreadnaughts—the *Arizona, Tennessee, West Virginia, Oklahoma*—seemed to wince and shudder like stricken humans. Black columns of smoke gushed up and the empty sky was suddenly filled with screaming planes which darted, dived, flew high and low, firing guns and hurling bombs into ships and buildings.

Dimly I heard the band playing. Never had the national anthem throbbed so slowly. The eyes of musicians and color guard rolled whitely at the young ensign Officer of the Deck who stood calm and straight-backed.

At last I realized these planes were Japanese. I ignored the ceremony and shot my camera frantically at the enemy. While the *Nevada* band still labored, an enemy plane dived in, machine guns blazing, trying to strafe the American sailors at attention. Suddenly, through the din of guns, bombs and blaring band music, came the unmistakable, piercing cry of Tarzan of the Apes. It came from Red, who had tilted back his head and was drumming his chest like Johnny Weissmuller himself. Thus alerted, everybody broke ranks and, as his cry died away, scattered like windblown sand to their battle stations. Red ran too.

Ordinarily I'm one of the world's leading cowards; in time of danger my thoughts center on self-preservation. But with a camera in my hands at a scene worth recording on film, I can act foolishly brave. That was one of those times. I was shooting my camera as if it were a rifle, first at the shuddering, burning battleships and then at the strafing planes.

There was a tremendous explosion down the row and the *Arizona* heaved up, then sank like a stone. Slowly the *Oklahoma* was turning turtle while scores of her crew scrambled onto the *Maryland,* moored inboard of her.

The *Nevada* was hit—by bomb or torpedo—and the deck shook as in an earthquake. Through the cries, the din, the rattle of enemy guns and roar of enemy planes, loudspeakers sounded the harsh summons of General Quarters. Dazed men groped through the smoke, shouting incoherently. Stumbling around and trying to get free of the smoke in order to take more pictures, I came on Red helping pass ammunition to the crew of a 3-inch gun. The men were remarkably grouped, as if posed, in a combination of stress and energy. I shot a picture.

In a moment I realized that the *Nevada* had cast loose and was making way down the bay. Apparently the intent was to get her out to the open sea. A fresh wave of attackers roared in firing at us while I shot back with all my remaining film. Enveloped in smoke and spray, the old *Nevada* rolled toward the harbor entrance like a ghost pursued by a swarm of angry spirits. This scene could best be shot from shore, I knew, but alas I was stuck in the vortex of events. Going below, I wandered among confused and angry men who could not understand my quest for more film.

At last there was a jarring lurch and the battleship seemed to go

dead in the water. In terror of being trapped below, I hurried topside
—better to die in the open. We were broached close to shore, and
groups were being assembled to fight a blaze in the stern. A man said
that someone at headquarters ashore had ordered the *Nevada* to
beach lest she sink and block the main channel.

By that time the attack had ended and the sky was empty except
for a few flecks of smoke from bursting antiaircraft shells.

I still did not feel this was *my* war. I knew I had witnessed something big—and terrible—but somehow all I could think of was my
pictures. I possessed an invaluable record, and I wanted to get it
away to safety as fast as possible.

It's not easy to extricate yourself from a burning battleship which
is involved in the outbreak of a war. I swam well enough that I could
easily have made it to shore, but what about my precious films?
Finding Red again, I explained the problem. At first he scarcely
seemed to hear me. Cap gone, shirt torn, he was streaked with sweat
and grime, but his face shone with the glory of battle. He had *partic-
ipated;* I could see he now felt it was *his* war. Yet he had the sense to
understand how I felt about my films and the loyalty to realize he had
been assigned to my mission. He also had creative ideas.

"Lieutenant," he said, "I know where there's a small life raft.
Let's use it to get the films to shore nice and dry."

We hurried to load films and equipment aboard the raft. The ensign
who had been Officer of the Deck when all hell broke loose suddenly
came upon us. His left arm was bandaged from a bullet wound. But
that was not why he would one day become a full admiral in the U.S.
Navy. Neither would he become a full admiral just because he had
acted bravely and wisely in the battle. I think that ensign eventually
became an admiral because he said to me: "Lieutenant, those pictures you took are the property of the U.S. Navy."

And because, even as I was arguing with him, he had three brawny
sailors take the film from Red and me.

It was a couple of hours before Red and I were able to head for
shore aboard a launch carrying wounded men. The carnage everywhere was awful. The chief American naval base in the Pacific looked
a shambles. Fires blazed on ships and ashore in a stench of oil smoke,
cordite, something like putrid meat. Every vessel in Pearl Harbor
appeared to have been sunk or hit.

Except for one. Spence's yacht, *Dove of Peace,* unscathed by even
a single bullet, had put out its boats to rescue men afloat in the water.

As we passed the yacht, I saw Spence at the rail looking more self-righteous than horrified by what had happened.

Eventually Red and I made our way back to our sedan and found it undamaged. It was almost dark by the time we returned to the field through traffic jams of hysterical people.

The slaughter at the field was almost as terrible as on Battleship Row. Dozens of planes had been destroyed by air attack, just as Goldman had suggested they might be. The armed guards had been killed or wounded, and the others had watched helplessly as the dive bombers dropped incendiary bombs.

As I looked across the field, I saw the General wandering around the strips among the wreckage of his airplanes, weeping like a child who had lost his toys, and I did not want to go near him.

2

The confusion of the military in Hawaii following the Japanese attack on Pearl Harbor and the airfields was incredible. People pretended to know what they were doing, but scarcely anyone did.

Headquarters Company, though not officially transferred out of the Air Corps (soon to be renamed the Air Force), was sent away off to the west coast of Oahu to perform Infantry patrol duty. Since we had lost nearly all our airplanes to the incendiary bombing and strafing of the Japanese, it must have appeared to the head brass that Headquarters Company was unnecessary. Actually, of course, it was vitally needed to bring some order from the chaos.

In my capacity as Court Photographer, I was listed as executive officer of Headquarters Company. I avoided all duties there except to sign or initial papers the first sergeant or the company clerk put in front of me. To my disgust, however, I was sent off on patrol duty because the General momentarily forgot me. I guess he had his own problems. Somebody said he was relieved of duties pending an investigation and sent to Fort Derussy, which lay between Honolulu and a thinly populated area known as Waikiki.

Headquarters Company, including me, rode in trucks through the pineapple fields to the wild west coast where we bivouacked in a yucca grove behind a coral slope. Apparently someone high up had decided it was a site of possible Japanese invasion.

We company officers made ourselves as comfortable as possible in large tents. The enlisted men patrolled constantly, always afoot, scrambling over coral and through brush by day and night, armed with Springfield rifles—a weapon which many of them never had touched before.

Red Jack did not seem to mind it much. Now that history had snatched him from obscurity, he was willing to sleep under a pup tent on the rock-hard ground. But he griped as much as everybody else about the lousy food.

Suddenly he and I were friends. It began with his imitations of Tarzan. He gave the Ape Man's cry perfectly, and made prodigious leaps while telling and acting out some of the scenes from the movies.

I missed my friend Goldman. He had been spared bivouac in order to serve as legal counselor to the General while our commander was preparing to face the investigating board being sent from Washington.

Red, to my surprise, was married and he gradually confided some of his history. One night when he and I were complaining about the latest dinner of soggy rice and hoary ham, he told me about his wife Rosemarie, a voluptuous, beautiful girl of eighteen. He showed me snapshots, and I understood why he longed for her. He had met her eight months ago while on a weekend pass in California, and had fallen in love instantly. She was a very special person, Red said. He claimed he could look clean through her deep blue eyes and see strange anxieties lurking on the other side. She was not exactly brilliant, he said, yet neither was she another dumb blonde: her lips were too generous, her jaw too firm for stupidity. When he met her, she seemed devoutly religious. They had been married only three months, then had four months of enforced separation, and Red wondered if she might forever be a stranger.

Rosemarie Hicks and her wacky mother had been members of a tiny California sect called the Pentecostal Church of the True Redeemer, a depressingly pious group opposed to all forms of pleasure while they prepared for the imminent Second Coming. It was obvious to Red when he met her that Rosemarie was virginal and would resist maybe forever men's efforts to overcome that unfortunate state. He thought at once of a stratagem—and was surprised no male had thought of it before. That Saturday night he went to the Pentecostal services and there, before Rosemarie, her mother, and many others, he announced himself possessed of the spirit of the True Redeemer and declared he was stopping forever his sinful ways of womanizing and boozing. From there it was an easy step to a tasteless Sunday chicken dinner prepared by the widow Hicks.

At that point a less tenacious man than Red might have abandoned the pursuit. No one ever had been more impossible than Mrs. Hicks. She was crazy, but Rosemarie did not seem to realize it, and she passively wore the long, shapeless dresses her mother prescribed as a means of warding off lustful men. Indeed, many a man must have failed to realize that Rosemarie had a lovely body under all that sackcloth. But Red, with his X-ray gaze, penetrated her disguise and was determined to make the conquest. It took him four more weekend passes to get her to the altar of the Pentecostal Church, and her submission to him that night was reluctant. It was, in truth, tearful and disappointing. Red was, nonetheless, as optimistic as he was tenacious. He was reminded of the time in high school when he wrote a play for the dramatic club and was told: "The material is all there, it just has to be organized."

Nevertheless, he was pleased to discover that Rosemarie wanted the marriage, even if only as a means of escaping from her mother. She was glad to move away from her mother and take a job clerking in an Army PX. Red felt he was making some progress as instructing her in the marriage arts when the Army spoiled everything by shipping him to Hawaii.

Rosemarie stayed behind. Though pregnant, she said she never wanted to go home to her mama again. Red didn't worry about his wife's fidelity the way so many men did. Within a couple of months she'd had a miscarriage and written him two dark blue letters. He replied encouragingly and passionately, reminding her that the syndicated poet Edward Guest had written: "If at first you don't succeed, try—try again." Though she had not answered, he was confident she would. She was as true to him as skin to flesh.

There in bivouac on the west coast he composed letter after passionate letter to her. A lyrical aspect in his nature found nothing banal in such similes as her skin to silk, her hair to spun gold, her breasts to ripe melons.

A week after we went to bivouac, First Sergeant Yaromski came blundering through the brush bellowing for Red, who hastily presented himself. Yaromski, an intelligent, large man shaped somewhat like a seal, had spent fifteen years in the Infantry before transferring to Air—a move he regretted vociferously after a run-in with the General. Reared on the Chicago West Side by Polish parents, he could speak in the accents of an Oxford don when he chose:

"My lad, do you have a picture of your wife?"

Red always carried a snapshot of Rosemarie. In fact, he carried three of them and had more in his footlocker. Pleased that Yaromski suddenly wished to be familiar, he said, "Sure, Sarge," and handed him three. Yaromski studied them solemnly while Red gazed admiringly around his shoulder and said, "Simply gorgeous, isn't she?"

"Charming," Yaromski replied. "Do you have a marriage certificate?"

"Not with me."

"I just came from company headquarters," Yaromski said. "She was there."

Red was aghast. "Rosemarie at the *Field?*"

Yaromski nodded. "She came looking for you. She's on a cruise and—"

"Rosemarie on a *cruise?*" He was close to shrieking.

Yaromski dropped his cultivated English accent: "Whyn't ya bastids nevah ansah ya lettahs? Ya wife comin' alla way ta the Field lookin for ya. She comin' right inna compny area. Pretty chick comin' inna the base like that mighten get *took,* ya know wot I mean."

Red did indeed know what he meant and insisted on a forty-eight hour pass into Honolulu.

Yaromski was reputed to be unimpressed by any woman, but Rosemarie had made a dent in him. He could regale us by the hour with his bizarre and obscene conquests of all manner of women under all manner of circumstances, but never had he known an enlisted man's wife to *cruise* from the States and march onto a post as if she were the United States Army Band. Besides, he admitted privately to me, Rosemarie was truly beautiful. He asked me to authorize the pass for Red Jack because the guy surely would go AWOL and lose his stripe if he didn't see his wife at once. Yaromski had personally conducted her to a reliable taxi at the gate and paid the driver to take the poor sweet soul back to Honolulu where she was staying at a place called the Missionary Hotel on Beretania Street.

"Anna nother thing," Yaromski told Red, "get ya wife offn Beretania Street. Ain't no place for a wife ta be. Ain't no place ta be inna place called da Mishnary Hotel. Sounds like ya know wot I mean."

Only later would I learn from Red what actually happened after he boarded the bus for town. On his way to Honolulu, Red remained fixated by the word *cruise.* Where had Rosemarie got the money to go on it? What was a cruise doing here now that there was a war? A cruise that came should be a cruise that went, so why hadn't she went with it? In downtown Honolulu service men scrambled by the dozens from the packed bus as it wound a serpentine way along Hotel, King and River Streets, where throngs milled in and out of movie houses, bars, restaurants, shooting galleries, trinket stores, shops reeking of rotted fish and vegetables. Dark stairways led to upper floors from whose windows whores leaned during their early supper break, most of them unfathomable mixtures of the Orient, with here and there a vacant Occidental face.

At Beretania Street Red leaped off. The smells of rancid grease and incense mingling with rotted fish in that crowded area usually made him think with pleasure how far he had journeyed from the drab New Jersey town of Glenwood. But in this late afternoon hour in the mellow golden light the smells became unpleasant. He felt queasy, almost scared. Where was Rosemarie? Why had she come here to interrupt his life in the Army? Was it disloyal to think such thoughts?

Two MPs closed in on him and demanded his pass. They took their time in studying it, and one said, "Okay, soldier. Just be off the street before nine. Curfew is twenty-one hundred hours." He asked directions to the Missionary Hotel. One just stared at him, but the other gestured straight ahead.

The Missionary Hotel had a sign so small that he almost missed it. His heart began to knock with anticipation, and then he halted as the odor of cheap perfume assailed him. This hotel might not be precisely a whorehouse, but he guessed from its smell it was a hangout for whores. He heard the sound of a woman's voice speaking resonantly, as if a radio had been turned loud.

Stepping into the tiny lobby, Red halted again. Three ugly, aging, Occidental whores sat in a row on an old sofa gaping at a woman on a high stool behind the clerk's desk who expounded to them in strident tones. The woman was Rosemarie and she was reading the passage from Revelation that her wacky Bible-spouting Ma had shouted out the first time Red went to Sunday chicken dinner:

"And the woman was arrayed in purple and scarlet color, and decked with gold and precious stones and pearls, having a golden cup in her hand full of abominations and filthiness of her fornication: And upon her forehead was a name written, MYSTERY, BABYLON THE GREAT, THE MOTHER OF HARLOTS AND ABOMINATIONS OF THE EARTH. . . ."

Rosemarie sang out the words as if they were an operatic "Anvil Chorus." Poor soul, he thought, she'd gone nuts, just like her Ma; when he'd married her, his lust had made him clean forget that insanity might be hereditary.

"Now listen to this—" Rosemarie laid her words like whiplashes on the startled whores— *"The beast that thou sawest was, and is not; and shall ascend out of the bottomless pit, and go into perdition; and they that dwell on the earth shall wonder, whose names were not written in the book of life from the foundation of the world, when they behold the beast that was, and is not, and yet is. . . ."*

Oh, lovely Rosemarie, whose plain gray Chambray dress failed to disguise the generous thrust of breasts. Instead of pity for her insanity, Red felt desire for her body.

"Rosemarie!"

She looked round at him, crinkled up her face like a child, and burst into tears. Then he was kissing her while the whores cheered and Rosemarie used the hotel desk as a barricade against his assault.

"Rosemarie!" he cried. "Throw me one of your curves and I'll hit the deck! What're you doing here?"

She had spent a quarter in a store raffle in Sausalito that offered a cruise from San Francisco to Hawaii as first prize, and guess who won? He'd forgotten how white and pretty her teeth were when she grinned.

"I mean what're you doing *here?*"

The ship had arrived in Honolulu on December 8.

"Rosemarie, why did you get off it?"

"To see you. Why else?"

"Then the boat went off and left you stranded?"

Her face became grave and she shook her head. "Red, I sold my passage back for a hundred dollars to a lady who wanted to go home. I aim to get a good job here."

Red felt a strange foreboding. "So as to be near me?"

"Well—" She looked dubious. "I want to have a good talk with you about a lot of things. Winning that cruise prize was a real sign to me. See, Ma got it in her mind to come live with me and I just can't take any more of that."

"I understand. But just now you sounded like the crazy old lady herself with that Bible stuff."

"I guess I yearn to believe in something. I came here because the lady who bought my ticket lived here. Mrs. Braucher, she manages the place, gives me a free room for tending the desk. The girls— Well — We're friends. Sometimes they get me riled up and I carry on like that with Bible readings. They like it. It's all that stuff about the body and pure spirit. You know?"

"No, I don't know," Red said. "Let's go to your room."

She shook her head firmly. "No sir. It's a terrible place, walls as thin as paper. But it's free. I've been writing you and phoning you and waiting for you to take me out of here. I'll fetch my things.'' Her long and lovely legs carried her up the steps two at a time.

The ugliest whore said to him, "Honey, that girl could be pure dynamite. Who're you to have her all to yourself?"

"Me?" He blinked. "Why I guess I'm the Red Jack of Hearts." And then, just for the hell of it, he did a gangling little soft-shoe until they burst into applause.

When Rosemarie came down carrying her two battered valises they went out into the street crowds and the suffocating stench of rancid food. "I hate it around here," she said. "It's like a honky carnival. And they call it *Hawaii?*"

Suddenly he hated it too. He had less than ten dollars, but she had more than fifty, all of which she gave to him.

"Now," he said, "we can afford to go to Waikiki and get us a big dinner and an expensive room with thick walls."

"Where we can talk," said Rosemarie.

Thus it happened that they found themselves on a Number 8 bus riding along Kalakaua beside the flashing sea where sails winked in the declining sun. Red put a hand on Rosemarie's thigh, and, though she moved away from him, he felt as content as he ever had. The view of the Pacific was magnificent, with the pregnant bellies of trade clouds exuding a golden nimbus and the deep green sea flinging waves in creamy scallops. A delicately balanced youth rode a surfboard on a towering crest while a poised brown girl watched from the beach.

A grandiose feeling settled on Red, like a crown on a monarch's head. It seemed a natural feeling far out here in the world's largest ocean, which pounded the shores of innumerable distant peoples and often lulled one into a false sense of security. *I am the king,* thought Red, *but who can find me in this vastness at the four corners of the trade winds?* He was not thinking lucidly. Yet he rarely did except while repairing something mechanical. Thus far his experiences in life had not made him wise; they had been, rather, signs of his fumbling search for wisdom.

People boarded and left the bus, but Red and Rosemarie rode on forever.

"Fort Derussy," the driver announced, stopping again.

They looked out at a lush Army preserve defended by well tended banks of orchids and poinsettias instead of gray stone walls.

After countless stops to let passengers on and off, the driver finally announced "Royal Hawaiian Hotel."

"Come on." Red picked up Rosemarie's luggage and they went slowly up the long path to the entrance of the Royal Hawaiian. The moment Red stepped to the desk to request a room he knew by the frosty glare of a clerk that he' had come to enemy country. There would be no room in this inn for Jesus Himself if He came as an enlisted man. Then Red committed the error of showing his money and demanding with bravado why it wasn't good there. Of course the clerk reproved him icily by explaining that his money was perfectly good but the hotel was *booked full*. It seemed that the dining room was booked full too.

"If this was a lousy movie," Red said to Rosemarie, "some rich, good American would step up and fix everything for us. But it's not a lousy movie, it's the lousy lobby of the Royal Hawaiian Hotel."

"I have our marriage certificate with me," Rosemarie said. "Would it help if I showed it to them?"

"Oh God, please, Rosemarie!" Red passed a hand across his clammy brow.

"I think you're aiming too high," she said.

They were no more warmly received at the Halekulani Hotel than at the Royal Hawaiian.

"Do you suppose there are any tourist homes?" asked Rosemarie.

"No." Red was furious. "There aren't even funeral homes in Waikiki."

They ate a dinner of hamburgers and milk shakes at the refreshment counter of a variety store where a waitress reminded Red that all enlisted men must be off the streets by nine o'clock. As they left the store he bought a couple of blankets and said they'd spend the night on the beach.

By the time I learned what was going through Rosemarie's mind, she had become quite a different woman.

She began to be angry with Red when he paid out $8.95 of their scant funds for the blankets. Never had she heard of such waste. Besides, she did not want to spend the night on a beach. Her resentment grew as she hobbled behind him just beyond the waves. She took off her shoes and stockings, but it was no fun going barefoot. Though the night was luminous with moonlight, she kept stumbling over things that hurt her feet.

"A thing to think about is pity," she called after Red.

"What?" He looked around at her, sounding annoyed.

"Oh, skip it." She was going to quarrel with him, the biggest quarrel of her life, but she wasn't starting it right. "Ever since I got here you haven't said you love me."

"You know good and well I do."

That still wasn't the way to start the quarrel. She couldn't care less whether he said he loved her, for she had decided she didn't love him. She was trying to figure out just *when* had she decided she didn't love him. Was it before she married him—or after? Before he went away—or after? Before the miscarriage—or after? There was something mighty sweet about Red—and something awful selfish, as shown by his horniness.

She lagged farther. "Where are we going?"

"To some private nook of leaf and sand."

Why did he talk silly a lot of the time? Nobody talked like that. She made her tone sarcastic: "How nice. The Leaf and Sand Hotel."

"Right, Rosemarie. Well said." She could almost *hear* him grinning as he trudged into the darkness with her suitcases.

"Don't put on airs with me!" she yelled suddenly. "Hell, you're nothing but a garage mechanic."

Red was shocked to the core, for he had never heard Rosemarie swear. He put down the bags and walked back to her. She realized he was not angry, just curious. "Rosemarie, did I ever claim to be anything but a mechanic?"

"All the time!" she flared. "It's all the time in your mind you're somebody else. Like Tarzan. Like you lots of times say you want to be an actor. Like you're the world's greatest lover boy. Like you're going to be the world's greatest pilot."

He turned from her with an air of weariness and resumed plodding along the shore.

She followed slowly, still seeking the precise, deadly way to begin the winning of the quarrel. There were sure signs the Lord was on her side, leading her toward some unknown Promised Land. How could she explain the signs to Red? First there came the sign that she no longer could bear to live with Mama or even be kind to her. Then came the sign of her miscarriage and her never wanting to be pregnant again. Next was the sign of winning the free cruise to Hawaii. And finally there was the sign of feeling troubled rather than happy when she met Red in Honolulu. Surely all these signs pointed to the true fact she must start a new life free of both Mama and him.

It was, she thought, the only way she ever would *be* somebody. Red never would have the money to give her some of the fine things she longed for, just as Mama never could offer her much. Only *she*

herself could get the comforts and pleasures she wanted, and even
the least of them would be denied her if she remained the wife of this
—this *garage mechanic* who seemed to want to keep her knocked
up.

"The trouble with you," she said, catching up with him, "is you
don't have pity."

He ignored her, trudging on like some single-minded Wise Man
toward an invisible Bethlehem. The waves crashed against the shore
and the night wind rattled the fronds of palms so that she had to shout
to make herself heard:

"No, I don't believe in any Second Coming! It was pity for Ma
kept me with her all that time. She went crazy with grief after Pa
died. You hear me? Crazy with grief! It's why she turned religious. I
pitied her so. What else was I to do but stay with her? But I've had
enough of that. I've run out of pity for everybody."

He seemed not to hear her, and she dropped down, hugging her
knees against the growing chill. After a long time he came back and
she told him, "Sit down, I want to talk to you." He obeyed. "I don't
want to get pregnant ever again." She was surprised at the cool way
she spoke her mind. "It's no fun having a miscarriage. But that's not
the point. I have to support myself, and I can't if I get pregnant again.
You know yourself, Red, you don't and can't support me."

He lay down, sulking, she thought. It was unlike him to sulk, however, so maybe he just couldn't think what to say. Wrapping herself
in a blanket, she lay down a distance from him, straining her gaze up
at the flood of stars beyond the moon and wishing she could count
them. After a while, hearing a man and woman talking and laughing
in the darkness, they got up and went on.

It seemed to Rosemarie they walked for hours, never breaking their
stubborn silence, sometimes wandering away from the sea to avoid
coral or brush, but always returning to it. They came at last to a small
sandy beach which appeared isolated from everything human. Wrapping her blanket tightly about her, Rosemarie dropped in numbed
fatigue, and the thud of waves washed her quickly into sleep.

Something moved across her left leg and she awoke with a start.
Her first thought was a snake, and she nearly screamed. Then she
realized it was only Red's hand. "Stop it," she said.

"Please." He sounded close to whimpering. "Please, Rosemarie."

"Not unless you've got something so I don't get pregnant."

"But I do!"

She still did not want to because it would make her unfaithful to her unspoken vow to end their marriage. She argued with him, but he always was a powerful persuader. He began to fool around, and she began to get bothered. Next she knew she was out of the blanket and out of her clothing, stark naked and protesting loudly.

"Liar!" she shrieked suddenly, trying to fight him off. He had not been prepared to save her from another pregnancy. But it was too late. "Dirty liar!" She drove a knee into his groin. Red, howling, rolled away. Springing to her feet, she raced from him and away from the sea.

She didn't care that she was naked. What mattered was that she might be pregnant again. Though her bare feet might be running over jagged coral, she felt no pain. All she felt was the will to escape from Red forever.

The Lord must have been on her side, for she found herself on a sandy road, running fast—faster as she heard Red coming behind and yelling to her. Ahead, the lights of a car approached, and she began waving frantically. Whoever was in that car could not be worse than Red, her mortal enemy.

3

Early that evening while Red and Rosemarie rode the bus to Waikiki, Goldman was at Fort Derussy lecturing our General on how to conduct himself before the investigating board. Goldman told me later that he was trying hard to feel sorry for him, but found it difficult because the General was such a cheat and a liar. For instance, something had gone wrong with him—maybe his balance fluid—that made him unable to pilot a plane anymore, yet he wore wings and collected flight pay by having competent pilots take him up for rides.

"Once more, sir," Goldman told him, "look at me as a member of the board. Now I ask you, 'General, do you mean to say you had absolutely no hint of the Japanese attack on Oahu?' "

The General made a bleating sound. "Please, Goldman, not that part. You've no idea what it's like to have your career blasted at the age of fifty."

Goldman sensed that the General was peering into the yawning abyss of his future in the face of a possible dishonorable discharge for reasons he felt beyond his control. Yet he, like other high-ranking Army and Navy officers in Hawaii, had received warning from Washington, where code-breakers were reading Japanese diplomatic messages. Hadn't Goldman himself suggested the possibility of an air attack early Sunday morning, and hadn't the General scorned the idea?

Several other ranking officers who had heard from the General about "Goldman's warning" would gladly have sent Goldman to the stockade for such smart-ass insubordination. There was even a rumor circulating that Goldman—variously referred to as Goldstein or Goldfarb or Goodman or that goddam Jew—had actually predicted *the date, even the very hour* of the Japanese sneak attack.

Curious things had happened to Goldman since that night years before when the Secretary of War had dipped into a goldfish bowl before a crowd in Washington and come up with his draft number on the very first scoop. The country was not then at war, and few believed it would be. All agreed it was ridiculous for a young man of Goldman's distinguished talents to leave Massachusetts Institute of Technology, where he was working for a master's degree in civil engineering, and wander around parade grounds picking up cigarette butts. All agreed, that is, but Goldman's local draft board and the draft appeals board.

He had no influential friends; his father ran a dry-cleaning establishment in Brooklyn. He and his family tried to think of him as spearheading a Jewish crusade against the maniac Hitler, and they believed that the Army would put his training to constructive use in the Corps of Engineers. It was a difficult faith to maintain, however, as he stayed on kitchen police duty at Camp Dix for day after dragging day.

Goldman found it even more difficult to clear up the misunderstanding that he was a lawyer. Then he was suddenly transferred from Dix to counterintelligence duty in Hawaii, a move that roused jealous resentment among fellow soldiers. How had he managed to obtain a military job that enabled him to prowl around in the Hawaiian sunshine wearing civilian clothes? Surely the transfer was the result of Jewish conniving.

Goldman understood, of course, that it had happened in spite of the fact that he was a Jew, but he was too wise ever to argue along that line. Accepting his assignment as a plum usually reserved for the relatives of Congressmen, he no longer mentioned he was a trained civil engineer until the General wanted to appoint Goldman his staff legal adviser. When the General heard Goldman's protest, he thought that Goldman didn't want to work for him; he assumed that this shrewd lawyer had something better lined up, that he must be very valuable indeed. And so the General grabbed him and promoted him to staff sergeant immediately.

Now, in their early evening conference at Derussy, the General sounded a bit plaintive: "Goldman, you have a good theoretical grasp of war and politics, but you have no practical experience at command level; you have no idea how impossible it is for an Army staff to coordinate with a Navy staff when all the time the goddam Navy insists it's top dog. . . ."

Goldman, still the young idealist, wished silently that someone in authority would just once make a simple admission of error.

"When I appear before the board," the General went on, "I want to make it plain that the responsibility for the defense of Hawaii lay with the Navy—"

"Excuse me, General, but as a member of the board I would reply, 'Then, sir, by your own admission there was no reason for you to have been here at all. With such an attitude, is it any surprise you failed to fulfill your duties?' "

The General worked his lips. "I'll say this again, Sergeant. If you can think of any excuses—I mean organization of facts and arguments—that can clear me with the board and restore me to duty, I promise you something. I'll get you a field commission in the Army of the United States—and none of that nonsense about going to Officers' Candidate School."

Goldman bowed his head slightly. "Again, thank you, sir. Since you accept me as counsel, may I suggest you're approaching the situation on the wrong track. Aren't you basically a fighter pilot?"

"Indeed yes! And the best in the Pacific."

"Right, sir. But where did you end up? In a bureaucratic maze of air defense and intelligence commands as deputy this and deputy that, but never with any real authority. See, sir, you're just not one of those paper-shuffling bureaucrats."

The General was amazed. As an expert bureaucrat, he saw what Goldman was driving at.

"Sir, you must tell the board you really had no responsibilities. You must disassociate yourself from the debacle. You were really there only as a kind of witness. The responsibility must be shifted upstairs, where it belongs. I'd say your heart has always been in a fighter plane. You're a fighting General, not a bureaucrat general."

"Yes!" He began to pace excitedly. "Make some notes."

"Then I'll skip that detail at the Royal Hawaiian?" Goldman asked, changing the subject.

That morning the General, even more incoherent than usual, had said his wife Dorothy had last night fallen under the evil influence of some psychiatrist named Fiddler who was conducting public symposiums at the Royal Hawaiian on what the General called "free love."

While declining to be specific, the General told Goldman that Fiddler had caused Dorothy, a large, jolly, somewhat dowdy bottle blonde, to start "talking dirty" and "making impossible demands."

The General frowned. "Indeed not. I'm going to get that bastard Fiddler if it's the last thing I ever do. And I need your help. How could Dorothy ever get into such a mess? She— *Listen, my wife is forty-eight years old!*"

Goldman had heard that was an age when women often acted their silliest, but he decided not to mention it.

"Get started now, Goldman," the General ordered. "Dorothy will be there. I trust you to infiltrate the group and tell me at 0800 tomorrow morning what happens."

During Goldman's counterintelligence service he had worked enough cases at the Royal Hawaiian to be acquainted with many of its employees. So he had no trouble in making the necessary arrangements. Disguised as a waiter, he took ice water to the meeting room Fiddler had rented. In the corridor outside was a poster inscribed:

FIND HAPPINESS
ACHIEVE HEALTH
THROUGH HYPNOSIS
DEMONSTRATION BY
MORTON FIDDLER, M.D.
FEE $5

At a table beside the sign a dark, comely young woman wearing a tight-fitting evening gown collected the entrance fees. Goldman took the ice water to the speaker's table and began arranging chairs. Before long he had counted nearly one hundred people present. The General's wife sat in the front row. As Goldman had anticipated, she did not recognize him. He had discovered that soldiers are faceless: people who knew him in uniform failed to recognize him in mufti, and those who thought of him as a civilian did not know who he was when he wore the uniform.

There was no mistaking Fiddler when he appeared. A Byzantine dome of black hair surmounted a large, square forehead. A bold nose arched above a black, ferocious mustache that failed to cloak voluptuous lips. The entire surprising facial structure was modified by wire-framed glasses perched before dark, melancholic eyes. Fiddler reclined against the table and began to speak:

"What higher goal can there be than human happiness? And how can we achieve it? Through a happy sexual life, of course. In my medical practice in New York City I analyze about ten thousand people a year, and nearly all of them need nothing more than a happy sexual relationship to be restored to a good, productive life. A basic problem with the people who come to me is that they think sex is dirty. That is not so, friends. War is dirty. Politics is dirty. Making profit from one's fellows is dirty. But there is nothing cleaner under the sun than good, happy sexual relationships.''

When Fiddler asked for a volunteer to undergo hypnosis, hands shot up. "First I'll take this young lady," he said and stepped to Dorothy. Leaning down and staring at her fixedly, he spoke for a moment. To Goldman it was obviously a put-up job, but the others seemed to think Fiddler actually hypnotized Dorothy.

When he asked if she had any sexual problems she replied in monotone that she personally had none but her husband did. She did not reveal the General's identity or more than her first name, but said he increasingly paid her less attention.

Fiddler said, "Do as I say, Dorothy. When you go home tonight, undress teasingly for your husband and throw yourself upon him. Then everything will be all right." He gestured, and Dorothy looked about blankly.

Goldman believed it all was phony. He stood with arms locked on his chest. Though advanced in his thinking, he was retarded in his sexual life. He was secretly embarrassed at being a virgin, but he had an abiding terror of getting a girl pregnant or contracting a venereal disease. Of course he had heard about condoms, but he had also heard that they were not semen-worthy.

"Waiter," Fiddler said to him, "why are you standing there looking so skeptical? Sit down and relax."

Goldman sank into a chair and Fiddler hovered over him, asking, "What are you thinking?"

"I'm thinking you're ahead of your time, Doctor."

Fiddler's dark eyes grew enormous and close to Goldman. "What else are you thinking?"

Goldman replied now in a monotone, "I wish I was two years old so I could enjoy the times ahead."

"What's your name, young man?"

"Ira Samuel Goldman."

"And where are you from?"

"Brooklyn."

"Ira, do you have any sexual problems?"

"Yes sir, I'm a virgin."

The people closest to Goldman stifled giggles. Fiddler asked, "Do you know why you're afraid of women?"

"Yes sir, I'm afraid a woman might destroy me by giving me syphilis or getting pregnant before I'm firmly established in my career as a civil engineer. You see, I don't just want a job. I want to help build whole new and better cities—"

"Okay," Fiddler said. "Now—"

"I don't want to be just an electrical engineer or—"

"Hush," Fiddler said.

"The work of the civil engineer underlies all groups. Foundations, simple or extremely complicated, are within his realm. He designs and supervises the construction of bridges, the—"

"Shut up!" cried Fiddler. "I'm trying to straighten out your sex life, not your career. Now listen to me, Ira. I say only one word to you. That word is rubbers. Have faith in them. From here go to the hotel drugstore and buy a pack of Trojans. Then walk up to the first woman who appeals to you and invite her to bed. The results will surprise you." He touched his shoulder.

Goldman, restored, had no recollection of what had happened. Leaving the room, he went to the drugstore and bought a pack of condoms with a vague feeling he should be prepared for a change in his life. From somewhere he remembered a brand name, Trojans, thus relieving himself of uttering the dirty word "condoms."

Returning, he looked at Fiddler's young and lovely assistant, then beckoned her into the corridor. Her long gown accentuated her body and her dark hair somehow emphasized her sensual expression. He imagined that she thrust her large, firm breasts up at him eagerly when he asked, "Where did you and Fiddler come from?"

"I never saw him till day before yesterday. He just stopped me on the street and offered me this job."

"Is he really a psychiatrist?"

"How should I know? All I know is he's making money here. Did he really hypnotize you?"

"Of course not." Goldman said evenly. He obviously had no conscious recollection of what had happened. "What's your name?"

"Vera."

"My name's Ira." His voice shook nervously. "Have a date with me?"

She looked at him levelly. "Depends what you mean."

He quavered, "As Cary Grant said in that movie, my intentions aren't strictly honorable."

"Wanna buy a duck?" she replied and returned to her seat.

What did she mean, wanna buy a duck? Didn't some comedian toss out that nonsense line back in the thirties? Goldman paced the corridor, trying to fathom what Vera had meant in saying that.

Suddenly she came out of the meeting room and said, "Look, I'm a professional."

"A what?"

"If you want to lay me," she continued, "it'll cost you fifty bucks an hour."

Goldman had more than fifty dollars in his pocket and felt the experience might well be worth the money. Vera's professionalism intrigued him. Losing his virginity now seemed easy, for what he had dreaded most about the event was that it would involve a lot of nonsense. So he made an appointment to meet her in the lobby at ten-thirty.

Vera Stacy had decided to become a professional while mulling Goldman's proposition. Till then she had not tried to be even an amateur in the oldest sport.

Early in 1941 her husband, First Lieutenant Henry Stacy of the Army Air Corps, who flew P-38s, had been transferred from Texas to Hawaii. Vera liked the lush beauty of Oahu and was delighted to have moved so far from her native town of Ozark, Iowa. She and Hank rented a bungalow close to a beach near Diamond Head; she drove an old Model A Ford to and from a secretarial job at Fort Derussy while he commuted between home and his base by motorcycle.

On Saturday, December 6, Hank phoned her that he had drawn weekend duty and would not be home till Monday. When the first wave of Japanese attackers came strafing and bombing early on Sunday morning, Hank ran for his plane on the strip. He was gunned to earth with such a vengeance that it took the official score-keepers almost twenty-four hours to identify what remained of Henry Stacy.

To her surprise, Vera's new status as widow brought her little grief, but rather a strange sense of relief. Now she would not have to decide what to do about Hank Stacy—the man she had married for his handsome uniform and flashing smile and the possibility of a life beyond Ozark. She would not go back to Ozark. The Army no longer could move her around at random. She could make her own decisions now. If the Japanese would fight for Oahu, she would fight for the tiny segment of it in which she had an investment. She must buy the bungalow, but where would the money come from? Hank's insurance would not go far. In addition to mortgage payments, the house needed a new roof, new plumbing; and they still owed for the car, the motorcycle, she couldn't remember what else.

Vera was worrying about finances as she walked along Kalakaua Avenue not long after Hank's death when Fiddler stepped up to her and said, "Pardon me, young lady, I'm not trying to proposition you, but . . ."

Fiddler's warm gaze exerted a hypnotic effect on her at once, but what was even more appealing to Vera was the twenty-five dollars he would pay her for each evening she served as his assistant.

At first she was shocked by what he wanted her to do. Then the desire for the money outweighed her reluctance. After she handled admissions at the door, Fiddler called her to the front later in the program and had her perform pantomimes with him suggestive of various positions in sexual intercourse. After she found that he acted impersonally, she—like the audience—found the pantomimes as graceful as ballroom dancing. "You'll note we remain fully clothed," Fiddler would say, "so there's nothing pornographic about us."

She did not know what to make of him. He claimed distinguished Armenian ancestry and a father who had been a prominent psychiatrist; he claimed a medical degree from Johns Hopkins and extensive graduate psychoanalytic work in Europe. But all his claims were gibberish to Vera.

However, she grew very fond of him. In their sexual pantomimes, Fiddler made her imagine a world of pleasure she never had experienced. Sometimes, when he put his arms around her while lecturing to his rapt audience, Vera felt stirrings of desire as never before. The second night following his lecture she hinted that she would like to go to bed with him.

"That's a broad hint," he told her with a straight face.

Though intelligent, Vera did not have a well developed sense of humor. "Well"—she was somewhat flustered by her new-found desire—"I'm not exactly propositioning you. But you make me think I missed a lot while married to Hank."

"Tell me about that," Fiddler said.

"I met him in Omaha where I was job-hunting after graduating from business school in my home town, Ozark, a real hick place. I couldn't find work, and my mother kept pointing out the possibilities the future might offer as an Army pilot's wife—like travel. So I married him. I lost my virginity on our wedding night. It was a—a very brief experience. I mean, I felt no particular pain or pleasure. No special physical sensation at all. I thought, *There's got to be more to it than this.*"

But there didn't seem to be. Worrying about being frigid, Vera feigned ecstasy of orgasm, which delighted Hank. Soon after they were married she had herself fitted with a diaphragm and vowed secretly never to become pregnant.

Hank's fellow fliers were much like him—dull; and so were their wives, while all of them acted very superior. Vera wished she could be different. She wanted to excel at something, though she could not decide what. She tried to immerse herself in secretarial jobs and popular fiction. Dressing and grooming herself meticulously, she became increasingly attractive, but it never seriously occurred to her to be unfaithful to Hank.

Now she felt frustrated that Fiddler would not make love to her.

"Try it with somebody else," he told her. "You and I must keep it clinical, or the whole act may fall apart."

She understood his wanting her as an accomplice only. But she was not sufficiently experienced to think of him as a consummate cold-blooded manipulator.

In any event, he taught her what a profitable subject sex could be to one who could exploit it cleverly. Cupidity, more than lust, made her consider becoming a hooker.

After Goldman and Vera agreed to meet later, he went to the kitchen and found a busboy who had done time at San Quentin for burglary and now was trying to go straight. The man had once helped Goldman during his counterintelligence days in his investigation of a suspected spy who turned out to be an innocent traveling salesman. As before, it took all of Goldman's persuasive powers to convince the man it would be patriotic to burglarize for his country.

They gained admission to Fiddler's suite with a pass key. Then, while Goldman kept watch in the corridor, the man rifled Fiddler's belongings. He found not a shred of evidence that Fiddler was a physician, not a stethoscope or prescription pad or license—just the usual traveler's belongings. "And these." He handed Goldman a couple of printed cards:

M. FIDDLER
ORIENTAL ART IMPORTS
248 WEST 37TH ST.
NEW YORK, N.Y.

The card confirmed Goldman's belief that Fiddler was not a physician or psychiatrist. The General could have him run out of Hawaii as a fraud.

After making some notes for the General, Goldman almost chickened out on his assignation. He did not realize Vera was as nervous as he, but had greater resolve. He had arranged with the management for a room, explaining that his case had taken a surprising twist.

After Vera turned on the lights and he put on the night latch, he said, "I've never paid for this before."

She had, of course, heard him explain under hypnosis that he was a virgin. Was that why she had decided to take him for money? Would she have had the nerve to play professional with an older, more experienced man?

She folded his money into her bag, and Goldman asked, "What's a nice, beautiful girl like you doing at a thing like this?"

"What's a nice, handsome boy like you doing as a waiter?"

"I'm not really a waiter. How did you get into your—uh—line of work?"

The fertility of her imagination pleased her. She had graduated from Vassar and married a cruel sot who deserted her, leaving twin sons to support. She had been promised a good hotel job in Hawaii, but it had fallen through and she had turned to the only way she could support her babies and herself.

Goldman listened sympathetically. Then he told her about himself, all lies, she thought. How he had graduated from Yale and gone to M.I.T. How he was an Army counterintelligence agent masquerading as a waiter. And he went on and on about being an engineer and nobody recognizing it. She realized that if she took up this career seriously she might find that clients wanted to talk with a sympathetic woman as much as they wanted the pleasure of her body. So she resolved that even with a client who was as much a liar as Ira Goldman, she would listen and act sympathetically.

He asked her, "Aren't you scared of venereal disease?"

She was scared to death of it, but she said, "No worry, because I pick my clients very carefully."

"Tell me frankly, do you think Trojans are safe?"

"Nothing safer." She was relieved to learn he had some.

He said, "Did you ever hear there's some kind of Catholic organization opposed to birth control that hires women at these condom factories to puncture them with needles?"

"No, Ira, I never heard of it. As a graduate of *Yale,* how can you believe such a crazy thing? If you're worried about it, blow one up."

Goldman blinked at her. "Blow one up?"

"Sure, like a balloon. If it's airtight it'll keep in or keep out anything you're worried about."

Goldman did as she suggested. As a light and air-filled spheroid took and held shape, he tied a knot in its end and began to laugh happily. He batted it like a volleyball to Vera, and she playfully batted it back to him.

At last, with a light heart, Goldman let Vera solve a problem that had troubled him for years.

Vera, on the other hand, became intensely serious. After all, if she were to succeed in this new vocation, she never must leave a client with the thought she herself had had with Hank: *There's got to be more to it than this.* Hank had liked to watch her undress, so she decided to make a show of that.

Goldman himself undressed carefully, as if preparing each article of clothing for a barracks inspection. He was looking around for an appropriate place to hang his trousers when he saw Vera's lovely breasts emerge as she lowered her evening dress. Gazing wildly at her white belly, black lace garter belt and the pink panties that swelled over the fullness of her crotch, Goldman discovered that his penis had sprung stiffly out of his GI underwear shorts.

"Sorry," he mumbled. "Where's the goddam Trojan I had ready?"

"You have a nice cock," she replied calmly. "The Trojan is on the dressing table near your right hand."

He barely got it on before he leaped toward her, winding his arms tightly about her waist and burying his face in her breasts. His body jerked awkwardly as he rubbed his penis against her thigh. Vera pried one of his frantic hands loose from her waist and moved it down between her legs, holding it tightly against her and pushing her hips forward to expose her crotch further.

He came, uttering moans of pleasure, before she could guide him into her, but he seemed not to know the difference. She made ecstatic sounds, too, as she used to fake them with Hank.

"That," said the still virginal Goldman, "is worth every penny of fifty bucks."

Vera, too, was beginning to feel a strange new pleasure. She was supremely excited by the idea of sex for hire and enjoyed it far more than the domestic brand she'd had with Hank. She did not need Fiddler so much after all, she decided. It was the combination of sex and making money from it that thrilled her. She knew she had started working in the most exciting and profitable profession she could imagine.

4

Vera left the Royal Hawaiian about eleven-thirty and drove her Ford toward home. She was pleased by the profit from her evening's labors: $25 from Fiddler and $50 from Goldman added up to far more than her weekly salary at Derussy. She would take a sick day off tomorrow because Fiddler had offered her $20 extra to come to his suite in the morning and act as his "nurse" during a consultation. Maybe it was time she quit her clerk's job. This new career, if Goldman was any indication, was easy, and at last she felt she was someone special.

The isolation of the bungalow on an unpaved road which led to a sandy beach had appealed to both Hank and her. There were no close neighbors, no sounds but the distant thud of surf, the murmur of wind, the muted calls of birds in the underbrush which covered the area. It did not occur to her to be afraid to live alone there. An innate self-possession made her heedless of dangers; Hank had not taught her much, and fortunately he had failed to teach her fear.

When she turned onto the side road leading to the bungalow, the moon shone brightly and there was a heavy scent of something like honeysuckle in the underbrush. Suddenly the calm was shattered by Rosemarie, nude, rushing into the headlights. Vera slammed the brake as Rosemarie screamed for help. Behind her Red, also naked, raced into the light. Though badly frightened, Vera had the presence to lean out her open window and call to Rosemarie to hop in. Rosemarie dashed to the right side of the car, jumped in, and slammed the door shut before Red could catch her.

Vera sent the car lunging ahead. Neither she nor Rosemarie spoke as they sped on. There was a circle near the beach where Vera swung the car around and then raced back in the direction they had come from. Red stood in the road ahead of them, waving frantically and blinking into the headlights. Vera did not take her foot off the gas pedal.

Rosemarie screamed. "Don't hit him!" Red leaped aside in time, and she began to sob. "Where are you going?"

"To the police. That man must be arrested."

Rosemarie begged Vera not to take her to the police in her naked state. The humiliation would be more than she could bear. "He's my husband. He's a soldier out on pass. We were on the beach together. That's where I left my clothes."

"Your husband? My God, I thought he was trying to rape you."

"Don't husbands often try to rape their wives? Mad as I was, I wouldn't have jumped into this car if you'd been a man. But since you're a woman I knew it was safe. Please take me back to the beach. Red and I are finished forever. I'll get my clothes and go on my way."

"If you go back there now, he'll be waiting for you. Let's drive around a while till he's out of the way, then I'll take you to my house."

"You're awful kind," Rosemarie said. "You saving me is one more sign of the direction I've got to go."

"What do you mean by that?" Vera asked.

"I've got to leave Red. I don't love him. Guess I never did. He was just a way for me to get away from Mama. Red lied to me back there on the beach. He'd have got me pregnant again. He treats me like I'm a whore set up for his convenience."

When they returned to the bungalow, Vera gave Rosemarie pajamas and a robe. Rosemarie was taller and larger than she: the most beautiful woman Vera ever had seen. While she made them toast and tea, Rosemarie admired the comfortable bungalow, which had two commodious bedrooms and a bath besides the large living room, dining area, and well equipped kitchen.

"To have your own place," she kept saying. "The most Red and me ever had was one room in a house with thin walls. I see your wedding band, Vera. What does your husband do?"

Vera had forgotten the ring. She slipped it off and never wore it again. She explained what had happened to Hank, and Rosemarie said she must miss him terribly.

"No, not really," she said. "He was never mean to me and we got along all right, but I didn't really love him. Sometimes I wonder how much people love each other except in stories."

Rosemarie nodded. "Maybe I came all the way to Hawaii to make sure I don't love Red. How are you going to make a living now your husband's gone?"

Possibly there was something liberating about becoming a hustler that led one to honesty of a sort. "I have a secretarial job with the Army, but the pay isn't enough. So I'm starting to sell myself to men. And for a darn good price, too."

Rosemarie's eyelids widened. "The girls at the Missionary Hotel do the same thing. And you all are the nicest people. A heap more decent than most Christians I know."

"I'm Christian too," Vera said. "I think Christians make the best hookers because their mamas try to keep them bottled up so long."

Next morning, before Vera left to keep her appointment with Fiddler, Rosemarie said, "I guess I have to go back to Red after all. Every stitch I've got is in those bags on the beach."

Vera spoke slowly: "If you go back to him now, you'll be with him the rest of your life. Maybe you'll get knocked up twenty times and have twenty miscarriages. But this time you have a choice. Maybe it's the last time you'll ever have one."

She was inspired suddenly by the notion that Rosemarie might become her partner—or, more profitably yet, her employee. With a body and face like hers, she could have men lined up all the way to Diamond Head. But she must proceed carefully.

"Stay here with me, Rosemarie, till you've decided what to do. Help yourself to my clothing. Tomorrow we'll get out and buy some things for you. Today stay inside and don't answer the door or phone. You must hide from Red."

The idea of hiding from him sounded comforting to Rosemarie.

"We must change your name." Vera lowered her voice conspiratorially. "We'll pretend you're my cousin from Ozark on a visit. What name do you like?"

Rosemarie began to smile. "I fancy the name Virginia Tucker. Let's call me Ginny."

"What a nice name," Vera said. "It's a deal, Ginny." She kissed Rosemarie's cheek. "See you later."

After he gave up hunting her, Red put Rosemarie's clothing into one of the bags, wrapped himself in both blankets and tried to doze off. But he could not fall asleep. Her strange disappearance left him frightened. How could a woman without a stitch disappear into the night?

Then he remembered with sudden surprise that it had happened before. Back in Glenwood High, when he was trying to be a writer, he used to have at least one story published every week on the "Junior Page" of the Glenwood weekly *Chronicle*. The coveted prize had been two Saturday matinee passes to the Royal Theater. At the time he created Rita Worldly he had been under the influence of Edgar Rice Burroughs' John Carter, Warlord of Mars, and was writing for the page under the pseudonym Stonewall. Miss Spofford, the overworked *Chronicle* reporter who edited the page and fixed up the spelling, punctuation and grammar of its contributors, had seemed to like his writing until he created Rita.

In his story, Red recalled, Rita had looked exactly like Rosemarie: a long-legged, gorgeous beauty with golden hair. Yet when he met Rosemarie, and until that very moment on Oahu beach, he had not thought about the close resemblance. He introduced Rita to the readers of the page as she was being chased across a pasture by a mad bull. In order to facilitate her swift flight toward safety he had had her strip off her clothing as she ran, thus giving him the opportunity to comment on "her beautiful naked body running in the sunlight." Despite Rita's grace and speed, the bull would have destroyed her had not Captain Omar appeared with his Venus spaceship in the very nick of time, killing the bull with his rocket pistol and wafting Rita off into space for further adventures distributed over a number of weekly installments.

Red had been shocked the next week to receive in the mail his story and a terse message from Miss Spofford: "Stonewall— How could you have written a story that was not original? Shame on you! You can pick up that piece of tripe at the office." Hurt and angry, he had brooded half an afternoon until his father found the letter. Though Pa had some shortcomings, discouraging Red from a writer's career was not one of them. When he read Spofford's slurring remark he became even more indignant than Red, declaring in his shrill voice: "Come on, Stonewall, we're going to sue that biddy for libel!" Noah Jack was something of an expert on libel, having been threatened with it often in a life devoted largely to socialism, atheism, printing, and business failures.

If Ma had been home that afternoon she might have prevented what happened, but she had a job clerking in Woolworth's basement that month. So there was no one to stop Red and his father from sailing down to the *Chronicle* and confronting Spofford—a gray, massive, forbidding woman who listened to Pa's shrill indignance for only a few seconds before cutting him off:

"Sir, this is a family newspaper and the Junior Page is for *children*. Do you think we can print such tripe as this?" She did not read the offending phrase aloud, but pointed to it with a blunt forefinger.

Pa had to put on his glasses to read it. When he finally made out "her beautiful naked body running in the sunlight," he peered at Spofford, mystified. "And what," he asked, "is the matter with that?"

Spofford, puffing up hugely, replied harshly: "What's the *matter?* As a parent, sir, you should be ashamed to ask such a question. A child like Andrew here could not even *think* such a thing. So he must have copied it from somewhere. Goodbye, sir."

However, Pa had the last word, yelling, "I hereby cancel my subscription to the *Chronicle.*" The victory had been Pyrrhic, for he had enjoyed reading that newspaper and missed it greatly.

So ended Red's literary career. His teachers said he had no possible future as a writer because he was poor at spelling and punctuation, could not remember the simplest rules of grammar, and had the lowest tastes in literature, preferring writers like Edgar Rice Burroughs to poets of such stature as Henry Wadsworth Longfellow.

There on the beach that chilly morning it cheered Red somewhat to stop thinking about Rosemarie and remember the old days in Glenwood. Then he began to feel guilty because he had written home so seldom since being drafted, rarely answering the weekly letters from his mother or his sister.

The car that picked up Rosemarie had come out of nowhere, as had Captain Omar's spaceship when it rescued Rita Worldly. It was as if an Author had planned it that way. But that was magical thinking, Red knew. In fact, it had been a Model A Ford driven by a woman, but Red had not been able to catch the license number. If Rosemarie didn't come back soon for her belongings he would have to go to the police, much as he hated to. He wondered what could be more embarrassing than to try to explain to a cop that his wife had been running from him in the nude? A cop would want to know *why*.

What had made Rosemarie go crazy? Because he had gone crazy, of course. How he loved her! It must have been fear of getting pregnant again that set her off. Yet he didn't insist on their having children right away. It would, in fact, be better to wait until the war was over. If only he had remembered to stop by the dispensary and pick up some condoms, Rosemarie would be snuggled up against him now. Thinking about that, he uttered a low wail. How he loved her!

A foggy dawn found him sitting up, clutching his knees and staring at the breakers that smashed the shore. He had become a pretty good swimmer since he watched Johnny Weissmuller playing Tarzan. Could he manage to drown himself? Rosemarie would come identify his body and, knowing she had killed him, grieve her way into a quick grave. All he had to do was throw himself into those waves. But they looked so cold and awfully *wet* that he could not bring himself to do it. He would rather die in a hot, dry place.

Hunger drove him off the beach about nine o'clock. Planning to return as soon as he'd had something to eat, he carried the luggage and blankets up the sandy road. When he came to a bungalow, he paused to inquire if anyone there had seen Rosemarie. But no one answered his bell-ringing and pounding on the door, so he trudged on.

At the main paved road he found a little coffee shop beside a service station overgrown with weeds. A woman behind the counter poured him coffee and started toast and eggs. When he told her he was looking for his wife, the woman asked, "How was she dressed, soldier?"

Red felt himself flushing. "You'll find this hard to believe, ma'm, but I've got all her clothes here in these suitcases." The woman stared at him. "I mean we were skinny-dipping there on the beach last night and—well! All of a sudden she just ran off without a stitch on and jumped into a car driven by some woman."

"Have you notified the police?"

He did not answer as he pondered what he had just told her. If he had heard the same thing from anyone, he would not believe a word of it. He had no alternative but to go to the police. Suppose Rosemarie had been kidnapped! If she had not returned to the beach by noon, he would report everything to the civilian police—not the Military Police, who had a foul reputation among enlisted men.

The woman served his toast and eggs, then went into a back room and talked on a phone. He had just finished eating when an Army car drew up and two MPs came in.

"Soldier, let's see your pass."

He showed it to them.

"What's your serial number?"

"42003183."

"Let's see your dog tags."

Unbuttoning his shirt, he held out the chained tags.

"What're you doing here this time of day?"

He told them what had happened, for it was apparent he would need plenty of help finding Rosemarie.

The MPs looked at him oddly and at each other. One said, "Private, you come with us."

Red wrinkled up his face. "I can't do that. My pass is good till tomorrow. You can check with Headquarters Company. I figure my wife will come back to the beach this morning looking for her luggage. I have to wait for her there." He described Rosemarie carefully. "You report her missing and I'll be there at the beach till noon."

One of the MPs gripped him tightly by an arm and said, "You're coming with us."

He would *not*. Picking up the bags and blankets, he went out ahead. Then, even though he knew he was acting crazy, he sprinted across the lumpy asphalt of the deserted service station toward the underbrush beyond. The safety of the brush was within leaping distance when a ton weight was dropped on his head and he went skidding down a long, spiraling funnel into darkness.

5

The General suddenly decided that I should make copies of photos I'd taken of him at the controls of various planes so that he could show the board of inquiry what a hot fighter pilot he was. He ordered me back from the wilds of bivouac, and I reported to him at Derussy the morning after Goldman had spied on Fiddler at the Royal Hawaiian.

When I arrived, he was telling Goldman, "I plan to attack the problem on two fronts."

"Excuse me, sir," Goldman said, "but which problem do you refer to?"

The General looked wretched this morning. His eyes looked like eggs which had been poached too long. He blinked slowly at Goldman. "Yes, yes, I have a lot of problems, don't I?" His tone was bitter. "Now I speak of Dorothy. I've arranged for a psychiatrist to treat her. And today we'll hang Fiddler. Follow me?"

Goldman did not, but he nodded sagaciously.

"Would you believe it, Goldman, I've been trying since six o'clock this morning, but I can't raise a single Army psychiatrist on the whole goddam island of Oahu. How would you like to have to explain that to the Chief of Staff in Washington? Now, I'll tell you the most ironic thing that's ever happened. I had to go to *Navy* for a psychiatrist to treat Dorothy! How's that for irony?"

"Incredible, sir."

"But true." The General made a wry face. "Through contacts I've learned there's a noted civilian psychiatrist from California here on active Navy duty who'll see Dorothy. I mean I had to go to Navy flag rank to get him, but, by God, I got him!"

"Congratulations, sir."

"Yes. Now, Goldman, I have a car waiting and I want you to go down to Pearl and pick up this Navy person. His name is Snook. And I want you to bring him right back here, and I'll take him to my quarters to treat Dorothy. And by the way, Goldman, this is none of your goddam business, and if you ever mention this among the enlisted men I'll have your balls shot off. My wife is *a very sick woman*."

"Yes sir."

"What d'you mean 'yes sir'?"

"Just agreeing with your judgment, General."

"Goldman, my wife came home from the Royal Hawaiian last night and acted absolutely insane. You wouldn't *believe* what she did. What really happened there? What did she do there?"

"Well, sir—"

"Never mind, I can't bear to even *think* what happened."

"But sir—"

"*Skip* it, Goldman. You're acting too nosy about my personal affairs. Those things are absolutely none of your goddam business. Understand?"

"Yes sir."

"I forgive you, Goldman. I appreciate your personal concern for me. Now, about Fiddler, how would you handle him?"

"I suggest, General, you have him deported back to the mainland. Let me give you my evidence."

"Don't be a dumb sergeant. I've scheduled Dorothy to leave for the mainland next week. I'll see to it that my wife and that lunatic Fiddler *are not on the mainland at the same time!* You know what I'm going to do?" His sudden grin made him look ghastly. "I'm going to have Fiddler put in safekeeping for the duration. *I'm going to have him inducted into the Army Medical Corps!* Then I'll have him shipped to Wake or one of those islands the Japs are about to capture, if they haven't already."

Goldman was incredulous. "But sir, I've reasonable doubt Fiddler actually has a medical degree."

"What difference does that make?"

"But sir, you can't just *draft* a middle-aged American citizen from New York who claims to be a doctor."

"Oh, can't you now? You'd be amazed how I can handle *Mr.* Fiddler. Now, start for Pearl and pick up this psychiatrist Snook from Captain Wentworth at the hospital administrative office. After you get back I'm sending you and an officer to the Royal Hawaiian to nail Fiddler's hide to the barn door. Now get cracking!"

Fortunately Goldman, an able bureaucrat who understood the importance of the telephone, was always armed with a plentiful supply of nickels. He used his first nickel to inform the General from a phone booth that Captain Wentworth had not heard of the plan to lend Snook out for Army service and was most antagonistic to it. The General said word should have been channeled to Wentworth through an Admiral Worth, who in turn should have received it from the Chief of Staff to the Commander in Chief, Pacific Fleet. Instead of being disturbed, the General expressed pleasure at the fact that Goldman was learning how impossible it was to coordinate even the simplest action with the goddam Navy.

Goldman wasted three hours and nearly a dollar in phone calls before admitting he was hopelessly entangled in red tape. Toward noon Wentworth personally informed him that no psychiatrist named Snook even existed.

On his last nickel, he endured a scolding, depressed that the General enjoyed his failure more than a report of success.

"Failed, eh?" the General shouted into the phone. "By God, Goldman, you're beginning to seem almost human! Well, come back, come back, stop wasting my time!"

I was on the General's end of this conversation, waiting while he looked through a pile of photos; his vanity was so enormous that he could spend an entire day looking at pictures of himself. I was almost as weary as Goldman when he returned.

"Now," the General said, "I'm going to send you both on a mission at which you cannot possibly fail. Boswick, you're going to administer the commission oath to a new member of the Army Medical Corps. Wait here." Then he left the office.

Goldman literally broke out in a sweat as he described the Fiddler case in detail to me. "Positively the guy is not a doctor. This is like —kidnapping." I agreed; I wanted no part of it.

When the General returned with administrative forms and sets of cut orders, I explained I was not commissioned in the Judge Advocate General's office and could not administer oaths. The General replied that was nonsense, any officer could administer an oath. I tried another tactic: any officer could, I lied, except a second lieutenant, and I was only a second lieutenant. But the General would brook no more argument. An order was an order. So it was either Fiddler's neck—or Goldman's and mine.

We took an Army sedan to the Royal Hawaiian, Goldman driving. While I listened, Goldman phoned Fiddler in his suite and identified himself as a Colonel Brawn:

"Dr. Fiddler, your symposiums have been of inestimable help to a person of high rank here in Hawaii. The person wants to remain anonymous, but he wants to reward you for your good work. He's sending around an officer and enlisted man to confer the honorary rank of major on you—Oh, no, *sir,* it's the *inactive* reserve. Strictly honorary, like being made a Kentucky colonel."

"How can you do this?" I asked Goldman after he hung up.

"Would you like to spend the rest of your life on bivouac?" he replied.

I offered to buy him a drink. At the time my grandmother was still alive—a dotty old lady in Chicago who professed to be terribly rich. I believed her because she'd send me hundreds of dollars from time to time. This left me with the unfortunate misconception that one day I would become the heir to great wealth and exaggerated my already cavalier attitude toward money. Although Grandma was to die broke, she had recently sent me a few hundred dollars which I had not had opportunity to spend.

Goldman said he didn't drink, but would have a beer with me. I said I didn't drink either, but would have a Scotch with him. While we were sitting at the bar bemoaning our ghastly mission against Fiddler we met a naval officer who eventually turned out to be a Lieutenant Commander Orville Snook (U.S. Naval Reserve).

Orvie Snook would have been surprised to hear the General describe him as a psychiatrist. For his specialty was gynecology, and he was at that time perhaps the most depressed gynecologist in existence.

Only a month previously he had been enjoying a prospering obstetrics practice in Fresno, California, where he lived with his wife and young daughter. He had lived circumspectly except for one indiscretion. In 1935 he had been talked into joining the Naval Reserve with the promise of a pension after twenty years of service. Being exceedingly fond of money, he had signed up with the understanding that he could switch to the inactive reserve if peace were threatened. By serving only a few hours a month and without ever setting foot on a naval vessel, he rose to the rank of lieutenant commander. After war began in Europe he did not resign but shrewdly had himself transferred to the inactive reserve. When the friendly captain of a minesweeper invited him to cruise to Hawaii at the end of November with a guarantee of passage back by battleship, Orvie was enchanted by the prospect of a vacation at government expense. Quickly arranging his affairs and saying goodbye to his family, he sailed from San Diego into azure seas. The minesweeper anchored in Pearl Harbor on Saturday evening, December 6, 1941.

On deck the next morning, Orvie thought they played remarkably realistic war games in Hawaii. The truth dawned on him after he narrowly missed death from a strafing Japanese plane. He felt he had been hoodwinked into a situation that really was no concern of his. That afternoon he thumbed a ride into downtown Honolulu and was astonished that the Western Union office refused to send his message to his wife: ESCAPED UNHARMED. RETURNING SOON.

On Monday afternoon Orvie trudged desperately to Headquarters of the Commander in Chief, Pacific Fleet. At the gate a Marine sergeant stepped in front of him, saluted, and asked, "Your mission, sir?"

Orvie, fumbling a salute in response, said, "Corporal, I'm Commander Snook. I want to arrange transportation back to California. You see, I'm in the inactive reserve."

The sergeant gaped at him. He had seen a lot of waffled officers since the attack, but this one was the worst. He finally sent Orvie off in another direction.

After blundering in and out of various offices, Orvie was taken into kindly custody by a Navy physician who recognized his medical insignia and confused state. The physician found him employment in the Ford Island emergency hospital where he spent a day bungling the treatment of burned and wounded men before someone thought it wise to utilize his specialty of gynecology and obstetrics. The trouble with that idea was that there were only a few women at Pearl Harbor at the time: nurses and the wives of officers—and, fortunately for them, none showed signs of pregnancy.

Orvie, having nothing to do, worked himself into a state of anxiety over the possibility that he might be killed in this war. He transferred anxiety over himself to anxiety about his wife: what would she do if he should die? Gradually he began to believe she did not love him and was being unfaithful to him. After considerable thought he decided that her lover was the family's young dentist.

The day before Goldman came looking for him, Orvie learned that a naval reserve lieutenant he had met was getting a medical discharge on psychological grounds. Eagerly Orvie pressed him as to how he had managed it. Evasive at first, the officer finally divulged he had acted on the advice of a noted psychiatrist named Fiddler, who was staying at the Royal Hawaiian. Fiddler's fee for discharge advice was high—$100 in cash—but the result was well worth it.

Phoning Fiddler, Orvie made an appointment for 2 P.M. He got a ride to the hotel, arriving more than an hour early. Though Orvie drank rarely, he wandered aimlessly into the bar because he could not find anyplace else to sit down. He was a short, scrawny man of thirty-two with thin lips and a mean, furtive look who bore little resemblance to the traditional U.S. Navy officer.

It was his mean and furtive appearance combined with the physician's insignia that made me look at him twice as he came up to the bar and frowned at the smiling countenance of a Hawaiian bartender who said, "*Okulehou?*"

"Fine, thanks," Orvie said. "And how are you?"

"No, Commander," I said to him, "he means do you want an *okulehou*. It's better known as an *oke* and made of strong Hawaiian liquor."

"How much does it cost?" Orvie asked.

"That doesn't matter," I said. "Have one on me. I just came into a small inheritance and my friend Goldman and I are screwing up our courage to take the next fateful step in our lives."

An *oke* should be drunk cautiously, even by a practiced drinker. But Orvie, relentlessly naive, bolted his as if it were water. He deserved to become uncouthly drunk, yet at first did not appear to. I, regarding him with awe, told the bartender to bring him another *oke*.

This loosened Orvie's tongue, and he told us, with occasional tears. the dreadful things that had happened to him since coming to Hawaii. He told us everything but his name.

Goldman and I had talked vaguely about having lunch, but we kept postponing it. We knew we had to nail Fiddler, but we kept postponing that too. It was Goldman who finally announced that we must proceed with our orders. We bade the still nameless Orvie goodbye but soon found him riding upstairs in an elevator with us. When we knocked on the door to Fiddler's suite, he was still with us.

Vera, acting as Fiddler's nurse, opened the door. She was so good-looking that I involuntarily muttered, "Oh boy!" Ignoring me, she exclaimed in surprise at seeing Goldman in uniform. He winked at her, but she ignored him too and said to Orvie, "Are you the Navy doctor who has an appointment with Dr. Fiddler?"

"Nnnn," he replied.

We crowded in together as Fiddler bounded out of his bedroom, crying, "I'm Fiddler. How are you, colleague?" He ignored us and wrung Orvie's hand.

"Nnnn," Orvie replied gratefully and sank into a chair.

Fiddler, still ignoring Goldman and me, said to Orvie, "So you're a gynecologist. In my family it's psychiatry. My daddy used to spend his summers with the Viennese Analytic Society at their summer retreat. Of course you've heard of Moshe Wolff, a good friend of Freud's and a great favorite of the group."

All of us gaped.

"Daddy used to say that Brill figured out old Moshe spent the equivalent of four consecutive years walking from his hotel room to the elevator and back to make sure he'd locked his door. Daddy said Moshe suffered from a compulsion to look down because he was afraid he might step on a duck liver. He was a kind man who spent much of his time looking for insects that had fallen on their backs and setting them upright. Doing this, Daddy said, made Moshe blush to the roots of his hair. But that shows you can't always trust a psychiatrist, not even your dear old daddy. Because I've had it on the highest authority that Moshe Wolff was bald as a billiard ball and kept his face wrapped in a woolen muffler except in the coldest winter weather."

"Thank you," gasped Orvie, shaking Fiddler's hand again.

"Most extraordinary thing happened half an hour ago," Fiddler went on. "Received a phone call from a high-ranking officer. Seems that in my symposiums here I've been of inestimable help to some high-ranking person and—"

"That's why we're here, Doctor," Goldman said. "I'm Sergeant Goldman and this is Lieutenant Boswick."

"How are you, gentlemen?" Fiddler said. "Didn't want to ignore you, but patients first, of course, for a busy doctor. Now I understand this honor being preferred me is in the *inactive* reserve—"

Orvie wanted to warn Fiddler against the treacheries of the military, but his jaws seemed locked. He could only say, "Nnnn!"

Fiddler went on, "You can understand how eager I am for active duty. Later, of course. Soon, I'm sure. But first I have my practice in New York to turn over to someone. As old John Milton wrote—Sergeant, Lieutenant, what can I do for you? Sergeant, you look vaguely familiar. Where could we have met?"

Goldman shrugged, and I said, "I have only a couple of questions before I administer the oath. You're a physician?"

"What else, Lieutenant? I don't run around with my diploma in my pocket, but I'm from Johns Hopkins. Specialty, psychiatry."

"How is your health?"

"The best. Never sick a day in my life. But look here, you say this is the inactive reserve. What's to prevent 'em from transferring me to active duty?"

Orvie made a strange sound while Goldman looked surprised and said, "Well, Doctor, consider the benign intentions of the high-ranking officer who wants to honor you. Would he want to make you a major and put you in the inactive reserve if he didn't want to protect you from active duty? See, they're bound to get all of you doctors sooner or later, but the ones they'll get later are those protected by being in the *inactive* reserve. Of course the active reserve are the ones they get sooner. And those who are in neither the active nor the inactive reserve they get first of all. So you can see what a favor the high brass is doing you. You'll have in your possession a document that says you're an inactive reservist."

Orvie made sounds of vehement protest, but Fiddler said, "Of course I understand perfectly. This is the nature of war. And can I wear a major's uniform when I feel like it?"

"Naturally," Goldman said. "Now, there are a couple of forms here for me to fill out and you to sign before Lieutenant Boswick administers the oath. I need your permanent address." Fiddler gave him the New York address which his card had advertised as that of a dealer in Oriental art. "And your next of kin?"

"None."

Goldman found that incomprehensible and questioned him at length while Fiddler insisted he had no wife, child, parent, not even a remote cousin.

"I'm Armenian," he said, "and it's the fate of Armenians to be just wanderers and finally become extinct. Nearly all of us were exterminated by the Turks years ago. I wish Turkey would join the Axis powers. Then I'd apply for active duty and go kill Turks, kill Turks, kill Turks!''

After answering more questions and taking the oath, Fiddler's eyes grew damp and he spoke with emotion: ''This may be the greatest day of my life. I've always wanted to be a soldier. I mean, I used to play soldier even before I was old enough to play with girls.''

He invited Goldman and me to meet him downstairs in an hour for a drink, then turned to Orvie. ''Now, what are the experiences, Doctor Snook, that make naval service difficult for you?''

Orvie was haltingly trying to explain as Goldman and I left. In the hall Goldman said, ''So there *is* a Navy Doctor Snook after all.'' Then we agreed not to waste more time. We stepped back inside, looking sheepish.

Fiddler smiled at us. ''Hi, men, forget something?''

''Dr. Fiddler''—Goldman lacked his usual decisiveness—''there's been a new development. A messenger just brought it to us. General Orders 516. Here it is, sir.''

Fiddler read the mimeographed sheet and said calmly, ''But I possess orders stating I'm in the *in*active reserve.''

''You see,'' I said, ''these new orders countermand your old orders. They have just *activated* you. And you'll note there in Paragraph 2 that you're to report to Schofield Barracks at 1700 today. We have transportation downstairs, sir.''

Orvie laughed hysterically, but no one paid him any attention.

Fiddler said, ''I want to consult a lawyer.''

I said, ''Everything has been done legally, Major. You were offered a commission and accepted it.''

Fiddler said, ''This is an invasion of my Constitutional rights.''

Goldman said, ''War is always an invasion of civil rights. Look how well off you are starting as a major. A lot of us—''

''Don't lecture me, you bastard!'' Fiddler cried. ''Now I recognize you. You're the *waiter!* What sort of game is this? I outrank you both and *command* you to tell me!''

Goldman and I just looked at each other.

''All right,'' Fiddler said. ''Okay, I'll take my lumps. I'll get my stuff and go with you.'' He went into the bedroom and shut the door.

Goldman turned to Orvie. ''Sir, a strange coincidence, Commander; this morning I went to the hospital looking for you—''

''Yeee!'' shrieked Orvie, frightening all of us nearly out of our wits.

Several minutes of confusion followed before Goldman demanded, "Does that bedroom have a door into the hall?"

Vera smiled. "Yes, and I hope he got away."

I phoned the General and told him Fiddler had escaped.

"Did he escape commissioned or uncommissioned?" the General asked.

"Commissioned, sir."

"Then he didn't escape," the General said. "I'll phone my friend the Provost Marshal of Honolulu. Fiddler's goose is cooked."

"Yes, sir. And Goldman and I will pursue him from this end. We'll follow up certain clues we have. It may be quite a while before we get back to Derussy."

"Yes, yes, follow that up, Boswick."

As I hung up the phone, Orvie stood up and said, "I've reached the end of my rope. I'm having a nervous breakdown."

"He's been working awful hard," I told Vera. "And this thing that just happened to his colleague Fiddler can't help but affect him. Besides, back in California his wife is being unfaithful to him."

"How do you know that?" Orvie demanded.

"It's all you talked about at the bar before lunch. Say, we haven't had lunch yet." I smiled at Vera, to whom I was strongly attracted: such a lovely face and figure, especially her tail, which wig-wagged me signals every time she moved. "Come on, honey, lunch is on me. My rich old grandmother just sent me more money from Chicago."

Vera rested a hand on a curving hip and gazed at me meditatively. "Why waste your money on food?"

"Would you prefer to drink lunch?"

"How about a good hot lunch?" she asked, shifting her weight suggestively to the other hip.

I boggled at her.

"Be my client!" Her expression turned radiant. "My name is Vera. I'm not some cheap B girl, I'm expensive, but you call my number and pay my price and something wonderful will happen to you."

Goldman blushed. "What she says is perfectly true."

Orvie looked at her sourly. "But what's your price?"

"Fifty dollars an hour."

"Outrageous!"

"I don't think so," I said. "See you later, Dr. Snook."

"Oh, I'm coming with you," Orvie said. "In my depressed state I shouldn't be left by myself—danger of suicide."

"I'm coming too," Goldman said, "even though I don't have fifty bucks."

We followed Vera's car to her bungalow in the Army sedan.

"This is my cousin Ginny from my home town of Ozark," Vera said. I didn't recognize Rosemarie, though I'd seen Red's snapshots of her; maybe it was because I didn't *associate* her with being there. My thought was how amazing that two such beautiful young women could be found under one roof.

"Ginny, we go by first names here," Vera said. "This is Boz, my client. Ira here is another client. And this is Orvie, who came along for the ride. After we have some tea, you entertain Ira and Orvie."

Rosemarie looked alarmed. "What do you mean *entertain?*"

"If either of them makes a pass, remember the fee is fifty an hour."

Rosemarie squared her lovely shoulders. "I won't do it!"

"Suit yourself, honey."

While we sipped tea we agreed the country could eventually win the war if everybody sacrificed enough. Orvie railed against the self-gratification of people in the States as described in a letter he had received only yesterday from his unfaithful wife: "They simply refuse to recognize there's a war on. I've written her about the terrible conditions out here on the fighting front, and what does she say? She writes she's having trouble buying good steak! Think of it!"

I asked, "Did she mention that young dentist?"

"How do you know about him?" Orvie demanded.

"Because you kept talking about him at the bar."

"I asked her specifically about him." Orvie's voice shook with anger. "And do you know what she had the gall to write? She tried to throw me off the scent by saying he had volunteered for Army duty in Spokane. Imagine!"

"Well," Rosemarie said, "it might be true."

"But *Spokane!*" cried Orvie. "Does she think I'm dumb enough to fall for a line like that? What would the Army be doing in *Spokane?*" Thinking Rosemarie was a call girl too, he told her sternly, "You get one thing straight, young lady. I'm being faithful to my wife even if she is unfaithful to me."

Rosemarie looked at him. "Why?"

Orvie, unable to think of a reason, finally said, "Just because."

When Vera took me into her bedroom she showed a sudden shyness that made me wonder if she really was a professional.

"Fifty an hour is an incredibly high price," I told her. "What tricks do you turn to make it worth so much?"

"Anything you want."

I still was skeptical. "Do you have any pornographic art?"

"A client stole it all last week."

"What do you have in the way of dildos?"

She had never heard of a dildo.

"You're a phony," I said. "A call girl has to be something special and you're not. You'd better stick to virgin servicemen. The fee for them is five bucks a lay. Anything more isn't legal under Roosevelt's wage-price laws."

She sat on the bed and nibbled at a fingernail, greedy, frustrated and thinking furiously. "There's one thing I can promise. Anybody who kisses my nooky won't get killed in the war."

"That's ridiculous, Vera. You can't prove it."

"Yes, I can. My husband never would and he was killed. All his friends who wouldn't were killed too. But those who liked to kiss it all lived. And the whole bunch of 'em were together at the Field when the Japs attacked."

She sounded convincing; not until much later did I learn it was a lie.

"What bullshit," I said, while already wanting to believe what Vera said.

Like the founders of all religions, she had a vivid imagination. Sitting there on the bed, she recited the genesis of the faith: the names of men in Hank's squadron who had become hamburger and the names of those alongside them who thenceforth had to pay fifty an hour for the privilege of expressing their faith.

"Do you make head?" I asked.

"Of course." She began to unbutton her blouse.

"What does that do for the guys besides the usual?"

She looked at me with utter seriousness and said, "Every last one of 'em has been given a medal. Some of the enlisted men only got the Good Conduct, but, after all, that's a medal too."

6

When Red made the long, exhausting climb back to consciousness he found himself in a cell. Within his head there seemed to be a blazing, crackling fire, and he stared through the cell bars as through glaring heat. Somebody was yelling, and it took him a while to realize it was himself. Gradually a figure on the other side of the bars assumed the shape of an MP, and gradually Red's sight became more normal, his voice more rational.

"Why'd you do it to me? My pass is okay. Let me outa here!"

Another MP appeared. "Shut up, soldier. We're checkin' you out for murder."

"Murder! Murdering who?"

"The woman you was on the beach with last night."

"That's Rosemarie! That's my *wife!* I told you what happened."

But they wanted to hear it all again. They took him out of the cell and handcuffed him to a stanchion while a grim lieutenant questioned him and a corporal wrote down what he said. Then they put him back in the cell.

He lay on the hard bunk, clasping his throbbing head and trying to think what might have become of Rosemarie. In time they brought him bread and coffee, but he couldn't swallow it. Later they brought him bread and lukewarm soup, which he managed to hold down. He did not so much sleep as lie in a dazed state, and after a long time it became the next morning.

Again they took him out of the cell and handcuffed him to the stanchion. Beside the lieutenant a big, beef-faced captain sat on a table, his small eyes drilling at Red. "Private"—his voice was weak for such a large man—"we have the goods on you. It'll go easier on you if you make a full confession now."

"Confession of what?" Red demanded.

"How you killed your wife. Drowned her, didn't you?"

"That's a goddam lie!"

An MP raised a short length of rubber hose, but did not strike him. After the officers failed to get a confession, he was taken back to his cell.

Silence closed around him as he lay on his bunk. Through the silence came the faint, distant droning of an airplane. Somewhere up there a free man rode through the blue. Red wondered if that man was maybe smarter or better than he; for sure that man was luckier.

He did not want to become an airplane pilot merely to fly through the air like Tarzan. He needed the money and privileges that being a pilot would bring him. If he became a pilot, he could give Rosemarie all the things he now could not afford. She liked pretty things, but he could only rarely indulge her.

An important thing about a pilot, Red thought, was that he had great responsibilities. There would be a lot of satisfaction in that—in knowing that the tasks he undertook were vital instead of merely time-serving. How could he manage to make the leap from motor pool driver to airplane pilot?

There was no point in blaming his folks because he had not gone to college. It was *his* fault. He had not done as well in high school as he could have; he always preferred to tinker with something mechanical rather than to work at math and Latin. His mother would have made every possible sacrifice to send him to college. So would his father, who admired the life of the mind so much that he sometimes seemed not of this world. Yet they had not been able to overcome Red's indifference.

His family—his father's family—had an interesting history. His mother's family was not so interesting; their name was Grote and they lived in Pennsylvania. But the Jacks were really interesting. Now that he had plenty of time to think about it, he had a very good and surprising name: Andrew Jackson Jack. But for the grace of his mother's interference, he might have been named Norman Thomas Jack, after the noted Socialist. His father, Noah, had been seventh generation over the Appalachians born. Back in the Revolution, a

Jack had come through Cumberland Gap and, turning off the long hunters' trail, gone into the big brush on the headwaters of the Kentucky River. Noah was fond of quoting the naturalist John James Audubon, who mentioned olden times on the Kentucky frontier in these words: *The simplicity of those days I cannot describe; man was man; each, one to another, a brother.*

Red felt that had a ring of truth, like life in the wonderful Tarzan books he began to read and cherish when he was very young. Man *is* man, he sometimes thought, *but the problem in these times is to make a brother of another.*

The Jacks had been a religious people, but Noah did not believe in God. The Jacks had been patriotic fighters, but Noah became a pacifist and decided there was something unfair to the majority of people in the structure of American society and government that could be repaired only by socialism. He left the back country, became a printer, and married Nina Grote, his opposite: dark to his red hair, large to his leanness, heavy-footed to his nimbleness, deliberate in thought and emotion to his quickness. Jenny, Red's older sister, resembled their mother. She stayed home after high school and found jobs during the lean Depression years that helped keep the family going. Jenny had no patience with Noah's socialist ideas and capitalist failures at job printing.

Remembering Depression times in Glenwood, Red thought his father had been wrong about one thing. Noah argued that a human is a rational social animal, that all experience is shared, that "We're in this together." But Red decided that a human is a lonely animal struggling against insurmountable odds. For, who was there to share his cell? And, if there were anything rational about humans, why was he being held incommunicado for a crime he had not committed?

After graduating from high school, Red had gone to work for Peck's Service Station at $18 a week. He wanted to get out of Glenwood, a dreary suburban town hedged in by equally dreary towns in the huge complex around Newark. But where was there to go? In those days the whole country looked poor and shabby, and his salary at Peck's gave him some freedom and self-respect, besides helping his family to get by, without being enough for his escape.

There in the cell he lost track of time. Twice more the MPs tried to get a confession from him. They did not offer Rosemarie's body for him to identify, and any fool knew there could not be murder without a body. It seemed to him that his headaches grew worse rather than better; he asked for a doctor, but they did not send for one.

He tried to distract himself by pretending he was flying an airplane. Tiring of that, he concentrated on Tarzan. Starting away back at the beginning of the first Tarzan book, he slowly told himself the entire story of that great man. He took time out from the telling to exercise on all the neighborhood trees from which he used to swing while uttering his piercing man-ape imitation. He trumpeted like Tantor, growled like Numa, whimpered like Cheetah. He went to the movies again, but the movies never had been as good as the real thing that existed within him. Johnny Weissmuller had been a better Tarzan than Buster Crabbe or Glenn Morris, but neither had lived up to Red's fantasy of the man himself. And Jane Porter didn't look at all like Maureen O'Sullivan; she looked like Rosemarie Jack.

One night a blinding light came in the darkness. For a moment he thought he saw and heard Yaromski. But he must be imagining it. Before the light came he had been riding the back of Tarzan's good elephant friend Tantor, and it was true that Tantor and Yaromski looked somewhat alike. While it seemed natural that Tantor should appear to him, he thought he must really be out of his head to imagine that he saw Yaromski.

Meanwhile, Fiddler also was in deep trouble. When he fled from the Royal Hawaiian, he took a taxi to Pearl Harbor. Having read in the Honolulu *Advocate* about Ivory Spence's appearance in his yacht, Fiddler shrewdly thought that Spence might save him. Surely he could persuade the billionaire to take him back to the mainland after he explained that he was a brother pacifist who was being per-secuted by the military. Fiddler easily convinced the guards at the Pearl Harbor main gate, after showing them his commission orders, that he was an Army intelligence officer assigned to arrest Spence for treason. Alas, Spence had sailed away yesterday aboard the *Dove of Peace*. The naval authorities had been relieved to be rid of him after he asked permission to leave the bay; they had enough troubles on their hands already.

Fiddler then told his taxi driver to take him to downtown Honolulu. He was in a travel agency, seeking to buy ship passage home, when MPs arrested him. He did not try to escape again after the Provost Marshal of Honolulu threatened him with execution as a deserter.

For three days Fiddler existed in the billeted officers' quarters at Schofield Barracks while undergoing what the Army called "process-ing." As in the processing of ham, it mainly involved a state of hanging around. He was inoculated against various diseases, he bought uniforms, he ignored daily admonitions to shave his mustache.

In vain he told everyone he had no medical training and was not a physician. His denial was the most absurd thing the Army ever had heard of. When, at last, the processing was ended and the Medical Corps ordered him to report to a colonel for assignment, the colonel was furious with him.

"What d'you mean you're not a doctor?" he cried. "I know you've the reputation of being a malingerer, Major, but this is really too much. Let's see—you're thirty-seven years old. This makes you an outright liar! Your record here clearly states you graduated from Johns Hopkins Medical School in 1929. D'you think the Army made that up?"

"No, sir," Fiddler replied patiently, "*I* made that up. *I* told a lie. It would be a simple matter for the Army to check and learn that no one named Morton Fiddler graduated from Johns Hopkins in 1929 or any other year. I have begged everybody to check on me and correct this ghastly mistake."

"Listen, Major, do you know the Army punishment for lying when applying for a specialist's commission such as you hold? I could quote from A.G.R. 49 dash 25, paragraph G. . . . Three years at hard labor in Leavenworth was the punishment for a man I knew who obtained a first lieutenant's commission in the Transportation Corps. He claimed a degree in mechanical engineering, and—pshaw— turned out he was just another unemployed accountant. *Three years,* Major! Sure you want to say you lied at this time when the Army needs doctors so badly?"

Fiddler blinked slowly and was interested to see that the colonel blinked in reply. During the incredible events of the past few days he had forgotten his powers of hypnotism. Maybe he could bring this man under his spell and have himself rejected. But nothing was working for him as it used to. The colonel slipped from under his influence and gave him the worst assignment available.

In the bivouac area on the wild west coast, Headquarters Company had finally set up a dispensary, consisting of a big, aged Army tent sheltering two cots, a portable medicine chest, and a couple of packing cases which served as chairs. Fiddler arrived there late on an afternoon during a driving rainstorm. He was soaked to the skin, and all his belongings, which he carried in two barracks bags, were a sodden mess.

Sloshing into the tent, he came face to face with Corporal Garfield Lincoln, a Negro medical corpsman who had been running the dispensary until a physician could be found. Lincoln sprang to attention and saluted smartly.

"Relax, relax," Fiddler said. "Who are you?"

Lincoln told him, and Fiddler said, "You sound like a Republican."

"No, sir, my friends call me Franklin Roosevelt. I'll help you with your gear, Major. I've been sleeping nights on one of these cots since we have no bed patients, but I'll go back to my pup tent."

"No need," Fiddler said. "There's a cot here for you and one, alas, for me. Under my plan we'll never have any bed patients. Anybody too sick to stay in his pup tent will be sent to the post hospital. Lincoln, this will come as a distinct shock to you, but I'm not a doctor."

Lincoln took the news calmly. "You'd be surprised how few there are in the Medical Corps, sir. Are you medical administration that got diverted?"

"No, I'm an importer of Oriental art that got diverted. Do you play chess?"

Lincoln smiled. "Yes, sir."

He had been a premedical student at Howard University when drafted, and he counted himself fortunate that the Army had not sent him to one of the labor battalions to which nearly all Negro draftees were consigned. He listened sympathetically to Fiddler's misadventures.

"It was a fit of insanity did me in. I was on my way home from Hong Kong with some Chinese junk for my New York trade. Met this silly, middle-aged woman who said I reminded her of a noted psychiatrist. And so, silly, middle-aged jerk that I am, I decided to pretend for a while I was a psychiatrist. I've read a lot of psychology and know some of the jargon. The role was pleasing. I mean I really liked myself better as Dr. Fiddler than as Mr. Fiddler. Among the stupid things I've learned is hypnotism. I really can hypnotize some people, though not everybody. Anyway, I decided to pause in Hawaii. . . ."

In his role as Army physician Fiddler had a horror of killing or harming some soldier he was supposed to treat. But Lincoln reassured him, explaining that treatment in the dispensary was simple: iodine for brush and coral lacerations, blue pills for diarrhea, pink pills for constipation, aspirin for everything else except fractures, which were transported back to the base hospital.

Besides being a good chess player, Lincoln turned out to be an excellent companion. On Fiddler's second day in the wilderness he thought of a way to amuse them both. The big Army tent which sheltered them reminded him of an old Mathew B. Brady Civil War photograph of President Lincoln and a general. Borrowing a Brownie camera, Fiddler pressed it on a surprised enlisted man who came stumbling through the underbrush seeking treatment for diarrhea and ordered the man to take their picture as they stood together outside the tent. Fiddler insisted that each thrust a hand inside his shirt in the old fashion of daguerreotype portraits, and the enlisted man kept snapping pictures which Fiddler said must be captioned "President Lincoln meets a general."

At that moment Yaromski marched solemnly toward the dispensary followed by two men carrying Red, unconscious on a stretcher.

"What's the matter with him?" Fiddler asked.

"You tell me," Yaromski replied. "You're the doctor."

"I've got news for you, Sergeant. I'm not a doctor."

"This Army," Yaromski declared, "has become so fucked up that things like that happen all the time. This here man is a good soldier, Private First Class Andrew Jackson Jack. We've been carrying him on the books for four days now as AWOL. All that time the fuckin' MPs have had him in a cell. He had a pass to go see his wife. She disappeared. Somehow the idiots got the idea Red murdered her."

Leaning over Red, Yaromski spoke tenderly in his low dialect: "Wheh's ya wife, ya crazy bastid?"

Red opened his eyes and smiled. "Jane's home in the tree, Tantor."

Yaromski wrinkled his face, as if to burst into tears. "He was whacked on the head when the MPs arrested him. He's been talking like this ever since I got him out of jail."

"Thinks he's Tarzan." Fiddler explained Red's literary allusions.

Yaromski said, "Like to read P. G. Wodehouse myself. Personally never went for Burroughs. Red's got a fractured skull from where the MP billy hit him. Concussion. I wonder about brain damage. The Provost Marshal's office claims it sent the company word of his arrest. We never received it if they ever sent it—which I doubt. But right now these whole Hawaiian Islands are so fucked up, anything can happen. Anyhow, Red's got to be taken to the base hospital.

Major—are you really a major? What I want from you is certification for him from this field hospital to the base hospital."

Fiddler quickly certified Red for admission to the base hospital, and Yaromski and his stretcher-bearers carried him away.

About four o'clock that afternoon the company clerk brought Fiddler a clutch of orders so fresh that they smudged his fingers with mimeograph ink. The orders, with their confusion of mysterious abbreviations, were incomprehensible to him, but the clerk interpreted them. He was to gather his belongings immediately and be driven to the Pearl Harbor Naval Base where some authority called SOPA-USN-YMS, a Navy cuneiform the clerk could not translate, would provide for his transportation to a strange command somewhere called DUMBO-USA, which neither the clerk nor Yaromski had ever heard of.

Fiddler's transfer was swift. At one moment he was watching the surprised expression of Lincoln recede into the brush, and at what seemed the next, a Navy yeoman was yelling at him in a noisy office on Ford Island. Darkness had fallen when he dragged his barracks bags down an incline into what seemed a dimly lighted pit. In it were the voices and smells of humans, and he demanded:

"Where the hell am I?"

"Siddown!" someone yelled.

Fiddler sank into what seemed a metal-lined latrine hole and cried out again, "I still want to know where the hell I am!"

A man seated next to him said, "You're on a Navy flying boat that's been converted to a transport."

"It hasn't been converted enough," Fiddler said.

"Take a blanket from your bag," the man said. "Roll it and sit on it. These seats are sunk to contain parachutes, but there aren't any parachutes aboard."

"I'm hungry," Fiddler said. "I never got any dinner."

"Who did?" the man replied.

Somebody said they'd been promised sandwiches and coffee in five minutes, and another said the promise had been made half an hour ago.

"Where are we going?" Fiddler asked.

"Let's see your orders." The man snapped on a flashlight, and Fiddler saw by the eagle pinned to his collar that he was a colonel. "Doctor, we're going there together. Dumbo is the code name for a newly activated installation somewhere in the Pacific."

In the distance a voice bawled that they must fasten their seat belts for takeoff and there was to be absolutely no smoking. Then the engines began to gag and gasp and finally snarl and the boat started to vibrate frighteningly. After a while they were vibrating less and someone shouted that they were airborne in the darkness. Dim lights came on, and Fiddler made out two rows of men, totaling about two dozen in number, facing one another along the sides of the cabin.

He said, "In this manner warriors were buried in the T'ang Dynasty, seated, facing each other, memorialized behind stone for eons."

"Thanks for the encouragement," the colonel said. "Where you from?"

Fiddler, weary with denying he was a physician, decided to maintain he was the best. He mentioned his practice in New York and his patriotic pleasure at being called to active duty while a Navy enlisted man crawled among them doling out dry bologna sandwiches and tepid coffee. Fiddler was so hungry he found the meal delicious.

At some dark and ghastly hour of early morning a harsh voice shouted to make sure their seat belts were fastened. They thought they were crashing. A Catholic Navy chaplain among them began to pray loudly and finger his beads. Then someone peering out a port yelled that there were lights below. They seemed to descend forever, and when they finally landed it was as if they had struck a stone wall. They bounced and struck again and tilted crazily. At last the engines were blessedly quiet, and they scrambled out fast through a doorway like a hole, as if escaping from a snake-infested cave.

They were at a place called Johnston Island, which at that time was ill prepared to receive visitors. But visitors they remained for two days while mechanics repaired a hole torn in the flying boat when they struck coral on that first bounce. Fiddler wondered then and later how a bleak and sandy bit of land could be plagued by both fierce flies and a harsh wind at the same time.

Fiddler and the colonel swatted at flies and became friends. The colonel's name was Charles Peter Basset, and before long he let Fiddler know he was a member of a distinguished family. Fiddler believed him because Basset was so casual in everything he said; indeed, he was flattered that Basset appeared to value his friendship. While Basset was forty-two and Fiddler thirty-seven, Fiddler seemed older, for he was plump and soft whereas Basset was lean and hard. And yet, curiously, the two looked very much alike, except for Fiddler's mustache and glasses. Both had the same color eyes, the bold nose, the domed forehead.

Basset revealed that he was the only surviving member of a wealthy family who had done well at the Military Academy, graduating third in his Class of 1924 before starting his career in the Corps of Engineers.

While Basset had been reared on the family estate on the Maryland Eastern Shore, Fiddler had grown up on the Manhattan West Side, where his father made a precarious living as a remittance man. He had held many and varied jobs before declaring himself an authority on Oriental art. In his studies at City College he had displayed an extraordinary talent for mathematics, but he never had been able to turn it into a career. While he liked to blame that failure on the Depression, it had more likely been a result of his own caprices. He lost an instructorship in mathematics at a Long Island college because he refused to pander up to the department head, He spurned job offers from accounting firms because he hated bookkeeping, at which he was very good. He was fired from a statistician's post on the very day he was hired because he fell into an argument with the manager over the existence of God. Deciding he loathed mathematics, he studied all manner of subjects in public libraries and earned a living at such things as operating a miniature golf course, serving as the publicity director of a small publishing house, and being the manager of a large Jersey City burlesque theater.

Though Fiddler had been many things, he never had been married. But he greatly admired photos of Mrs. Basset and their son Roger. Helen Basset was beautiful; her name seemed apt, for she was like Fiddler's notion of that mythic woman of Homer who had caused so much trouble at ancient Troy: dark, patrician, sensual—and somehow vulnerable. Roger, a handsome child with a petulant mouth, was photographed in military uniform.

"We're going to make a soldier of him," Basset told Fiddler. "He's only ten years old, but I've got him in military school over my wife's objections."

Fiddler was surprised that military schools accepted such young students, and Basset replied, "Oh yes, some will take 'em at age eight. Roger's a little hell-raiser, and I'm not home enough to discipline him properly. But that school will knock some sense into him."

"How does he like the school?" Fiddler asked.

"What difference does that make?" Basset replied.

During two searing, fly-stinging days on Johnston they played chess on a small traveling board. After the flying boat took off once again, one of the passengers with navigational experience said they were shaping course more to the south than the west. Fiddler and Basset were the only two bound for Dumbo; the others had different, equally mysterious destinations.

At last the rising crimson sun flooded a turquoise sea with yellow light. Black specks grew on the gray southwestern horizon, and they began to descend.

It happened suddenly. There was a popping sound, as if someone had exploded a paper bag in another room. They tilted wildly and began to career downwards, so fast that their shrieks of terror seemed not to keep pace with them. It was something to hear men, Fiddler hearing his own voice among them, screaming like children frightening themselves in night games.

He never could reconstruct precisely what followed. Apparently, when they struck, the flying boat split like a ripe grape. Fiddler, in a paralysis of terror, had failed to fasten his seat belt. Possibly that saved his life. He was hurled through the air like a projectile and presumably lost consciousness briefly. And, finally, his death was delayed by something that had made him a butt of humor on the flying boat: he had insisted on wearing his uncomfortable life jacket from the moment they left Johnston. Despite his many adventures, he was basically conservative. There were things he did not trust, and one of them was airplanes.

At some point, while somersaulting through the air or after hitting the sea, he instinctively inflated his jacket. When restored somewhat, he found himself floating in choppy water while the yellow recovery dye from his jacket spread around him. Bits of wreckage floated everywhere. Stunned, he watched a man with chalk-white face raise a hand and then sink beneath the sea.

A life raft had somehow been flung loose, and another man, moaning in pain, was clinging to it. Fiddler paddled to the raft and saw that the man was Basset.

"Oh, Christ, my back!"

With great effort Fiddler struggled onto the raft and panted, "Easy, easy, I'll help you." He grasped Bassett by the shoulders.

Basset screamed. "Don't touch! Back broken! You doctor! You know don't *touch!*" Basset's voice failed in a gargling sound, his hold slipped, and he would have sunk if Fiddler had not clung to him.

At last he dragged his friend onto the raft. Basset was dead. And Fiddler had the terrible conviction he had killed him. For a time he felt as though he would go out of his mind. He thought he could have saved Basset's life if he had truly been a physician. It was intolerable to go on pretending he was a doctor. Basset's had been a life worth saving while his was not. Basset must not die. Fiddler must die before he killed others in his ignorance. Fiddler should be reborn as Basset, thus saving Basset's life.

Basset in his meticulous military way, carried his orders, ID card, pay record, and the photos of his wife and son, along with a little cash, in a waterproof belt. Fiddler took the belt off Basset, strapping it around himself, then exchanged their collar insignia. He put his dog tags around Basset's neck and hung Basset's about his own, noting that they had the same blood type and that his serial number now was 0-929585. Suddenly he noticed Basset's wedding ring and West Point class ring. He had some trouble in getting them off the lifeless fingers, but they fitted on his own as if they had been made for him.

Grasping Major Morton Fiddler about the waist, he shoved him into the sea where he sank like a stone. Then Colonel Charles Peter Basset fell back on the raft and awaited rescue.

7

Around the time Morton Fiddler was on his way to Dumbo and becoming Colonel Charles Peter Basset, Vera asked for my help in recruiting Rosemarie into her profession. As an Army public relations officer, pimping came easy for me.

I had already reported Vera's gospel to Orvie Snook: he who went down on her would never go down under enemy fire.

"Ridiculous," Orvie said.

"Isn't it, though?"

"The most ridiculous thing about it," Orvis said, "is how expensive it is."

"Well, you don't have to do it. There are lots of other things you can do. She's a very capable woman. There's a certain pagan delight even in her missionary position."

Orvie pondered for a while, then said, "It's very important to survive this war."

"Nothing is more important."

"There's the survival of the country, of course." I had rarely heard him sound such a patriotic note.

"True. Next to my own survival I hope most that the country survives this incredible thing."

Suddenly Orvie expressed an interesting idea. "Why don't I become Vera's gynecologist? Bet you anything she could use a new diaphragm. I make hellishly good diaphragms. At home my patients used to say, 'Snook's diaphragms fit like a glove' or something like that. I have all the equipment for 'em at the hospital. And I haven't a blasted thing to do all day. Boz, how do you pass your time?''

"Just fucking around, you might say. I know, it's terribly dull.''

"The point is, I could get a cut rate from Vera if I was her gynecologist. And I think I really ought to get in on this stupid superstition. Nothing to it, I'm sure, but I feel I shouldn't pass up anything in the survival department.

"I know, Orvie. My own feeling is leave no stone unturned.''

Vera was pleased with Orvie's idea and brought her price down to ten dollars an hour for him. "And I want you to fit Ginny with one too.''

Rosemarie, or Ginny, as we thought her to be, had never heard of a diaphragm—only a condom. News of it struck her the way the wheel must have enchanted primitive man. Of course she wanted one. "As a precaution,'' she said, "in case—you know.''

When Orvie came to fit her, they would not let me watch. I had to stand outside and only listen. It was especially interesting when Rosemarie shrieked with laughter and said, "Doctor, your eyelashes are tickling me!'' Orvie mumbled, "Lie still, I need a good view of this thing.'' When he came out his face was flushed and he said to me, "I had some very unprofessional thoughts in there. Did you ever think we're all becoming decadent?''

"I always was,'' I said. "I just never had such a grand opportunity for it till this war came along.''

Orvie left to put in a few hours of duty, but Vera asked me to linger. My time was my own because the General had suddenly been hailed before the inquiry board and had taken Goldman with him. Vera took me aside and said:

"I think my cousin Ginny would like to get into this business with me. She's just timid about asking. I need your help, Boz. Ginny likes you and—''

"No thanks,'' I replied. "I've got enough bad marks against me. I'm not going to add corrupting virgin youth to the list.''

"Ginny's no virgin. Back home in Ozark she'd lay anybody—for free. It's taking money for it that bothers her. Please talk to her.''

Somehow this put the matter in a different light. I asked Rosemarie to sit down on the divan while I discussed something important with her. To my surprise, she snuggled up close and fixed her blue eyes on me with a look of such expectation that it reminded me of yearning.

"Ginny,'' I began, "in my undergraduate days I was an outstand-

ing student of economics. I had a professor, old Professor Teeterbaum, who taught me something I'll never forget. It's known among
economists as Teeterbaum's Law, and it goes: 'Never give away
anything you can sell.' It's really at the foundation of modern economics. Darwin used it in his great work on the survival of the fittest,
You've heard of that, of course.''

"No, Boz, I haven't." There was a huskiness about her voice that
was enchanting to me. "I don't have much education. There are so
many things I just don't know anything about." She rested a warm
hand on my thigh. "But I love to listen to you talk. You're so—
brilliant. You must have been a great student and enjoyed all the fine
things of life."

She made me feel dazed. Why was I setting her up for Vera? Why
couldn't I have her to myself—at no cost? Never mind her lack of
education; I had mind enough for us both, and wanted her body for
myself alone. Suddenly I didn't know what to say next, but there was
no need for me to say anything as she went on:

"I've missed fine things. That's what I've missed. All because I
don't have the money to buy the fine things of life. I've been thinking
since I came to Vera's, is there anything really wrong with her charging for it?"

"Yes," I said. "I mean no." I put an encouraging arm around her
shoulders. "It's good that you're thinking about it. Teeterbaum's
Law, you know. Economics. Survival of the fittest. Origin of spe-
cies." I put my other hand on her thigh. "Yes. And yet no. Keep
your opinions—well rounded."

"Yes." She stroked my thigh. "I've been afraid of—you know—
having babies. But this new thing gives me—confidence."

"You should have utter confidence," I said. "It'll bring you life's
finest things."

"The trouble is I'm so shy, Boz. I don't really know the first thing
about it. Can I watch you and Vera and see what you do?"

I demurred. Though my faults were too numerous to count, exhi-
bitionism was not one of them.

"Please, Boz."

"Well, all right. When?"

"How about right now? Vera doesn't have an appointment. You
ask her. I feel shy about asking."

"Yes!" Vera exclaimed when I asked her. "Right away. This is a
real breakthrough!" She invited Rosemarie into her bedroom.

Rosemarie entered, blushing. "Good afternooon," she said and sat down in a chair at the foot of the bed. I think it was her saying good afternoon that got me.

"Undressing teasingly is very important," Vera told her as she began to unbutton her skirt. "It arouses the man. You'll see how Boz reacts."

But I was not reacting at all. I just sat there on the bed, intensely embarrassed.

"Boz dear," Vera said, "start to undress."

"Just go right ahead as if I'm not here," Rosemarie said.

I took off first one shoe, then the other—next one sock, and then the other. "Come on, Boz," Vera said. I wiggled my bare toes and looked at them. "It's helpful," Vera told her, "to leave on just your garter belt, stockings and shoes like this for a while. Sometimes it helps when the man acts shy, like Boz is playing it today, to help him undress." She began to unbutton my shirt.

At last she and I were lying naked on the bed, but still, nothing. "What's the matter with you today?" Vera asked peevishly. "Sometimes," she told Rosemarie, "for some reason nobody understands, the man can't get it up."

"Unbelievable!" Rosemarie exclaimed. "I never heard of such a thing!"

"In that case," Vera said, "there are ways the woman can help him. Watch carefully." But she was of no help at all to me.

"That's sweet and sort of sad," Rosemarie said.

I became aware that she was standing beside the bed, watching us and breathing quickly, her face flushed. Reaching out, she touched the root of my embarrassment and instantly it sprang to attention.

"Well I'll be damned," Vera said.

"Poor, pretty Boz." Rosemarie made a humming sound and began to stroke me.

"Take off your clothes, dear," Vera said, "and lie down where I am."

Rosemarie showed a bit of embarrassment, but complied. What a stunning creature she was!

"I've got the thing in me so I can't get pregnant," she said. "But first I'd rather try it this other way I just heard of."

Vera offered suggestions with barely contained excitement, but the phone rang and she left to answer it. Her departure dissolved Rosemarie's inhibitions.

Until then Rosemarie had known none of the pleasures of oral sex, she said later, but once she discovered the candy cane she could not get enough of it, licking and mouthing it up and down with little cries of surprise and delight while her hands played happily with every bauble of mine and her own in reach. She came quickly to a shuddering climax. Then I taught her that this was not a swift rabbity event but a consuming life experience. I would like to think that I was an extraordinary teacher, but the truth is I was a mere device, a key as it were, to a treasure trove of pure sensuality. Rosemarie took to it all like a duck to water and once she caught onto the concept of multiple orgasm there was no stopping her. Within an hour the teacher had turned pupil and I was writhing in delicious agony at the shocking uses Rosemarie had found in her tongue. After two hours I was a weak-kneed shadow of my former self and Rosemarie was an enthusiastic professional.

In this way I corrupted Rosemarie. That afternoon she agreed with Vera to split every fifty-dollar fee. That evening I spent two hundred dollars in happy testimony to her professionalism. And she was astounded to earn so much money for such great pleasure.

Next morning the General dispatched me to the Field for some records he and Goldman wanted for his defense. While there, I heard that Red was in the hospital under mysterious circumstances.

When Yaromski had told me a few days before that Red was AWOL, I'd found it hard to believe. He was too enthusiastic a soldier, I insisted. Yaromski agreed, but said things were so fouled up that enthusiasm was of no help any more. Yaromski himself had applied for transfer back to the Infantry and hoped for quick action.

As soon as I'd completed my errand for the General, I hastened to the hospital to see Red. He had been there two days and was sitting up, head swathed in bandages but chipper as a blue jay.

"They say I had a clot on the old brain," he told me. "Made me go a little zombie. But I'm okay now. I remember everything. I remember things I don't even want to. Yaromski told 'em it happened when I fell off a cliff on bivouac so as to keep my record clean. I know I can trust you not to squeal, Lieutenant Boswick. You're the one officer in the world I can trust."

"You sure can," I said. "The way to do that is, don't think of me as an officer. That's easy because most responsible people think I'm not. Tell me what happened, Red."

He described it all in great detail. As I listened, I grew increasingly uneasy. I began to have an inkling about the true identity of Vera's cousin Ginny.

After a while Red brought out his snapshots of Rosemarie, and I was aghast. Ginny was indeed Rosemarie. Until then I had not thought of myself as a bad man, only as a careless, incompetent, cowardly one. But it was *I* who had corrupted this Rosemarie whom Red loved so intensely that tears came to his eyes when he spoke of her. Yet I could not tell him what had happened without betraying her. Guilt had come to the Garden of Eden, if you could so call that patch of Vera's in Waikiki.

After leaving Red, I hurried to the General's office hoping to find Goldman. He was there. The hearings had adjourned early that day; things were going so badly for the General that Goldman had prescribed a sedative and sent him to bed. Like a good Catholic come to confession, I poured out the sad tale of my corrupting Rosemarie to Goldman.

"I don't think you did corrupt her," he said after I finished. "I think she had already decided to corrupt herself—her marriage to Red. You were merely the—uh—agent of corruption."

I suddenly realized what a great comfort he must be to our General in his time of trial.

"What we must do now," he said, "is convince her to return to Red and give up this—you know. Poor Red! I never realized how moral I really am."

"Me neither," I said. "But I always turn the most moral after I've committed some crime."

We drove to Vera's and found the young ladies unattended. When I confronted them with the truth, Vera became angry and Rosemarie tearful. Goldman made a stirring appeal to Rosemarie about the sanctity of marriage and the need of her returning to Red.

"But I don't *want* to!" she wailed. "I don't ever want to see him again. I want to have my own career and amount to something."

"But—" Goldman began.

"Listen, *Reverend* Goldman," Vera yelled, "you just mind your own goddam business and stop butting into other people's affairs! You too, Boz! If ever there were a couple of lice on the wall that have no reason to act pious, it's you two. Someday we girls are going to get our rights."

"My God," Goldman said, "I think you already have."

Although we had come to convince them, they wound up convincing us that Rosemarie's decision was hers alone to make.

"I'm not going to be ashamed of what I'm doing," Rosemarie said.

"I don't want to live under a phony name. No more calling me Ginny. I am Rosemarie, and that's what everybody's going to call me."

After we drove away I wondered to Goldman if I should tell Red what had become of her.

"No." Goldman drawled out the word slowly. "Stay out of it, Boz. There's so much guilt around these days that a little innocence is a good thing. Let him find out for himself. If you tell him, you betray Rosemarie. And that would just pile more guilt on your head."

Striving for a nobility I lacked, I resolved never to visit Rosemarie or Vera again and spent all the time I could seeing Red. Headquarters Company was moved back to the Field, and Red, released from the hospital, returned to it. We continued to see a lot of each other.

Gradually, in our conversations, Red talked less about Rosemarie and more about missing his father, mother and sister. It was strange, he said, for he had not yearned to see his family during the many months since he was drafted. He wrote two letters home within four days. He didn't mention Rosemarie's coming to Hawaii or his trouble with the MPs; it seemed that even a hundred pages could not begin to explain the crazy things that had happened to him.

His father had not written since Red sent home a snapshot of Rosemarie with a letter announcing their marriage; it was as if he had taken one look at her picture and decided she was pure poison. But his mother and Jenny always politely mentioned her in their letters. Now Red all but begged Pa to drop him a line. His father was, after all, the smart one in the family, Red said. He saw through Rosemarie as he had seen through the sham of patriotism and this stupid war.

On the day in 1940 when Red's draft number was drawn, Pa had grieved instead of gloated. "This day is a curse to our family! If the capitalists can't destroy us with a depression, they'll do it with a war!" He had begged Red to take the conscientious objector's route out of military service.

Red, remembering it aloud to Garfield Lincoln and me one evening, mourned that he had not done it. "I just didn't have the courage. My father's got more character than me. He quoted an English writer from way back, Samuel Johnson. According to Pa, this Sam Johnson said, *Patriotism is the last refuge of a scoundrel.*"

Lincoln nodded. "That's pretty good. Your pa must really have character. So does my old man—in a different way. He's a Pullman porter. I say that with respect. About the best a nigger can aspire to these days is to be a Pullman porter. I mean, if I ever do really make it into medicine it won't be any greater than my old man's effort to become a Pullman porter in his time." He pondered for a while. "Why should he be a patriot? I mean, he's not dumb or a scoundrel. That man Johnson must have been quite a writer. A line my old man likes to quote from him is, *How is it that we hear the loudest yelps for liberty among the drivers of Negroes?*"

"I would like to point out something to you," Yaromski said, employing his high dialect. "I would like to use an analogy I think you're intelligent enough to understand. A person can have doubts about the Virgin Birth and still be a good Catholic in his actions, if not in the opinion of the priests."

"But I'm not at all religious," Red replied stubbornly.

Yaromski lapsed into low dialect: "Ya dumb bastid, ya know wot I means! Yer in dis Ahmy till it's ovah an' don' get any udder ideas!"

Red indeed knew what he meant. Yaromski and Lincoln were his friends, and on the basis of their friendship he would try to be a good soldier. He would forget about Rosemarie. Yaromski had reported her disappearance to the civilian police of Honolulu, but no policeman ever came to question Red about her. Maybe no one cared about a missing person except the one who missed her. He did try his best to be a good soldier. He was in that mood when Yaromski talked him into requesting transfer to the Infantry.

8

Colonel Charles Peter Basset, born Morton Fiddler, was spotted by a PBY search plane soon after the crash and picked up by a Navy patrol boat from Dumbo.

His fit of insanity had passed and now seemed to him a spate of genius. As Colonel Basset he might find a way to escape home safely to the States, but as Major Fiddler he would have been fated to destroy innocent men while playing doctor. As Basset, however, he retained the shrewd survival instincts of Fiddler. So, when the patrol boat came alongside his raft, he feigned shock, for he needed time to learn something about himself and what was expected of him.

Understanding came to him quickly. Dumbo was the Army code name for an island called Masa-Masoa in a group possessed by France. Only the military mind could have made something ugly of a name like Masa-Masoa, but even the military could not altogether destroy the natural beauty of the island. Basset never forgot his approach to it in the rescue boat.

Its extinct volcano soared grandly, the green rain forests of its flanks ending well below its summit, creating the effect of a stern gray Puritan hat silhouetted against a blue sky. As Basset approached, the wind formed a long slender cloud that seemed to pierce the volcano as an Indian arrow might a Puritan crown. Coral reefs surrounded the island with a garland of foam. Unfortunately for the good of the inhabitants, the reef was broken by a passage into a small, well shel-

tered harbor. This gave it value to the American military and made it
another pearl on the chain the Americans had planned to string from
Hawaii to Australia even before the outbreak of war.

A wide and fertile plain at the foot of the volcano had for centuries
blessed the people with a rich cornucopia of coconuts, oranges, lem-
ons, bananas, pineapples, papayas, and many vegetables. The
blessed plain had turned into a curse, however, because it was flat
and wide enough to make an ideal landing field for military planes. At
that time the Seabees were mainly an idea only, and so the building
of an airstrip on the island had fallen to the Army, while the Navy
improved the harbor. For a month before Basset arrived, Army
troops had been gouging and destroying the Masoans' means of suste-
nance and promising them flour and corned beef which failed to appear.

When the boat entered the harbor that afternoon Basset, lying on a
stretcher, saw that a crowd had gathered on a recently completed
quay. He was relieved that he was able to discard the glasses he had
used in his guise as psychiatrist. He gave his orders to the solicitous
young ensign commanding the boat, then pretended to fall unconscious as the boat was tied up.

"Jesus!" a man on the quay exclaimed. "One survivor, and it has
to be Basset!" Through narrowed lids Basset saw that the speaker
was a stringy, hard-faced major of engineers.

"He should be hospitalized," the ensign said.

"As you know, there is no hospital," the major replied. "There is
no doctor since Captain Janis got drunk and drowned himself. There
was supposed to be a good surgeon coming on that flight, but he was
killed and we got Basset instead."

Basset was lifted into a truck and taken on a jouncing ride to the
scattered tents which composed Dumbo headquarters. A medical
corpsman whose breath smelled of alcohol listened to his heart
through a stethoscope and heard it beating. He spoke to another
enlisted man who came into the tent: "I don't know what ails him.
Hit on the head, I guess. You heard what Major Chute said about
him?"

"Everybody's heard. The guys up at the strip are suddenly working
like mad today just because they heard he's coming. They've been
told the Warden is taking over. That's some name the Army pinned
on him. The Warden! Chute says he's so tough and mean that he
shaves with a blowtorch. The Engineer Corps hands him only the

hardest assignments. They started calling him the Warden after he got mad at the Mississippi River. Said he was going to pen it in for life. And they said he just might have done it if they hadn't called him off. You can see why they sent him here. Chute's way behind schedule in building the strip. Oh, God, I want to be transferred!''

Basset felt there must be some mistake. Maybe there were two Colonel Bassets, and, in a typical Army foul-up, they had sent the wrong one here. For the Basset whose identity he inherited had seemed mild-mannered and decent. Surely a lovely wife like his would not have stayed married to a mean man like the Warden.

But apparently there was no mistake, for Chute came in and said, "That's him, grown older and pussier, but still the mean son of a bitch I spent the most miserable month of my life with on the Twin Fork Dam back in '32. Have you figured out what's the matter with him?''

"No sir, not yet, but I'm working at it.''

Another officer came in and said, "So that's the Warden. He has a mustache.''

"That's not regulation here by my orders,'' Chute said. "If he ain't dead, he's supposed to succeed me as island commander. And my last official order is to get rid of that mustache. Corporal, shave it off the son of a bitch.''

"Right now, sir?''

"Right now.''

Basset opened his eyes and sat up slowly. Then he rose calmly to his feet while the two officers and two enlisted men shrank from him in terror.

"Major Chute,'' he said, "I've heard everything you said, you bastard. The inspector general's office has enough on you to hang you by the neck. But I've been sent here to string you up by the balls because you won't complete the airstrip.''

Chute's lips worked in his pale face, but he uttered no sound.

Basset turned to the other officer, a portly captain. "Who the hell are you?''

"Captain Delaney, sir,'' he stammered. "Quartermaster.'' Then he thought it a good idea to salute.

"Captain, you're carrying a lot of beer on that belly.'' Basset took a roll of it in his fingers and pinched so hard that Delaney yelped. "We'll have to give you some special exercises.'' He turned to the corpsman. "Corporal, stop drinking that rubbing alcohol unless you want to join your medical officer. All right, Chute, haul your ass out of sling and take me to my headquarters. I want a fast rundown on everything.''

Within a day or two Basset realized that a military command was little different from running a newspaper stand or any other enterprise. It had its special language, like any business, but essentially it was a matter of organizing a confusion of detail into some purpose. In the case of Dumbo the purpose was the building of an airstrip. As in running any endeavor, the trick was to delegate authority. And, of course, the crucial art behind the trick was to decide whom to trust.

Basset was surprised at how the armed forces had managed to assemble so many untrustworthy misfits on Masa-Masoa. The only professional career officers were Chute, a competent engineer, and Lieutenant Commander Duffy, the capable chief of naval construction. Apart from their engineering competence, however, both had serious flaws of character: they were jealous, scheming liars. Chute had been island commander, a post which Duffy longed for, but which Basset now held. Each warned him against the other. And both warned him against Major Joseph "Pappy" Hoyle, a Georgian sprung from the National Guard who commanded the Infantry battalion of 228 Negro draftees assigned to build the strip with inadequate equipment under Chute's direction. Both also warned him against Major Sebastian Rinaldo, a National Guardsman from Rhode Island who commanded an all-white antiaircraft battalion of 236 men recently arrived from Texas to serve as the island's protective force. And absolutely everybody joined in warning him against Delaney, who commanded the quartermaster service company that supplied the battalions.

On his first morning Basset rode to the Infantry area with Chute at 0600 and was surprised to find the entire battalion doing cadence drilling and calisthenics while Pappy Hoyle passed benevolently among his black troops, uttering encouragement and tapping behinds with his swagger stick.

"Is Hoyle doing this for my benefit?" asked Basset.

"No," Chute said. "He runs 'em ragged for half an hour five mornings a week and has a full field inspection on Saturdays. Wants to keep 'em in condition."

Every eye in the battalion was on the Warden as Hoyle approached him, saluted twice, puckered up his face real friendly, and said, "And how are *yew* this morning, Colonel?"

Basset returned the salute and said, "No more morning drill and exercise."

Apparently Hoyle had read that book about winning friends and influencing people, for he maintained his determinedly friendly air and said, "Well, Colonel, I know they're niggers and never will be sent to combat, but according to Hoyle this conditioning is according to regulations."

"Well, Major, from now on things are done here according to Basset. Our objective is to build an airstrip in the shortest possible time. The men are getting plenty of exercise working on the strip. From now on work will begin there at 0600 in the cool of the day and people will get compensatory time off in the heat of the day."

He and Chute rode on to Rinaldo's headquarters through a beautiful glade coursing through the lower forest of the volcano. A sergeant had to awaken Rinaldo, who stumbled from his tent in panic and gave Basset a quick tour of the gun positions. They were poorly sited and pathetically weak: two 90-millimeters and four 50-caliber machine guns.

"Aren't the Japs beyond attack range?" Basset asked. No one knew. He sent for a map which, when it arrived, was still neatly folded in its original envelope. Rinaldo spread it out on the field table and leaned over it, his finger trailing back and forth from one dot to another, until he found Japan. He paused, frowning, then returned to the search. At last he stood back, smiling, his finger marking their location, a spot about a thousand miles from where he'd thought the island was.

The Americans were keen on comfort in their bivouac areas. Shrewd migrants, they had a sharp eye for dwelling place, drainage, refuse disposal, and water supply, and had hired the comeliest Masoan girls as laundresses and the brightest youths to keep their tents and areas tidy. There was order in the apparent chaos of the encampments. About the AA gun emplacements the bivouacs sprawled like Gypsy camps with bits of colored cloth and potted plants arranged to try to disguise the regulation olive drab and khaki which were the wretched fabric of the men's uprooted lives. There were portraits of Betty Grable, Rita Hayworth, and nuder, lesser known women, but none of home or mother. Several men had fashioned elaborate shaving stands from wood scraps with helmets inset to serve as basins. Two had captured and penned a half-wild pig which they sought to tame rather than to eat. There were many mongrels, a goat, a jungle cat that looked as fierce as a leopard. These AA men had nothing to do except to clean their guns and hold a daily half-hour dry-run drill. They dared not expend live ammunition in target practice, for Rinaldo explained they had almost none, and the Navy refused to supply them with more unless they came up with something worth trading.

Basset thought that if he were to accomplish Dumbo's objective he must develop more than a reputation for cruelty: he must be feared as utterly mad. Thus, surprising a soldier who lay in a hammock reading Henry Adams' *Mont-Saint-Michel and Chartres,* he shouted so loudly that the terrified young man fell out of his hammock. "Reading a book at *eight* in the morning? What sort of outfit you running, Major?"

Rinaldo had a habit of dancing from foot to foot when under stress. "Sorry, sir. Should we burn the book?"

Basset adopted a sinister tone, a mad leer: "If you burn that book, Rinaldo, I'll have your ass burned at the stake. Order the child to hide it in his footlocker till I've left the area. Then let him resume reading while he still has the chance. Great changes are about to be wrought, Major. *Great changes!*"

His inspection of the quartermaster company revealed even more sloth than in the AA battalion. There was an atmosphere of corruption about the company such as he had not sensed since he used to deliver tribute to the office of a New Jersey political boss. It took him only a few minutes to smell out the chief source of corruption: a huge, hidden cache of beer which the company had waylaid on its course to Corregidor.

"Well, sir"—Sweat broke out on Delaney's pallid brow—"things ain't getting through to Corregidor any more. I mean they mainly need ammunition out there."

"I'll tend to you later, Delaney!" Basset marched away.

At noon that day he interrupted the chow and siesta of every Army officer with a summons to headquarters. Totaling twenty-three, they were too numerous to crowd into his tent, so he had a corporal carry his canvas armchair outside. He sat down in the shade facing the officers while they stood in the sun and stared into the distance. These men wanted to kill him, he realized, but fortunately they lacked the nerve. Silently he looked into the eyes of each; but not one could meet his gaze, as much from guilt as from the sun.

At last he began in a low tone: "There are going to be some changes. . . . Henceforth *everybody* but the radar men of the AA battalion is going to work on the strip. There will be no drill, no inspections, till the job is done. Then," he concluded, "we can resume playing war games."

Basset had no idea how an airstrip should be built, but he was not much worried by his total lack of engineering experience. He had always felt that even a country clergyman who had a sufficient air of authority could run General Motors, that General Motors pretty much ran itself. All the head of a vast and complex undertaking need do was to say yes or no. He simply had to be a good guesser in order to maintain power.

After dismissing the assembled officers, Basset detained Chute and asked him, "Essentially what the hell's the problem in the airstrip operation?"

Chute crinkled up his face like a baby crying. "They order an all-weather strip, but they won't send any steel matting. We need sixty-seven tons of it and we haven't got an ounce."

It was news to Basset that concrete required matting. He said, "We must find a substitute."

"Find a substitute for matting," snarled Chute, "and you've discovered something like perpetual motion."

"Then we'll have to find the real thing. Goddam it, Chute, shake your ass loose and *get* us steel matting!"

Chute looked at him with the horror of one trapped by a dangerous madman, then uttered a whinnying sound and galloped off through the palm trees.

Basset sat down to a lonely luncheon of greasy sausage, dehydrated potatoes and lumpy bread prepared by a cook who had been a high school algebra teacher before he was drafted and sent to baker's school. After a couple of tentative bites Basset pushed aside his plate and went for a walk around the headquarters area. As he strolled among the palms, hands clasped behind him and pondering the problem of the matting, he heard the staccato of Morse code from the headquarters message center tent. Stepping in, he found a thin corporal listening but not taking down any message.

"Good afternoon," Basset said. "Who are you? What do you do?"

The Corporal got to his feet quickly. "I'm Merwyn, sir. Radio operator. I run the message center."

"What are you listening to?" Basset asked.

"Key TBS—that's talk between ships—in Force Seven. That's the code name of a convoy coming near us on the way from Panama to

Australia. They're supposed to maintain radio silence, but they get so
bored they bust out talking to each other every once in a while.''

Basset meditated. ''Do you know the call designation of Headquarters Pacific Ocean Areas?''

''Of course, Colonel. We have to report to them at least three times
every twenty-four hours. That's Zebra Eight Four Comgenpoa. We
have three different codes on that network.''

''Could Comgenpoa reach the commander of Force Seven?''

''Yes sir. But he'd have to channel it through Cincpoa—that's
Navy—because—well, sir, I guess you know this is sort of the
Navy's war out here. I have the Navy code book for such a message
and can read it, but I'm not allowed to send in it.''

''Yeah. Well, Merwyn, I've just allowed you to. I want you to send
the following message to Concom Seven: Divert sixty-seven tons of
steel airstrip matting and 12,000 rations of fresh meat to Dumbo. Sign
it Comgenpoa.''

Merwyn stared at him. ''Sir, Cincpac-Cincpoa monitors absolutely
every message sent in the Pacific. It's said they even listen to conversations between seagulls.''

''Yeah. Well, Merwyn, if those fat cats at Pearl have that big a
snooping operation going I'll bet their left hand knows not what their
right is doing. Send the message. That is an order.''

Merwyn did not hesitate. Basset sat down and listened to the incomprehensible dit-dah until Merwyn looked around at him with an
expression of awe. ''Colonel, sir, it's roger all the way. The matting
and the meat will arrive tomorrow afternoon.''

''Thank you.''

Basset walked back to the chow tent where Chute picked dourly at
a curled bit of sausage in his mess kit.

''The steel matting will be here tomorrow afternoon,'' Basset told
him. ''And at the same time we'll be getting 12,000 rations of fresh
meat.''

Two tears coursed down Chute's haggard face. But whether they
were expressive of joy or rage or utter insanity Basset could not tell.

The next morning Basset sought out Merwyn and asked him, ''Do
you happen to know anywhere on this island an honest man who
doesn't drink?''

''Yes sir, Pfc. James Lubbock is a thoroughly honest man who's
opposed to drinking anything stronger than milk. He's a Seventh Day
Adventist. You know they're pacifist and not supposed to do military

duty. Well, Lubbock got saved in Dallas right after he finished basic. He made his salvation known to his captain, but they wouldn't discharge him.''

"Fetch me Lubbock."

He was a big, ambling, gentle-mannered man who acted as unafraid of Basset as Merwyn did.

"Lubbock, I hear you're as opposed to beer-swilling as I am. And it has come to my attention that hidden on this island is a reservoir, a veritable ocean of stolen beer that is being swilled by certain thieving parties. Lubbock, I want that dried up. If beer is to be drunk, it will be fairly apportioned. Sipped, that is, in moderation by thirsty, hardworking men. Lubbock, I appoint you in charge of the beer detail. You're relieved of all other duties, whatever they might have been. Select the men of your detail carefully on the basis of character. Arm yourselves, and we'll publish it broadside that twenty-four-hour guard has been mounted over the beer with instructions to shoot to kill. Lubbock, I want you to make a careful count of the bottles and report the total to me personally. Come on, son, I'll show you where the stuff is hidden.''

Merwyn went along too, and, as they emerged from the shade into bright sunlight, Basset observed that the young corporal had not shaved his upper lip that morning.

The attitude toward Basset began to change from fear to awe after two ships put into the harbor late in the afternoon with steel matting and a quantity of fresh meat along with two huge refrigerators and an auxiliary power generator. It was a reflection of Basset's powerful personality that while he put Chute in charge of unloading the vessels he left him with the distinct impression that he was in fact directing the operation himself.

Actually, he paid no attention to the labor of the troops and crews as the tons of goods were craned onto the quay, for he was preoccupied with a project of his own. After he organized the beer detail that morning he busied himself with two pieces of torn old sheeting in which he snipped numerous holes. On either side of each sheet he sewed round Rising Suns cut from red cloth, then trampled both thoroughly in the dirt before fixing each to a small pole.

After the first ship tied up at the quay he paid a courtesy call on its skipper, taking one of his creations with him. While the ship's officers plied him with Scotch and steak, he showed them his captured Japanese battle flag and regaled them with the story of how he and the brave remnants of his men had captured the flag when they seized the island. "You can see our bullet holes here in the flag. . . . *'Banzai!'* they screamed on their last charge. . . . We took no prisoners. . . . Their C.O. committed suicide. . . ." A junior officer wondered aloud why the people at home hadn't heard about the capture of Masa-Masoa. "Didn't dare," Basset explained, shaking his head sadly. "Our casualties were frightful. The waters of this harbor literally ran red with American blood."

It took great persuasion on the skipper's part to get Basset to part with his captured Japanese battle flag. But he finally consented in exchange for two cases of Johnny Walker Red Label and six boxes of Havana cigars. When he visited the second freighter with his second flag, he found an even more receptive audience: he departed with three cases of Johnny Walker Black and eight boxes of Havanas. Both Scotch and cigars he placed in the safe deposit of the beer cache, for Lubbock had made certain that the members of its guard detail were non-smokers as well as teetotalers.

Life as the commander of Masa-Masoa so engaged Basset that he could not imagine why he ever had wanted anything but a military career. It was not that he coveted power so much, but rather enjoyed trying to solve difficult problems.

The problem of completing the airstrip in another six weeks before the start of the local monsoons was difficult indeed. With the help of beer, however, he thought he might achieve his goal. His plan combined ideals of both socialism and capitalism. There would be equality in work and rationing of beer, but hard workers were offered the incentive of beer dividends. Teams were formed, rules of achievement laid out. Many tried hard to obtain additional beer which, if one didn't drink it, could be traded for the desired possessions of thirstier, lazier men. Since money was of little value on Masa-Masoa, beer became a potent medium of exchange. Basset was even able to obtain the use of idle Navy bulldozers, essential to quick completion of the strip, in trade for several cases of beer.

Vigorous, unceasing work began to show on him. He grew thinner, harder, moved faster, carried himself with military aplomb. Helped by Merwyn, whom he promoted to master sergeant and put in charge of headquarters, he quickly learned the language and special customs of the Army. In the process some of the past slipped from him. For instance, recalling his past ability at hypnotism, he tried it a few times on likely subjects but found that the skill seemed to have left him.

One thing about him did not change, however: he kept his mustache luxuriantly fierce. As a result of his fairness in administering the beer and his genius in obtaining fresh meat for the men, nearly every soldier on the island began growing a mustache a couple of weeks after Basset arrived. While soldiers still called him the Warden behind his back, it was said now with esteem.

In his devotion to duty he forgot about his personal life. When a ship bearing mail brought a letter from his wife Helen, he opened it with interest. Not liking the name Charles, he was pleased to see that she addressed him as "Dear Pete." Her letter was full of surprises. She was teaching at a school for retarded children in New Jersey and enjoying it. Roger hated military school and was doing badly. "I don't care what you say, Pete, I'm taking him out of there unless things start going better. After all, he's *my* son too." But his biggest surprise was to learn that he and his dear Helen had been estranged for the past couple of years while maintaining a facade of congenial marriage.

"I know our lousy marriage has had its effects on Roger," she wrote. "I'll abide by your wish and wait till this war is over to get a divorce. But then I want to be free. Sometimes my twenty-eight years seem awfully long. Until then I'll try to believe in the resolve you expressed before you left: that you want to earn respect, even affection, instead of fear and mistrust. . . ."

Basset adjusted the photos of her and Roger on his field desk and typed a long letter. He told her he had been lucky to survive the crash, and in Fiddler's death he mourned the passing of a friend. "Sorry to hear about Roger's problems," he wrote. "If he hates it, pull him out of there. I can't remember his address. Will write him if you provide it." He signed it off, "Love and devotion, Pete."

He could forge the Warden's signature in imitation of that in his pay records, but he could not maintain the forgery throughout a letter. Yet what difference did it make? He might never hear from his estranged wife again.

However, she wrote back quickly.

"My dear Pete," she began, "What an astonishingly delightful letter from you. You *have* changed! I never knew you possessed such a grand sense of humor. Shame on you for barking at that poor boy in the hammock who was reading Henry Adams. And I didn't think you even knew who Henry Adams was!" She gave him Roger's address, adding, "Don't expect him to answer. You'll have to admit you've been pretty hard on the little kid and he's not about to do a quick somersault in his attitude toward you."

She went on to speculate about his personality having been shaped by the fact that he was a foundling who had struggled hard for everything, especially to win an appointment to the military academy. She also speculated about having been attracted to him because he was much older than she was and he had seemed a father figure to an orphan like herself. She ended the long letter, "As always, Helen."

So Basset had lied about his background in a wish to impress. From what Helen wrote, there at least would not be relatives or in-laws asking about such things as Fiddler/Basset's appearance and background in case he ever ran into them. But that must never happen. He must not even communicate further with her for fear it might lead to a tragic confrontation some day.

However, the role of father suddenly appealed to him, and he could not resist writing Roger a warm note. Then he decided to write Helen once more just for the hell of it. Giving himself over to enjoyable rhetoric, he wrote how he longed to see her. "Perhaps it will be sooner than we realize, my dear. The destinies of people in war are settled by strangers in distant places."

9

Like most wars in their early stages, our war seemed to be going nowhere. American forces in the Philippines were quickly penned up on Corregidor Island and the Bataan Peninsula; before long, the Hero commanding them would flee to personal safety in Australia, and they would capitulate to the enemy. The Japanese Navy was superior everywhere. All over the Central and West Pacific the Americans and their allies were outnumbered, outmaneuvered, forced to surrender.

In Hawaii, the General followed Goldman's advice when he faced the board of inquiry and was cleared of blame in the Pearl Harbor defeat. He was not returned to his command, however; he was kept at Derussy with nothing to do while awaiting a new assignment. Surprisingly, he kept his word and obtained a second lieutenant's commission for Goldman.

Goldman, however, was dismayed rather than pleased by his commission. For incomprehensible reasons he was commissioned in the Infantry rather than the Air Force. By that time he had served the General long enough to hate him thoroughly, yet dreaded to be separated from his patronage. Since he had never had basic training or fired any weapon or known anything about close-order drill, he visualized himself being court-martialed for incompetence.

I was as unhappy as Goldman. I had no worthwhile function, and life seemed pointless. Often I yearned to go to Vera's, but I refused to give in to my lust. This forced nobility of character sometimes made me melancholic, especially after my kooky grandmother sent me a check for a thousand with a letter admonishing me, "You're not killing enough Japs." I thought about the twenty hours of pleasure that Grandma's generosity could offer me and suffered alone.

One day Goldman paid what he insisted was only a social call at Vera's and came back piqued. "Vera is downright uncivil. She kept calling me Reverend Goldman and asked if I'd come to hold prayers. But Rosemarie seems very happy. She asked about you and said she misses you. I told her you were broke."

Red and I continued to see quite a bit of each other, an unusual situation in the Army where officers and enlisted men are so rigidly segregated. He was bored with the motor pool and restlessly awaiting transfer to the Infantry, a move he hoped to make in the company of Yaromski. In his mood of disenchantment he thought he'd never make it to flight school.

On the last Saturday in January he was given a one-day pass into Honolulu along with just about everybody else in the company. Yaromski warned him to be very careful not to run afoul of the MPs again. As a precaution, Yaromski put him in the charge of their mutual friend, Corporal Willie Willowboe, better known as Cherokee, a full-blooded Indian who, at six feet five towered above them all. His massive chest and arms assured him of never being crossed. Red, Cherokee and Lincoln took a bus to town together.

On Hotel Street they separated, Lincoln going to a bar frequented by Negro enlisted men, while Red and Cherokee entered the Fireside Cafe. On the ride from the Field the warm splash of the Hawaiian sun made Red think of freedom—and Rosemarie. He'd brought along swimming trunks in a bowling bag, and told Cherokee he knew a great place out in Waikiki where they could go for a swim. But Cherokee wasn't partial to the idea: no sir, they were not going to waste perfectly good drinking time by going all the way to Waikiki. Yaromski had put Cherokee in charge of Red, and he outranked him anyhow, and he was not going to let Red out of his sight, so that was that.

But Red had other ideas. He had read that murderers liked to return to the scenes of their crimes. Or maybe, like a great detective, he felt he could unravel the mystery by starting again at the scene where it began. In any event, he wanted to go back to that beach just once more and *look*.

Telling Cherokee to keep an eye on his beer, Red went to the latrine. Cherokee was unconcerned because there was only one door to the latrine. But he forgot to reckon on its window. By the time Cherokee went into the latrine looking for him, Red was two blocks distant.

He was making for the Number 8 bus that would take him to Waikiki when he saw three men from the company approaching and ducked into the bar of the Meacham Hotel to avoid them. Ordering a beer, he put nickels in the jukebox to play two of Rosemarie's favorites—Bing Crosby singing "Smoke Gets in Your Eyes" and Frances Langford doing "I'm in the Mood for Love." Tears came to his eyes as he thought about Rosemarie while Crosby moaned, *When your heart's on fire . . . When a lovely flame dies . . .*

At that moment I stepped to the bar and saw him. Goldman and I had planned to go downtown that afternoon and see *Citizen Kane,* a movie each of us had seen and enjoyed before. But at the last moment the General snared Goldman while I contrived to escape. Arriving too early for the film, I went into the Meacham bar for a beer.

There I saw Red and stepped through the crowd to his side. When I saw the tears in his eyes, I thought something awful had happened. Well, from his viewpoint, it had.

"That's one of Rosemarie's favorite songs," he told me. "You know, I've got her so under my skin I don't think I'll ever recover. Where *is* she?"

I felt stricken. Why had I bumbled into this bar when there were many others around the movie house? Maybe everything would be better if I never saw Red again.

"I'm going out to Waikiki," he said. "I'm going to search that whole area." I became upset as he told me his plans and how he had escaped from Cherokee. "Yes sir, Lieutenant Boswick, that's what I'm going to do. I *know* I can trust you not to squeal on me."

"I won't squeal, Red, but—" I was lecturing him on the dangers of going to Waikiki and running into the MPs again when the bartender suddenly called out:

"No colored here! Move!"

Seeing Lincoln's reflection in the mirror, I told the bartender, "This man's my friend."

"I don't care, Lieutenant. House rule. They have their own place."

"Hi, Lieutenant." Lincoln turned to Red. "Cherokee's looking for you."

"I know. I've got to get on to Waikiki."

We went outside, and I said, "Everybody wait a minute. Everybody's got to hold a pow-wow while I buy everybody a beer. Lincoln, what place will they let you into?''

"There's a colored place around the corner on King. They don't much like whites coming in there, but they daren't throw us out, you being a lieutenant. Red, Cherokee is mad at you. Yaromski's in town, and he's mad too. They've got everybody looking at you. Why did you run out?''

"I've got to get to Waikiki," Red said. "I've been thinking about it. Rosemarie is hiding from me somewhere near that beach. I *know* she is.''

"You know nothing of the sort," I said. "Now let's knock off this silliness.''

"Let's go to the New Emma Cafe instead of the colored place," Lincoln said. "Yaromski and Cherokee have set up search headquarters there. Turn yourself in, Red, and they'll be over their mads in a minute. Or better yet, let me turn you in. I'll make points with Yaromski for doing it.''

"Ass-kisser," Red said.

"I'm not! You do what Lieutenant Boswick says.''

"That's a direct order, Private Jack," I said. "We're going to the New Emma Cafe.''

"Look out!" Red yelled. "Here they come!''

I whirled around, but saw no one familiar. By the time I wheeled back, Red was running away, with Lincoln after him. I went on to the movie, but had difficulty concentrating. It was a while before I learned what happened next to Red and Lincoln.

They ran into another bar where no one seemed to notice Lincoln was Negro. "You ought to be ashamed of yourself for disobeying our friend Lieutenant Boswick," Lincoln panted.

"I'll obey him tomorrow," Red said. "But not today." They had two or three more beers while they argued, then Red said, "Goodbye, Corporal Lincoln, I'm on my way to Waikiki.''

Lincoln drank up his beer and said, "I'll follow you at a safe distance. If somebody recognizes you, I'll holler and you start running. That way I won't be implicated.''

After they got off the bus in Waikiki and walked down the road toward the ocean, they would not have called themselves drunk; but they had drunk a lot of beer, and felt happy. As they approached Vera's bungalow, Red said, "I want to investigate that mysterious house.''

"What's mysterious about it?" Lincoln asked. "It's just an ordinary bungalow."

"It has an air of mystery about it," Red said. "We'll go up and ring the bell."

"Not me," Lincoln said. "If you look real close, you'll see my skin is black. And there's one thing a smart black-skin learns at an early age. Unless you've really got to, you don't go to strange houses ringing doorbells. Because inside there may be a big ole white man with a shotgun who shoots first and asks after, 'Nigguh, what you doin' at my door?' I'll just wait out here." He disappeared into the brush as Red climbed the steps to the porch. Seeing that the door was open beyond the screen, he rang the bell.

Rosemarie, wearing a new flowered dress, had just come from her bedroom to greet a client. He was a frail young Army lieutenant, who took the hand she extended and kissed it, "You're lovely!" he exclaimed.

At that moment Red, receiving no reply to his ring, shaded his eyes and peered through the screen. "Rosemarie!" he shouted. Then, seeing that an Army officer had grasped his wife by the arm and was about to attack her, he tore open the screen door, crying, "Leggo my wife, you dirty son of bitch!"

Rosemarie, staring at Red, uttered a terrified scream that must have been heard as far as the beach. Certainly it pierced to Vera in her bedroom and to her client, a Navy ensign, and to Lincoln lurking in the underbrush beside the house. Her scream completely unnerved the lieutenant, who staggered backward as a red-haired madman rushed at him, swinging wildly.

Rosemarie's fright gave way to a consuming rage at Red's discovery. While he and the lieutenant danced around each other, she shrieked curses at him. Neither she nor Vera ever did remember who had left a golf putter in the living room; suddenly, however, it was in Rosemarie's hands, and she swung it hard at her husband, hitting him on the side of the head and decking him.

Lincoln, believing by the noise that a crowd was attacking Red, dashed into the house to aid him just as the ensign galloped naked from the bedroom with Vera, also naked, yammering in terror behind him. The ensign's athletic prowess was not confined to sexual games; he had boxed as a middleweight at Annapolis. Seeing Lincoln and thinking he had gone crazy and invaded the house, he went at him coolly in approved ring fashion; one-two, two-one.

Lincoln's knees collapsed. In a sudden, awful silence, as he sank toward the floor, he heard a bird in the brush calling *per-chic-o-ree, per-chic-o-ree-ree-ree,* like flaxbirds along the creek beside his home near Front Royal. But as he fell asleep he realized he must be mistaken. For Cherokee, who knew a lot about birds, had vowed there were no flaxbirds in Hawaii.

The MPs carried off Red and Lincoln, both groggy, while Rosemarie wept hysterically. Yaromski's excellent intelligence system notified him immediately after Red and Lincoln were arrested. He and Cherokee arrived at Vera's quickly, and the lieutenant answered the door.

Yaromski said, "Sir—" and the lieutenant saluted *him* while backing into the living room, where Yaromski saw Rosemarie. Yaromski, pressing on, said, "With your permission I'd like to talk to you or the lady." The lieutenant, deferring to Rosemarie, left the room.

Yaromski at once revised his original impression of her. Beautiful, but definitely not innocent, he thought; she was as tough a broad as any he had known.

"Mrs. Jack," he said, "let me put it to you this way. The Army ain't no place for a lady like you, but your husband's a good soldier. It's his career. Please don't proffer charges against him. If you do, you ain't going to look like the lady you are and your lieutenant friend could suffer. If you don't, I promise to have your husband sent to a tropic island thousands of miles away for the rest of the war."

Without hesitating she agreed to drop assault charges against Red.

Yaromski took the frightened young lieutenant to the Provost Marshal's office where, to the astonishment of the jailers, the lieutenant beseeched them to release the enlisted men. About eleven o'clock that evening Yaromski routed me out of my bunk to go to the office and sign orders reducing Red and Lincoln to privates and sending them to Dumbo.

"You're the only officer I can trust not to make a Federal case of it," he told me. "I just want Red out of harm's way before he gets into deeper trouble, and I have to give Lincoln the same treatment because he was involved too."

In the office Red acted sheepish, Lincoln angry. Then Red squared his shoulders and said, "Lieutenant Boswick—Lieutenant Boswick, I found Rosemarie. She's being unfaithful to me."

I tut-tutted him, saying something inane like he must be mistaken.

Lincoln turned on him angrily: "You ruined me, and I was only trying to help you."

"You didn't have to," Red replied. "It was your own fault. Did you see the way I knocked out that lieutenant?"

"You never touched him. What I saw was your wife knock you out with a golf club. My God, you whites are *savages!* Things like that don't happen in a respectable colored family. From now on, boy, I'm looking out for myself."

They left next day for Dumbo. I gave them my paternal blessing, doubting I would ever see either again. I knew I'd miss Red, but agreed with Yaromski that he'd be better off away from Hawaii. Maybe, in truth, I was relieved that I would no longer have to face the man I'd unwittingly betrayed.

When Red and Lincoln landed at Dumbo in a rainstorm and hauled their barracks bags to a little tin shelter which served as the air depot, a yawning corporal rang a couple of people by field phone. After a long time a truck driven by a Negro private arrived and they rode off through the mud till the rain and the truck stopped simultaneously. Climbing out, they found themselves in a palm grove that shone like silver from the rain.

Everywhere Red looked he saw Negroes; and gradually all of them stopped whatever they were doing and looked at him. "Why are there so damn many Negroes around?" he asked.

Lincoln smiled for the first time in days. "Now you know how I feel. For years I've been asking myself why are there so damn many whites around."

They went into a big tent where three Negro enlisted men stared at Red. Finally one, a big master sergeant, studied his orders and said, "I've got to call Major Hoyle on this one." He rang the field phone connection to Hoyle's tent. "Major, we've just received two men from Hawaii, and one is white. . . . Yes sir . . . Yes sir . . . But sir, he has red hair. . . . Yes sir . . . Well sir, his eyes are sort of green. . . . Yes sir . . . Right, Major . . . Yes *sir!*"

Hanging up the phone, he continued to gaze expressionlessly at Red. "Well, soldier, welcome to the all-Negro 108th Infantry Battalion. Major Hoyle says there's a question about you being colored with a little white blood mixed in. Major Hoyle says they never make mistakes about things like that in Hawaii. And you understand Major Hoyle *never* makes mistakes himself."

Next morning in the headquarters tent Merwyn said to Basset, Colonel, the Army's turning this place into Devil's Island. Three from the Schofield stockade last week. Now they're even *flying* 'em in. Two busted enlisted men on that mail plane yesterday. I had 'em sent directly to Hoyle's battalion without even seeing them. There are asterisks after their names. That's the new code in this theater for a trouble-makin' nigruh."

"There can be mistakes in asterisks, Merwyn. If you didn't see 'em, how do you know they're Negroes?"

"By their names. Straight out of 'Amos 'n' Andy.' Can you imagine a white being named Andrew Jackson Jack?"

Basset, remembering Red, stared at Merwyn. "As a matter of fact I can."

When Basset arrived at battalion he asked Hoyle, "Did you receive a white soldier yesterday named Jack?"

"No sir. But we did receive a nigger soldier named Jack with a lot of white blood in him."

"Send for him."

Hoyle looked embarrassed. "Colonel, I'm proud of my record of not a single AWOL."

"You mean not an AWOL on the books, Hoyle. You forget to record your many overnight absences. If the poor souls had any way of escaping from this damn island, you wouldn't have a man left. Now, fetch me Jack."

"That's what I'm leading up to, Colonel," Hoyle labored on. "The son of a bitch went on one of those overnight absences. I think he must have been *passing* as white in civilian life, and when the Army got to the truth of the matter about him being black . . ."

The truth of the matter was that when Red had been assigned to a tent he had walked in its front entrance and out its rear and headed into the jungle with a vague notion of emulating his old god Tarzan. After spending the most miserable night of his life stung by insects and haunted by a mortal terror of snakes (of which there was not one on Masa-Masoa), he was found by a native who directed him to the tent area. Swollen from stings, he presented himself meekly for punishment soon after Basset arrived.

"*There* he is!" cried Hoyle.

Basset, seeing that Red was indeed the one he had sent to the base hospital from bivouac when he was Fiddler, told Hoyle, "This man is white."

"He *looks* pretty white," Hoyle agreed, "but he *can't* be. Colonel, I know my niggers. And they don't make mistakes in Hawaii."

"You making me out a liar?" roared Basset. "The man is transferred to my headquarters immediately. Soldier, get your gear and come with me."

As they left, his eyes met those of Lincoln, who was standing nearby and watching. He hoped so much that Lincoln did not recognize him that he convinced himself momentarily that Lincoln did not. At headquarters he turned a dazed Red over to a surprised Merwyn: "Quarter him, have him fed and given some stuff for his bug bites. Then I'll interview him personally."

When Red appeared, Basset told him, "That was a stupid thing to do."

Red, who had been delirious at their previous meeting and naturally did not recognize him, mumbled, "Sorry, sir. I'm not against Negroes, I'm just not Negro myself."

"I know," Basset said. "Now tell me all that's happened to you between the time you arrived in Hawaii and got here."

After listening sympathetically to Red's tribulations he told him, "Forget about your wife. Good riddance. What sort of work do you like best?"

Within the hour Andrew Jackson Jack, once more a blithely spirited Pfc., took charge of the headquarters motor pool. The pool consisted of only two rickety trucks, but Red was elated to be in charge of them. It was not long before he once again yearned for flight school.

Late in the afternoon, while Basset was reading an old magazine at his desk, he heard a familiar voice address Merwyn beyond the canvas flap: "Sergeant, Private Garfield Lincoln asks permission to speak to the commanding officer."

"About what?"

"I want to talk to him about the strange death of a good friend, Major Morton Fiddler. Just tell him that and he'll understand."

Basset panicked. Putting on his sunglasses, he called to Merwyn, "Send the man in, Sergeant."

Lincoln stepped in, saluted smartly, and said, "Private Garfield Lincoln has permission to speak to the commanding officer. Sir, I'm inquiring about a friend who is reported to have died in a plane crash, a Major Fiddler. At least, that's what a man in Major Hoyle's battalion told me."

"Fiddler? Fiddler?" Basset, in trying to disguise his voice, caused it to squeak unbelievably. "Yes, he died in a crash that I survived. You shouldn't bother me with such things. I'm busy running a whole island. Now go along."

Lincoln held out that snapshot showing the two of them in front of the medical tent on Oahu, hands thrust into shirts Napoleon-style. "*Colonel,* don't you recognize Major Fiddler?"

"Yes, I recognize Fiddler. I was deeply grieved by his death in that crash. I remember him telling me about you in our flight from Hawaii, *Corporal.* In memory of Fiddler I'll be glad to make you a corporal, Corporal, and send you to a nice berth in our lovely dispensary."

But Lincoln shook his head. "Well, *Colonel,* after what I've been through I figure I'm deserving of sergeant."

Basset demurred. "It takes time—a few weeks at least. If you make sergeant too fast, where else is there to go?"

Lincoln leaned toward him. "As far as I'm concerned, the sky's the limit. I wouldn't object to being Lieutenant General Lincoln. And when that happens I'll really believe I'm fighting for a democracy."

Basset hesitated. "Well—all right—Sergeant. Now—"

"Colonel, did you ever hear about that case where an enlisted man suspected that his commanding officer was an imposter and the whole thing was taken to the inspector general, and after . . ."

Basset squirmed and wiped his brow.

"Deciding the man had murdered the officer he pretended to be"—Lincoln's voice sank low—"they sent him to Leavenworth for forty years. I guess you know how they did it. I guess you forget that officers are *fingerprinted.*"

Basset's neck chilled. "Interesting. Very interesting, Staff Sergeant Lincoln."

Probably he had gone far enough, Lincoln thought. Staff sergeant was a much higher rating than he ever had remotely imagined achieving. Fiddler, who obviously had assumed the role of the dead Basset, had been kind to him during their brief time together in the bivouac dispensary tent. Lincoln would not actually betray him, and he did not want to blackmail him beyond reason. However, never had he had such a golden opportunity to get even with the white man for a whole lifetime of injustices. If he could make master sergeant, he'd be able to save a lot of money to help grease his way into medical school.

Breathing deeply, Lincoln said, "I'm more ambitious than just becoming a staff sergeant, Colonel."

Basset made that bleating sound that seems to afflict military people when they're in trouble. "Staff Sergeant Lincoln, I can't make you a tech sergeant because the chief enlisted man at the dispensary already is one."

"Sir, who said anything about wanting to be a tech sergeant? I want to be a *master* sergeant."

"But think how unfair that is to the poor guy at the dispensary who's doing a good job and—"

"Colonel, you don't understand. I don't want to work at any old dispensary. I want to work right here at headquarters. I don't want to resume my medical career till I go to medical school."

"Now, there I've got you," Basset said. "I'm forbidden by order of the theater commander to have a medical corpsman on a headquarters staff. You'd have to be transferred to the Infantry. Which carries the threat of combat at any time. No man in his right mind would want to be transferred out of the nice, safe Medical Corps."

But Lincoln's eyes glittered with vision of the power entailed in those stripes and rockers of a master sergeant. "Well, Colonel, *this* man in his right mind will take his chances on being an Infantry master sergeant."

"But this headquarters already has a master sergeant in charge."

"Make him a first sergeant, Colonel. Hold out the promise of his becoming a warrant officer. I'm not greedy. I don't want to be in charge of the whole place."

"But why would you want to move in with a bunch of double-crossing whites?"

"I reckon I can stand 'em if I'm a master sergeant."

Basset whined, "But what can you *do* here?"

"Colonel, I type real good with two fingers."

Thus it happened that Merwyn was promoted to first sergeant and Garfield Lincoln became the only two-fingered clerk-typist in the Pacific with a master sergeant's rating.

10

My military career had been running downhill fast, but about three weeks after Red and Lincoln disappeared in the direction of Dumbo it took a decided skid for the worse. And so did Goldman's.

If I had been smart, I never would have let the General take me out of the company to become his aide, along with Goldman. There are many things you can't avoid in the Army, but you can duck being an aide. At first, however, I thought I was lucky to escape from the boring routine of the company.

The officer succeeding the General was a hard-nosed colonel aghast at the disarray of his command. He had everyone at the Field working twelve hours a day trying to bring some order from the chaos there. At that time, in February 1942, an Air Force headquarters company was essentially a housekeeping outfit, and, much as we had loathed bivouac, nobody liked to return to the dull routine of counting nuts and bolts and filing triplicate reports.

Yaromski and Cherokee had gone to the Infantry, and I no longer had a friendly guide who would show me what bits of paper I must sign and precisely where the signature must be affixed. Another depressing aspect was that I could not interest the new colonel even slightly in photography. At first he was surprised that a second lieutenant rather than a first was executive officer of the company. However, after briefly observing my work, he pronounced me unfit for promotion and expressed surprise that I ever had been commissioned in the first place. Yes, I was an incompetent officer—and for good reason: I knew enough by now to realize that competent officers were sent into combat where they were killed either by the enemy or their own men. So a worthy first lieutenant became the company exec and I became an aide to the General.

Even after Red left Hawaii and I did not have to confront his innocent, friendly countenance any longer, I stayed away from Rosemarie and Vera. So did Goldman, and we became rather smug about our principled conduct. It was not always easy, since neither of us could find a pretty, companionable young woman to date.

Goldman and I had found that one of the worst military fates is to be employed by an unemployed general—and we were beginning to think our General might be permanently unemployable. He had a desk at Derussy and was on a couple of routing lists so that he could shuffle papers with an air of importance, but he remained as devoid of responsibility as a log rotting on a beach. An experienced bureaucrat who felt stripped of authority, the General took out his frustration on Goldman and me.

He made us do the damnedest things, like calling him from payphones so that people around his office would think he had important connections and weighty responsibilities. Since he never reimbursed us for our nickels, it became expensive as well as boring.

Then, suddenly, he went on a kick that Goldman and I didn't at first understand. Since Dorothy was safely ensconced Stateside with her senile parents, since Fiddler was safely dead in far southwestern waters, and since his career was awaiting a new development, the General decided to have what he called some fun. He made this known to Goldman and me with what he intended to be a merry twinkle, but it came across to us as a lecherous leer. We withdrew to the officers' latrine for consultation.

"And now by God," whispered Goldman, "he wants me to perform as pimp. I will not do it!"

"Why not?" I asked. "Just consider it a form of supply work. Think how many men are proud to be in Army Supply."

We returned to our General and I casually told him about the legend of Vera. "Kiss her nooky, sir, and you'll have eternal life in this war. It only costs fifty bucks."

"Oh!" The General clapped a hand to his paunch, as if mortally wounded. "Oh! Oh! I've never heard of such a disgusting thing. Filthy, Boswick! Filthy! Filthy! Shame on you. Did you say fifty dollars?"

"Yes sir."

"Well, let me tell you, Boswick, never once in my life have I paid for it."

Knowing how penurious he was, this did not surprise us at all.

"When I say fun," the General went on, "I mean—well, for instance, something fun to look at."

Goldman and I withdrew to the latrine again, and held another consultation.

"He must mean he wants to look at dirty pitchas," Goldman whispered. "Make him some dirty pictures, Boz, and it all will pass."

"No," I said, "I'm interested in almost every kind of photographic art, but I decided a long time ago to draw the line at the pornograph. With my sensual nature I'd probably do very good dirty pitchas, and after that I might never do anything else. It would—well, goddam it, I'm corrupt enough already without corrupting my lens as well."

Goldman could not talk me into it, so I drove a command car down to Beretania Street, then the center of the Honolulu pornographic industry, and spent ten dollars of my hard-earned money on a stack of dirty pictures. After I brought them back, Goldman and I built a little stockade of manuals on the General's desk and had him hide behind it to look at the photos.

"Oh! Oh!" he kept saying as he leered and chortled. "How can a woman stoop so low?"

"They say, sir, that the chief requirement of a whore is to be limber in the knees."

"Boswick," the General said, "you're a disgusting disgrace to the United States Army."

"Yes, sir," I agreed, "it would be best for the service if I was separated from it immediately."

After a while the General said, "You two young bucks must know plenty of nurses."

"No, sir," Goldman said, "I've never met a single service nurse."

"Me neither," I said. "Every time I used to go on sick call there was only a hairy male to take care of me, so I quit going."

"But you are *going* to get acquainted with a couple of nurses." Suddenly the General's tone bore a portent we did not understand. "I want you to bring two of them to my quarters at 2100 tonight."

It was our turn to bleat.

"Don't you bucks try to hold out on me." Now the General sounded savage. "Bring your nurses to my quarters at 2100. That is an order. If you fail, I'll have you both shipped off to combat outfits tomorrow morning.''

Goldman uttered a moaning sound, and I let loose with a wail. But the General came back with something like a snarl. "Dismissed till 2100. Do not fail!'' He buttoned the dirty pictures into a pocket and marched out of the office.

"What we'll have to do," Goldman said, "is round up a couple of prostitutes and pay them ourselves. That's the most evil thing about the old son of a bitch: we'll have to pay for them ourselves. How much money do you have, Boz? Do you know any prostitutes?''

"Of course, and so do you, dummy. I just never think of Rosemarie and Vera as prostitutes.''

We drove to Vera's to negotiate. I had a few hundred dollars, and Goldman, who was almost broke, promised to begin paying his share out of next month's pay. Neither of us objected to spending money; we just didn't want to waste it on the General.

"Hi, Boz." Vera, who was painting her toenails in the living room, greeted me cordially. "Long time no see." Her tone turned cold. "Good afternoon, Reverend Goldman. Neither of you made an appointment for therapy.''

"Is that what you call it now?" I asked. "And is this, then, the clinic?''

"Boz! Ira!" Rosemarie came from the bathroom, where she'd been washing her hair. "Nice to see you." She clasped our hands. "Yes, this is the clinic, Boz, and we're therapists trying to help the sick. It's really true, I think. So many men have problems about sex. Speaking of problems," she continued, "do you know where they sent Red?''

"The same place they sent Fiddler, wherever it is. But Fiddler never got there. We heard a couple of days ago he was killed in a plane crash.''

Vera let out a wail. "Oh no! He was such a wonderful man. She fixed us with a vicious stare. "*You two* sent Fiddler to his death!''

"No, we did not," Goldman said. "The General did. Boz and I were only acting under the General's orders. That's war: his ass or mine. You had as much of a role in Fiddler's death as Boz and I did, Vera.''

"*I* had something to do with Fiddler's death?" Vera's eyes filled with tears in an extraordinary display of emotion. "I *loved* Fiddler. *Now* I know that. Oh, how terrible, the dear, innocent man.''

"Please think logically for a change, Vera." Goldman sounded like a judge. "Of course you had a role in his death. We all did, but none of us was the master planner. The General was. *He* is to blame."

Vera blinked, trying to grasp what he meant, and her blinking appeared to induce tears in Rosemarie, who suddenly cried out, "Oh, I hope I didn't send Red to his death too!"

"Please," I said, "stop worrying about the past. Ira's life and mine are in jeopardy right this minute unless you help us. We want you to make a house call."

"No house calls," Vera said. "We've got all the practice we can handle right here in the clinic."

"If you don't visit this patient," I said, "Ira and I will be sent to our deaths in combat."

"Tell me one place in the Pacific except the Philippines where there is any combat. And nobody can get to the Philippines."

"There is much combat out there." I pointed a finger to the west. "They're keeping it out of the papers because the casualties are so high. But we have top secret reports on it. When are you girls going to stop sending men to their graves?"

Rosemarie continued to weep silently. Vera said that for house calls she charged $100 per hour per therapist. We haggled.

"Think!" Goldman thundered. "You never would have got a start in this lucrative profession if it hadn't been for us. It's as if we paid your way through medical school."

Rosemarie, ever more tender, prevailed on Vera to relent after we revealed the General's identity and his threat. It was agreed they would charge only $50 apiece for one hour of therapy and we would provide the transportation.

We arrived at the General's quarters promptly at 2100. We presented Nurse Vera and Nurse Rosemarie to him. He wore his uniform and all his ribbons, which were not numerous.

"No formalities," he said. "You girls just call me General. Where you stationed? I can help your careers." As usual, he did not want answers to his questions. "Let's all have a little drinky."

"Well, sir," Goldman said, "Boswick and I will take off now. See you in exactly one hour."

"Halt!" Suddenly I realized that the General, who did not handle booze too well, had been priming himself with Scotch for whatever erotic experience he planned to undertake. "Goldman, serve us a drink. No, Boswick, you serve the drinks. Goldman, you goddam Jews—and I don't mean anything personal in that—are too stingy with drinks."

He fell back on a sofa and indicated to the women that they should sit on either side of him. When I came from the kitchen with Scotch for the General and ginger ale for the women I nearly dropped the glasses in astonishment. The General's right hand was pawing under Rosemarie's skirt on his left, and his left hand was doing the same to Vera on his right. The faces of both women were white with outrage; they had never experienced anything so degrading since entering their profession. I, remembering my attempts to feel up girls in my days at military school, knew that never again would I bring myself to insult a woman in this fashion. Goldman had gone to a corner of the room and turned his face to the wall, like a child being punished.

"Ah, Boswick"—the General's expression and the position of his crossed arms made him look like a man strangling from the effort to hug himself—"caught in the act, eh?"

"Yes sir." I couldn't think of anything else to say.

"Goldman!" The General untangled his hands from under the women's skirts to take the Scotch I proferred. "What are you doing in that corner—amusing yourself by abusing yourself?"

Goldman just shook his head.

The General fumbled and dropped the glass of Scotch I had just handed him. I was groveling around the floor trying to clean up the mess when the General said, "Enough of this fooling around, you gals come with me."

They cast me looks of contempt, as if I were to blame for everything, as he led them into a bedroom and slammed the door. The ensuing silence was awful to contemplate.

Goldman, giving up his stance in the corner, said, "I'm going to throw up. I'd better do it outside." I followed him out and found him, head tilted back, staring in anguish at a fat moon in a starry sky. "It smells like summer roses in Prospect Park," he said and retched. "I can't even vomit because I couldn't even eat any supper."

I went back inside where the silence remained ominous. A whimpering sound coming from the bedroom made me break out with sweat. Then the door opened and the women filed out, staring at me glassily. The muffled sobbing in the bedroom must come from the General; it was such a dreadful sound to hear that Goldman, who had staggered back inside, clapped his hands over his ears.

"He can't do it," Vera said to me. "Take us back to the clinic."

As they went out, the General stopped sobbing and called, "Goldman! Boswick!" We stepped hesitantly to the door and peered in at him fearfully. A light was on, revealing his khaki shirt with its gold star and line of ribbons crumpled on the floor. He was sheeted to the throat in bed.

"You men should have been here," he said, eyes still teary. "I laughed till I cried. I don't know what those nurses might say, but I will say this: they were quite overwhelmed by my—uh—powers." Maybe there was something about the way we stared at him that made him close his eyes. "Uh— Uh— Uh— You men needn't report for duty till ten in the morning."

As we drove the women home, Vera said, "Usually I feel sorry for men when they get that way. But not him. There are ways a woman can help a man. But not him. He made us promise not to tell about it, so that's why I'm blabbing right away. Your General is a complete bastard."

When we arrived at the bungalow, she said, "We didn't earn our money tonight. Nobody else is scheduled. Would you guys like to come in for an hour?"

"Please do," Rosemarie urged us.

We needed no coaxing. Rosemarie had made her own decision about how she wanted to live, and I was sure I never would see Red again. After all, since Rosemarie was doing it with everyone, what good would it do if I abstained?

I intended to spend an hour with her—and Goldman planned equal time with Vera. But we wound up staying the night. My delight with Rosemarie was so great that I would have paid a fortune for our time together and gone away with the feeling I had not spent a penny for the love she lavished on me. Already she had become that accomplished as a courtesan.

Goldman and I, somewhat fatigued, were a bit tardy in arriving at the General's office next morning. He was not there. I had the wish that he had suddenly been transferred. But when an enlisted man sent us to look at the bulletin board, I saw that it was Goldman and I who were being sent away—to Dumbo.

Our air passage to Dumbo was similar to that of many unfortunate souls who had preceded us. Goldman's journey was complicated by personal misfortune: he ate a poisonous liverwurst sandwich, which made him violently ill. When the airplane landed, he was weak from vomiting and diarrhea, his head throbbed, and his eyes were glassy with fatigue.

After the door was opened and the humid heat of Masa-Masoa

smote us, Goldman would have crawled back into the airplane if I hadn't shoved him down the ladder.

Standing wretchedly in the sun-glare, we gazed at Red Jack. Goldman farted and moaned.

"Lieutenant Boswick!" Red cried. He saluted us and then, laughing in delight, he clapped me on the back. "Welcome to Dumbo! Welcome, Lieutenant Goldman."

"Oh God!" Goldman groaned again.

Liking Red as much as I did, I should have been glad to see him. But I was not. All I could think of was sporting with his wife on a bed in Waikiki.

"Where," quavered Goldman, "is the nearest latrine?"

Red pointed off into the sun-glare, and Goldman ran in that general direction.

"Is there anything you can recommend about this place?" I asked Red.

"Well, the native women are ugly and there's no bar. The worst is the monotony. I work at headquarters, and the C.O.—Colonel Basset —he might be the best guy who ever lived. Maybe at first he'll sort of try to scare you. But he does that just to relieve the monotony."

Goldman finally crawled into the truck cab with us and asked, "What's the medical service like on this post?"

"Hideous. We got a new doctor last month, but Colonel Basset swears he was a chiropractor in civilian life. The one before that he swore was a veterinarian."

"Is that a latrine over there?" cried Goldman. "Stop the truck."

Red stopped the truck. "Lieutenant Goldman, this whole island is one latrine. Help yourself."

I asked for more information about Basset. "What's his full name? What are his weaknesses?"

"Charles Peter Basset, and he has no weaknesses."

When we reached headquarters, Lincoln greeted me with hilarity: "Lieutenant, what did you went and *done* to be sent here?" He wrung my hand and slapped my back in most unmilitary fashion.

Meanwhile, Merwyn announced us to Basset. Goldman stepped ahead of me around the canvas drop, raised his hand to salute, and pitched on his face in a dead faint.

Coming behind him, I understood why he had fainted as I stared at Fiddler's startled countenance. I wanted to hide. But then, in my consternation, I realized that Fiddler was as frightened as we.

"Wha— wha— wha—" he quavered. "What's the meaning of this? Medic!"

The enlisted men dashed in and gathered around Goldman, perplexed. Lincoln rolled him over, and Goldman opened his eyes.

"I'm your commanding officer, Colonel Basset," snarled the Warden. "What's the meanin' of you comin' in here an' faintin'?"

"Sir," whispered Goldman, "I thought—for a second I thought you were somebody else." Still flat on his back, he raised his right hand to his brow in a feeble salute. "Second Lieutenant Ira Goldman reporting for duty, sir."

"Carry him away," snarled Basset. When the room was empty, he turned to me. "What's your specialty?"

"Public relations, Colonel."

"Oh, great!" roared the Warden. "Here we are on the brink of invasion, with the troops all keyed up, an' they send us a public relations officer! What public are we supposed to relate to, Lieutenant? Why d'you come bustlin' in here all laced up with camera straps like a goose trussed fer the Christmas oven. You tryin' to put somethin' over on me?"

I spoke evenly: "Bluster will get you nowhere. Lieutenant Goldman and I are counterintelligence agents. We've been sent here to investigate the murder of Colonel Charles Peter Basset."

Fiddler/Basset exuded a sound like air escaping from an inner tube. He did not so much sit down as shrivel in his chair. Tears came to his eyes and he whispered, "Why do you fiends pursue me so? What diabolical plot is there against me? Did I ever commit any sin except to be born a homeless, friendless Armenian?"

"Lieutenant Goldman and I can be merciful," I said. "Of course certain—uh—discrepancies have been observed by higher authority. For instance, the signature of the commander of this place. But a decision in the matter is left to our discretion. Perhaps, Major—Colonel—whatever the case may be—a full confession to us is the best way."

"Yes," he whispered. "I like that. Keep your voice down. The enlisted men listen all the time. I've no one to talk to here. They must never know, I'd rather shoot myself than be humiliated in front of them. Yes, yes, I have a great need of confession. I don't suppose you legal eagles can understand that. I've thought of writing it all to Helen."

"Helen?"

"Basset's wife. My wife. The wife of the commander of this place who writes me all the time. Let's go off among the palm trees so I can talk to you where nobody can hear."

"No rush," I said. "Lieutenant Goldman and I are tired from our trip. He is half dead from a fecal sandwich. We need a shower, a chance to rest a bit before we talk. Is there any place you can get a drink on this miserable island?"

"Yes, yes." He smiled wanly. "I have booze. Do you like Scotch? I have Red Label. I have Black Label. How about a good Havana cigar? Come with me."

11

Fiddler/Basset took to confession avidly. He relished it, luxuriated in it, found emotional peace in telling us more about himself than we wanted to know. For the better part of two days we sat listening to him in a secluded place among the palms, taking notes on what he said and then burning them when we returned to our tent.

We had him completely under our influence when, just before the cocktail hour on the second day, I stopped him in midsentence and said, "We've heard enough."

"Are you sure? Are you sympathetic to my case?"

"Give us five minutes to pass judgment." Goldman and I withdrew deeper into the palm grove while Fiddler paced nervously. We agreed, returned, and I said: "Fiddler, we find you innocent of murdering Basset. In fact, we find you are Basset. We'll so report it to our headquarters—by mail, not radio, so nobody here will know."

"Thank you—thanks, thanks." He wrung hands with us both. "I suppose they'll be pulling you out of here now that you've finished the investigation."

"They might not," Goldman said. "They might be so annoyed with us for finding you're Basset and it really was Fiddler who died in that plane crash that they might leave us here."

"To wither on the vine, so to speak," I said.

"I'd be delighted," Basset said. "You're good company. Goldman, you could help train me to be a credible engineer. Boswick, you

could be my public relations officer. Take pictures, send out releases
—that sort of thing.''

"Sort of put Dumbo on the map, you mean?''

"Exactly. A project is greatly needed here now. It's been the motto
of my crazy life: 'Try to get into mischief before mischief gets into
you.' ''

The airstrip had been completed, the rains had come, the beer had
run out—and the idle, miserable troops had begun to mutter against
the Warden and blame him for their lot. As soon as the airstrip was
finished, someone far upstairs had decided that a bigger, better strip
should be built on a distant island which was on a more direct route
between strategic places. By the time Goldman and I arrived, Chute
had been shipped away to work on that project, but no one else left
the island except for an occasional enlisted man or officer who
feigned madness so convincingly that Basset rewarded him with recommendation for a Section 8 discharge.

Now, airplanes shunned Dumbo as if it were ravaged by a plague.
The men who had toiled hard to build the strip blamed Basset because
it was so little used. Since he was the one who had urged them on,
they decided the airport had been *his* idea and he had shown great
lack of foresight in electing to build it on Masa-Masoa.

"I've resigned myself to being loathed,'' he told us. "In that way
I think I show real capacity for leadership. I've decided that only
followers who pretend to be leaders strive for popularity. A curious
change has come over me. I've begun to take my military career
seriously and stopped having frivolous ideas of escaping. The point
being that you *can't* escape.''

Then, just as we thought he had rid himself of confession, he made
still another one. He showed us a letter from Helen. "It has me
scared shitless,'' he said with the refreshing candor of a born leader.

She wrote him: "An odd thing happened yesterday. Two F.B.I.
agents—not one, but *two*—came to see me about you. They said it
was just a 'routine spot check.' But I wonder if you're being considered for some important promotion. They wanted to know about
your friends, what organizations you've belonged to, things like
that. . . .''

Sweat literally broke out on Basset's brow.

"Should I confess all? But to whom should I confess? Pappy
Hoyle? The Secretary of War?''

"If you were to confess your entire history,'' I said, "the recital
might run on for weeks.''

"Confess nothing," Goldman advised. "Maintain your innocence to the end. Above all, don't let them fingerprint you."

"Yes, yes. Anyway, for the time being my goals have changed. For a long time I wanted to stop being Basset and become Fiddler or somebody else. But now I'm going to try to be the best Basset possible under the circumstances. Goldman, I'll start studying engineering under your tutelage. Send to Hawaii for manuals. I'll need dozens of manuals. Meanwhile, I must think of the welfare of my troops. They must find something worthwhile to do, as I have."

Next day the enlisted men at headquarters began painting signs and standing them all over the island: PUT DUMBO ON THE MAP.

"But how?" Basset asked. For once even his, Goldman's and my fertile imaginations failed. "The men are asking the question everywhere. Rinaldo is even having a symposium on it. We'll hold a discussion of our best minds at headquarters."

Nobody had any idea. When Lincoln wondered aloud if the place was really worth putting on the map, he was booed loudly for negativism. Red raised a hand, and Basset told him to speak up.

"Why not," he said, "let us build a secret air base here and send out releases and pictures of it to all the papers?" There was cautious silence. "We would hollow out the mountain and then have a huge hangar door open and the planes would come roaring out."

"It sounds like an awful lot of work," Merwyn said.

"Not really," Red said. "See, we'd only *pretend* to hollow out the mountain. Everybody would make model airplanes and there'd be a contest and the winners would get prizes. Boz—Lieutenant Boswick would make pictures of the model planes and we could say this is an aerial view of 'em."

"What a wonderful idea!" Basset exclaimed.

"But what would the prizes be?" somebody asked. "The beer's all gone."

"I'll contribute a bottle of Scotch I just happen to have in my possession," Basset said. "I'll try—I won't guarantee, but I'll *try* to offer a grand prize of a week in Hawaii."

"For that," I said, "even *I* will try to make a model airplane."

"You're not eligible," Basset said. "You're one of the judges."

A semblance of contentment came to Dumbo for a couple of weeks as nearly everyone worked on a model airplane. Rather late in the wave of enthusiasm Goldman thought of something.

"Are we," he asked Basset, "in danger of incurring the wrath of the high command for revealing military secrets?"

"What's a military secret about a fleet of three or four hundred model airplanes?" Basset countered. "I expect to be commended. But if they don't like it, I'll say I knew nothing about it. Claim it was the work of an overly enthusiastic public relations officer who acted without my authorization."

I had growing misgivings as I saw that it was as impossible to stop the model plane contest as to stifle the winds of a hurricane. The ingenuity of these Americans in obtaining and shaping the materials for their models would have delighted Thomas A. Edison. But none was as ingenious as Red, who somehow wormed his way into the Navy machine shop down at the quay and built a beautiful six-inch model of a P-38 with wing flaps which actually moved—all from shining metal!

Of course he won first prize. His work was so superb that no one questioned his right to first, no one remarked that he was Basset's favorite.

"Private Jack," Basset said at the huge ceremony attended by everyone on the island, "congratulations! Hello, Hawaii—I hope. If that cannot be arranged, is there some other way we can honor you?"

Red stepped to the microphone and said, "Thank you, sir. I'll give up the Hawaii prize for something else. I don't even *want* to go to Hawaii except on my way to somewhere else." There were shocked outcries from the audience. "Where I want to go to, Colonel, is flight school. I think that if you can arrange to send me to Hawaii you could send me to flight school instead."

So the Hawaiian furlough prize went to a Negro sergeant in Hoyle's battalion who had made an excellent replica in wood of a B-17.

Afterwards Basset said to Red, "You're always talking about being a pilot, but I never seriously thought about sending you to flight school. How are we going to get you through two years of college?"

"By a little falsification, Colonel. I'm going to write Harvard and ask for my records. When they write back that they can't find 'em, I'll type in above the Harvard signature that they're looking and will send them along. You can send the letter with your recommendation of me."

Basset looked sad. "You disappoint me deeply, Red. You are one man I thought I could count on to retain his integrity. But now I find you're growing up. Too bad! But of course I'll do it because you have to have a prize."

Now it was my turn to do something about putting Dumbo on the map. I took a picture of the mountain. ("'Looks like an ordinary mountain, doesn't it?'') Then I took a picture of one of its jungle-clad sides. (''Did you ever see such perfect camouflage?'') Next we laid out a couple of hundred model planes on the floor of an empty tent, and after dark I took a flashbulb picture of them. (''Who would guess these are hidden inside?'') The following morning we outlined runways in the sand and arranged more than three hundred models; I was helped up a palm tree from which I shot more pictures at a downward angle. (''Aerial view of the mighty American secret air base at Dumbo. For further information about it write the P.R.O., APO 746, San Francisco.'')

The photos were incredibly lifelike, but Goldman was disgusted. ''Nobody's going to print this stuff, Boz. Every newspaper man in America knows about national security and the War Secrets Act or whatever it's called. And if some nut did publish your pictures, you'd go to Leavenworth for life. Even after they found out they were only pictures of model planes, the Army is so humorless they'd probably get you for *intent*.''

I told him I'd already figured that out. Without telling anyone at Dumbo, I was going to send the photos with an explanation to military intelligence headquarters in Hawaii and suggest that they be used to fool the enemy.

Military intelligence authorities never did reply to me. But they sent Basset a letter commending his scheme to dupe the enemy and saying he would receive the Legion of Merit for it. Scores of American newspapers carried the pictures, which were officially released by the Army. However, Dumbo itself was never named—only referred to as a secret American base in the Pacific. So Dumbo never did get on the map, but Basset did.

Although Basset was disappointed in Red for trying to fake a college education, he was fonder of him than anyone else at Dumbo. He continued to mention to me Red's ''utter lack of guile.'' Brimming with guile himself, Basset could not but admire one so lacking in deceit and cunning—apart from his effort to go to flight school. Of course he put through Red's request with the highest recommendation, and all of us waited expectantly.

Basset pointed out to Goldman and me that the noble Lubbock had nowhere near Red's strength of character. For it turned out that, although Lubbock neither drank nor smoked, he would sink to depths of treachery in order to satisfy his passion for candy bars.

Red and I became even closer friends. During those days he talked more about his past, and I developed a sympathetic understanding for him. So did Basset after I told him privately what had become of Vera and Rosemarie.

"I feel to blame for that," Basset said.

"Help yourself if you enjoy feeling guilty. Lord knows there's enough guilt around to share with anybody who wants some."

"But Vera was a real nice woman, Boz. I never laid a lecherous hand on her, but I think I broke down her—inhibitions. I led her into prostitution through sheer carelessness."

"She's still a nice woman," I said. "She's just become more practical than she used to be. Inventive, too. I mean she practically made up a whole new religion. You'd be amazed at the number of guys who are glad to pay for the privilege of—uh—worshiping at her shrine."

"You sound even more cynical than I am," Basset said. "The rest of us go around here confessing everything all the time, but you never confess anything. Where you from?"

"Biloxi, Mississippi."

"You can't be from Biloxi. You don't talk like anybody who ever came from Biloxi."

"I always check my accent at the border when I leave, and I never aim to go back and pick it up."

"Do you hate your mother?"

"I don't know. She died when I was too young to remember her."

"Then it's your father?"

"Used to think so, but I'm not sure any more. Got a letter a couple of weeks ago from my father's third wife. When she got through complainin' 'bout the sugah sho'tage an' the plenty o' the nigruhs an' that man in the White House Ah felt right sorry for mah ol' man."

"Seems only yesterday there were too many parents," Basset said. "And now suddenly there aren't enough. You've got none, Helen's got none, I got none, Basset the First had none. Goldman's the only one I know has parents."

"Maybe that's why he acts serene most of the time," I said. "I never knew a Jew didn't have at least one parent tucked away somewhere."

"Red must have parents," Basset said, "because he's the most serene Wasp with an unfaithful wife I ever saw."

"Red has a mama he cherishes, but his papa has ceased to function for some reason."

Red, in his long conversations with me, talked constantly about his mother, father and sister back home in Glenwood. He wondered why his father never wrote him. He finally asked his sister, and he showed me Jenny's reply:

"Pa doesn't seem much of this world any more. It's like he couldn't turn the world into the way he wants it to be and so he won't pay any attention to it. He's working steady now as a linotyper for the Newark Evening News but he acts sad all the time and goes for long spells when he scarce speaks to Ma or me. There's no sense to the way he acts because we're better off than we've ever been. He reads your letters over and over and just sighs. One time he said What good thing can I write to Andrew? I said Well then write him what's bad but for Heavens sake *write* him something! But he just sighs and goes back to reading one of his ancient books."

Occasionally Red would talk about Rosemarie. He was worried that he might have judged her unfairly and felt that he should apologize for that awful fight with the lieutenant. He even might have written if he had known her address.

One day I said to Basset, "Why don't I write Rosemarie and give his address and see if she writes him?"

Basset shook his head.

"Then what would happen if I came right out and told Red what Rosemarie has become and to cut her out of his life for good?"

"Never! The real truth about life is so awful that people can't bear it. They make up religions to avoid confronting it. One time when I was a lot younger and my name was Fiddler I was so in love with a woman that I wanted to marry her. She loved me too, but insisted she must first confess something about herself. Please do, I urged her. Nothing could make me love you less. Well, she did, and within minutes I wondered how I could ever have been such a jerk as to love her at all. If she hadn't worried about the truth we might now be married and living happily ever after instead of my sitting here on a speck of coral in the world's biggest ocean pretending to be somebody I'm not. Boz, we must not tell Red the truth about Rosemarie. We must preserve his innocence and happiness."

Basset's remarks made me reflect on the ambivalence of his character. He could be a real good guy. And then he suddenly could switch to a selfish son of a bitch. For instance, he was delighted to receive the Legion of Merit and acted as though he really had conceived the idea that Red thought up and I helped to develop; in no way did he try to reward me, though he did recommend Red for flight school. Goldman and I privately came to the conclusion that he was a manipulator and opportunist who was smart enough to be a bit skeptical of us because we shared those traits. Yet Basset could be wonderful and generous with innocents like Red was and Vera had been. Was he maybe just a consummate role-player and actor who was, in some ways, a shell of a man?

Early in August, despite Basset's admonition, I wrote Vera and Rosemarie, telling them Goldman and I were on the same island as Red and gave the address. It didn't seem to me that I was tampering with fate. I was simply offering choices—I was weary of the notion that we have no control over our destinies. I wanted to believe that Rosemarie and Red—and everyone—had the power to make choices that would determine what became of them.

It was eight months to the day after the Japanese attacked Pearl Harbor before the Americans mounted a ground offensive against the enemy. The place was Guadalcanal in the Solomon Islands, August 7, 1942.

Two days later Lincoln came running from the message center. "It's happened!" he cried. "Dumbo's getting a new commander!"

Basset's hands were not steady as he read the message from Hawaii stating that he would be superseded as commander of Dumbo. But by whom, and when, and would he be moved elsewhere?

The Army often did things by halves, especially in its messages. Late that afternoon our headquarters received the second half of the message informing Basset that he "and staff" should prepare to move tomorrow to a different command code-named Button. Trying to make light of an uncertain situation, Basset wandered about saying, "Button? Button? Who's got the Button?"

He was deeply worried. After deciding to make the best of his Army career, he had worked hard to learn all he could about civil engineering, helped by Goldman and dozens of manuals. But what was going to happen now? What would he do if the Army ordered him to build a dam—a road—a bridge? He could bluff many things, but no mortal could counterfeit a bridge.

Suddenly Red spoke up: "Colonel Basset, take me with you. I don't think I'm ever going to be accepted at flight school—and if I am, the orders will catch up with me wherever I go."

Basset, vastly pleased, nevertheless spoke roughly: "I suppose so. It says here 'and staff.' But it could be someplace a lot worse than this."

"I don't care," Red said. "I want to go with you."

Suddenly it dawned on Basset that in all his promoting of enlisted men he had forgotten to promote Red, his favorite. Forthwith he told Merwyn to cut orders making Red a buck sergeant.

At that moment Goldman came in from a day-long absence at Pappy Hoyle's battalion. Poor Goldman had gone a little touched in the head and for several weeks now had been trying to learn to be a good infantryman when he wasn't directing Basset's engineering studies. It was sad to see such a fine mind torturing its body into a mass of coordinated muscles. Every day Goldman went to Hoyle's battalion and did calisthenics with the troops; he became a sharp-shooter and tossed grenades and filled our tent with manuals on small-unit actions and leadership until I became quite annoyed with him.

Now Goldman stood with eyes half closed trying to imagine where Button might be while Basset baited the rest of us. Wouldn't we like to come with Red and him? All demurred. But suppose, Basset said, he was being transferred to a cushy Stateside job where the women yearned and the booze flowed?

"Colonel, I'm thinking in the other direction," Lincoln said. "I'm thinking they might need you on Guadalcanal."

The armed forces radio news had been jabbering all day about the heroism of the Marines on that God-forsaken island.

"That's mainly a Marine operation," I said. "God bless the U.S. Marines. They feel this is their war here in the Pacific and I think they're fully entitled to it. God bless those brave lads and may they all get dozens of medals."

"The Army's in on the operation too," Lincoln said. "It says on the radio that Japanese airfield the Marines took has to be enlarged and made operable. So they might well be looking for an engineering genius like yourself, Colonel."

"I see what you mean." Goldman spoke reflectively. "That's a real possibility. So, Colonel, I won't volunteer to accompany you."

"You don't have to," Basset crowed, "because I've already got you on orders to come with me. See these words, 'and staff'? Well, Goldman, you're 'and staff.' "

Goldman held his hands to his head.

Basset turned to me. "How about you, Boz? Wherever I go, I'll need a public relations officer. And your work here has been out-standing. Personally, I feel they're sending me to Governor's Island in New York Harbor. Think, gay blade, what a figure you'd cut on Broadway."

I should not have thought about it, but I did. Though not a lucky gambler, I was a daring one. I longed to see my native land. Even England, land of ale, women and song, would be a welcome diversion from the Pacific wastes. After brief deliberation I volunteered to go with them.

"Bravo!" Basset clapped my back.

That night before we were to leave, destination still unknown, Basset broke out a couple of bottles and a box of cigars for a farewell headquarters party that began hilariously and ended mawkishly. A sodden Merwyn delivered a mostly incoherent speech in which he referred to us four as "the Boy Allies."

In the painfully sober gray dawn an urgent message set things straight. Our airplane would arrive from Hawaii bringing the new commander of Dumbo. Then it would fly on to the west with Basset, Goldman, Red and me. Button was the code name for Espíritu Santo in the northern New Hebrides, which was the advance staging base for Guadalcanal.

"God save us!" I howled.

"How can He," countered Basset, "when you don't believe in Him?"

Merwyn, still reading the urgent message aloud, said, "The new commander of Dumbo will be—" He named Goldman's and my very own General.

"I can't wait to get out of here!" cried Goldman.

"There really are some things worse than Guadalcanal," I agreed.

In a deluge we four Boy Allies gathered under the little tin roof at the strip with Lincoln, Merwyn, Lubbock, Pappy Hoyle and Rinaldo. Basset's luggage, except for toilet articles and a change of underwear, consisted solely of the remaining Scotch and cigars which he had bartered from the merchant skippers. He said it was smart to carry trade goods when venturing among savages.

The airplane bumbled in, almost shearing off the tops of the palms, and we trudged to it. The doorway was opened, the ladder put up, and the General appeared. He came down cautiously in the rain, followed by a frightened-looking retinue. We waiting men saluted, the General replied, and finally he spoke:

"Where is the honor guard?"

"Oh no!" murmured Lincoln. "Colonel, take me with you!"

Basset, holding his salute, stepped close to the General and gazed into his eyes. He said something no one but the General could hear. He thought it probably wouldn't work, he told us later; not in months had he tried to hypnotize anyone, and no doubt he had lost the knack. But it did work. The General's salute froze to his helmet liner, his gaze became fixed somewhere distant.

Basset, turning his back on the General, shook hands with his astonished friends, then led us up the ladder into the airplane. A few minutes later, after the plane had taxied around for takeoff, we looked out the ports. Our friends waved frantically while the General remained rigidly at salute and stared vacantly into space.

12

When we made an overnight stop at Nouméa in New Caledonia, Basset reported to the major general in command of Army operations in the Solomons. He returned to us, looking grim and acting sour.

"The worst has happened. From here we're to fly north to Espíritu Santo. There we'll take a ship to Guadalcanal. The Marines claim firm control of the airstrip the Japs were building there. My assignment—*our* assignment—is to finish it. I have authorization to use whatever hands are available in any branch of the services to finish the job."

Turning to me, he said, "Damn you, Boswick, I didn't get this assignment just for finishing the airstrip at Dumbo on time. The major general said he'd been impressed by my model plane ruse at Dumbo. *You* are to blame for that!"

Of course the idea had been Red's, but I didn't want to blame him. Red, wanting in turn to shield me from Basset's anger, reminded him, "Colonel, *I* was the one got that idea. Blame me for it."

"Nothing to blame you for," Basset grumbled. "Boswick is the one can foul up the best of ideas."

I kept silent. It occurred to me that Fiddler never would have sounded thus. Was this strange actor finally completing the great transition into another role?

Goldman asked if there was earth-moving equipment on Guadalcanal to expand the airstrip.

"It was sent," Basset growled, "and ended up in the Fiji Islands. Everything's fouled up. That strip is still only 2600 feet long, but those optimists in the Marines pronounce it fit for fighter operations. There's not enough cement, pumps, pipes, valves, runway matting, or prefabricated sections for fuel storage tanks."

The major general, whose forces were to cooperate with the Marines in seizing Guadalcanal, had explained all to Basset.

The Navy insisted that it direct the task of evicting the enemy from the Island, as Guadalcanal was beginning to be called. Watchtower, the grand name of the operation, actually was a shoestring affair, hastily conceived and carelessly executed. Basset learned that the admiral appointed to command Watchtower showed little talent for lacing together shoestrings and was receiving small help from the admiral who commanded his expeditionary force. (Both eventually would be removed to quiet posts far from the vicissitudes of combat. The major general who talked with Basset was, on the other hand, a smart, tough officer who would become one of the outstanding commanders of the war.)

Meantime the waters off Guadalcanal and its satellite islands were aptly becoming known as Ironbottom Sound, a grave of sunken ships, and an area where sharks feasted on humans. The result there of the first naval engagement after the American landings early in August was that the Japanese inflicted the worst defeat ever suffered by the U.S. Navy in a fair fight. The major general said that the American public was not judged prepared to hear of this failure on top of so much other bad news and informed Basset of the defeat in strictest confidence; Basset informed Goldman and me in strictest confidence; we informed Red in strictest confidence; and he went around informing in strictest confidence everyone he met—all of whom said they already had heard about it.

The brunt of the effort to seize The Island was borne by the Marines, who were ill prepared for this combat. Led by brave and able officers, the Marines were selected mainly because of the prevailing Navy notion that the Army always was unprepared for anything. However, Army elements already were moving in too.

"What is an element?" I asked.

"We four are an element," Basset replied seriously.

Winging north from Nouméa next morning on a Catalina Flying Boat, we came into one of the most beautiful areas on earth. To the west the Coral Sea surged as far as the eye could see, bright blue and flecked with whitecaps stirred by the fresh southeast trades that would fling it against Australia's Great Barrier Reef a thousand miles distant. Here on the eastern fringe of the sea the airplane flirted with the white puff clouds of the New Hebrides. We passed over jungle-clad islands where lofty, purple volcanoes shouldered the rising sun. Below us the coastal waters, transparent as air, revealed submerged reefs of peacock colors and ancient colonies of polyps flaming redly among the shoals.

While Basset and Goldman dozed, Red and I moved about the airplane, staring out the dirty ports at the unsurpassed beauty of the sea and islands. We smelled the breath of the passenger who had been drinking from a whiskey bottle and caught his blurred words: "These Hebrides are nice to look at, lads, but beware 'em. They reach for you like a beautiful woman with syphilis."

He was a ravaged-looking Australian civilian who had boarded at Nouméa after returning from leave in Brisbane. Saying he had spent much of his life as trader and planter in the islands, he claimed to be on his way back to some nameless spot in the Solomons. There, he said, he was employed now by the Allies as a coastwatcher; living with natives, constantly on the move, radioing out reports of Japanese troop strengths and movements, he lived on the edge of betrayal, capture, torture, death.

Red and I had met his likes many times in literature, but never in the flesh. Red accepted him instantly, but I thought it was quite possible he could also be a cement dealer from Brisbane trying to negotiate a profitable deal. He told stories of hair-raising experiences in the far-off islands so convincingly, however, that Red became almost speechless with awe.

Toward noon the base code-named Button on the island of Espíritu Santo came into view. Our flying boat settled on the sparkling waters of a harbor where dozens of ships were anchored within a submarine boom. We clambered onto a float pier and breathed good ancient smells of hyacinth and woodsmoke that the stench of diesel oil could not obliterate.

We made our way to a transportation office housed in a huge tin-roofed shed without walls. There a noisy bustle of men, typewriters and mimeograph machines displayed the customary military confusion. Our top-rated priority, assigned by Headquarters Commander in Chief, South Pacific, was of no consequence to the officers and enlisted men harried by streams of conflicting priorities.

Basset finally obtained an interview with a distracted major. "You'd think," Basset told him, "we really want to go to Guadalcanal from the efforts I'm making to get us there."

The major passed us along to a corporal, who finally obtained passage for four aboard a converted seaplane tender which was sailing for The Island next day.

After spending a miserable night in a muddy tent area, we returned to the transportation office and were ordered to a pier where men sprawled listlessly with their belongings while waiting for lighters to take them to ships in the harbor. A voice barked incoherently and almost continually over a loudspeaker.

Basset, pulling his helmet liner over his eyes and resting his head on a barracks bag, appeared to be asleep when Red nudged him and said, "They're calling you, Colonel."

From the loudspeaker came: "Monal Dasset reporta tida Maja Mumph inna trapstortation shet."

"Will be back soon as possible," Basset told us. "If I don't make it on the next tender, I'll be on the one after that. You guys take my gear, please, if they move you before I get back."

A few minutes later we were ordered into a lighter and took Basset's gear, consisting mainly of Scotch and cigars. He was not aboard the next lighter or any of those following. While we anxiously scanned the shore, the ship gave signs of weighing anchor and sailing. When I protested to the bridge that our most distinguished passenger was missing, I was roundly cussed out by a lieutenant commander.

We sailed in midafternoon, still scanning the shore and reassuring one another that Basset must have boarded another ship and we'd see him "there."

As I learned later, Basset went to the transportation office in search of "Maja Mumph" after he left us on the pier that morning. There he was confronted by a young captain who saluted and asked, "Colonel Basset?"

"Yeah."

"I'm Captain Eugene Swisher, WDGS."

"What?"

"War Department General Staff."

Basset found Swisher's appearance surprising. Of medium height, he had a large, round and hairless face. His arching brows appeared to have been painted above brown eyes and his fine brown hair looked to be painted on too. The effect was somewhat that of a clown made up for a circus act, and, as if Swisher knew it, his expression was constantly one of astonishment that nature had given him such an appearance.

He spoke petulantly: "You don't look like the photos I've seen of you. How do I know you're Colonel Basset?"

Disguising his alarm with an air of weariness, Basset said, "So I'm not Basset. Keep looking, Captain." He turned away.

Swisher dashed around in front of him. "Colonel, what's your serial number?"

"0929585."

"Maybe you're Basset." Swisher sounded disappointed. "That's his number all right."

"Who the hell are you and what the hell do you want?"

"That sounds more like the way they say you talk, Colonel. I just came off the morning flight from Nouméa. Been chasing twenty-four hours behind you all the way from Dumbo. Have orders for you to accompany me."

Basset, frightened, gave a snarl. "Well, I've got news for you, buster. I'm on my way to Guadalcanal under SOPAFA orders, than which there is nothing whicher in this theater. Pack off!"

Swisher sighed. "Maybe you're Colonel Basset after all. Everybody says he talks like that. Sir, there's nothing whicher than WDGS orders in any theater. Look!" Swisher thrust a sheet of orders at him, but Basset did not try to penetrate its thicket of jargon.

"I'll get my gear," he said and hurried away.

He intended to run as soon as he was out of Swisher's sight. Once he was aboard the seaplane tender, Swisher could never catch him. Guadalcanal might be the safest hideout on earth, because no chair-bound WDGS officer would ever follow him to such a dangerous place. When he broke into a run, he glanced over a shoulder and saw that Swisher was running gamely behind him. He ran faster. So did Swisher.

A Marine sergeant, inspecting a stack of lumber, looked at Basset with surprise—a colonel *running?*

"Help!" gasped Basset, galloping around the stack. "They caught me in the nurses' quarters!"

"Nurses?" cried the sergeant, eyes wide, and began to gallop alongside him. "They got *nurses* here? Where? Duck in here, sir."

Basset halted, panting, in a small bay amid the lumber piles, and the sergeant crowded after him. "*Where,* sir?"

"Up there." Basset pointed wildly. "Nubile, prurient nurses the Army shipped in secretly."

"Nubile? They got *black* nurses?"

"No! No! No! They're all white and they're horny from confinement. That captain has the key to their pen."

Swisher cantered past, and the sergeant went after him while Basset peeked around the stack. "Captain!" the sergeant called to Swisher. "This is a restricted area!" Swisher, finding himself in a dead end among the lumber piles, started to run back the way he had come. "So," the sergeant said, "tryin' to steal Navy property, huh?" and flattened him with a left hook.

As Basset ran on toward the pier he saw the sergeant searching Swisher's pockets for the key to the nurses' quarters.

Seeing that we had gone to the ship and taken his gear with us, Basset waited for the next lighter. There was no need to worry more about Swisher, he believed; that Marine sergeant had taken care of him for a couple of hours. But in a few minutes he saw Swisher running toward him again. In panic and dismay he could not find anyplace to hide on the pier; he was trapped.

"Got to get to that ship!" he shouted. "Got to get my gear!"

"Oooo!" Swisher wobbled a bit as he ran and his right jaw was puffed where the Marine had hit him. "Sorry. Got into a restricted area and was arrested by shore patrol. Colonel Basset, are you trying to run away from me?"

"My gear!" yelled Basset. "Got nothing but my wallet and my orders to Guadalcanal. My men! Can't be separated from 'em."

"Get 'em later." Swisher fought for breath. "They're holding the Nouméa flight for us. Come on!"

Basset was aghast. "What priority have you to hold up the Nouméa flight?"

"I told you the highest. Didn't you read your new orders? Colonel, you're headed for the War Department in Washington."

The seaplane tender on which Red, Goldman and I sailed from Espíritu Santo for Guadalcanal was "converted" only to the extent that it no longer tended seaplanes. In the reeking spaces below decks were jammed Marine replacement specialists and a company of Seabees on their way to try to dislodge a destroyer transport which had run aground in Ironbottom Sound. Above decks were lashed supplies ranging from cases of condensed milk to drums of aviation gasoline. For three hours of every four we were confined to cramped, fetid bunk space near the engine room; in the fourth hour it was our turn for rotation to the upper decks.

On the third day after we sailed, we entered the Bismarck Sea and the azure waters became gray. The zestful air turned humid, and the lava shores of distant islands were as drab as though hammered out of iron.

When we went above at 0500 the following morning there was an oppressive dead calm. We felt rather than saw the imminence of a land that was curiously disturbing. It exuded a rank stench of slime and jungle that made some of us on deck start coughing. In the distance was a *bup-bup-bup* of artillery fire, a chatter of machine guns.

The ship barely moved. The light grew, but this dawn brought no joy; it succeeded, rather, in merely lighting the lava crests of a satellite island and giving them the eerie look of humpbacked monsters rising from the sea. At last the spreading light revealed the matted jungle shores of Guadalcanal about three hundred yards distant. No bird called a greeting to the dawn; there was no sound but the thud of artillery.

Someone said, startlingly loud: "This place gives me the creeps!"

Red, Goldman and I went aft to see if the other ships in our convoy were still with us. Suddenly the quiet erupted in a cacophony of gunfire, joined by the little 20-millimeter peashooters of the tender. Looking about wildly, we could not make out what everybody was shooting at.

But then we saw it: a plane coming in low, flying incredibly slowly through the bursting flak. It seemed to be aimed at me; instinctively I ducked behind a pile of cargo.

At once my eardrums sucked under a concussion so deafening that I did not even hear it. I seemed simply to be flying, gracefully, while gray sea and sky tumbled awkwardly over one another.

13

I died. But I was soon reborn, thrashing and trying to disgorge salt water from my throat. I would have sunk and died for the last time if Red had not rescued me.

Then we were swimming side by side away from the ship and the flames billowing into the dawn sky. Others were swimming too. I thought I should pull off my boots, but, remembering Basset's tale of sharks, I did not want to take the time. I swam faster, and so did Red. We flailed the water frantically, like contestants in a dead-heat race, till my lunging hand struck something pliable that made me nearly cry out at the thought of shark. It was a rotted log. At last I found myself standing to my waist in water, with mud oozing above my knees, while Red floundered nearby.

It seemed we would never recover breath or still the knocking of our hearts. Red clutched at a vine to steady himself, but it turned out to be some kind of moss that disintegrated at his touch. Where was Goldman? The ship still burned, though its glaring flames were lost in the blaze of the rising sun, and a couple of men still swam for shore. Suddenly one of the swimmers screamed, and I saw a flash of shark fin. The man screamed again and again, raising himself almost out of the water, and then his head disappeared in a bloody boil of brine as he flung up a red stump of leg and went down forever.

I screamed too. "That's Goldman!"

"Looked like him!"

In the silence a strange sound seemed to come from the brush around us. Gradually I realized the sound was of Red and me retching.

Terror of sharks sent us floundering into the swamp and a new horror: the ooze sucked at us like bottomless quicksand. If others had made it to shore, we could not see or hear them.

I wept for Goldman; I had not realized I loved him as a brother. Thinking back to the days when we served the General, I remembered our times of joy and sadness together. But the thought I could not shake off was what a stupid waste of life this was.

As Red and I struggled on, trying to help each other, swarms of insects attacked us. At last we clambered from the slime onto muddy land. Next I knew, we were breaking a way through matted brush, taking turns leading each other. Even the tangled shrubs seemed to give off a stench like sewer gas, or rotting animal flesh. Then, through the brush, I made out a field of grass.

Croaking encouragement to Red, I pressed ahead with the intent of flinging myself in the lovely field. But the grass turned out to be *kunai,* very tall, and with blades like bayonets. Moaning, I sank down and wished I had died with Goldman. After a short rest, Red urged us on, and slowly we worked our way around the *kunai* until we came upon a miracle.

A faint path wound into the jungle. With Red leading, we blundered gratefully along the trail until a fresh terror made us halt in consternation. Were we within friendly or enemy lines? Suppose the path led to a Japanese camp? Cautiously we went ahead until the jungle opened abruptly on a glade where tents were pitched. It was a Marine rest camp, but no one welcomed us. Two more mouths to feed—and Army mouths at that!

A lieutenant sent us on to battalion headquarters with a youthful guide who took wry joy in reporting bad news: the Marines were about to be pushed into the sea. They could not hold the airfield. They were starving. They were short of ammunition. The Island was swept by a plague of dysentery that reduced men to skeletons in two days. And if the diarrhea didn't kill you, the malaria would. All of it, the youth explained, was the fault of Franklin Delano Roosevelt, who had personally picked out this island as the best place to destroy the Marine Corps, which he hated because it had refused to commission one of his sons a general.

At battalion headquarters, where everybody looked and smelled filthy, there was some merriment over the Army finally deigning to send two men to The Island. My announcement that we were supposed to help expand the airstrip met with jeers. Then a kindly lieutenant scrounged around and found for each of us essential things which had been lifted from the dead: canteen, mess kit, helmet and liner, a Springfield, a belt of ammo, a bayonet, a trenching shovel, blanket, poncho.

Rations were so short that the battalion was down to two meals a day served at nine in the morning and four in the afternoon. Red and I ravenously spooned up hash and glutinous boiled rice and washed it down with tea captured from the Japanese. The Marines showed us where and how deep to dig foxholes, and warned us not to raise our heads from our holes after nightfall no matter what happened.

As we began our toil amid swarms of mosquitoes, Red asked, "Boz, are you sure that was Goldman who was killed by the shark?"

"No, I'm not sure, but it looked like him."

"We must write letters to his parents," Red said, "but we won't tell them a shark did it. Let's have him die like a hero, leading his men against the enemy."

We curled into a fetal position in our foxholes, and covered ourselves and our rifles with the blanket and poncho and fell asleep. Almost instantly we were awakened by a thud that shook the earth. The cannonading did not stop all night, and when I crawled out of the hole at dawn I was so exhausted that I almost envied Goldman his death.

That morning we struck out for the airfield. We believed Basset had probably arrived safely there aboard another ship. Red even imagined that if he had been unable to obtain ship passage he would have hitched a ride aboard one of the combat planes out of New Hebrides that flew bomb strikes on Guadalcanal. So great was his faith in Basset.

However, no one at the airfield had heard of him. A squad of Air Force ground crewmen and their captain had arrived aboard another ship in our convoy, but the captain said he would not accept us unless we could show orders assigning us to the unit. Our orders had gone down with everything else—my precious cameras and film, Basset's Scotch and cigars. The captain said that was tough shit for us, his supplies were too short for him to feed a couple of strays. When my eloquence failed to move him, we wandered away feeling like social outcasts.

We applied to the Marines at the field, like migrants seeking employment in a foreign country.

"Look, Lieutenant," said a weary Marine captain, "what can you do?"

I lied, claiming that Red and I were civil engineers.

"Shit on that," the captain said, "I used to be a civil engineer myself till I got into this mess. I see no chance to lengthen this strip. I just hope we can keep it operable. We have no earth-moving equipment, so we're stuck with pick and shovel."

Because Red and I worked hard with pick and shovel we won grudging respect from the others, even though we were not Marines. Twice a day we ate their monotonous slops and, like everyone, we tried to sleep in holes dug at the edge of the field.

When it rained, as it did much of the time, the field turned to slough, and afterwards the hot sun baked a mud crust that crumbled and blew as choking dust. An Air Force squadron of P-400 fighters, an export version of the P-39, flew missions off the strip. Lacking adequate oxygen equipment and superchargers, the P-400s were incapable of high-altitude fighting. Within a few days after its arrival, almost the entire squadron was wiped out, and it was expected that Marine fighter planes and dive-bombers would soon arrive. Meantime the Air Force planes were being serviced by a detachment of Marine specialists. No one hoped to make the wrecked planes operable again; the idea was to strip them of working parts to service other planes.

When a plane crash-landed on the strip one day, Red watched with interest as men picked at the wreckage like vultures feasting on carrion. Before long he began coaching a green hand on how to remove a fuel pump. The man was so inept that Red finally took wrench and screwdriver from him and quickly performed the task.

"You!" A Marine tech sergeant tapped his shoulder. "Come wid me."

Red did not resume toil with pick and shovel, and it took him another day to con the maintenance detachment into accepting me as an equally expert mechanic. Fortunately, I was manually adept, and with Red's coaching I was soon able to perform passably.

The Japanese pounded the field every night. Though they did not inflict many casualties, they turned the nights into hell for us. Anyone was lucky to get two or three hours of interrupted sleep; nerves grew taut, tempers short. Then a new epidemic of dysentery affected everyone; and at the peak of it, the toilet paper supply ran out. That week a ton of cups and saucers arrived. Malaria was on the rise; the new drug Atabrine, reported to keep the disease in check, was dispensed liberally, but many men would not swallow the yellow pills because they believed a rumor that Atabrine would leave them impotent.

The Marines felt sorry for Red and me. We were not being paid and did not exist administratively. They sent reports about us, but nothing came of them. Red, wanting to become a pilot more than ever now that he was working on planes and meeting men who flew, offered to enlist in the Marines. However, someone higher up said that was impossible.

In the meantime, the Japanese, commanding the waters and air space of The Island after dark, which the Americans claimed to control during the day, had decided on an all-out effort to drive us off Guadalcanal. It began at 0140 one morning. A sound like a huge door slamming brought Red and me wide awake in the cave we had dug deep underground and covered with metal sheeting. Dirt began to rain on us as the roar of shelling became deafening. We covered our heads with our blankets and plugged fingers in ears, but the awful din continued to hammer us with the concussive force of flailing fists.

For seventy minutes (the historians reported long after) two Japanese battleships poured more than nine hundred rounds of fourteen-inch high-explosive shells onto the field while a cruiser and seven destroyers thickened the fire with five-inch shells. It was the heaviest bombardment of the Pacific to that time. The roaring grew as fuel dumps went up in flames and stored bombs and ammunition began to explode. Even in our cave deep underground we thought we felt the searing heat. Worse, however, was the awful noise. Before long we truly did not hear it, but simply felt it beating at our chests and heads until we were ready to die.

The shelling ceased abruptly at 0250, but it took everyone still alive many minutes to realize it. We were stone deaf. We understood the shelling had stopped when our heads did not throb as painfully. Slowly deafness subsided into a loud ringing through which our shouts to each other came as whispers.

We scrambled up our ladder onto the field where the leaping flames of dozens of fires made it as light as day. Here and there men moved like wraiths. Where palms had stood were only torn stumps. A huge slab of steel airstrip matting had been hurled a couple of hundred yards and imbedded itself upright in the earth like a giant discus. A can labeled "HAM," eviscerated, was neatly lodged in a broken airplane propeller.

At dawn we counted only twenty-one whole fighters and dive bombers where last night there had been ninety-nine. Of those surviving, nearly all needed repairs. More than forty men were dead and more than twice as many incapacitated with wounds at the airfield alone. We surviving ground crewmen worked feverishly to repair as many planes as we could while the others struggled to fill in the deep craters in the strip.

Throughout the day rumors spread that the Japanese had thrown in large ground forces at several places with the aim of encircling and seizing the field. The U.S. Army had finally landed its promised regiment. But where in God's name was the U.S. Navy? Was there even a U.S. Navy still in existence?

Yet the airfield still existed, and in late afternoon planes took off on scouting missions.

That night the Japanese Navy bombarded us again, almost as heavily as before. And the next day we quickly set about repairing runway and planes once more.

The passage of time became blurred. Our exhaustion never quite ended in the collapse we would have welcomed. We carried on like sleepwalkers.

One day in mid-October I came out of a supply tent and had the illusion that I saw Goldman. Closing my eyes and groaning, I wondered if madness could be far behind hallucination. I opened my eyes and still saw Goldman staring at me. At least it looked like the remnants of Goldman: the young face had become wizened; the generous princeling nose had turned as sharp as a Saracen scimitar; filthy fatigues hung from this skeleton.

"Yeee!" cried the creature, recoiling from me.

"Yeee!" I replied. Only Goldman could recoil so expressively.

We sort of hugged each other and made yammering sounds. Then we went looking for Red, who was at first as frightened by Goldman's ghost as I had been.

"You look hideous," I kept telling him. "What's the matter with you?"

"So do you," he said.

I saw for the first time that Red and I were wraiths too.

Goldman had swum ashore when Red and I did, and, believing we were dead, had fallen in with a unit of Marines, who put him to work as a stevedore in an unloading zone. Life with the Marines had been so arduous that he'd run away to the Army when its first Infantry battalion had landed. Amazingly, he was beginning to make a happy home for himself in the Infantry as a platoon commander. To add to his good luck, Yaromski was the first sergeant and Cherokee one of the noncoms in the company where he had elected to come to rest.

"But the best thing about D Company," Goldman said, "is that I'm no longer administratively lost, no longer missing in action. D Company has put me back in existence again."

This might have seemed an extreme statement coming from a man who had been intelligent enough to forecast the attack on Pearl Harbor. But to Red and me, *in extremis* from having been lost administratively for a long time, it sounded perfectly rational.

Next day, at Goldman's invitation, we took our rifles and hitched a truck ride to D Company's position, where Yaromski and Cherokee greeted us warmly and we ate tastier chow than we had in weeks. The company commander, a pleasant Carolinian named Brown, known to everyone as Farmer Brown, was so eager to replace his casualties that he offered me command of a platoon, an honor I declined.

In its defensive position the company had dug its lines in the jungle at the edge of a large field of *kunai* grass which sloped to a knoll about a thousand yards away. Fields of fire had been cut through the tall, sharp grass. The lines had been prepared for assault with barbed wire on which shell fragments were strung to jangle a warning if the enemy tried to cross it after dark.

Yaromski said the company had been in a fire fight the night before; seven men had been wounded and evacuated to the field hospital. It was the ninth day of combat, and the men were gaining self-confidence. Tomorrow they would fall back as battalion reserve, so they were having it easy compared to what the Marines had endured.

Yaromski and Cherokee came along when Goldman took us to his platoon sector after chow. Cherokee had a bullhorn which he'd swiped during the landing, and somewhere down across the *kunai* there was an English-speaking Japanese soldier who also had a horn. His voice came to us in a cultivated accent:

"Blood for the Em-pe-ror!"

Cherokee raised his horn and replied: "Blood for El-ea-nor! Blood for Frank-lin!"

"Blood for the Em-pe-ror!" came the answer.

I remarked that the Japanese sounded too intelligent to mean what he was saying.

"He means it, all right," Yaromski said. "He's an illiterate little bastard. Listen to this." He took the bullhorn and snarled: "Tojo eat shit!"

Back came the Japanese: "Babe Ruth eat shit!"

"See what I mean?" Yaromski said. "Babe Ruth is no longer one of our leading cultural symbols, but that illiterate little bastard down there doesn't know it."

When the enemy began to lob in mortar shells, Red and I crawled deeper into the platoon command post dugout. We had planned to start back to the airfield after chow, but only an idiot would have tried to make his way through the fire storm the Japanese were laying on rear and forward positions.

At last Goldman brought us rifle ammo clips and spoke cheerfully: "I think it's going to begin sooner than expected." So we would have to pay for our lunch. Rain was starting to fall when, at Goldman's direction, we raced after a corporal to a forward dugout.

From an aperture Red and I stared down a fire-field lane through the *kunai*. Behind us two mortars were zeroed on the lane while their crews sat in the rain and played gin rummy with waterproof cards. The corporal said nothing would happen till after dark.

Suddenly, however, the Japanese lifted their fire, and through the rain we made out a brown mass stirring in the *kunai*. Then the enemy came up the lane at a run, and our mortars began barking behind us while hidden machine guns chattered on either side. The running mass of Japanese slowed, but soon came on again. When they were within rifle range, the corporal moved between Red and me and we began to fire steadily.

It was war as I'd fought it when I was a kid at Saturday movie matinees, bang-bang-banging away at the Indians charging the wagon train. We killed them by the dozens. It was so easy that I felt stunned. We just fired at moving figures, and some fell.

After so many dead and wounded had piled in the lane that those behind could not climb over them, the living fell back the way they had come. Red and I stopped firing and looked at each other with wonder. "It's like knocking over lead ducks!"

I didn't realize that the enemy mortars had gone into action again when a mosquito stung my neck sharply. I put a hand up to the bite and thought it must have been a huge mosquito because my fingers were covered with blood. Then I saw that Red's expression had changed from wonder to horror. He started toward me with hands outstretched. Suddenly feeling dizzy, I decided to sit down. One of the mortar men had sat down too and was clutching his stomach with a surprised look, as if stricken with indigestion. As Red knelt beside me, my dizziness grew and I thought I'd feel better if I lay back and slept for a while.

14

"Why," Basset asked Swisher after they took off from Espíritu Santo, "does the War Department send somebody in person to escort me? Am I incapable of traveling by myself? Things haven't been done this way since Bonaparte was First Consul."

Swisher stared at him solemnly from the adjacent bucket seat. "An interesting question, Colonel. Your grades in history at the Academy were so poor I didn't think you'd know Napoleon was ever anything but Emperor—if you even knew that. Let's see, your class was '23?"

" '24." The date was on the Academy ring Basset had inherited.

"Oh, yes." Swisher frowned. "It was my idea I come and get you. You're my case."

"Your *case?*"

Swisher formed a small, deprecatory smile. "I've made something of a name for myself since receiving a direct commission in G-2, WDGS. I was a lawyer in civilian life—criminal law. And I'm earning the reputation of being the best in Army investigative work."

"Congratulations." Basset yawned and closed his eyes.

"Don't you want to hear the answer to your question?" Swisher sounded petulant.

"Which question?"

"Why I came to the Pacific to fetch you personally."

"Answer fast. I want to sleep."

"You're being investigated for a vitally important job of the highest top-secret classification."

Basset, dismayed, opened his eyes. What did engineers do but build bridges, airstrips, and such? And what could possibly be classified about them?

"Understand that you have not been picked," Swisher went on. "You're merely a candidate. I can't say more than that."

"You can't say more because you don't know more. You've said too much already for anybody who really knows anything."

"You puzzle me, Colonel. Sometimes you sound literary, sometimes illiterate. There are so many things. Even your handwriting has changed. The letters you sign to your wife don't look at all like your writing only a year ago."

"You son of a bitch, you've been reading my mail!"

"Why not? How do you think three-way investigations are carried out?"

"By the Army, Navy and FBI, but not by reading my mail, you bastard. Swisher, you're a menace to society and I'll have to destroy you."

Swisher's eyes seemed to bulge. "You *threaten* me?"

Basset, reaching out, tugged at Swisher's left eyebrow, wondering if the curious-looking thing would come off in his fingers. But it didn't; it grew there firmly. Swisher uttered a piercing shriek, and everybody in the airplane stared at them.

"What are you?" cried a Navy commander. "A couple of Army faggots?"

Swisher swelled with rage; he was so furious at Basset that he wouldn't speak to him until they reached Nouméa. That was fine with Basset, who pretended to sleep while contemplating this weird and frightening twist in his fate.

Traveling with Swisher on WDGS orders offered royal comforts; all obstacles were removed, every effort made to speed them on their way with ease. In Nouméa, Swisher arranged for Basset to buy fresh uniforms, got him advance pay, and obtained them access to a renowned Army-Navy club for officers of highest rank where they dined on succulent filets mignon, crisp French fries, a salad of fresh Australian greens and baked Alaska. After another Scotch on the rocks, Basset was ready for a good night's sleep. But Swisher pressed on relentlessly. He sent two brigadier generals into paroxysms of fury by having them bumped from the next flight east so that he and a grumbling, sleepy Basset could take off into the night.

As they were nearing Johnston Island, Basset opened his wallet and looked at his photos of Helen and Roger. Swisher asked who they were.

"My wife and son."

Swisher let out a loud, frightening sound. "Got you! Don't know whether to have you arrested now ⊕r later. Colonel, that woman is not your wife!"

Basset thought Swisher had gone totally insane. He must get rid of him, then turn himself into a civilian when he arrived back in the States. It would be certain death for him to go to Washington, where Helen and others would expose him as a fraud.

As they approached Hawaii in fading light, Swisher warned: "Don't try to get out of my sight."

Basset was still muttering at him when the passengers filed off the plane and into the reception center. Observing several MPs on duty, Basset beckoned one, who approached and saluted. "Corporal," he murmured, "keep an eye on that captain there ahead of me. He's been making homosexual advances to me all the way from Johnston. The filthy beggar even put a hand on my leg."

"My God, yes, sir, Colonel. You want to proffer charges now?"

"Not just yet. But don't let him out of your sight."

After they had been checked through reception, Basset went into a stall in the officers' latrine. Swisher, following, had just unbuttoned his pants at the urinal when Basset let out an unearthly yell in his stall. The MPs rushed in, seized Swisher, and dragged him away, kicking and shrieking.

"You were right, sir," the corporal said to Basset. "He sure was exposing himself."

"Guess that's what a man has to do here if he's using the facilities," Basset said. "But you and I know, Corporal, that man was exposing himself *with malice aforethought*. Remember to use that phrase when you book him, son."

"Yes *sir*. Will you come along with us?"

"I can't just yet. I'm scheduled to conduct an all-night top-secret briefing session for the commanding general. Have the man held incommunicado all night. He's very dangerous and I'm sure his orders are phony. He pretends to have WDGS orders like mine. I'll be there in the morning to sew up your case."

Basset went to the billeted officers' quarters, intending to get a night's sleep before using his priority to take the first morning flight to San Francisco. Then he would fly on east and turn himself into a civilian under a different name. By paying a couple of hundred bucks to a New York racketeer he knew, he could obtain a phony draft registration card, essential to employment—and in a Bowery Savings Bank Morton Fiddler had a ten-thousand-dollar account.

After a cafeteria dinner he was struck by the crazy notion that he'd like to speak to Vera one last time. She had moved, but the telephone operator provided her new number. When she answered, he said, "Hi, there, I'm a friend of Boz Boswick's."

"Oh," she said, "well, we're booked solid tonight."

"Don't want a professional consultation. Just send Boz's regards. Ira Goldman's too."

"Hey," she said, "who *is* this?"

"Charlie or Chuck, Pete or Peter Basset. I—"

"Fiddler!" She rang it out. "I'd recognize you anywhere. My God, and I thought you were dead! Honey, where are you?"

He found himself grinning. Rather than being frightened that she recognized his voice so easily, he felt pleased. "Wanna buy a duck?" he asked her.

"You bet I wanna buy a duck, Fiddler. The hell with the patients, you come right out here to the clinic."

He gave her directions to a taxi driver, who took him to a much grander house than the bungalow which she now owned and rented out. The large two-story home of California-Spanish design, was on another road that led to another beach in Waikiki. Vera had bought it and the surrounding brush-covered five acres for a modest price with her earnings, figuring that the property would increase in value after the war.

A pretty Hawaiian girl opened the door and smiled at Basset. "Hello, I'm Lulu. Do you have an appointment?"

"Tell Vera that Chuck Charlie Basset is here."

"Fiddler!" Vera appeared instantly and flung her arms about him. "And they said you were dead!"

"I am. I mean he is. Will you swear to keep a secret?"

"I keep more secrets than the War Department. What's yours?"

"My name is Colonel Charles Peter Basset and I'm an engineer career officer in the U.S. Army."

Vera yelled with laughter. "That's the wildest secret I've ever kept. Who but Fiddler could think it up?"

She stepped back, admiring him, and he noticed that in her long brightly patterned gown she looked prettier than ever.

"Professional life seems to suit you," he said. "Quite a hospital you have here. How many operating rooms do you have?"

"Boz and Ira must have told you all about us. How are they?"

"All right, I guess. I got separated from 'em. They're on some lousy island and Red is with them. Where's Rosemarie?"

Vera glanced about swiftly and her gaze settled on Lulu, who listened with an animated expression. "Secrets, Lulu. Hush about Red, please, Fiddler. Rosemarie seems to have got over him, and I don't want him coming back to her mind. Okay?"

"Sure."

"I really think of this place as a clinic," she went on. "I mean I really think we're doing something good for the war effort. These poor lonely men so far from home. Lulu here is an intern. Besides Rosemarie and me, we now have three interns and one resident."

Lulu cast Basset a droll look: "When we interns aren't taking care of the Johns, we're scrubbing the bathrooms."

He laughed, but Vera frowned and told her, "Stop pretending you're Groucho Marx. Some of the patients have complained about your one-liners. Therapy is a very serious experience for them."

"Expensive too," Lulu said to Basset.

"If you have a better mousetrap," he replied, "the world will beat a path to your door."

Lulu grinned, but Vera was thinking of other things. "After you phoned, I canceled everything that needed my personal attention. Let's go somewhere private and talk."

"Just one thing, Miz Vera," Lulu said. "I mean two things. Two young ensigns. They're in the same engine-room watch of the cruiser *Northampton* that's supposed to sail west in the morning. They had the regular fifty-dollar treatment with Dr. Henrietta and Dr. Mary. Then they heard about your Lucky Special from that commander who's undergoing therapy with Rosemarie. They offer to pay twenty-five dollars each for it."

"Can't somebody else take care of it?"

"No ma'm, they know who you are, and they say it's got to be you or no dice."

Basset thought that while Vera had changed in many ways, one thing that remained the same was her facial expression at the mention of money. He could see her mentally computing her possible fees.

"This'll only take a moment," she told him. "Just a brief clinical thing. Did Boz tell you about this power I have to offer men safe conduct through the war?''

"He told me about your *claim* to such power, Vera."

"I made it up on the spur of the moment"—She spoke reflectively —"but you know, Fiddler, I'm beginning to wonder if it may not be true because— This is the reception room."

She opened a door, and he followed. "Emergency cases only, eh?"

The two young ensigns leaped to their feet. It was astonishing, Basset thought, how every day the fighters in this war seemed to be getting younger; soon the fleets and armies might be composed entirely of children led by a few tired old admirals and generals.

"I am Vera," she told the young men.

"Yes ma'm," gasped one. "We know that."

"Do you know that all who go through this initiation ceremony have emerged unharmed from all sorts of dangers?"

They nodded eagerly.

"The rules are simple. You pay Miss—Lulu— the fee. You remain fully clothed. You kiss the sacred cleft and receive my promise of lasting life. If you touch any other part of my body a very terrible thing will happen to you." She turned to Basset. "Wait outside with Lulu."

Lulu sat on a divan reading an old copy of the *New York Times Book Review*. "What's the matter with you," Basset asked, "are you a bookworm?"

"Yes," she said. "I graduated first in my high school class in Honolulu. I want to go to Radcliffe."

"Well, a couple days of interning in this place and you should have money for a year's tuition."

"It's not a lack of money," Lulu said. "Not a lack of brains. I did brilliantly on the college boards. It's my name—Lulu Halekalunakalawai—and my race. The Radcliffe admissions office can't even spell my name."

"Shorten it to Hale. They'll think you're a descendant of Nathan's and accept you."

"It's the color of my skin—my hair—my face—my race—Americans think Hawaiian girls can't do anything but the hula."

One of the ensigns stepped out with a dazed expression, and Basset said, "My God that was quick." The ensign stared at him vacantly, and Lulu said, "That will be twenty-five dollars more, young man." He paid and passed into the night.

"I don't see how Radcliffe could have anything on this place,"

Basset said. "Lulu, you don't know when you're well off. I figure women are the only winners in a war."

"Do you call *this* being a woman?" Lulu asked indignantly.

The other ensign hastened out with a furtive look, thrust his money at Lulu, and fled. "Holy smoke!" Basset said. "Hurry, hurry, hurry. This place is like the automat."

Vera appeared, holding her robe tightly around her. "Sometimes," she said, "it seems a crime to take their money. Fiddler, honey, I want to talk to you."

Basset went with Vera to her private room. "It's not my public bedroom," she explained. "I don't want you even to look at that. You're the only one, except for Rosemarie and the maid, I've ever let in here."

It was the most extraordinary bedroom he ever had seen. Except that it contained a large bed and dressing table, it was like an office with a desk and filing cabinets. It was like a real estate information office, walls festooned with photos, ads, posters of Hawaiian and California mansions, bungalows, even hotels of all shapes and sizes. Above the desk on a bulletin board were tacked numerous memos and a couple of interest-amortization tables.

"Sexiest damn bedroom I ever visited," Basset said gravely.

"It's my refuge," Vera said, "a place to get away from it all. Fiddler, honey, tell me everything that's happened since I saw you last."

He enjoyed a long confession that concluded with his plans for turning himself into a civilian.

"If that's possible." She traced a finger around his mustache. "They're really going to be after you. Whatever happens, I want you to stay in touch with me. I'll give you my downtown post box number and the name I use there. Now that I've found you again, I can't bear to let you go. Fiddler, I've finally fallen in love. With you. At first I thought I wouldn't mind having you see what I let those ensigns do to me, but all of a sudden I couldn't stand that—I've never been in love before. But now I am with you."

Eventually Fiddler would admit that his chief trouble was in being too plastic. Suggestible. A chameleon. Yet gallant, too, in his fashion. When an attractive woman like Vera said that she loved him, he found it natural to reply that he loved her too. So he declared his undying love for Vera.

They exchanged a kiss, and Vera said, "I never kiss the men I do business with. When the war is over, I can afford to retire. Then there will be just you and me, Fiddler. This is merely a way to make some money.''

He understood that, but, whatever her circumstances, he did not truly love her. When she had worked for him at the Royal Hawaiian last winter, he had been fond of her because she had been an innocent and needed protection. However, now that she had become more worldly and was making her way as a hooker, he felt that he could make love to her without actually loving her.

The door to Vera's room was opened slowly, and a woman spoke in the gentlest tone Basset ever had heard: "Vera?''

He glanced over a shoulder at the most beautiful woman in the world. She was naked; her fingers hooked a robe which hung over her shoulder. Surprised that Vera had a guest, she apologized for coming in and quickly swung her robe as cover—but not before Basset saw her full breasts, the exquisite joining of her long and slender legs to her lithe torso.

As she started to back out the doorway, Vera said, "It's okay, dear. Pete, this is Rosemarie. Rosemarie, this is Pete, the most important man in my life. You've often heard me speak of him.''

"Well.'' Rosemarie smiled doubtfully.

Basset realized that she would not have heard his name before: the incredible thing about this woman might be less her beauty than the fact she found it hard to lie. Red's Rosemarie! Lovely as her body was, it did not surpass the beauty of her face and golden hair.

I want her! Basset formed the thought just as she closed the door and disappeared.

"Red's Rosemarie!'' He sounded shocked.

"But no longer Red's,'' Vera said. "Now she belongs to—to the world. Pretty, isn't she?''

"Yes.''

"Prettier than me, Fiddler?'' Vera asked with a jealous gleam in her eye.

"No prettier than you,'' Fiddler lied. "No reason for you to be jealous,'' he continued, supporting one untruth with another. "I'm awful fond of Red. I'd be disloyal to him if I—''

"That's sweet.'' Vera stroked his face. "That's my Fiddler. The sweetest guy in the world doing some of the world's zaniest things. Dear Fiddler, you and I have a lot of lost time to make up before you leave.''

It felt strange to be called Fiddler. Yet who, he wondered, was he really? He had been trying to be Basset, and now he suddenly wanted to be Fiddler again. Vera claimed to love Fiddler. Could she manage to love Basset? Maybe he could have a satisfying relationship with a woman only when he was playing the role of someone other than himself. But then he had an arresting thought: If he played different roles long enough, would he eventually lose his own identity completely?

He and Vera made love half the night: the finest experience Basset could remember. What made it exceptionally exhilarating was that in the dark he pretended Vera was Rosemarie.

He had planned to leave early in the morning, but delayed going. A C-54 took off for San Francisco every hour, and, with his priority, he could bump anyone on any flight. He was drinking coffee with Vera and Rosemarie when Lulu brought in mail.

"Look!" Rosemarie exclaimed to Vera. "Here's a letter to the both of us from Boz." It was the letter written from Dumbo about ten days earlier.

Vera told her to open it and report on what Boz had written. In a soft, chirping voice that made Basset think of swallows nesting, Rosemarie began to read the letter aloud. "Oh!" she exclaimed suddenly. "Oh, listen to this! Boz says, 'Red works in the headquarters where Ira and I are. He's a good, cheerful soldier and a real close friend.' And listen to this, Vera, just listen"—tears sprang to Rosemarie's eyes—" 'Rosemarie, Red speaks often of you' "—her voice broke—" 'with love and respect.' " She dabbed the back of a hand to her eyes. " 'Goldman and I have never told him we know you. If you ever want to write him and say you and Vera are hairdressers in the same shop, this is his address—' " Rosemarie began to cry like a child.

Vera was furious. "That goddam Boz, poking his nose in where it's none of his business," she said to Basset as she drove him to the airport. "At least he didn't spill the beans and tell her you were the commander at Dumbo."

Basset was even more upset than Vera, though he tried not to show it. He had conceived a shattering passion for Rosemarie and now suddenly was being separated from her with no hope of ever consummating it. How, except through Vera, could he get in touch with her again? He had hinted broadly of his wish that Rosemarie ride to the airport with them, but neither she nor Vera understood how he felt.

At the same time he felt tormented by a sense of disloyalty to Red. And the most distressing aspect of it all was that Rosemarie had said she was going to devote the rest of the day to writing Red, telling him how much she loved and missed him.

15

I found myself in a charnel house after being hit by shrapnel on Guadalcanal. There was a smell of formaldehyde and chloroform, of feces, urine, vomit, sweat, putrefied flesh. The *bup-bup-bup— ba-up* did not come from mortars; it was the slowly dying fire of my heart.

"Mother!" a boy cried nearby. "Mom!" another called. "Mother! *Mother!*" The first boy's voice grew more insistent. "Mama! *Ma!*" The cry was taken up elsewhere in the charnel house. Why were so many boys there? The Marines and the Infantry were supposed to be composed of men, but this place was full of boys.

"Give this one another pint." Someone leaned over me and spoke: "Raise your right hand." I raised my right hand and said, "I do solemnly swear—" "Raise your left hand." I raised it and said, "Address me as sir, soldier, I'm a brigadier general." The voice came again: "Raise your right leg, smartass." I did so, and then my left leg.

"For a smartass you were very lucky," the voice said. "The fragment missed your spine, otherwise you'd be paralyzed for life or maybe dead. You've lost a lot of blood and you've got a hole in your neck where your head used to fit." I raised a hand and touched my head, relieved to find it still firmly on my shoulders.

"*Mother!*" shrieked a boy who seemed to be lying almost on top of me. "Mother, I'm *blind!*" His voice rose in a piercing wail, and other boys took up the chant for mother till I thought I couldn't stand it another instant.

I tried to speak, but the effort to speak started blood running down my throat. I began to choke and retch. As I struggled to sit up, a hand pushed me back and a familiar voice said, "Swallow it, smartass, don't fight it, you'll be okay."

My death was delayed a couple of days so that I could be evacuated from The Island in torrential rain. This clever move by the authorities enabled me to puke myself half to death in the suffocating hold of a rolling ship. Not yet alive, I arrived at a base hospital in Nouméa. I thought I was familiar with base hospitals from what I had read, but the Nouméa base hospital was not what I expected. For one thing, all the nurses were males.

About a month later, I had finally convalesced to the ambulatory stage. I wandered out of the officers' wing one day and came face to face with Red. Our joy at finding each other again was uncontained.

Red's left foot was in a cast as a result of a bullet wound which he'd suffered after well-meaning friends had arranged his transfer to D Company. "My next transfer is going to be to Air Force gunnery school," he said. "If I can't arrange that, I won't play any more. I'll just arrange to get discharged—and how can they ever hope to win the war without me?"

I said I was trying to arrange a discharge myself and finding it difficult.

"You ought to see Goldman," Red said. "He acts as if he wants to be a general with a chest full of medals. Already he's made first lieutenant and is the company exec. Farmer Brown calls him a great soldier. Even Yaromski admits he's not bad. Sometimes he acts downright fearless. The way he tried to explain it to me—he's been through so much on that damn island, he figures nothing can hurt him now."

"Gone nuts, eh? Poor Goldman. I can remember when he was a pretty bright guy."

"Have you heard anything about Colonel Basset?" Red asked.

"Not a thing."

"Neither have we. I wonder if he was killed."

"You can't kill off Basset. He's just hiding from us somewhere."

"I don't think so," Red said. "I'll bet he tried to get us off The Island and heard we were missing in action. If he's still alive, I bet he'd give his colonel's eagles to try to help us."

"He can't have tried very hard because we're all three back on the country's books. I even got paid last week."

Red and I spent most of our waking hours together, talking and reading and playing gin rummy. He seldom mentioned Rosemarie, but longed to hear from his family. Then, a few days after we came together, a letter arrived from his sister Jenny. He handed it to me.

"Bad news, Red, bad news," the letter said. "Mama died suddenly of a heart attack last Friday. . . . she had been put in charge of the notions dept at Grants. She got a job there in August and rose real fast. Anyway I came in from work maybe ten minutes after Ma and there she was sitting on the bottom step of the front stairs and she says Jenny I feel terrible and I says Ma I'll help you up the stairs and let's you lie down. I thought it was the flu. She says If I get taken real sick don't let on to Red cause he's doing a fine job serving our country and all I'm doing is serving Mr. W. T. Grant. Then she tries to laugh, but the pain hit her again and that's the last thing she said. Dr. Flynn says it was a massive heart attack. And we didn't even know she had heart trouble. . . ."

I looked at Red, trying to think of something good to say—I never have figured out what to say at such a time—but Red made things easier by getting up and walking away.

I should have stopped reading the letter then, but I went on till I saw Red's sister in a new light. She told how much the casket cost and what she paid the preacher and how she had become engaged to the head bookkeeper of the company where she worked and what his salary was and what kind of house their combined income would enable them to buy and how Pa would have to fend for himself now. "Red I just can't stand that man any more. All he does is sit and cry over Mama but when she was alive he'd go for days and barely speak to her."

Her letter reminded me of those from my own father and stepmother that ran on about money, cars, housing and rationing. Nearly all service people overseas got such letters—reports from another world—while they knew they might soon belong to no world at all. Often it was easier not even to try to reply.

I forgave Jenny Jack her greed for money and her impatience with her frustrated father and hoped Red would too, if he even caught the implications of her letter—which I wished he would not. But his reply showed that he had:

Dear Jenny,

   I am sad. I didn't know how much I'd miss Ma till now that she's gone. Tell Pa to write me sometime if he ever feels like it. Congratulations on your coming marriage. It sounds like you and Bill will have everything you need to make you very happy. I expect to leave the hospital any day now and go back to active duty.

Love,

Red

I was silently admiring the simple dignity of his letter when he said, "I don't want ever to go back to Glenwood or any place like it. I'd rather die in this war than go back to the Glenwoods of our country."

"I understand what you mean," I said. "But I don't agree on the death part. Once you're dead you've lost the chance to make things better than they are."

"That word 'love' there in that letter," Red went on, "I don't really mean it. What's happened to love anyway? I loved Rosemarie, and she left me. I loved Ma, and she died. I loved Pa, but he won't even write me any more. I loved Jenny, but now I know she doesn't care about anything except money and the appearance of things. I didn't exactly love Colonel Basset, but I was really fond of him and he went away and acts like I don't exist."

However, it was not in Red's nature to stay depressed for long. He was always ready with a joke or up to some kind of fun.

When we tired of one sort of corn, we tried another as we sat out the rains of Nouméa. We decided to collaborate on a musical comedy, but didn't get far past Red's title: "Who Wuz It Hid de Spanish Fly Inside de Vaseline?"

My application for a medical discharge was turned down, and Red's new application for flight school got lost. One afternoon late in November Goldman, wearing first lieutenant's bars and a yellowish Atabrine tan, appeared in the rec room where Red and I were playing gin rummy.

"Ten-hut!" I exclaimed, leaping to my feet and holding a salute to him, while Red followed suit. "Good afternoon, sir."

"Oh, knock it off!" Goldman was very embarrassed as he shook hands with us.

D Company and its battalion had been pulled out of Guadalcanal in order that some other outfit "get blooded" in combat, as the generals far to the rear liked to describe such movements. The battalion had been terribly mauled in the course of making some gains against the Japanese lines on The Island; all the officers in D Company except

Goldman had been killed or wounded out of action, leaving him the acting company commander.

"*You* a company commander?" I said. "The situation is indeed desperate."

"It really is," he replied seriously. "If things could be intelligently organized—as things never are—Yaromski should be company commander. But he's a difficult, stubborn man—he won't even allow them to commission him because he has a low opinion of officers."

Now what remained of the battalion was floating off Nouméa on its way to some Pacific island for a new euphemism used to describe one kind of tedium: rest and recreation. Goldman had come ashore for a couple of hours, accompanied by Yaromski and Cherokee, who would be along to see us soon.

"An amazing thing happened," Goldman said. "As we climbed out of the lighter from our ship, somebody let out a loud whistle from a Negro work gang on the pier. It was Lincoln. The poor guy didn't last twenty-four hours at headquarters after the General took over at Dumbo. Then, as he put it, he was sold into slavery and ended up in one of those all-Negro work battalions. I offered him Infantry employment in D Company, and he jumped at the chance."

"He must have turned soft in the head," I said.

"Not necessarily. You've never been employed in a work battalion."

"But who are you to perform miracles of transfer? Where did you get the power?"

"From Division. Every company commander now has the power to recruit volunteers—enlisted volunteers, that is—from noncombat units to combat units like ours. I could even arrange a transfer for you if you want to volunteer."

I let out a mock scream of horror. My discharge from the hospital only awaited final signature, and I was hoping for a public relations assignment someplace.

"Did you know," Goldman said, "that there are noncombat jobs within combat organizations?"

"Oh, no you don't," I said. "Haven't you heard of the inactive reserve?"

"I wouldn't con a friend." A kind of sanctimony came into his manner that made me understand why Vera sometimes called him Reverend Goldman. "There's a new job in the battalion table of organization that calls for an orientation officer."

"As Basset would inquire, to orient who to what?"

"Us troops to the"—Goldman waved vaguely—"the big picture
of the war. You deliver lectures and show slides and put out newslet-
ters—things like that."

Red urged me to come along with D Company, and then Goldman
leaned toward me confidentially: "Boz, this orientation job gives the
officer a camera and an unlimited supply of film—"

Thus it happened that I became the orientation officer of the 9th
Battalion with the privilege of living among my friends in D Company.

If Livau had not been infested with American soldiers, it would
have been a delightful place. The easterly trades blew fresh and salty-
sweet on the island where the temperature never rose above ninety
or sank below sixty. Behind beautiful beaches, groves of tall palms
gave an effect of extensive parklands.

The food was the best we'd had since the outbreak of war. The
battalion commander, Lieutenant Colonel Naylor, was a superb officer because he was an utterly reasonable man—a West Point graduate who made my whinings about military schools sound puerile.
Naylor called me disorientation officer. Realizing that no one in the
battalion cared what was happening in Libya and other distant places,
he saw my role in the way I did: to try to help create as strong morale
as possible.

I did my best at scrounging, borrowing and stealing feature-length
movies with the impossible goal of showing a different film every
evening. Besides serving as "movie officer," I used my camera to
take pictures of virtually every man and officer in the battalion which
he could send home to his family or girl friend. Naylor liked my
military work in this area so much that he put me in for first lieutenant. But nothing came of it.

Goldman made captain, as deserved. Red became the enlisted
leader of the second platoon and was promoted to staff sergeant, not
because of his friendship with Goldman and Yaromski, but because
he truly qualified for the job.

Red stopped answering Jenny's letters, which were mainly concerned with the costs of things and how her husband Bill was doing
in his job. He did not mention his father after Jenny wrote that Noah
had moved into a boarding house while she and Bill had bought the
house they desired. Then Red received a letter which did not bear a
return address; he read it excitedly, and showed it to me.

Dear Andrew,

I have been remiss about writing you and wish to make amends. I am sorry you were wounded and trust you are now fully recovered. Yet what good thing can we expect to come from war? I have been reading Max Eastman's translation of *The Three Sources and Three Constituent Parts of Marxism,* by Nikolai Lenin, and have underlined a few passages that may give you food for thought, wherever you are:

"Political institutions are a superstructure resting on an economic foundation."

"Capital, created by the labor of the worker, oppresses the worker by undermining the small proprietor and creating an army of the unemployed."

"Capital has conquered throughout the world, but its victory is only an earnest of the victory of labor over capital."

For amusement I tried reading some of this to Jenny's Bill. Thought he was going to have a stroke. He is an ass.

I have not become a Marxist any more than the noble Norman Thomas is a Marxist. But I like to keep an open mind and read the best and worst news from all camps.

I still miss your mother, but have got used to her death. Always remember, Andrew, what a fine woman she was.

I haven't put the address on this letter because this is not the place to write me. It's a boarding house, a terrible place. We get cabbage for dinner on Monday, Wednesday, Friday and Saturday, and the stench lasts the entire week. I'm moving on.

Next month I plan to marry Mrs. Mabel Rothstein, who has reminded me how remiss I've been in not writing you during my depression over this dreadful capitalistic war. Mrs. Rothstein is a widow, a good woman with a good mind, used to work for the state employment office in Newark, enjoys reading, has a pension and a small flat in Irvington. Will write my new address when I move.

My warmest regards,

Pa

However, Noah Jack did not write again; or, if he did, Red did not receive the letter. He asked Jenny for his address and received a quick, indignant reply in which she carried on against Mrs. Rothstein because she was Jewish; if Jenny knew Noah's new address, she forgot to supply it. Another letter came soon, more hysterical than the previous, in which Jenny said that Pa and Mrs. Rothstein had broken up and he had gone off she knew not where. Red gathered that she had had something to do with breaking them up, and he told me he never would write his sister again. All he could do, he said, was wait to hear from his father.

Since his family ties had weakened, his loneliness turned his thoughts to Rosemarie again. He told me he had decided to have the Red Cross try to find her. With my help he told their representative all we knew about where she might be in Waikiki.

By well into 1943, when we had been on Livau more than four months, it became evident to even the most obtuse soldier that our purpose there was not one of rest and recreation but of military training. About six weeks after we arrived, the Marines brought the amphtracs to Livau like salesmen proudly showing a new model car.

Goldman took one look at the vehicles and said, "My God, they're like open coffins."

Yaromski turned on him. "You shouldn't say that. It's real bad luck to say a thing like that."

The amphtracs, or LVTs, were track-driven amphibious vehicles propelled by gasoline engines which, the Marines insisted, offered the best means of carrying assault troops over a fringe of coral reef. The vehicles were twenty-five feet long, ten feet wide, weighed just under twelve tons, and could crowd in twenty-five men or four tons of cargo, like a bunker on wheels.

D, E and F Companies each received eight amphtracs. It was not surprising that the Marine trainers should pick Red, with his mechanical skills, to be a vehicle operator. But everyone was amazed when they yanked Lincoln out of his comfortable dispensary berth to become an operator.

"We find nigruhs make superior amphtrac operators," explained the Marine lieutenant in charge of training. "Everybody knows a white man's smarter 'n a nigruh, but somehow they got a feel for handlin' amphtracs."

Lincoln liked his new job as much as Red enjoyed his.

From the time we received our amphtracs we knew we were destined for an invasion somewhere. If anybody was frightened, none showed it, for we had become party to a military phenomenon. The training process had involved a softening of our minds as well as a hardening of our bodies. There were few, if any, individualists left among us; we had come to count on and trust one another, and so we would move in a mass, as directed. How we would act in the showdown had nothing to do with a sense of loyalty to the United States of America. It involved, rather, devotion to D Company, self-pride, a wish for the respect of our peers. We took comfort now in being unknowns submerged in a mass of humanity. We had an illusion of safety in such anonymity. They had worked us over till they had us precisely where they wanted us: so compliant to authority that we would go wherever we were told and kill anyone who stood in the way of our getting there. Good soldiers all.

At last we were told that the place we were to attack would be known to us simply as The Atoll. It was not a mindless military excursion, but a carefully planned operation. In the grand strategy of the Pacific war we were being led by the Navy in the westward advance, while the Army led a thrust northward through New Guinea and the Philippines for what the briefing officer kept calling "a huge pincer move" against Japan. In its advance westward the Navy, with the cooperation of the Marines and the Army, must seize reef-surrounded islands known as atolls which possessed anchorages or air strips that could serve as necessary American bases.

Afterwards I asked Goldman, "American bases necessary to what?"

"To the advance westward, stupid."

"And the advance westward is necessary to what?"

"You heard what the man said. To the huge pincer move against Japan."

"If we only put our minds to it, there should be an easier way. If Basset were here, he'd point out the trouble with this operation is that one atoll leads but to another."

Goldman sighed. "I know. I wonder what ever became of Basset."

"I think he ducked out and is now a safe civilian."

"I doubt it," Goldman said. "I don't think there's any escape from this at all."

16

After Basset left Vera and flew east he lectured himself severely. He was guilty of incredible naiveté in thinking there was such a thing as a whore with a heart of gold and then becoming obsessed with one. He would forget Rosemarie. He would forget Vera too, with her plan to make him king of her Hawaiian real estate empire; now he was more than a little afraid of her affection. Indeed, he would try to forget he had inadvertently involved himself in this huge, senseless war in this huge, senseless ocean. The uniformed Basset was about to disappear forever and Fiddler be reborn in a civilian suit of undistinguished gray worsted.

The airplane made its American landfall more than ten hours after takeoff. It was early on an August morning in 1942, and the hills north of San Francisco looked like golden heaps of grain. Basset had not realized how much he missed his country.

Carrying his orders, he went through reception and was about to head for the finance office when a man said, "Colonel Basset?" He faced a young first lieutenant who smiled pleasantly, saluted, and gave his name. "Isn't Captain Swisher with you? His name isn't on the flight manifest with yours."

"I thought he came on without me. He disappeared two days ago."

"Disappeared?" The lieutenant sounded alarmed. When Basset said he had last seen Swisher at Hickam Field, the lieutenant followed him into the finance office, and, giving him no chance to escape, conducted him to an eastbound flight.

Basset's flying luck was bad. A propeller developed reverse pitch, and they were held eight hours in St. Louis for repairs. Then the Washington area was socked in fog and they had to land at Langley Field, far down the Virginia Peninsula near Hampton Roads. There the passengers were put on a bus for a jouncing five-hour ride to Fort Myer, across the Potomac from Washington.

Basset intended to take a taxi over the river to Union Station, where he would board a train for New York and oblivion, but he was so tired from his long journey that he decided to catch a few hours' sleep in the Myer bachelor officers' quarters. Eight hours later he awakened from sound sleep with a sensation that his right fingers were sticky and someone was holding his hand.

Opening his eyes wider, he saw that Swisher had him by the hand while a major stood nearby. Swisher had smeared his fingers with ink and was trying to put their prints on a sheet of paper. Basset, springing to his feet, smeared his inky fingers across Swisher's face while the major backed away embarrassed and said:

"Colonel, we didn't want to awaken you just for your fingerprints."

"You sons of bitches are going to get more than my fingerprints!" roared the Warden. "You're going to get dishonorable discharges!"

"That's what I mean! That's what I mean!" Swisher cried, dancing about and trying to wipe the ink off his face. "He's always threatening everybody. I *know* he's the one got me arrested on trumped-up charges in Hawaii. I just can't prove it yet."

Basset collected his toilet articles and went to the latrine, where he showered and shaved. When he returned to his bunk, Swisher and the major had gone. Dressing and putting his few belongings in his small bag, he went to the Fort Myer north gate and told a taxi driver to take him to Union Station. As they crossed Memorial Bridge he looked out the rear window and saw Swisher and the major tailing the cab in an Army sedan.

"Never mind Union Station," he told the driver. "Go to the War Department Building at Twenty-first Street and Virginia Avenue."

His orders directed him to report there. So he would postpone his date with oblivion for a while. Now, instead of being frightened, he was thoroughly angry; it seemed far more important to end the career of Captain Swisher than that of Colonel Basset.

The receptionist in the weakly lighted, high-ceilinged hall of the building was an old master sergeant who told him to sit on a bench, then went off someplace with the copy of his orders. Each time the door opened and closed as people came and went, Basset saw Swisher and the major lurking outside. They peered in at him occasionally like curious children forbidden to enter.

After a time a woman came in and paused at the vacated reception desk. She seemed to glance at him from the corner of her eye. She was pretty, auburn-haired, and carried her well-formed body superbly. Although small, she gave an impression of great strength. As Basset watched her, Swisher and the major came through the doorway and looked from her to him.

The woman glanced at them, then around at him. Her face lighted, she opened her arms, and exclaimed, "Pete!"

"Surprise!" Basset rose. "Wondered when you'd recognize me." He gathered her into his arms, and her blue eyes remained wide with wonder while he kissed her.

The major stepped forward. "Mrs. Basset, is this truly your husband?"

"Who else? Who are you and why do you ask?"

"Counterintelligence, WDGS. It was my office asked you to come to Washington to greet your husband."

"Well, I just have." She made a regal gesture that caused the major to step back; with such a gesture Elizabeth I must have sent poor Raleigh to the Tower. "Don't you people do anything besides play games? Haven't you heard there's a war on?"

The major fell back another step, then turned angrily on Swisher. "You've carried your nonsense far enough. Next stop for you is the psycho ward at Walter Reed."

Tears formed in Swisher's eyes as he followed the major out.

The old sergeant had returned; he spoke to Basset: "Sir, the General is waiting to see you. Come with me."

Helen Basset, staring at him fixedly, said, "'I'll wait here for you, Pete."

He was ushered into the presence of a three-star general whom he had heard described as a supply and logistics genius. The general and Basset had known each other in the past, for the general came around his desk with hand extended.

"Warden, you're looking sufficiently beastly. I've had so damn much to do these last months you'd slipped my mind. Well, not exactly. Someone misinformed me. I heard you were doing something very important in England and couldn't be touched. But all the time you were assigned to purgatory in the Pacific. No doubt the work of one of your enemies. Why in the hell didn't you write me and complain?''

"Well," Basset said, "for all I knew, you were the one sent me there."

"Balls, Warden, balls. You and I had our rounds. You were the only one had the guts to stand up to me." Three Stars smiled wryly. "Of course you were wrong ninety percent of the time, but you did stand up. I have personally recommended you for what undoubtedly is the toughest job in this whole goddam war."

"And I should thank you?" growled the Warden.

Three Stars grinned. "Yes sir, that's my baby!"

"May I ask, General, what the job is?"

"You may ask, but I won't tell you—not yet. You and I are going to a meeting at nine o'clock tomorrow morning here in this building. It'll be the most important meeting you ever attended. The Secretary of War will be there. So will the Chief of Staff. And various other luminaries. Come here to my office at eight-thirty in the morning. So long till then, Warden, I've got work stacked to the ceiling."

Basset left Three Stars' office like a sleepwalker. When he saw Helen waiting on the bench, he dropped beside her. It seemed difficult for him to breathe as he said, "Things are happening too fast for me."

"You can say that again," Helen said. "Who are you?"

"Fiddler."

"I wondered about that." Her surprise grew. "When he—I mean you—wrote about Fiddler dying in the plane crash, I wondered—Fiddler the physician!"

"No, just plain Fiddler."

"Who *are* you?"

"At this point I'm not sure. Let's go somewhere and have a drink."

"At eleven o'clock in the morning? What are you—an alcoholic?"

"Not that I know of. What are you doing here?"

"They told me to come here from New Jersey. I knew there was trouble of some kind, but I didn't know what it was."

"Thanks for helping me."

"What else could I do? You really look very much like him, and I felt sorry for you sitting so forlorn on this bench."

They took a taxi to the Willard, where the bar had just opened. Seated at a table, he ordered a double Scotch and she a Dubonnet on the rocks. He had developed an affection for this woman while corresponding with her from Dumbo. Yet now that he met her in the flesh he had a vague unease. She had the mind of the woman with whom he had enjoyed exchanging letters, but not the physical appearance. He had corresponded with the woman in the photograph, the woman with the eyes of an innocent, a vulnerable expression. Helen, this wife he faced across the table, did not seem at all vulnerable. He knew immediately he could never hypnotize her, no matter how long and often he tried.

"Want to see pictures of yourself and Roger?" He handed her the photos.

She put down her glass and her eyes filled with tears. "That lousy son of a bitch!" She tore the woman's picture in two.

"Any idea who she is?" Basset asked.

"No. Probably he bought the picture at some commercial studio to act out his fantasy. No woman who looks like that would have anything to do with him. The corollary is, what does that make me?"

"Nice. Beautiful in a different way." He touched her hand. "I grew fond of you as a pen pal."

"No, I think you were fond of the beautiful woman in that picture." She shrugged. "Well, anyhow, why did they call you to Washington?"

"I don't know yet." He described his brief interview.

"Oh, my God! And you're not even an engineer?"

"No."

"Wouldn't it be best to make a clean breast of it all?"

"How can I prove I didn't kill Basset on the raft? And now you've just implicated yourself by identifying me as him."

"Oh, my gosh, I never thought of that! Don't confess anything! What possessed you to switch identities?"

"Possibly some inadequacy of childhood. But a more pressing motive was that I don't know how to practice medicine."

Midway through his account she started to laugh. "Please forgive me, I'm not usually given to hysterics, but— Say!" She stopped laughing suddenly. "That man over there—I know I sound paranoid, but that man keeps moving from empty table to table to get closer. Is he *following* us?"

Basset turned to see Swisher, wearing a civilian suit. "That's Swisher of counterintelligence. Persistent cuss."

"Then they're really serious about this!" She sounded alarmed.

"They're not," Basset said. "Only Swisher is. If we just hang on long enough, Swisher will receive the punishment of all serious people—jail or an institution for the insane. Let's go to lunch."

They went to O'Donnell's Seafood on E Street. Swisher followed them into the restaurant, but he was seated at a booth so far from theirs that he could not hear a word they said.

"So what are you going to do?" Helen asked.

"It's my instinct to stick around and meet the Secretary of War and Chief of Staff. Such opportunities don't come often to a draft-dodger like me."

"That's my instinct too. What shall I call you? Not Pete, because, even though you look alike, you're totally unlike him. I hate the name Morton. Not Fiddler. How about Ted? When I was young I was in love with a boy named Ted, but he never knew I existed."

Just as, Basset thought, Rosemarie did not know that he existed. What in God's name had come over him? There he sat with possibly the finest woman he ever had met—his wife, though not his wife. Helen was comely enough, witty and wise enough, with greater instinctive loyalty to him than he ever had found in anyone, yet her features seemed to fade across the table and in their place he saw Rosemarie. He must remember that Rosemarie was Red's wife, that he loved Red like a son, that he wished Red and Rosemarie happiness such as had eluded him.

"Don't call me Ted," he said sharply. "Please, I'm afraid things are mixed up enough already."

"Sorry." Her gaze fell. "I understand."

"Call me Pete."

After a while he said, "I have some men—three men—got hook-ered onto Guadalcanal. I must get them off that island and back to so-called civilization."

"Do they know who you really are?" she asked.

"Two of them do."

"I think that's wonderful of you, Pete."

When they left the restaurant and made their way through the warm afternoon, Swisher followed at a careful distance.

Helen said, "Will he never give up?"

"In time they'll force him to give up—public pressure versus frustrated genius. You say you have a room at the Willard?"

"Yes, the intelligence people booked it for me, and that major made it clear I'm paying for it."

"Swisher tailing us back there makes it necessary for me to come up to your room." He glanced at her. "Don't worry, I won't—try to take advantage of the situation."

She did not say anything. She was lovely in a different, unexpected way from the photographed woman. He liked her as if she were his sister, a relationship he never had experienced. But he had no urge to make love to her. Would he have desired her if she had turned out to be the beautiful, innocent-looking creature of Basset's photo? In the confused state of affairs that entangled him the only one he wanted was Rosemarie. After all, his theoretical marriage to Helen was a situation created by others to which he never had been a party.

Her small room at the Willard was almost filled by twin beds. A few minutes after they entered it, Basset opened the door and saw Swisher lurking at the end of the corridor.

"Is he really that stupid?" Helen asked. "Does he think we don't know he's trailing us?"

"He's not stupid. He's a smart guy who believes in himself."

He realized that if it were not for Swisher tailing him he could light out of there, take a train from Union Station, and disappear in New York. In fact, he could elude Swisher if he wanted to. But the altogether weird fact about the situation was that he did not want to elude him; for some reason he did not want to escape and become Fiddler again.

"Do you need any money?" she asked as they sat on uncomfortable chairs. "I can give you some."

Her concern touched him. "Thanks, I'm okay. But what about you? I notice by the pay record that the old Colonel's allotment every month to you was mighty slim pickin's."

"It covers Roger at military school. That's what he mainly cared about. Not really about Roger himself, but just about Roger being in military school."

"I never heard of a kid ten years old in military school."

She grimaced. "It happens. There was nothing I could do about it. I was raised Quaker, and Pete—well, let's call him the old Colonel —and I used to have our rounds about that. Sometimes I thought he insisted Roger go to military school just to taunt me."

"How's the kid doing? He never answered my letter."

"He's doing badly. He didn't answer because he hates his father. I don't want him to meet you. He'd know at once you're not his father and it would confuse him badly. I'm going to pull him out of military school and have him live with me as soon as I can get reorganized. I'm teaching way out in the country and there's no decent school for Roger to attend. But I have to support myself and—''

"Why do you teach the retarded?"

"Because they need me. I'm working on a degree. I drive ten miles nights to take courses. The qualifications for my present job are mainly patience and a fondness for children. My students can't learn a great deal, but every small gain makes it all worthwhile."

"And you were cheated out of his insurance!" Basset said. "I never thought of that. If I remain Colonel Basset, I'll arrange a decent allotment for you and Roger. If I become Fiddler again, I'll send you a reward for saving my life."

"Is there any doubt about who you're going to be?"

"Some, yes."

She asked, "Do you by any chance like to dance?" He nodded. "So do I," she said. "But my husband didn't and wouldn't and it used to make him jealous when other men danced with me. When I got my orders to come here, I slipped in a gown that would be nice for dancing."

"Then let's do," he said.

He went out and bought fresh suntans while Swisher followed and watched, then he ducked Swisher long enough to try to obtain a room for himself at the Raleigh Hotel, where a clerk explained that there was not a vacant hotel room in Washington. Basset in turn explained this to Helen, shouting through the closed door of her bathroom while changing clothes.

"Don't worry about it," she shouted back. "As President Roosevelt says, you have nothing to fear but fear itself."

At seven o'clock they were in the Starlight Room at the Carlton. Swisher, who had recovered the scent, took a table across the room a minute later. Three Marines with their dates at a table adjoining theirs wanted to buy them drinks after they saw Basset's Pacific ribbon; Basset reciprocated.

Helen was a superb dancer—and so was he. "Holy cow, sir," said one of the Marines when they returned from the floor, "just like Rogers and Astaire." They danced again, and when they came back to their table, they found a penciled note from Swisher saying simply: *Basset never danced.*

"I'm getting tired of this," Helen said.

Basset spoke to the Marines: "That 4-F civilian over there"—he pointed out Swisher covertly—"just insulted our dancing. Are we really that bad?"

Next thing Basset and Helen saw, Swisher was leaving the Starlight Room in the company of the three Marines, but by some curious magic his feet were not touching the floor. When the Marines returned to their table, one said, "Sir, that 4-F just passed out in the men's latrine."

Basset and Helen returned to the Willard after midnight; he lay on one bed and she on the other. He was half asleep, thinking of Rosemarie, when Helen said:

"Pete, you're a tremendous dancer."

"So are you," he replied. "You're the best dancer I've ever known. Thank you for a wonderful time. Good night, Helen."

She sighed. "Good night, Pete. That was the nicest first date I've ever had."

Next morning Basset was shown in to Three Stars at the appointed hour and listened to him attentively:

"You're my candidate, Basset. It means you're the Army's candidate to take charge of this complicated project as technical officer—provided the Secretary of War and Chief of Staff agree with my judgment. That, as always, is far from certain. Understand?"

"Yes sir."

"I still can't tell you what it's about. If things turn out as I hope, you'll be working with the greatest array of geniuses ever gathered in one country at one time. You never saw such a collection of oddballs. They've come to America from many different countries, and many of them speak English badly. They're proud, temperamental, each pretty determined to have things his own way. The reason I picked you is not because you're a great diplomat—you're the world's worst. I picked you because you're tough and stubborn, and get things done. And I think not the least of your talents is your ability to sling the bull. In America, and maybe in other places, that's essential if you're going to get things done. If I had the time, which I guess I never will, I'd write a book titled 'Bullshitting: The Art that Made America Great.' "

Three Stars conducted him to a room whose vaulting ceiling dwarfed the men gathered around the long table. Perhaps it was this dwarfing process that made the men look ordinary—and therefore human—to Basset.

The Secretary of War was aging, frail; he looked like a Massachusetts country banker Basset had once known. The Chief of Staff, who sat on the Secretary's right, had the sour look of an apple farmer whose orchard had been blighted. On the Secretary's left sat an aging, pipe-sucking civilian who might have been the town physician about to report to the selectmen on a measles epidemic. Ranging down the table on either side were several other unremarkable-looking men.

As Basset raised his eyes heavenward, perhaps in unconscious supplication, he glimpsed something that finally lent a bit of distinction to the men assembled there. On the high ceiling, someone had painted in faithful detail the Great Seal of the United States of America.

While all stared at Basset, the Secretary called out in a reedy, slightly impatient tone, "Yes, General?"

"Mr. Secretary—gentlemen—I present Colonel C. P. Basset."

"Well, sit down—sit down," the Secretary said, fiddling with some papers, while everyone else continued to scrutinize Basset, who sank into one of the two empty chairs at the end of the table. "Colonel—uh—Basset," the Secretary said, "I'm informed that in Army circles you're referred to as the—uh—Warden. And I'm further informed you received this—uh—appellation because of your announced determination to pen in the Mississippi River. Is that so?"

"Yes sir." Basset never had sounded more assured. He understood that the Secretary was amused; and he understood that the Secretary did not want *him* to be amused.

"Tell me—uh—Colonel, were you serious?"

"I was angry, sir. The Mississippi takes a dreadful toll of lives when flooding. I believe that by a process of damafooling—"

"What in the hell is damafooling?" demanded the Country Doctor.

"A term I use to describe a system of strategic damming of tributary headwaters," Basset went on serenely. "It *could* be done, but it would be very costly and present certain dangerous hazards to the environment of the rivers involved. But to answer your question, Mr. Secretary, yes, I was serious."

The Secretary put on his glasses, peered down the table at him, and then took them off.

The Chief of Staff spoke: "Colonel"—his tone was surprisingly gentle for such a sour-looking man—"I understand you've just come from Guadalcanal. What were conditions there when you left?"

"You were misinformed, sir. I never got to Guadalcanal. I was on my way there when I received orders derailing me at Espíritu Santo and bringing me back here."

"Were you glad to come back?"

"No sir, I'd rather be on Guadalcanal. What's the sense of being a soldier if you don't go to combat?"

Chief of Staff cast him a bleak look that was intended as a smile.

"Well—uh—" The Secretary looked about. "Any more questions?"

"Yes," said Country Doctor. "Colonel, do you know what uranium is?"

He recalled the stern drill of his high school chemistry teacher. "As I remember," he said slowly, "uranium is a radioactive element of the chromium group, found—if I remember correctly—in combination in pitchblende and certain other rare metals, and reduced as a heavy, hard, nickel-white metal."

Country Doctor took his pipe from his mouth and said, "Good."

A bushy-haired man asked in a thick accent, "Do you know what an isotope is?"

"No sir, I do not."

The man raised his hands and eyes appealingly to the Great Seal on the ceiling and demanded, "How can we work with a man who doesn't know what an isotope is?"

"Well, sir," the Warden answered harshly, "I have no idea what it is I'm supposed to work at with you. I'm sure I could learn what an isotope is. Do you know how to build a pontoon bridge? Or let me ask you this: Is it necessary that a theater critic know how to construct a theater?"

Country Doctor laughed—an uncontrolled cackle, and the Secretary almost grinned. He said, "This project has been placed under the production control of the Army. Personally I favor your candidate, General. Does anyone here seriously object?" When no one said anything, the Secretary went on, "Good luck, Colonel. All of us appear to agree. Both the Chief of Staff and I are too busy with many other things to devote substantial time to this project. My thought is that it be guided by a committee of five."

Basset, still having no idea what the project was about, spoke up in the tone of the Warden—that role Three Stars called essential to the job: "Mr. Secretary, sir, I raise a question. I've never known a committee of five to accomplish anything. If a committee is necessary at the start of this project, I urge that it be confined to three members."

"He's right," said Chief of Staff.

So it was agreed while the scientists present argued and babbled among themselves.

For briefing he was turned over to Country Doctor, who became his friend. Thenceforth he called this distinguished American physicist Doc. After the meeting broke up, Doc and Basset went into an isolated room to talk, and Doc began their discussion.

"In 1938 some physicists in Germany split the first uranium atom. Since that time scientists in many countries have decided that a bomb with incredible force can be built if enough fissionable material can be produced. This material has to be either plutonium or U-235, a rare isotope of uranium. By the way, an isotope is one of two or more types of the same element, having the same atomic number and hence occupying the same place in the periodic table. They're almost identical in their chemical behavior but they're different in atomic mass. Plutonium is a newly discovered element. As far as we can tell, nobody knows as much about plutonium as scientists working in the United States and Britain. Many of those scientists, by the way, are refugees from fascist countries. Now, Colonel, can you tell me what an isotope is?"

Basset repeated what he had just been told, adding, "That's by rote. My real understanding is limited."

Doc looked pleased. "That's okay, Colonel. Everybody starting in this new program has one limitation or another when it comes to understanding, but a retentive memory such as you display is a good beginning. Our big problem is how to produce large amounts of U-235 or plutonium. We have five different methods that are being put forward by their various advocates. The methods offered for separation of U-235 are electromagnetic, centrifuge, and gaseous-diffusion. The methods involving production of plutonium are by heavy-water reactor or by graphite reactor. I know all these things must be new terms to you, and not yet sufficiently described, but would you try to repeat what I've just said?"

Basset repeated it perfectly.

"Naturally all of this is top secret, Colonel. In fact, we'll have to have some security designation even higher than top secret. We know the Nazis are working as frantically as we at trying to develop a superbomb. We think—we hope—we hold an edge. It's a tremendous race—the biggest race the world has ever known. Whoever wins it will win the war and maybe control the world. Which means to people like you and me that it's vital we win. Because it's vital that whoever develops this weapon and holds this secret be a benign power. That is, not concerned like the Nazis and Japanese with ruling the world, but with keeping the world *in balance*. The Army's job in this—*your* job—is like that of one who has to manufacture what us crazy inventors give you the patent to.''

"A question," Basset said. "If such a bomb can eventually be manufactured, do you have any idea of its force—of what it means in terms of human life?''

Doc was silent a long time. At last he said, "You aren't supposed to ask questions like that, Basset. It's why they've turned the production problem over to you—to the Army. *'Theirs not to reason why.'* Do you know Tennyson? It doesn't matter. You're not supposed to know Tennyson. You're supposed to do or die. This is a war, and you are the Army, and your job is to win the war.''

So, Basset thought, they didn't know what the damn' bomb would do. Maybe, for all they knew, it would blow up the whole damn' world.

"There's one thing we're positive about," Doc said. "This bomb is necessary to the saving of hundreds of thousands—maybe millions —of American lives. We don't know what it will do in terms of enemy lives. But that is the problem of the enemies who started this war. Beyond the saving of American lives, of Americans who otherwise would die in combat, there can be no humanitarian aspects to this situation. All we're supposed to think about at this point is how to win the goddam war.''

At precisely forty-five minutes past midnight a bugle blared reveille over the attack transport's loudspeakers, notes squawking loud enough to rouse the dead. When Red and I climbed to the upper deck, we saw that the bugler appeared to have roused instead, the moon, for it came up as if hauled by ropes, lighting the surrounding sea with a mellow light that seemed created by stagecraft.

From other ships maneuvering in ghostly formations came faint, tinny notes of other bugles. By some magic we had made our rendezvous with the gathering great armada. But all the talk about surprising the Japanese on The Atoll must have been in vain, for there was such a stillness on the sea that you could hear a man cough a mile away.

From the galleys rose a fragrance of coffee, steaks, scrambled eggs, which the messmen of the attack transport—called an APA—ladled without stint. After going below and eating our fill, we climbed up again with Lincoln and Yaromski. Now the ships were making their final wide turn in formation and setting course due east in order to close The Atoll while it was still silhouetted by the moon.

Somebody sneezed over the loudspeaker system, and a hoarse voice said, "Crews, man your amphtracs."

We visited the head, then collected our gear. I carried a carbine and ammo, three meals of K rations, two canteens of water. Everyone had the same, besides something special—a belt of grenades or a part of a mortar. My own special was a camera. Naylor had some understandable doubts about my prowess as a fighter, but he knew I was handy with a camera and he had a sense of history that made him think it a good idea to record The Atoll invasion. I had elected to ride in the company command amphtrac, operated by Red, with Goldman in the bow.

The amphtracs clustered on the deck in the moonlight looked like a tightly packed herd of hippos. Lincoln was in the cab of the vehicle adjoining ours, trying to read something by the moon's light.

"What ya readin'?" Red called to him.

"*Uncle Tom's Cabin,*" Lincoln called back. It was a letter from his father he had read and re-read several times.

Red's two crewmen, Sawyer and Polowetsky, had taken their stations: each sat clutching his knees beside the mounted .50-caliber machine gun. Why did they wake us so early only to make us wait? Waiting gave us time to think. Most of us were afraid of being afraid and found it best to think instead of what good companions we had; no better company of men ever existed.

At last a voice speaking rapidly over the loudspeakers startled us: "Load your amphtracs! Load your amphtracs!"

The ship seemed to lie dead in the water as the men of D Company, wearing mottled green fatigues and cloth-covered steel helmets, swarmed into their assigned LVTs. Goldman took his place in the bow of our amphtrac and looked across at Yaromski in the bow of Lincoln's. Cherokee was in the vehicle astern. Eight bells clanged and a voice said:

"This is Chaplain Marston. Wherever you men are, pause and give a prayer to—uff—" His voice died breathlessly.

"This is Father Kane," snarled the Catholic chaplain, who possibly had dug an elbow into the midriff of his Protestant brother. "Blessings on you in the name of—uff—"

"Boats away!" roared a third voice. "Let 'em go!"

The cables locked to our amphtrac grew taut as a cargo boom lifted us quickly, swung us unceremoniously over the side, and set us lightly on the calm surface of the sea. Red and his crewmen released the cables swiftly and signaled that we were free. As Red started the motor, battleships and cruisers somewhere over the horizon began their barrage of The Atoll.

The amphtracs formed bow to stern on Naylor's lead craft and circled slowly as prescribed while the thundering batteries of the big warships winked in the growing light. The sun, appearing to be hauled up by brute strength as the moon had been a few hours earlier, cast a malevolent red eye on The Atoll. We could see nothing except clouds of smoke in which flashes erupted. The flashes proved dangerous, however: Japanese four-inch guns began to straddle transports which had not finished boating their troops, and soon the vessels withdrew to a safer distance. For precisely twelve minutes air bombardment took over, and then the naval fire resumed.

Still the amphtracs circled, waiting. In the din of guns and bombs we could not hear our craft's motor but we could feel it pulsing steadily. The long wait began to make us uneasy. A westerly wind was rising and kicking up a chop that started the amphtrac rolling and several men vomiting overside.

Suddenly two minesweepers appeared full steam from the north and, screened by smoke, swept a channel from the transport area into the lagoon. Behind them tore two destroyers. The forward guns of all four blasted straight on at the enemy batteries as they slowed inside the lagoon.

D, E and F companies were in the first wave of twenty-four amphtracs designated as Landing Team One and scheduled to land on Beach Red One at the head of The Atoll airstrip at H hour. The two teams following our 9th Battalion, each consisting of a battalion of Marines in an equivalent number of amphtracs, were scheduled to land at three-minute intervals on adjoining Beach Red Two and Beach Red Three to our right.

At 0630, on signal, Landing Team One left rendezvous for the departure line about three and one-half miles distant. The schedule allowed us one hour to cover that distance, but we realized we were going to be late.

In the choppy sea the ungainly amphtracs rolled and bucked, threatening now and then to swamp, while the wind that chopped the sea cleared the sky of haze and left it pristine blue, like a fine autumn day back home. At times we felt we made no progress, but gradually we left behind one yellow flag after another marking our course until we reached the last buoy at the break in the reef that marked the entrance to the lagoon. My watch read 0805.

The enemy four-inch guns no longer flamed from the smoke-shrouded island inside the reefs. Maybe, we hoped, the furious naval and air bombardment had knocked out the defenders. But no one in our amphtrac dared mention it for fear of jinxing the operations. We bobbed raggedly for a while on the departure line where we had to make a ninety-degree turn for a three-mile approach through the lagoon to the island. The signal came, and we gasped ahead—faster now as the chop receded. Glancing astern, I saw the second landing team of Marines take off from departure and the third forming to follow. The naval barrage lifted suddenly, and only the two destroyers in the lagoon continued to fire at the shore.

By 0855 we were close enough that we could make out a deadfall of palms and a smashed wharf through the pall of smoke covering the island. We saw, too, that the tide was much farther out than had been promised. The briefing officers on the transport had been very specific about that: "You will land at high tide. Your shore treads won't have much work before you're on the beach itself. We planned it that way. Don't worry. We promise the tide will be high."

But their promise had been broken.

When we had almost reached the pitted, jagged coral which extended at low tide to the beach, there was a flash and clatter of machine-gun fire to our left. It was like the eruption of a volcano. The shore ahead seemed to explode in a roaring sheet of flame as the Japanese unleashed machine guns, mortars, rifles, coast defense guns, antiboat guns. That heavy naval bombardment had not even dented the enemy defenses.

The stern of our amphtrac sank and its bow reared high like a maddened horse and piercing screams rent the roar of gunfire. Bullets and shrapnel pinged on the armor like hail smashing glass. Slowly the bow settled again. Goldman was no longer in it. Sawyer and Polowetsky began firing their machine gun blindly at the shore: it was like a slingshot against armor. Almost at the same time both gunners toppled backward, and two brave men—Smith on the left, Muhler on the right—took their places.

I was utterly terrified—I didn't have the stuff to be a good soldier. Later someone commended my coolness for taking pictures in this holocaust, yet there was nothing cool about me. In a frenzy, I began shooting pictures one after another. I did not really know what I was doing as I went berserk with my camera.

The amphtrac's treads, finding a grip on the coral, made a hideous grinding sound that came through a slight lull in the enemy fire. Then Smith pitched down, and Muhler fell too. Nobody moved to take over the gun; this amphtrac was fresh out of heroes. What in God's name had become of Goldman?

As if in answer to my frantic question, he came scrambling over the side, his usually calm expression somewhat cockeyed. He had been tossed out of the plunging amphtrac and apparently was uninjured. It was impossible to know what he should do in his role as leader except to seek cover along with everybody else. Maybe the inferno of enemy guns that seemed to have started hours ago had been blazing for only a couple of minutes. In the gory wash of the amphtrac bed you could not tell how many were dead or wounded among those cowering for cover.

Red, as skipper of this monstrous contraption lumbering over the jagged coral, was reluctant to seek cover. His stubborn pride forbade him to desert the fragile cab and thus halt our clumsy progress. Shrapnel had pierced the thin armor of the vehicle in several places, but miraculously he was thus far unscathed.

I glanced across at Lincoln's amphtrac, which clawed and jounced abreast of ours over the coral. Yaromski stood boldly in the bow, clutching the gate. In the next instant he pitched backwards. I glimpsed Lincoln's face, but whether it was contorted from horror at Yaromski's fate or from some grievous wound of his own I could not tell. Ahead of us, Naylor toppled from his command vehicle, dead. And behind us I saw Cherokee's body.

Our amphtrac halted suddenly, whether because the motor had died or the treads were stuck on some insurmountable object, I could not tell. The gate dropped of its own volition without Red touching the control lever. I had the weird feeling the machine had taken control of the situation and we were mere robots under its direction. Goldman scrambled to his feet, shouting encouragement that no one could hear in the din, slapping the backs and buttocks of the living, the dead and the wounded indiscriminately. Goldman was the bravest there as he raced off the amphtrac toward the beach and we tried to follow him.

Something unaccountable happened quickly. The left side of the amphtrac rose, as if lifted by invisible hands, and spilled everyone, including Red and me, out the right side. Probably it was caused by the concussion of an exploding shell; whatever, we scrambled dazedly to our feet and started off in the direction Goldman and a couple of others had gone. In the dense pall of smoke we could not make out anyone. Lumps of coral looked like human bodies, and bodies were mere coral. Somehow I had lost my carbine, but I still had camera and film.

It seemed that Red and I were the only ones not yet hit. Seeing men to the right running toward shore, we swerved in that direction. Then we saw that Lincoln's amphtrac had stalled too; a few men were fleeing from it while Lincoln stayed in the cab.

"Come on!" Red shrieked at him.

But Lincoln sat still. Thinking him dazed by the cannonade, we sprang to his vehicle to drag him out of the cab. Red and I both reached for him at once, then pulled back in horror. His fatigues were drenched with blood from a bullet which had pierced his breast. He was dead.

I felt numbed. Red wept wildly as we ran for cover. Yaromski. Cherokee. Lincoln. Red wanted to die too. Maybe it would have been better for me if I could have wept; instead of grief, I felt a growing consummate rage at all this senseless suffering and dying.

We ran after a soldier I did not remember seeing before, and, gasping for breath, finally flung ourselves down beside a concrete wall at the edge of the beach where a half-dozen others huddled.

"Who're you?" a youth asked dully.

"D Company."

"There ain't no D Company. They got wiped out."

So Goldman had been killed too. We believed it without question: Goldman was dead.

A young first lieutenant materialized, seemingly from the sky that must be somewhere above the smoke. He said something unintelligible through the crash of gunfire.

"What'd he say?" I yelled to Red.

"Fuck him," the youth said. "He ain't in my company. I dunno what he said anyway."

"We got to attack that bunker!" the lieutenant cried.

"Shit on him," the youth said, then followed us as we clambered over the wall, which was about four feet high. My only weapon was my camera and extra film, but I felt perfectly secure with it.

The world had turned weird: no more sequences, just bits and pieces, nothing stemmed logically from something else. Once we had scrambled on top of the wall there was no other side to drop into. We were on a flat concrete surface—six or seven of us clustering there while a machine gun rattled nearby. Someone asked the young lieutenant *what* bunker we were supposed to attack, and he looked about dazedly, not knowing how to reply.

A stroke of genius came over Red and he yelled, "*We're on top of the bunker!*"

The barrel of a four-inch gun suddenly thrust from an aperture below us like the black snout of an enormous clam, and its blast nearly knocked us off our feet. Red asked for a grenade, and somebody gave him one. Pulling its pin, he dropped it down an air duct into the bunker. I took a picture of him doing it. In a few seconds there came a distant popping sound. The four-inch thrust out its snout once more, but it did not fire again.

"Good thinking!" cried the lieutenant while I snapped his picture. "Let's find another bunker and climb on top of it!"

The machine gun went on and on, as insistent as an unanswered phone. It dawned on us that the gunner was trying to hit us, but for some reason could not. All of us flattened ourselves except the lieutenant, who yelled, "Come on, you gonna be shit-head cowards?" As if to demonstrate how invulnerable we were, he took a couple of steps to the left and was riddled by machine gun bullets. I took a picture of him as he fell dead.

"Dumb, fuckin', shit-headed lieutenant bastard," the youth said.

In siting a machine gun to cover the bunker, the Japanese had erred slightly on its fire-field and thus there was a zone of safety on its top. The youth took a grenade, stood up slowly, pulled its pin, waited an agonizingly long time, and then hurled the grenade at the machine gun embrasure like a baseball catcher throwing out a base-stealer at second. It was a perfect throw. There was a sound like someone dropping a tray of dishes, and the machine gun was silent. I took a picture of the youth completing his throw.

I did not see the American dive-bomber coming in, but Red did. Grabbing me, he flung us both off the top of the bunker onto a stretch of sand.

In the blinding flash, the deafening crash, I died for the thousandth time. After what seemed like hours, I saw that Red, lying on the sand near me, still was alive. Through the whistling in my ears his voice came as a feeble chirp:

"That goddam plane was one of ours! A Curtiss Helldiver. Killed everybody! We came down feet first."

I saw that someone who had been with us on top of the bunker had come down only one foot first. A few yards away a leg severed at the hip was planted to its ankle in the sand.

It reminded me that the lower half of my own body might be missing. Since I felt no pain, I probably had no body. Otherwise, I would be in some kind of torment, for it was the nature of bodies to suffer pain. Maybe I was just a severed, thinking head lying there and looking at Red. It took all my will to look down at my body. Behold, all of it was there, not even a small part missing, while the worst headache ever reminded me that I was alive.

"You all right?" I asked Red.

"Yeah, I'm okay. I just don't have the wish to get up and go on."

"I know, neither do I."

After a while, aware that the enemy firing had subsided considerably, I sat up and took a picture of the severed leg in the sand.

"What are you going to do with that picture?" Red asked.

"Put it in a history book for kids. They used to plant flags at the advanced posts of empire, but now they plant legs. This picture will give the little bastards a better idea of what war and empire is all about."

There was no firing near us now. An LCI was disgorging Marines onto the beach. I could not remember if the LCIs were supposed to come in the second or third support wave, but I didn't care. Red and I drank warm water from our canteens and I asked him what he aimed to do now.

"Lie right here till carried away." He spoke mildly, almost cheerfully. "I just quit this war."

"Me too," I said. "That makes two bodies they have to carry away."

A few minutes later a couple of Marines looked down at us. "Lieutenant," one said, "where are you and the sergeant hit?"

"Don't know," I said. "Got blown off this bunker by a friendly bomber."

"I can't feel nothing from the neck down," Red said. "Send the medics."

One of the Marines picked up my camera, which lay beside me, and I half sat up to snatch it back from him. "That's D Company property, Mister."

"Well," he said, "at least you ain't paralyzed from the neck down, Lieutenant." A dozen more Marines ran past, led by a captain, who ordered the first two to follow along.

I got to my feet, feeling dizzy, and Red said, "Lie down like me if you want the medics to carry you away."

"There's got to be another way out besides this," I said. "If the medics carry me away, they'll take my camera."

"So what, Boz? There's lots more cameras in the world, but you may never get to play with any of 'em unless you let them carry you away now."

We were arguing foolishly, he lying on the sand and I supporting myself against the bunker wall when a Marine chicken colonel came running, followed by a sergeant who packed a walkie-talkie on his back. "Set up shop here," he told the sergeant, and to me he said, "You really did it, Lieutenant."

"What did I do now?" I asked defensively.

"You drove in the wedge—you and your men. I watched it as we were coming in. This bunker, that machine gun site. Gives us a toehold we can enlarge. Very, very good, Lieutenant. The way you did it, thought you must be a Marine. But got to give credit where credit's due." He had his sergeant take down my name and outfit. "Tough casualties."

"It was that goddam Navy bomber killed everybody here but us two."

"A Curtiss Helldiver," Red said, "and I'm paralyzed from the neck down."

As the Colonel turned to the unlimbered radio set, he told me, "Navy planes don't bomb friendly forces."

"The hell they don't, Colonel. That one just—"

He frowned around at me and repeated testily, "Navy planes don't bomb friendly forces!" Then he began issuing orders into his radio set.

Other Marines came piling in and fanning out, as disciplined as a champion football team, if you could view what they were doing that benignly. When medics appeared, I had them put Red on a stretcher and trotted alongside back to the beach.

There I came upon a grim-faced officer, leading others, who had just sprung from an LCI and was waving forward an enlisted man unfurling an American flag in the smoky breeze. All, unconsciously grouped in postures of great energy, formed a perfectly balanced picture.

As I lowered my camera I saw that the leading officer wore two stars on his helmet and recognized him from press pictures as a man the Marines adored, Old Grizzly. Almost instantly an officer grabbed me by an arm and demanded my picture in the name of God and the U.S. Marine Corps. I argued only briefly, for I was outnumbered and didn't want my camera and the rest of the film confiscated.

Old Grizzly, glimpsing what had happened, cast us an odd look as he lumbered past and said to the officer, "Beckwith, take the guy's name and give him credit for Chrissake."

And so the officer, a major, took my name and outfit as well as the film before I hurried after Red and the medics.

18

Vera began to see that she must increase her staff at the clinic. She was thinking about it one afternoon as she came down the stairs and found that Lulu had just admitted a comely woman.

"I'm Mrs. Bonham," the woman said. "From the American Red Cross. I'd like to speak to Mrs. Andrew Jackson Jack."

Vera tensed. Red had not answered the letter Rosemarie wrote months before; she never mentioned him any more and appeared to have forgotten about him. Vera had come to think of Red as her enemy, a menace to trade, because when Rosemarie had him on her mind, she lost interest in business.

Mrs. Bonham looked at Vera descending the stairs and said, "How do you do, Mrs. Jack, I'm Mrs. Bonham from the American Red Cross."

Vera made up something Fiddler might have said: "As long as you're not from the Canadian Red Cross. We had somebody here from the Canadian Red Cross last week."

Ruth Bonham was not stupid, but devoid of a sense of humor. She could not understand why the Canadian Red Cross would be seeking money in Hawaii, and said, "Well, I guess you might as well take it any place you can get it."

"That's what I always figure too," Vera said. "Mrs. Jack isn't in. I mean she doesn't live here any more. What's it about?"

"Her husband, Staff Sergeant Andrew Jackson Jack. He's arranging to send her an allotment of seventy-five dollars a month from his pay and wants to get in touch with her.''

Vera, fearful that Rosemarie would come downstairs at any moment, said, "Come into my—uh—parlor, Mrs. Bonham.'' In the reception room she poured Ruth a Scotch and poured herself some of the caramel-colored water she pretended was booze while explaining that she didn't know what had become of Rosemarie. There was something about Ruth Bonham—petulant eyes, a businesslike style to her short chestnut hair, a well-formed and supple body—that made Vera wonder if she had found a candidate for her staff.

After they had talked a while she asked, "What do you do for fun, Mrs. Bonham?'' Ruth blushed and stiffened, but Vera had learned that the stiffer they are the quicker they break.

Ruth had to admit that she never had fun any more; it wasn't even any fun being a volunteer for the Red Cross the way it used to be at home in the States. Her husband was the skipper of an LST in the southwestern Pacific. In civilian life he'd been a law firm partner in a large eastern city; a patriot who held a naval reserve commission, he had volunteered the day after Pearl Harbor. He had strong political connections that enabled him to bring her to Hawaii, but then he had been sent farther west, leaving her alone.

"Are you poor?'' Vera asked.

"Oh, Lord, no,'' Ruth said. "All we've got is money. No children. No fun. Just money in the bank.''

"What do you mean by fun?'' Vera asked. Then, realizing that Ruth was too straitlaced to explain, she volunteered: "Good sex?''

Ruth blinked and said indistinctly, "Nobody ever said that to me before! I never even—I mean, uh, you know . . .''

Vera exclaimed in pity. "You said your name is Ruth? Poor Ruth, good sex is something a woman should never be without. I'll bet you never even had an orgasm.''

"Well, I guess—no.'' She let Vera pour her another drink. "But who are you going to tell that to? I can't tell my husband. All my life —I mean a lot of my life—I've been faking orgasms to him. Who you going to tell? I mean, who—in—the—hell—you—going—to—tell?''

Vera was sympathetic. "I know a submarine officer back from patrol could probably solve your problem. Want a date with him tonight?''

"Suppose I got pregnant?''

"Don't you have a diaphragm?''

"I *did* have. But after we came to Hawaii and my husband saw how many loose men there are around, he took my diaphragm with him to the Southwest Pacific to make sure I stayed faithful."

"What's your husband going to do with your diaphragm in the southwestern Pacific?" Vera asked wonderingly. "Maybe somebody will shove it up his ass."

"No," Ruth said seriously, "Gregory wouldn't stand for that."

"You don't have to worry about your diaphragm with this submarine officer. He's oral."

"Oral who?" asked Ruth.

Vera realized there was much to explain, and Ruth listened to her with fascination. "I've often wondered about that," she said, "but Gregory says it's very nasty and dirty and would never let us try it. But you say it's not?"

"Absolutely not. It's thoroughly cleansing."

Ruth sighed. "I'm so glad. It's like a weight has been lifted off my shoulders. Where do I meet this submarine officer?"

Ruth found no moral problem in becoming a prostitute after Vera convinced her, very easily, that she really was serving as a therapist to deeply troubled men. She took to the work with such enthusiasm that Vera quickly made her assistant high priestess in the servicemen's cult of lasting life. Gullible wanderers of the war zones accepted the word that she was Vera herself and happily worshiped at her shrine. Ruth was so delighted with the kneeling ceremony that she cried out in excited pleasure while it was under way.

"It's wonderful," Vera told Rosemarie. "From no orgasms she's up to more than twenty a day. How's that for therapy?"

"Well," Rosemarie said noncommittally.

Ruth never returned to her Red Cross chapter, but at Vera's suggestion she phoned and explained that Rosemarie had joined the WAVES, no one knew where, and that she herself must resign from the Cross because she was so deeply involved in another volunteer charity. She accepted Vera's explanation that Red was an evil influence on Rosemarie and never mentioned him to her. Ruth, indeed, accepted Vera's word on everything. She had heard, for example, that prostitutes charged men two dollars for their favors, and was pleased to hear Vera say that she could not be called a prostitute since she charged nothing for what she did—Vera merely gave her a good expense account.

Orvie, who fitted Ruth with a diaphragm and became fond of her, asked Vera one time what she was doing with the huge profits she was making from the clinic.

"Buying real estate," Vera said. "I'll buy up every inch of Waikiki I can."

"You're crazy," Orvie said. "After the war is over, everybody will go back to the States and the Hawaiian Islands will become known as the Deserted Islands. You'll lose your shirt, Vera."

"Want to bet?" she replied. "You always find things out too late."

He was a good technician, she thought, but otherwise a know-nothing.

One thing neither Orvie nor anyone else knew was that Vera continued to hear from Basset and to write him under the name of Fiddler at a postal box number in Washington. To her distress—and his own, he had not been able to escape and now was in charge of a huge Army laundry. Vera was bothered by a subtle change in the tone of his letters as time passed. He did not *sound* like Fiddler, but like someone she didn't know—Basset perhaps? And why did he ask so many questions about Rosemarie? He kept saying he could arrange free transportation to and from Washington for them both as a vacation; however, Vera replied that they were too busy with the grind of work. Was it possible, she wondered, that she could not stay in love with any man? She hoped not. But she admitted to herself that the acquisition of a man could not bring her the same satisfaction as did acquisition of another acre of virgin land.

Since Orvie did not have sufficient Navy employment as a gynecologist, his superiors had him qualify as a psychiatrist—a branch of medicine increasingly in demand as the war progressed.

One afternoon during a lull, Vera and Rosemarie were talking about Orvie and Ruth, who was upstairs entertaining a Chinese planter from Kauai.

"Orvie's beginning to enjoy her more than us," Vera said. "He says she really throws herself into her work. By the way, have you noticed the word she's started to use about patients? She says she *interviews* them."

"I noticed," Rosemarie said. "You'd think this was an employment office."

Lulu answered the phone and said that Commander Snook wanted to speak to Vera immediately. Rosemarie could hear his voice honking all the way across the room.

"Speak slower," Vera said. "I can't understand a word you're saying. You sound like you're being transferred." She looked surprised and turning to Rosemarie. "But he *is!* They're sending him to sea."

"Oh God!" exclaimed Rosemarie. "They've finally scraped the bottom of the barrel."

Hanging up, Vera said, "He'll be right out. He's terrified. They're sending him off in a hospital ship."

"Why would they want to send a gynecologist off on a hospital ship?"

"He's going as a psychiatrist—tomorrow."

The Chinese planter, a frequent and pleasant client with the secretive smile of a Persian pussycat, prowled down the stairs and paid Vera his fee. "The new lady is very nice," he said. "Thank you very much." He went out and climbed into his Rolls and drove away.

"Maybe," Rosemarie said, "if we could get four or five more like Ruth, we could quit work and just play."

"Too risky," Vera said. "You can't trust everybody. In fact, you can't trust anybody. Now the problem is, who will be our gynecologist while Orvie's at sea?"

Ruth came downstairs wearing the satisfied expression that came over her after interviewing a patient. "I never thought I'd want to interview a Chinese," she said. "But he really is very nice. Such a thorough gentleman. And he gave me some gasoline ration stamps."

"You need gas stamps?" Vera asked. "Why didn't you say so? I know the guy who *makes* the ration stamps and I'll give you all you want."

They were discussing the stupidity of the government in rationing gas, meat and other essential things when Orvie came in. His lips were tight, his eyes moist, as if he were returning from the funeral of a beloved one. "If only I'd stuck to my specialty," he said, "they'd never have sent me to sea."

"Oh, come on, Orvie," Rosemarie said, "there's not a thing to worry about. You're going on a hospital ship. They have big red crosses painted all over 'em and the enemy pays no attention to 'em."

"That's what you think!" Orvie cried. "I've heard all about it at the hospital. Do you know that Jap planes and subs will go around any number of battleships and things just to get at a hospital ship? Do you know *why?* They *want* to sink hospital ships so as to destroy our limited supply of doctors and nurses."

"Yes, I've heard that," Ruth said.

Orvie looked at her in alarm. "You *have?*"

"Yes, but I don't believe it because there are more doctors and nurses around than we know what to do with. Dr. Snook, I should think you'd be *proud* to be going to sea to serve our country."

"Oh, I am, I am, Ruth." Orvie, playing with his cap, somehow managed to look modest. "Of course I don't really know any psychiatry, but I guess that doesn't matter. Why do they need a psychiatrist on a hospital ship anyway? And it will be a great satisfaction to me if anything happens to me at sea." His eyes moistened. "I think I mentioned to you that my wife is being unfaithful to me in Fresno. Can you imagine how terrible she'll feel, Ruth, if I should die in action?"

"That reminds me," Vera said, "what are we going to do about a gynecologist while you're gone?"

"I have a replacement arranged," Orvie said. "He's a nice young lieutenant fresh from a residency in gynecology at New York University Hospital. He understands the arrangements and will be in touch with you next week."

After giving all three an examination, Orvie said he would like a few more words with Ruth. They went upstairs so that she could conduct the interview in private.

On The Atoll, Japanese resistance, which had seemed unbreakable in the morning, had just about ended in midafternoon. The enemy firing had become so desultory that it was deemed safe for a gleaming white hospital ship to sail into the lagoon and anchor among many other American vessels.

Red lay in an improvised field hospital on the beach, and I sat beside him, feeling very tired and still dazed. "Do you really want to go through with this?" I asked.

"You bet. Don't you wish you were?"

I did, and yet I did not. Anyway, it was too late to claim paralysis from combat fatigue. I had gone looking for D Company and the 9th Battalion, but could not find them; some Marines said the Army unit had been "wiped out," others said, "knocked out." I was like a child lost in the woods. Still clutching my camera, I returned to the field hospital and Red. The medics paid no attention to him because he had no visible injury and they had more severely wounded men than they could handle.

Everything seemed to be happening accidentally. By accident some men had been killed and others wounded; by accident I had been separated from 9th Battalion and could not find it; by accident Red was lifted up and carried to a lighter with seriously wounded men. I went along, simply because I did not know where else to go. A corpsman trying to bring some order from the chaos at the lighter accepted my word that I was "taking my man" out to the hospital ship, but another corpsman said, "You come right back, Lieutenant, you can't go aboard that ship." He made a note of my name and unit and the fact that I had gone to the ship.

As I sat beside Red among the wounded on the lighter while it made its way to the ship in the lagoon, I wished I'd done as Red had. I wanted never to set foot on that atoll again.

The wounded were lifted by crane onto the reception deck of the Navy hospital ship with a care that amounted to tenderness. I went up the ladder, and no one prevented me from stepping to the side of Red's litter on the deck. Many of the wounded were unconscious and a few were dead by the time they were hoisted aboard. Two corpsmen read the diagnosis tag on each patient and had him rolled aft to the appropriate ward or surgery room.

"This," said a corpsman after reading Red's tag, "was found on the beach wearing an Army uniform with staff sergeant's stripes. It says here he's deaf, dumb and paralyzed from the neck down."

"That sounds like Army," the other said. Drawing a sterile needle, he jabbed Red in the buttocks. Red writhed, but did not cry out. "His paralysis is receding." He jabbed again, and Red yelped. "He may be deaf, but he's not dumb."

The first corpsman leaned over Red and asked, "Pardner, are you able to piss?"

Red shook his head, and the corpsman said, "He's not deaf, but he may be sort of dumb. Send him to the psycho ward." He looked at me. "What's the matter with you, Lieutenant?"

I had an inspiration. "I want to use your darkroom."

"Darkroom? Darkroom?" The corpsmen looked at each other. "Have we got a darkroom?"

"The Admiral says you do. He ordered me to develop this stuff and get it back to him as quick as possible."

"If the Admiral says we got a darkroom," one said, "I guess we must got one."

"I know," the other said, "he must mean the X-ray room." He beckoned to a child in sailor's costume who looked to be all of four-teen years old. "Take this gentleman to X-ray and tell the yeoman the Admiral gives his work priority."

I told Red I'd see him later and followed to X-ray where the technician in charge led me to a well-equipped darkroom adjoining X-ray. There I became happily absorbed in developing my film. With surprise and considerable distaste I found that from a kind of reflex I had made many more pictures than I remembered taking. What kind of creep was I to photograph such horrors? And yet I had recorded the horror of war with stunning, dramatic shots. None would appear in the *New York Times;* they were too ruthlessly terrible to appear in any newspaper. Nevertheless, as a craftsman, I began to be pleased with them. I had not had time to plan and aim; I had been, so to speak, shooting from the hip. Despite my terror, my subconscious had been working perfectly. It made me think about having a civilian career as a photographer if I could survive this mess. Suddenly I felt very good as I began to think about a peaceful, satisfying life beyond the grave of war. Devout Christians must feel that way when contemplating heaven from their deathbeds.

I bundled my prints and negatives into a big envelope I found in the darkroom and went looking for Red. There were no patients in the psycho ward. A physician stood with his back to me fretting to a corpsman named Truro over the lack of patients.

"It's soon yet, sir," Truro replied. "The troops haven't had time yet to make up their minds they're going crazy. But here's one."

The doctor turned. To my total astonishment he was Orvie Snook. But my astonishment was no greater than his. His eyes bugged and he quavered, "Boz!"

In my best Mississippi accent I replied, "You mistake me foh someone else, suh. Ah am Gen'l Robuht E. Lee an' Ah *did* win the Battle o' Gettysburg. Any repo'ts to the contwawy, suh, is the wuhk o' Yankee histowians who wanna discwedit me."

Orvie was close to tears; I was touched because I hadn't realized he cared so much about me. "This distinguished officer," he said to Truro, "this Lieutenant Boswick, who served with me at the Battle of Pearl Harbor, this man, Truro, had one of the most promising careers in the U.S. Army. What happened to him?"

"Well," Truro said, "guess that's what we have to find out, eh, sir?"

"And look," Orvie said, "he carries a camera he's found somewhere. He was always fond of cameras. Now he's like a child who can't be separated from his favorite toy. Boz, your fatigues are in tatters and you look pretty bad. You just stretch out on a bunk and take it easy."

"Only," I said, "if you addwess me respectfuwy by mah true name o' Gen'l Lee."

"Here comes another," Truro said.

As an attendant rolled Red into the ward, a nurse passed. She was quite ugly, but she must have looked beautiful to Red, who had not seen a white woman in more than a year, for he raised his head and smiled at her.

Truro read the tag and said to Orvie, "This here man is Army too, like General Lee there. He's deaf, dumb and paralyzed from the neck down."

"Well, fella," Orvie said to Red, "we'll have you up and talking in no time."

"He can't hear you," Truro said.

Orvie said, "Both of these men are suffering from battle fatigue."

Red nodded enthusiastically, and Truro said, "He hears you, he's beginning to hear better."

"Good!" cried Orvie. "We're beginning to get somewhere. Can you hear me, soldier?" Red nodded and smiled. "What's your name and outfit, soldier?" Red rolled his eyes wildly. "Don't worry about it," Orvie told him. "Things like that can slip your mind and then— whoof!—they pop right out at you. Can you hear me, Boz?"

"Ah told you, young man, mah name is Robuht E. Lee. Ah'm Commanduh in Chief o' owah Confed'ate fohces."

"Excuse me. General Lee, can you hear me?"

"O' cohse Ah heah you. No cause foh yew tew shout at me!"

"Now I'll tell you both," Orvie went on, "in a second here I'm going to give you both something that's doing wonders for men with battle fatigue. It's called sodium Pentothal. It puts you only part way asleep. Then we'll talk together and the things bothering you will just—well, wash away. Come on, Truro, let's go get the Pentothal."

After they had gone, Red asked me, "You really going through with it and try for a discharge?"

"It's tempting. I started this just horsing around. Sometimes horsing around is the way I make up my mind about something important."

At that moment a man we knew from D Company, head bandaged and one arm in a cast, looked in the doorway and greeted us. "You two don't look bad off. Where you been? Goldman's looking for you." *Goldman alive?* "He sure is. He's wandering round, trying to find what's left of D Company. And you're about it."

An attendant sent the man on, and I said, "I'd sure like to say goodbye to Ira."

"Me too," Red said. "I hate to think of him left way out here by himself in the middle of this stupid damn ocean."

Orvie and Truro returned with the Pentothal and a syringe the size of a horse pistol. Orvie said, "I'll try Boz first. Swab his left arm, Truro."

"Doctor, aren't you supposed to stick him in the ass?"

"I don't think so," Orvie said. "The time I saw it done at the hospital they stuck the guy in the arm."

It was alarming to learn that he'd never used this stuff on a patient before, so I said, "Jes a teensy-weensy bit, Gen'l Longstreet." When he stuck the needle in my arm I hollered, "What the hell you doing, Orvie?" and pulled away.

"Did you hear that?" Orvie's voice came in a kind of shriek to Truro. "Boz! Boz! You recognize me?"

"Of course I recognize you, Orvie. Where am I?"

"A miracle!" cried Orvie. "Oh, the miracles of modern medicine!"

"Well," Truro said dubiously, "I don't see how the stuff had time to take effect."

"How can you be so skeptical?" Orvie was indignant with him. "Why are there always skeptics when modern medicine performs a miracle? Boz, how do you feel?"

"Okay." I finally had made up my mind what I was going to do: I'd return to The Atoll and try again to find Goldman. "Last I remember a bomb or something went off, but I'm all right now. Orvie, what the hell are you doing here?"

"Practicing psychiatry and enjoying every minute of it." He was all hyped up by having cured me of battle fatigue. "Now I'm going to see what I can do for this man here."

Attendants were beginning to wheel in patients more seriously troubled than Red and I—two writhing in straitjackets, two weeping hysterically—but Orvie and Truro paid no attention to them as they set up Red for an injection.

"Just give him a very little bit," I advised.

"Who's practicing psychiatry here?" Orvie asked me.

"Nobody at all that I can see."

"He's all better," Orvie said to Truro. "He has a very caustic personality that always wants to express itself." He eased the needle into Red's arm and said, "If you can hear me, repeat after me, 'Yes, I can hear you.' "

"Yes, I can hear you," Red said, unaffected by the tiny bit of sodium Pentothal.

Orvie made a crowing sound. "Did you hear that, Truro? I've got him *talking*."

"Remarkable, sir."

"Tell me your name," Orvie said to Red.

"I don't remember."

"Where do you live in the States?"

"I don't remember."

"What's the last thing you remember?"

"Unnecessary death and destruction. Good men dying for no good reason. All of us victims of the capitalist system. No living politician anywhere ever said a truthful thing."

"Never mind about that! Don't talk that way!"

"A few more remarks like that," Truro said, "and he'll get twenty years in the stockade instead of a psycho discharge."

Red, having fun, went on, "Politicians are corrupt, like generals and admirals. They—"

"Shut up!" cried Orvie. "I won't help you if you carry on like a damn Communist. Listen to me. What do you want most?"

"A discharge from the Army."

"What else?"

"A good piece of ass."

"Ah ha!" Orvie said to Truro. "Now we're getting somewhere. This man is sexually frustrated. He went into battle sexually frustrated and—well, you can see the result yourself." He peered at Red, who peered back at him through half-closed eyes. "How would you like me to get you a piece of tail?"

"Right here and now?"

"No, no, there are only nurses on this ship. They're not allowed to have sexual intercourse."

"That is," Truro said, "not with enlisted men."

Orvie said, "I'm talking about when we get back to Hawaii. If I promise you a magnificent piece of tail, will you promise me to—uh —reassemble yourself? Just look at the great progress you've already made under my care. You can talk and you can hear. I want you to get a thought into your subconscious mind. Now hear this. If you get up and walk and tell me your name, I'll arrange for you to get gloriously laid in Hawaii."

"How much?"

"Fifty bucks."

"That's a lot of dough."

"But this is a lot of woman. I mean women. You can take your pick. There's Ruth and Lulu. There's Vera and Rosemarie and—"

I began to babble to try to divert them, but no one paid me any attention.

Red stared hard at Orvie and asked, "Rosemarie who?"

"Rosemarie Jack. She's a gorgeous blonde—" Red's look of growing rage made Orvie's voice trail off.

Propping himself on an elbow, Red shouted, "Listen, you son of a bitch, I'm Staff Sergeant Andrew Jackson Jack of the United States Army! Rosemarie is my wife. And when I get back to Hawaii I'm going to beat the shit out of everybody who laid her."

Orvie was struck dumb. His lips moved, but no sound came. Suddenly he sagged and seemed to become smaller. He did not as much leave the ward as simply disappear.

"My God," I said to Truro, "Red's name is right there on his dog tags."

"I know, but the doctor forgot to read them."

Red remained propped on his elbow, scowling at Truro, who finally asked, "Sergeant Jack, may I bring you some dinner?"

"I'll go get it myself when I feel like it."

Truro made a wide gesture with both hands. "These things happen. I mean names get mixed up. Commander Snook didn't mean any offense. I mean you can see yourself what a jerk he is. You being all psyched up and everything just now, this could be a case of mistaken mental telepathy identity. You know what I mean?"

"Get out of here!" Red said.

He lay back, staring up, smoldering with rage, while Truro went away and I sat down on his bunk. "There could be some mistake, Red."

"There's no mistake." His green-eyed gaze seemed to shaft clean through me. "So she became a whore. Do you know anything about it?"

"No," I lied.

He believed me. His believing my lie should have been the worst thing that had yet happened to me, but I felt only sweet relief.

"I feel funny." Red's voice broke, but he did not weep. "I never felt so funny before. In my mind, I mean. Mixed up is what I mean. Maybe I'm not just pretending to be crazy. Maybe I'm really crazy. What made Rosemarie do it?"

"I don't know, Red. I'm going up on deck and get some air. I'm suffocating."

He grabbed my arm and hung on hard. "Stick with me. I'm not going back to Hawaii and fuck out of the Army. I'm going ashore and look for Ira and what's left of D Company. If I go back to Hawaii I would only look up Rosemarie and bust her jaw. But I don't want to do that. I don't want ever to see her again. Let's get something to eat on this tub and then go ashore."

As we left the ward, the public-address system, which seemed never to stop jabbering, got through to me: "Loo-tent Bos-vick reporta tida spetion deck, Loo-tentant Bos-vick—" Red went with me.

A yeoman said I was to go ashore on the lighter waiting below and report to Old Grizzly's headquarters on the beach. Somehow they had traced me to the hospital ship. "Come on," I told Red, but the yeoman would not let him pass. Despite all my angry arguments, an order was an order was an order. Loo-tenant Bos-vick was ordered ashore, but Red could not leave the ship without a special order.

We went back to the ward and pleaded with Truro for a dismissal order so that Red could go with me.

"Sarge," Truro said, "I never thought you were nuts till now. I don't have the power to write the order. Anyway, why should you want to go back to your beat-up outfit on that stinking atoll? This ship sails for Pearl Harbor first thing in the morning. They may not give you a Section 8 discharge, but they'll never send you back to combat."

Red said, "I want to talk to Snook."

"The trouble with that is that Snook doesn't want to talk to you. And since he happens to outrank you, he doesn't have to. You might as well relax and take a nap, Sarge, because once you get on one of these hospital ships, they never let you off till they reach home port."

Two more berserk Marines were brought in and lashed in strait-jackets as Red and I went above again.

"It's an easy swim," he told me. "I know you can't swim with me because of the camera and that folder of pictures. So I'll see you ashore. Tell Goldman I'm on my way."

The moon was up early, gleaming on the lagoon. The guns were silent at last, and fires flickered here and there on the island. We found a coil of line in a lifeboat and tied an end to the rail in a dark part of the deck. If we said anything else, I don't remember what it was. Red tied his boots around his neck by their laces and then for some reason we shook hands rather formally, like people parting at a railroad station. Red went down the line, hand under hand, and swam away silently. I pulled up the line, put it back in the lifeboat, and took the lighter ashore.

19

Old Grizzly could have slept comfortably on a ship in the lagoon, but chose to spend the first night ashore where his troops were engaged with the Japanese—an admirable gesture that many two-star generals failed to make during the war. His command post was almost in the front lines.

Although there was generally less chicken in the Marines than in the Army, there nevertheless were a few bones and feathers. Hard by Grizzly's command post was the headquarters of Major Beckwith, the Marine public relations officer for the operation, to whom I was directed after I went ashore from the hospital ship. The invasion was barely twelve hours old, but already Beckwith and his men were churning out words and pictures that portrayed a great Marine victory.

"I don't understand your being Army," Beckwith told me rather peevishly. "You're too talented. This is a terrific picture." He handed me a print he had had developed of my shot of Grizzly and the color bearer coming ashore. "The General is highly pleased with it. He said he wants to congratulate you personally soon as he can find you. What happened to your fatigues? They look more like shorts and halter. Haven't you had a chance to wash your face?"

"Goddam Navy bomber blew me galley west," I said.

Beckwith said, "Navy bombers don't bomb friendly forces."

"I'm telling you, Major, it was a Curtiss Helldiver."

"Navy bombers don't bomb friendly forces," Beckwith said.

Grizzly's command post had been thrown together from tin, wood and canvas in a place that appeared more sheltered than most on the coral atoll. The General sat on a small keg at a field desk in the dimness of a heavily shaded Coleman lamp, surrounded by maps, schedules, men, wires, phones. He was as big as a bear, and had the fangs and sharp nose of one; in fact, the command post smelled like a bear's den. On a box beside him sat a Navy captain who raised eyes that appeared as dark and suffering as those of a martyr.

"Nice picture," the General told me. "Beckwith, how you going to caption the thing when you send it out?"

"We're working on that now, sir. Will have you approve it."

"My God, I don't have to approve picture captions. You have any ideas, Lieutenant?"

One came to me. "How about slugging it 'Old Glory and Old Grizzly.'"

His lips curled back on his fangs in a wide grin. "By God, I want this man transferred to the Marines. Where's our lawyer? Where in hell is Stavisky?"

"Right here, sir!" A major came into the dim light. "A transfer isn't easily arranged, sir. It has to begin with the wish of the individual to be transferred and—"

"Nothing's easy," Grizzly grumbled, "when you goddam lawyers start messing with it. How about it, Lieutenant, want to be a Marine?"

No, I did not. I said, "Marines have too many atolls to land on, sir."

He grinned good-naturedly. "A smart answer. What happened to your fatigue uniform? You look like you've been in a dog fight."

"Goddam Navy bomber blew me off a bunker."

"Navy bombers don't bomb friendly forces," the General said.

The Navy captain at his side said, "Of course they do, Grizzly."

The General looked surprised. "They do?"

"Sure," the Captain said. "They hit anything that moves. I'm sure it was a terrible experience, Lieutenant Boswick."

The sympathetic way he said it made me almost want to thank him for the terrible experience, but I only said, "It was a Curtiss Helldiver, sir."

"All right, Lieutenant"—Beckwith spoke sharply—"we'll go along now. The General's busy."

"I'm not busy." Grizzly sounded aggrieved. "I'm just sitting here watching everything run itself. It's like a complicated set of electric trains where you just throw a switch now and then. When I was a kid — Hey, Boswick, I don't know how you got into combat with a camera, but do you have any more pictures?''

I took a couple of dozen out of the envelope. Grizzly and the Captain drew their heads together to look at the pictures while Beckwith leaned over their shoulders. In a moment the Captain said, ''I think I'm going to throw up.'' Grizzly, studying a photo grimly, said, ''Don't do it now, Carl. It stinks bad enough in here already.''

Beckwith spoke to me accusingly: ''These are terrible pictures.''

''I know they're not technically good. On most I don't even remember aiming. I was scared shitless and just working the camera because there was nothing else to do just then.''

''You'd never make a Marine,'' Beckwith said. ''Marines don't get scared shitless.''

''The hell they don't,'' Grizzly said, studying another picture. ''But it is true, Beckwith, that you are full of shit.''

''Yes sir.''

''What d'you mean 'Yes sir'?'' He made a grumbling sound. ''Tell a man he's full of shit and he says 'Yes sir.' Why doesn't he say, 'No sir, I ain't'? Any time a man answers me with that I'll promote him on the spot. What d'you mean, Beckwith, that these pictures Boswick took are terrible?''

''Well, sir, I mean that they do nothing to promote the war effort. No family newspaper is going to publish these things. You just heard Captain Cook say they make him sick to his stomach.''

''That,'' Cook said, ''doesn't prove anything except that I have a weak stomach. These pictures compose a graphic, ghastly record of war as it is. They're important to any serious history of this one.''

Beckwith, who could be stubborn, said, ''But nobody will print 'em, sir. If nobody will print 'em, you might as well destroy 'em.''

''If you destroy these pictures,'' Grizzly said, ''I'll have you strung up by the balls, Beckwith. How about it, Boswick, want to team up with us? You might even make first lieutenant someday.''

Captain Cook spoke: ''Maybe that can be arranged later. But right now I have another mission for Lieutenant Boswick. I want him to come out to the *Newark* with me when I go back tomorrow and bring his pictures—including the one he made of you, Grizzly.''

Grizzly made menacing, rumbling sounds. ''Goddam Navy! I know the Navy's in charge here, but it doesn't signify that because I finally got me a good photographer you can steal him for the Admiral.''

"You can't *give* a photographer to the Admiral," Captain Cook said. "He hates publicity."

"That's what he says," Grizzly said, "but that's not what he means. He just hates mediocre publicity. Well, so long, Boswick, I've got to get back to taking this atoll. Thanks for making that pretty picture of me."

Of course I was highly pleased that they liked my photographs. I didn't expect any newspaper to print them, but I was not working for newspapers. I really was working for myself, trying to develop my skill and grateful for all the encouragement I could receive.

It was arranged that I would report to Captain Cook there at 0700 next morning. Meanwhile I asked for the whereabouts of D Company from the operations clerk and learned that what was left of it had been drawn into reserve at the end of the beach and would be evacuated tomorrow. Famished, I took a can of rations from a pile and, having lost my spoon, I lifted one off a corpse and ate as I stumbled along the beach in search of D.

The company was sprawled in darkness that a pale moon failed to penetrate; a crazy sentry almost shot at me before I could convince him who I was. I could not see Goldman distinctly as our hands fumbled in a clasp and he welcomed me back from the dead.

"Red's on his way too." In a whisper that no one else could hear I told him about Orvie and all that had happened. "It'll be an easy swim for him. He'll be here long before daylight."

"I wouldn't blame you guys if you'd sailed away." Goldman sounded hoarse and exhausted. "There was a while today when I'd have goofed off myself if there'd been any place to goof to." Counting Red and me, there were only 28 live and unwounded bodies left in D Company. He did not yet have a report on the entire decimated battalion.

Goldman should have been pleased by my word that the company would be evacuated tomorrow, but he said, "Who knows it's going to happen? A clerk writes down what he's told—and tomorrow somebody comes along and changes everything. People like us are the pawns, moved and forfeited."

Red had not appeared in the D Company area when I left in the morning and I wondered anxiously what had become of him.

When I returned to Grizzly's command post I was as tattered and dirty as I'd been the night before. Cook told me not to worry about my appearance. Gray, round-faced, with a habitual look of anxiety, he was chief of staff to the Admiral, who wore three stars and was responsible for leading the American drive west from Hawaii under the direction of Cincpac, as the Commander in Chief of the Pacific was called. While the Admiral had the difficult job of conquering, Cook had the equally perplexing task of arranging for it to be done.

As we boarded a small craft to go out to the *Newark,* he said, "Your tatters are just right for what I'm trying to prove to the Admiral. Our heavy casualties on The Atoll are caused by two factors— not enough bombardment, and misjudging the tides. You and your pictures can be a great help to my arguments. I want the Admiral to *see* for himself."

I asked why we attacked the most heavily defended atolls.

"Because they're the ones with the best and longest airstrips. The Japanese have been busy at them for years and are dug in much more deeply than we realized. We have to have these strips to go on west."

The Admiral's flag, three white stars on a blue field, flew at the truck of the *Newark.* In days of peace the cruiser had displayed a handsome teak quarterdeck and was noted for impeccable ceremony, but now she had been stripped for war: teak deck removed, and the admiral's barge and accommodation ladder dumped ashore as excess weight. Cook and I climbed up a vertical sea ladder and were piped aboard by a boatswain's mate wearing dungarees. I glimpsed a thin, suspicious face with large ears peering down at us from the bridge.

Cook had me wait while he stepped onto the open bridge deck. The Admiral's voice came, austere as a north wind: "Carl, who's the disheveled creature you brought back with you?"

"An Army lieutenant who was in the first wave. He has some interesting photos I want you to see."

"Well, first get him properly dressed."

"Ray—"

"Please, Carl, get your man dressed, shaved and showered too. Why are you dramatizing so?"

"Because I want you to hear from him what it was like."

"Maybe I don't want to know what it was like. If I know what it was like it might affect my judgment. This job of mine is no place for a humanitarian like you."

"And do you think my job is? The message I bring you from Grizzly is that future bombardments must be fifty or sixty times heavier."

"Did you say fifty?"

"No sir, I said sixty."

"By simple arithmetic would you please multiply the weight of shells fired at that atoll by sixty and tell me where in the Pacific Ocean you're going to find available ship bottoms to transport that ammunition to an operational scene?"

"There's plenty of available tonnage on the West Coast."

"All right, all right. I still don't see why it was necessary for you to spend last night ashore with Grizzly."

"Let me get the pictures and show you."

"No, not now." Suddenly the Admiral sounded tired and petulant. "I'm trying to get in my hundred laps on this deck before I go back to work."

Cook turned me over to an ensign named Gibbons who saw to it I was washed, shaved and dressed in a fresh set of Navy suntans. While I ate in the junior officers' cafeteria mess, Gibbons gave me the lowdown on the higher-up. He was a bright political science major from Harvard who sounded as if he had written a treatise on the current state of command in the U.S. Navy.

Cook, he said, was the brightest man in the Navy—brighter than the Admiral, brighter than the Commander of the Pacific (Cincpac) and, God knew, brighter than Cominch, as the Commander in Chief of the Navy was called. The trouble with Cook, Gibbons said, was that he was made vulnerable by a sensitive conscience and prone to do unnecessary things like spending last night on The Atoll in order to share the suffering of the troops.

The Admiral was bright enough, Gibbons explained, to understand the single great necessity of successful military command: Never be vulnerable. His frosty attitudes, which some blamed on shyness, really came from his efforts to maintain his air of invulnerability. He spent ten hours in his bunk every night, sleeping and reading detective stories, because it separated him from his staff and the danger that he might show some weakness in their presence. He paced the deck for hours because no one dared interrupt him while he was doing it. He ate quantities of raw onions with the excuse that they were good for his health, but actually because their smell tended to keep people at some distance.

The Admiral had to make very few decisions. Cincpac above him and Cook below stacked all the options so obviously that a grammar school boy would have seen what to do. The Admiral got along well with Cincpac back at headquarters in Hawaii because he always did precisely what Cincpac wanted him to do. And Cincpac got along well with Cominch back in Washington because he always did precisely as Cominch wished.

But Cominch got along with no one, not his thousands of inferiors in the Navy, or his peers on the Joint Chiefs of Staff, or the President, or the Congress, because Cominch did only what *he* wanted to do. Cominch, said Gibbons, was the orneriest, meanest son of a bitch wearing the uniform of any nation anywhere. Nevertheless, by instilling fear in everyone who knew, or knew of, him, he had pulled the U.S. Navy up by its bootstraps after the debacle at Pearl Harbor and was turning it into a respected, fighting organization.

Long ago, Gibbons told me, Cook had had a run-in with Cominch, who had vowed to block further promotion of this brilliant officer.

"But hope springs eternal," Gibbons said. "Cook is so tolerant himself that he can't really believe there's anyone as intolerant as Cominch. Lately he's been campaigning with the Admiral and Cincpac to get a promotion to rear admiral. I see a dual purpose in his bringing you aboard. One was what he told you—to convince the old man there have to be heavier shore bombardments. His other purpose is selfish."

I asked Gibbons to explain.

"He knows his old buddy the Admiral inside out. Cook knows he'd like to be accepted as a warm, human leader. But the Admiral's scared that any effort in that direction will only make him look corny—vulnerable, that is. There's nothing corny about that picture you took of Grizzly and the color-bearer because it's such a natural, spontaneous shot. I think Cook wants you to do something similar for the Admiral. And he feels that if you do, the Admiral out of secret gratitude will throw all his weight into getting Cook that promotion."

20

I'd hoped to be put ashore that afternoon and rejoin Goldman, Red and D Company, but events prevented it. When the Japanese on The Atoll staged a strong counterattack from an interior line of deep defenses the Americans did not even know existed, the big warships thickened their bombardment. Naturally, everyone aboard the *Newark* became too busy to have any time for me.

Instead of being happy that I was not ashore and shot at, I was filled with anxiety for Red, Goldman and my own future. The horrors of that invasion yesterday had unsettled me as nothing ever had: I was not content simply to be comfortable today; I wanted to be sure I'd be safe tomorrow.

They found me a bunk vacated by a wounded man, but I could not sleep in the hot, cramped stateroom which shook to the crash of the cruiser's guns. The bombardment went on all day and all night and I finally fell asleep on a wardroom sofa from exhaustion. It seemed I had barely dozed off when Gibbons was shaking me awake. The guns had stopped, the temperature cooled, the ship was moving.

"Boswick," he said, "it's very exciting."

"What is?" I was sleepy and cross.

"We may be going into battle. It could be one of the historic battles of the war."

"Fuck history," I said. "I'm sleeping."

Gibbons was one of those people who never stops being reasonable. He said, "If you fuck history, history is bound to fuck you."

"It'll do that anyway," I said. "What do you plan I should do about this historic event?"

"Captain Cook suggests you come topside and take pictures."

"Is there any shooting up there?"

"Not yet."

"Then I'll follow his suggestion."

It was a pearl-like dawn with pastel colors spreading across and above the silent Pacific. The Atoll and its din of battle had evaporated, leaving our ship and a few others hastening toward the black and distant bulwark of night. I found myself watching the changing colors of dawn and thinking that all this frightened scurrying around by Americans and Japanese was of no more consequence than the crawl of snails in a splendid Garden of Eden.

As if fearing to interrupt the growing dawn, I spoke in almost a whisper: "Is there anything important you can tell me about this coming historic event?"

"Only that it may not occur at all—a symptom, I might add, of all historic events."

"Then why did Cook have you wake me?"

"He wants you ready to do as you see fit."

"Gibbons, are you trying to tell me I should sneak some shots of the Admiral on the bridge?"

He nodded. "At least I *think* that's what Captain Cook means. I'll show you a place you can stand on the flying bridge."

I loaded and we climbed and stood. Gibbons said, "The Captain suggested we could just be standing here talking casually."

"That's nice of him to wake me from the first decent sleep I've had in weeks so we can come up here and talk casually. I see no sign of the Admiral. What are we supposed to talk casually about?"

"Well, since nobody can hear us, I can tell you what I know about what's happening. About four hours ago we unscrambled a top-secret message from Pearl Harbor saying that a large—maybe the main—enemy fleet is approaching from the west. They gave some coordinates. The Admiral has to make a decision. They let him borrow fourteen warships from Souwespac down in New Guinea waters for two weeks and his loan is about to run out. For the moment he seems to have advantage in ships and planes to the enemy. Is this the golden moment for him to engage with intent to destroy? Yet his primary mission is to cover The Atoll till we've secured it. If he leaves all those troop ships unprotected back there and the enemy force eludes us and gets to 'em—well, what a mess. What should he do?"

"What did Cincpac say in his message he should do?"

"Cincpac didn't say. The Admiral commands on the scene."

"What does Cook say he should do?"

"Cook doesn't. He never offers opinions till asked, and the Admiral hasn't asked."

"Gibbons, you seem to have firm opinions on everything—what would you advise if asked?"

Gibbons rolled his eyes and shrugged. "Beats the hell out of me. I'm no great strategist. All I want to do is get back to New England and start teaching poly sci on a nice quiet campus that's handy to good skiing. What would you do, Boswick?"

"I'd sail on west and keep my search planes out—the way you can see he's doing now with all those planes around the horizon. I'd do what Drake or Nelson would have done—find and close with the enemy and destroy 'em. Become a national hero and run for President or something. Right?"

"Wrong, Boswick, wrong. I mean I *think* you're probably wrong. Drake and Nelson weren't lucky every time. There's a lot of economics involved. You might run out of fuel if you go too far west. Men are always replaceable, but all those troop ships back at that atoll cost a lot of money. This is a business you've got to run, not a joy ride to take—Pssst, there he comes."

Cook had come into our view of the bridge with a kind of mincing step that I realized was his way of bringing out the Admiral, rather the way a trainer coaxes a lion from its cage.

"Go ahead," Gibbons whispered.

"Go ahead at what? I should waste film on the back of a man's head? I can't get any decent shots from up here anyway. I'm going down there."

Fear struck Gibbons for the first time in his fearless monologues. "Oh, my God, don't do that!"

But then I saw something amazing. The Admiral had become aware of my camera presence and in a coy way was inviting its attention. Chin up! Profile against the horizon! "I'll be a son of a gun," I said to Gibbons, "under all that austerity he's as big a ham as a general I used to work for. Do me a favor and get word to Captain Cook that Lieutenant Boswick requests permission to appear on the bridge. Explain, if you can, that angle and distance are wrong from here."

Gibbons went off and returned quickly, looking surprised. "You know what you're doing after all. Permission granted. But you may not speak to the Admiral. He has a tremendous decision to make and can't be bothered with trivialities. He doesn't even want to be aware that you're present. By the way, he finally did look at your shot of Grizzly, and Captain Cook says he likes it very much.''

The word had been spread among the flunkies on the bridge that I did not exist. It's an odd feeling to be a nonexistent photographer taking pictures of a great commander on the bridge of his flagship. However, the Admiral was perfectly aware of my existence and in his tacit way cooperated thoroughly with me while pretending not to, which proved that he was as vain as every man. I got some dandy shots before he indicated with a wave of the hand to Cook, as if he had just discovered my presence, that I should be banished from the bridge. The cruiser's darkroom was at my disposal immediately. Soon the Admiral's flag lieutenant arrived to complain about how slowly my prints dried. They were very good pictures, but the flag lieutenant did not thank me before he skipped off with them, secure in the knowledge that I did not exist.

I clambered into my bunk and had fallen into deep sleep when awakened by Captain Cook himself. He was enthusiastic about the pictures. "Get up, Boswick. The Admiral would like you to stroll with him when he takes his constitutional at 1600.'' I observed that it was then only about 1400 and maybe I could get a little more sleep, but Cook said, "You need to shower and shave and put on fresh suntans before you walk with the Admiral.''

Naturally I was excited by the invitation. Dreams of glory flooded my mind, making my thinking a bit damp. I visualized one of my photos of the Admiral on the cover of *Life*. The editors would be so pleased by my work that they would arrange to have me discharged from the Army so that I could become one of the great photographers on their staff. I'd be sent to Paris where the wine was cheap and the women loose. But then I remembered that, besides *Life* not yet having hired me, the troops had not yet retaken Paris.

After suiting up, I asked Cook about the coming historic sea-air engagement.

He shrugged. "That will have to wait for another day. We have positives from two reconnaissance planes that the enemy force has turned back and is withdrawing to the northwest. The Admiral won't be drawn out and overextended, you know. You might call this the triumph of discipline over daring. Grizzly reports things well under control on The Atoll, so we'll take up watch just to the north of it and await developments.''

I was relieved that I apparently would not become involved in the continuing battle ashore. But what about Red and Goldman? When the enemy mounted a strong counterattack yesterday, had it been necessary for Grizzly to throw in ragtag reserves such as D Company?

"Oh, by the way, Boswick," Cook said, "when you walk with the Admiral, it would be good if you had some patter."

"Patter?"

"The Admiral enjoys small talk. Stay on neutral subjects. Like photography. He's become quite a bug on photography. But don't mention newspapers. I imagine you must have had some news photography experience to do the sort of thing you do." There was no point in my mentioning that I had none. "Just don't say newspapers to the Admiral. He hates any sort of cheap publicity. You must have noticed there's not a single correspondent or photographer on board his ship. They're all over on the *Knoxville* and quite upset about the Admiral not talking to them. There's nothing anybody—even Cincpac—can do about his poor relations with the press."

At 1558 that afternoon I was waiting in the wings, and at a signal from Cook, strode on stage. He presented me to the Admiral, whom I saluted without, as I had been known to do, sticking my thumb in my eye. The Admiral waved a hand vaguely at his forehead and stared over my left shoulder, giving me the impression I still was nonexistent.

"Ee-la-bo-rumpf," I thought he said.

"Yes sir!" I did a few fancy skips to get in step with him as he charged across the deck.

"An-a-da-rooo?" It sounded like a question.

"Yes sir!"

"Where?" he asked distinctly.

"Where, sir?"

"Yes, where did you have this photographic studio?"

"Oh," I lied, "in my native Biloxi, Mississippi."

"You don't talk like anybody I ever heard from Mississippi."

"Well, sir, I guess the Army scared it out of me."

"Oh, yes." He shook his head slightly. "Army—dreadful—terrible—awful. What became of your little photographic studio after you —uh—marched off to war?"

I explained that I'd left it in charge of my dear wife Josephine, who didn't really know a flash bulb from a lens and who was waging a losing battle to prevent the shop from falling into the hands of evil, draft-dodging creditors. The Admiral winced visibly, as if winged by shrapnel, and quickly changed the subject so that I knew I somehow had stumbled out of matters Cook would have called neutral. He began to talk about camera technicalities, a subject on which he was very well informed, and to ask my opinions.

Suddenly he asked, "Lieutenant Bobdick, why do you think it is that various photographers can take pictures of the same person and every one make him look different?"

My answer was not spontaneous. The notion had come to me one time when I was drinking at a bar in Honolulu and it had troubled me now and then since. I said it seemed to me a kind of ethnic thing.

"If an Italian takes your picture, he'll make you look slightly Italian, German the same. When an Englishman takes a picture of a Frenchman, he makes him look English. Jewish photographer? All their subjects look Jewish. I even know a good Negro photographer who somehow and perfectly unconsciously thickens the lips and noses of his subjects. He can make a pure Anglo-Saxon appear to have a trace of black blood."

"Yes, yes, yes! What a fascinating idea!" The Admiral sounded as excited as it's possible for one wearing three stars to be. "You must ride back to Pearl Harbor with us, and we'll talk about photography along the way."

It was more than three weeks before the *Newark* returned to Pearl. During that time I did not buddy it up again with the Admiral, who was preoccupied with his own seclusion and what no doubt were intricate matters of tactics and strategy.

Neither did I have more than a word or two further with Cook, who gave me back my horror prints of combat and said that the Admiral simply refused to look at them. I had been of what use Cook could make of me, and now, so to speak, he had put me in reserve. I begged him to try to find out what had become of D Company, and he said he would, but when I checked later at the communications center, there was no record of messages sent or received on the subject, and a snotty lieutenant told me, "Look, man, this isn't the radiogram office of a cruise ship—we've got *important* things to do."

It's as boring to be unemployed on a busy big warship as in a small back-country town. Gibbons remained my only translator of what was transpiring, and sometimes his reports were confusing. When we took up an ocean station, Gibbons said that The Atoll had been captured and we were waiting for some command decision that even he could not divine. We rolled in bright sunlight with numerous ships about us at a respectful distance one from another while patrolling planes and submarines made us feel secure from all danger.

I was on the afterdeck talking to a couple of crewmen that afternoon when an LST came in view making a course that would pass about a thousand yards to our port side. We were speculating over how such a cumbersome vessel could survive Pacific storms when a destroyer came plunging from the opposite direction. The two appeared to have the entire ocean in which to pass each other. Suddenly they crashed, bows-on, with a sickening ripping, and equipment flew up from both vessels in a kind of slow motion.

It was like two trains racing at each other after a switch had failed. The LST sank quickly while the destroyer remained feebly afloat like a wounded bird. Rescue operations took the rest of the afternoon, and the accident was a topic of conversation in the fleet for days.

I became weary with the argued merits of who was innocent, who guilty, but I was not allowed to forget it because it was my misfortune to have the rescued skipper of the LST assigned to the bunk beneath mine. He was a tall, good-looking reserve lieutenant commander named Gregory Bonham, who had survived the accident in the flesh only; in spirit he had become deeply disturbed. All day long he talked about his innocence until everyone fled at the mere sight of him; at night, whenever he fell asleep for a few minutes, he ground his teeth. Both day and night I avoided him as much as possible and took to napping in odd corners at odd moments like a cat.

A large ensign named Timmons who had starred at football for one of the Big Ten Conference teams and now served in the *Newark*'s engine room, tossed on the bottom bunk beneath Bonham. "Listen," he said forthrightly to Bonham one day when all of us were steaming in our bunks, "look at it this way. Even if they bust you to ensign, you're going to spend weeks in Hawaii while they fool around about the court of inquiry. All that time you can have fun getting all the ass you want."

"But I can't," Bonham said despondently, "because my wife's in Hawaii."

Timmons sat up so suddenly that he bumped his head on the bottom of Bonham's bunk while I looked over the side of mine to see if the man had at last irrevocably lost his mind.

"In many ways she's a fine woman," Bonham went on, "but she's just not a good piece of tail. Too shy and reserved. Even so, I made sure she didn't play around while I was away. When I sailed from Pearl, I took her diaphragm with me."

Timmons, holding his bumped head, got out of his bunk with a dazed expression and said, "Let me look at it. It'd do my soul good just to *see* one."

"Don't have it any more," Bonham said. "It went down with my ship."

Timmons swore. "When you get back without your wife's diaphragm, what's to prevent her from getting pregnant?"

"*I* am," Bonham said. "Haven't you heard of—of whatchamacallit?"

"Buggery?" Timmons asked helpfully.

"No, no—continence. I'm not going to sleep with Ruth any more. I don't even want to."

"My God!" Timmons exclaimed. "Did that accident leave you impotent?"

"No, no, I'm potent enough. But I'm in the mood for a more exciting piece of ass than Ruth can offer. When we sail into Pearl I'm not even going to let her know I'm back right away. I'm going to sniff around and see if I can't have a little fun before I go home."

Even though I avoided Bonham, I felt sorry for him, but did not intend to take a hand in his personal problems. During the year I'd been away from Hawaii I had changed in ways I did not at first fully realize. I had developed a tendency to be more concerned about my own welfare. Of course I still cared about my friends, but to my grief I'd discovered how little I could do to help others.

What, for instance, could I have done to save the lives of Lincoln, Yaromski, Cherokee? They lingered in my thoughts as vividly as if I had just passed them on the deck of this warship. Having long since given up Basset, I had only two close friends remaining in the Pacific —Red and Goldman, whom I remembered often. Yet what could I do for them? I could not help Red realize his ambition to go to flight school. I could not arrange a military job for Goldman that was worthy of his intellect.

That flashing blade Boswick had become a bit nicked from wear. Once I would have invited a half-dozen of my shipmates to come enjoy the women in Waikiki, but now I felt that would be pandering. Subtly I let only Gibbons know that there was expensive pleasure to be bought out near Diamond Head, and he replied less subtly:

"Thank you, comrade, but no. Sex is all in the mind, you know. And it's in my mind that most of its pleasure is in the search-out and selection by two partners where there is no exchange of coin."

I would not forget his remark. I had begun to think I was polyga-
mous because I'd not found reason to be otherwise. But I wondered
if I could establish a satisfying relationship with a woman whether I
might become as lastingly monogamous as many men. But how to
find that special woman? As my grandmother, who was not so sappy
after all, wrote me once: "You can't marry somebody you don't
know." (She also was the author of: "How do I know what I'm
thinking till I hear what I say?")

The *Newark* berthed at Pearl one afternoon, and by early evening
Gibbons and I were standing at a packed bar where we had to shout
to be heard. I plied him with drinks in slight reciprocation for his
many kindnesses to me at sea. Gibbons shouted that the flag lieutenant had said just an hour ago that Cook had made an all-out pitch
for promotion with the Admiral, but the Admiral had told him flatly
he would not antagonize Cincpac and Cominch with another request.
So Cook had told him as flatly that he was requesting transfer back
to the planning board in Washington, where he could enjoy his
family.

And then Bonham worked his way to us at the bar. He was horribly
drunk, so drunk that I hoped he would not recognize us. His jaw
appeared to have come unhinged and his eyes might have popped out
of their sockets if not held in by firmly slitted lids, but—unfortunately
—he recognized us and lurched through the crowd.

"She's gone!" he bellowed in a voice that stilled all conversation
in the room. "Ran out on me! Nobody knows where, goddam her!"

He sobbed and stumbled off through the crowd.

Early next morning I went to Army headquarters with a letter Cook
had signed that explained I'd been on detached fleet duty. There I
tried to learn the whereabouts of D Company, but they didn't even
attempt to check, they just sent me to the officers' replacement pool
at Hickam Field because my basic branch was Air Force.

After hesitating for reasons I did not fully understand, I phoned
Vera.

"Boz! Are you all right? Orvie says you went psycho after a terrible battle."

"Orvie's the one who is psycho. How are things?"

"I'd like to talk to you," she said. "Just social. It's only ten-thirty
in the morning and everybody but me and Lulu and the day maid are
still asleep. Can you shoot out here now?"

I took everything of value with me, since signs warning of thieves
were posted around the BOQ, and arrived in half an hour at Vera's

new palace. Lulu let me in, and Vera and I kissed in our brother and sister fashion.

"You look great, Vera. And what a mansion. I remember when you were just a small cottage industry and suddenly you've grown into U.S. Steel."

She introduced Lulu: "Working her way through Radcliffe." Lulu rolled lovely dark eyes: "Yesterday a lowly intern. Today a full-fledged resident. Tomorrow a college freshman."

Vera and I went to her private quarters, where a maid brought us coffee and pastry while I recounted some of the things that had happened and explained I didn't know what had become of Red, Goldman and Fiddler. When I told her about the scene between Red and Orvie, she begged me not to mention it to Rosemarie. I said I wouldn't think of doing such a stupid thing.

"I'm really glad it happened," Vera said. "That should make Red get over any notion he had of their reconciling. I wish you didn't have to mention him at all when Rosemarie asks you about him, as she's bound to. She gets upset whenever she thinks about him, and that's no good for her—or for business. Last time she got moody about him I thought she was going to quit. And I can't afford to lose her."

I realized that I had indeed changed. I used to be amused by Vera's greed, but now I found it quite unsettling.

"Bear in mind, Boz, that Rosemarie doesn't know Red tried to contact her through the Red Cross." Vera smiled. "The volunteer worker who came looking for her is now—uh, on the staff. In fact, she's living in. Her name is Ruth. I think you'd enjoy her."

Ruth is not an unusual name, but I inquired if her last name were Bonham. Vera was as surprised as I at the coincidence: "Thank heavens you let me know. I'll make sure that no lieutenant commander named Gregory gets an appointment here." I asked if she didn't want Ruth to know her husband was back from sea duty. "Of course I don't want her to know," Vera said. "She's an invaluable addition and is very happy. She doesn't give a damn about her husband. Fact is, Boz, I've decided there's hardly a woman alive loves her husband—and vice versa—and even those who do, need only one opportunity to be unfaithful to 'em." I put up a struggle on Bonham's behalf. It seemed cruel and excessive punishment that the poor guy should both lose his wife and face a court of inquiry about the collision at the same time.

But Vera said, "No, sir—N-O, Boz, I'm not going to run the risk of losing Ruth. We've made a kind of contract together and I've put her on salary. Why don't I set you up with her for this afternoon? I'd enjoy being with you myself, but I have real estate appointments all afternoon and into the evening. I hope to buy ten acres more at a really good price. I know Rosemarie likes you, but then you have this thing about her being married to your friend, so—''

She could not understand why I would not make an appointment with Ruth just because I'd met her husband, so I changed the subject and berated Fiddler/Basset: "Red and Goldman and I had every faith in him, but he never tried to get us out of the mess he put us in.''

"Maybe he couldn't do anything." Her gaze lost mine. "I always could talk better to you, Boz, than anybody else—except him. He's in Washington." She described his visit in great detail and told me they corresponded secretly. "Nobody else except you and Goldman knows he's really Fiddler. I think I'm in love with him. Imagine! Can you give me a single good reason why?''

I answered that one easily: "You two are irrevocably separated forever, so it's perfectly safe for you to be in love with him. There's not the slightest danger of his ever interfering in your life.''

Fiddler himself could not have made a platitude sound more imaginative and penetrating.

Rosemarie, hearing from Lulu that I was there, burst in with a delighted cry. She wore a bathrobe and revealed none of the fatigue signs that women are said to show from continual night work. Fresh from sleep, she had a rare quality of maidenly innocence. Her voice was girlish, her breath as sweet as clover when she flung her arms about me.

"Boz, honey, you don't look at all like that stupid Orvie said. What about Red? Orvie knew nothing about him.''

I won the struggle not to show the passion I suddenly felt and the desire to crush her in my arms. I acted fraternal—paternal—however it is that you're supposed to act with the wife of your best friend. Red was all right, I said.

"I'm glad to hear that." She poured herself some coffee. "I wish him well, I really do, but we were just never meant for each other. I'm going to divorce him soon as I can." She curled up next to me on the sofa. "If he'd ever wanted to get in touch with me after I wrote him, he could have found a way. But he didn't even try. I'll bet he's found a home in the Army. He's just that shiftless.''

Vera gave a little smile, as if to say that she had Rosemarie well in control and Rosemarie appeared to be getting me in control, and so all was well. She left to dress for her business appointments.

As Vera closed the door on us, Rosemarie said, "Truly, Boz, I've missed you like I never did Red. Tell me what you've been doing." Her right hand touched my knee and her fingers absently traced a pattern there.

I wanted to tell her to stop, but I didn't even move my knee. Instead of putting an arm around her, I sat and suffered, as I never would have done in the old days.

Suddenly I had a seizure of seriousness. I was disgusted with Vera for her greed and angry with Rosemarie for not understanding Red.

"You have no idea how much Red has suffered," I told her with the thought that she must suffer too for having deserted him.

She was such an amenable woman that she wanted to comply with my wish to feel guilty. Ceasing to toy with my knee, she asked me to describe his suffering.

I told her about Guadalcanal and the hospital and The Atoll, carrying on about pain and loneliness until I manipulated her emotions as cleverly as in the past I had roused her sexual feelings.

Soon I had her in tears, and she said brokenly, "Oh, Boz, I know it's all my fault Red was shipped off and suffered so." But then, strong woman that she was, she blinked at her tears and said, "Maybe it wasn't really as bad for him as you make it sound."

"It was even worse," I said. "Let me show you." I got the pictures from the bag I'd brought along and began showing her my shots of the invasion. "There's Red driving the LVT. Look at his expression. . . ."

Soon she started to tremble.

"That's Yaromski—what's left of him—Red's close friend. He's the sergeant came to the bungalow the day Red began swinging at Goldman—"

"And I was the one sent him off—" Her voice shook and died.

"This is Red setting off a grenade that silenced a bunker."

Why was I punishing her so severely? I think I was trying to push her back to Red.

"This kid—"

"*Stop it!*" She swung to her feet, hands raised to her eyes, and screamed piercingly. I thought her scream would bring everyone running, not realizing that Vera had had the walls of the place sound-proofed. "Boz—I—just—can't—take—any—more!" Her words were barely coherent through racking sobs.

I was penitent. Rosemarie clung to me; if I had not supported her, she might have fallen. At last she grew calmer and raised her tearful face to mine.

"I understand, Boz. I understand you don't want to—be with me because of him. That's the most wonderful thing I've ever heard of. That's the way *I* am going to be."

She said it with such conviction that I believed her. She left the room, and I gathered up my pictures and went out too. Lulu, the perfect receptionist, sat there reading a fat book.

"What's the matter with Rosemarie?" she asked. I shrugged. "Did you make an appointment with her or Vera?" I shook my head. "Anything wrong, Boz?"

"Quite a bit, apparently, but I don't think this clinic can fix me up. What's that book you're reading?" She held it up, and I saw it was Spengler's *Decline of the West*. "Let me know how it ends," I said, and left.

I went back to the bachelor officers' quarters at Hickam because I couldn't think of anywhere else to go.

A sergeant sitting on my bunk sprang to his feet as I approached and babbled, "Lieutenant Boswick? Lieutenant Boswick?" I wondered what I had done *now*. "Lieutenant Boswick, they're looking everywhere for you! You're supposed to come with me right away to the commanding general's office. You've been awarded the Distinguished Service Cross for extraordinary heroism in combat."

21

Despite the fuss about getting me quickly to the commanding general's office, there was only delay when I arrived at headquarters.

A warrant officer reading a magazine told me to wait. I was convinced there had been a mistake, that the true hero would arrive at any moment and they'd send me back to the barracks. Of course I remembered the Marine colonel who had mistakenly praised me at The Atoll, but I did not see how his commending me could have led to the Distinguished Service Cross. After a while I asked the warrant officer, "Which medal are you talking about?"

"The second from the top." He sounded bored. "The top is the Congressional. And then comes this one. I suppose you feel you don't deserve it."

"That's right, I don't deserve it."

"All you damn heroes are so damn modest," he said. "The delay is that the General is arguing with Cincpac over making it the Congressional for you. It's not that he necessarily feels you deserve the Congressional, it's just he feels the *Army* deserves one. All this long time the war's been going on in the Pacific and they're handing out Congressionals to Navy and Marine people like popcorn at the ball park, but there's not been a single one to the Army. That makes the General look bad."

A bald, fat colonel came along, looked at me, and asked, "Is this the one?"

"Yes sir, this is—um—er—Boswick."

"Nice to meet you, Boswick." He shook my hand genially. "I'm Plover. Well, the General has lost another round to Cincpac. You don't get the Congressional, Boswick. You get the Distinguished Service Cross. The trouble is they can't find one. The General has sent men out looking for one so he can pin it on you." Plover studied me as if I were a horse he might buy. "You'll do, son. You're photogenic enough. You'll fit the package."

"The package, sir?"

"Yes," Plover said. "I'm WDGS and we're putting together a package of medal-winners for the Treasury Department. A bond tour in the States. As things stand now, I'll have two heroes from the European Theater and two from the Pacific. Nice duty, eh?"

"Yes *sir*."

"What ribbons do you have?"

"The Pacific—I'm due three stars on it—and the Purple Heart."

"Well, now, I'll tell you, Boswick, you've got to have more ribbons than that if you're going to make a hit on our bond tour. The General wants you back here at 1800, so I'll tell you what you do. I'll give you written authorization and have you driven to the PX to pick up a Silver Star ribbon and a Bronze Star ribbon and while you're about it you might as well get a Good Conduct too. You have authorization to wear these extra ribbons only during the tour. Let's see, that will make six, counting your Distinguished Service, and then everybody can wear the American Defense ribbon. Oh yes, have you heard of El Salvador?"

"Vaguely. A little country down Latin American way."

"Yes. Well, El Salvador wants to give what we call its Matching Medal to every American serviceman who wins the Silver Star or better. Guess they think it'll help their tourist trade after the war. Very handsome ribbon. Looks like a flaming prick. Now, I don't know where you got that Air Force insignia you're wearing, but for the purposes of our tour you're supposed to be Infantry. Pick yourself up some crossed rifles while you're at the PX and get yourself some better-fitting suntans. Be back here at 1800 sharp."

I thought of something. "Colonel Plover, if you're putting together a package, have you thought it would be good to have a Jewish war hero in it?"

He stared at me. "Yes, I've thought of that. It would be especially helpful, Treasury says, when it comes to selling bonds in the New York City and Miami areas. I had one being flown in from the European Theater, but the son of a gun went and got himself killed before I could land him. Do you have someone in mind?''

I told him about Goldman in glowing terms and even showed him a picture of his back as he led the charge onto The Atoll. Plover, enthusiastic, had the warrant officer take down Goldman's name and outfit and then send off an urgent message for him to come at once. Next I asked Plover if he didn't need a Sergeant York hillbilly type, and he replied, ''Give me another Sergeant York and I can raise fifty million bucks for the war effort.'' So I manufactured a great hero and Kentucky wisecracker, Sergeant Andrew Jackson Jack.

Plover said, ''He'd fit perfectly into the script I have in mind.'' He had Warrant add Red's name to the urgent message, and then asked to see the rest of my photos. Not a career officer but a wartime import from Broadway, Plover had a theatrical sense of give and take. That is, he never wanted to give anything without taking something in return. Having given me extra medals (even though temporarily) and having invited my friends to embark on a Stateside pleasure tour with me, he asked for my invasion pictures with this candid explanation: ''I want my superiors in Washington to see what I've been through during my three-week tour here in the Pacific.'' I was glad to give him the prints. I still had the negatives.

I picked up the stuff at the PX and had the driver take me back to the barracks so that I could spruce up. This time there was a corporal sitting on my bunk. ''Lieutenant,'' he said in a quavering adolescent voice, ''your wife is waiting for you in the company office.''

There are some benefits to the military experience. You learn, for instance, to accept the impossible with a smile and a shrug.

It might somehow be to my advantage to have a wife.

I went to the office and there sat Rosemarie surrounded by about twenty officers and enlisted men who had appeared on one pretext or another just to look at her or even try to exchange a few words. When she saw me, she cried, ''Boz!'' and rushed to me, flung her arms about me, and burst into tears.

''Gentlemen!'' I said to the assembled multitude. ''Please! Is there no private place where I can speak to her?''

The most private proved to be out in the hot, sandy barracks area where I asked her, ''What in the hell is this all about?''

''Please, Boz, you've got to help me. You're the only one can. I know you will, you're smart enough to do it somehow. I've left Vera's forever. I want to go back to California and never see Hawaii again. I drew my savings out of the bank. There's a certified check here in my bag for over thirty-five thousand. But no matter how much money I've got, there's no way I can get home from Hawaii except as a serviceman's dependent. Will you help me?''

Of course I would try. "Why are you doing this? Does Vera know?''

"Vera doesn't know anything. I left a note she can read when she comes back this evening. I'm doing it because I'm ashamed of what I've been. If I was a Catholic, I'd become a nun. There aren't any Protestant nuns, are there?''

"Millions of 'em, not all by their own choosing. Is what I told you about Red what's making you do this?''

"Yes. I'm going to learn to love him again. I want to be worthy of him. I'm going to get a job on an assembly line or something in California and live like a nun and wait for him.''

Plover was not the only one who could write scenarios. I was making up a very good one while I talked to Rosemarie: Red and Goldman would be flying to Hawaii within a day or two; Red and Rosemarie would be gloriously reunited; then all of us would fly to the mainland, where Goldman could have a happy reunion with his family. What a wonderful ending to our travail. All that this stunning scenario of mine required was the total cooperation of everyone.

"Where's your luggage?" I asked Rosemarie.

"In that office where all those men are. I came to Hawaii in two bags and I'm leaving with two. Only they're much better bags than the ones I came with and the clothing in them is a lot better too.''

I left her in the office while I put on uniform and ribbons. Then I took her and her luggage in the sedan back to headquarters. On the way she said the men in the office had told her I was to receive the Distinguished Service Cross.

"Red deserves it far more. So does Ira," I said.

"You generous dear." She squeezed my hand and sat closer to me and I wished there was a kind way to tell her to stop doing things like that.

When we came to the warrant officer's desk, he got to his feet with an amazed look and pointed wordlessly at Rosemarie. I introduced my wife, and Warrant tripped over a wastebasket and nearly fell down as he went to fetch Plover. When Rosemarie offered him her warmest smile, Plover said, "Boswick, you never told me.''

"You never asked, Colonel. Rosemarie has been working as a hairdresser here while I was"—I waved vaguely—"out there. I want to arrange transportation home to California for her.''

"My dear"—Plover kept patting her shoulder—"your priority will be the highest. I see a change in my script, Boswick. Your wife must accompany us on the tour. One beautiful woman is better than a thousand medals when it comes to selling bonds."

I suddenly foresaw a problem with my own script and wondered how to revise it. When Red arrived to pick up his medal and join the road show, how could he be happily reunited with his wife if everyone thought she was married to me? That part would require a lot of reworking, I thought. I must somehow get to Red ahead of everyone else and persuade him that Rosemarie's and my relationship was perfectly innocent and I was doing all these things for everyone's good.

"The photographers and press are waiting," Plover said. "The public relations people are waiting. The General is almost ready. With you in the pictures, Rosemarie, they should get world-wide circulation."

She drew me aside in alarm. "Suppose the picture gets in the *Advertiser* and Vera sees it?"

"There's nothing she can do. Maybe there's nothing she *would* do."

Warrant disappeared, reappeared in an open doorway, and announced sonorously, "The General is waiting."

The General smiled at Rosemarie and paid scarcely any attention to me. He was so busy looking at her that when he pinned the medal on me, he pricked his finger, no doubt the only time he ever was wounded in action. Reporters asked Rosemarie and me a few questions which we answered vaguely. It was over quickly, and Plover said we must come to dinner with him and a couple of other officers.

Stopping at Warrant's desk, I asked if there was any answer yet to the urgent message concerning Red and Goldman.

"Damnedest thing," he said. "Goldman—it's Major Goldman now —must work for the toughest colonel ever. The man refuses to release him for promotional work. Says he's essential where he is. A field commander has the right to do that, of course, and the General won't overrule him."

I felt stunned, and Rosemarie asked, "Where is he now?"

"Back on Livau, rebuilding the battalion."

"What about Red—Sergeant Jack?"

"Sorry to report this," Warrant said. "Sergeant Jack has been missing since The Atoll and is now listed as dead."

Rosemarie started to weep, and I felt my eyes begin to sting. Tears had never been as handy as laughter to me, but I had not fully realized how fond I was of Red until I started to cry.

"Rather not go to dinner?" Plover asked sympathetically.

I thought that a good idea, but Rosemarie said, "We'd better go. It helps to forget things if you keep busy."

Plover and the others took us to the Royal Hawaiian, where everyone but Rosemarie drank too much, especially me. Plover provided a room for us at the hotel and helped me into the double bed I was to share with Rosemarie. ("Don't worry about the bill, it's on the Treasury Department.")

After he had gone and Rosemarie was starting her elaborate woman's ritual before going to bed, she said something that kept me awake a few seconds longer: "I know Red is dead, Boz. But there's something I can't take—even me, who can take anything. I cannot be widowed and married again on the same day."

Next morning I awakened to one of my famous hangovers. Rosemarie, who had phoned room service for coffee, sat wearing a flimsy negligee and reading a Gideon Bible.

"Now hear this from Revelation—" She sounded as if she were shouting through my headache— "*And the woman was arrayed in purple and scarlet color, and decked with gold and precious stones and pearls, having a golden cup in her hand full of abominations and filthiness of her fornication: And upon her forehead was a name written,* MYSTERY, BABYLON THE GREAT, THE MOTHER OF HARLOTS AND—"

The door burst open to admit room service, who turned out to be —instead of a gentle Hawaiian boy—a fierce-looking officer wearing only a peaked naval cap and jockstrap. Seeing and hearing Rosemarie reading the Bible, he blanched, set down the tray and fled.

"Boz, did you see that?" Rosemarie shrieked. *"They call that room service?"*

As I got up, made my way to the door and locked it, I reminded her that the Royal Hawaiian had become a rest center for fatigued submarine officers, one of whom obviously had seized our tray from the room-service boy. "Plover shouldn't have let you spend the night here."

"There's nothing to worry about," she said, "because I'm going to turn over a new leaf."

"I thought we already had."

"Yes, I have." She nodded vigorously. "And I'm indebted to you for starting me on the—the new leaf. Boz, you're such an honorable man. . . ." Her description of me as honorable, brave and good, though inaccurate, was pleasing to hear. "I don't know another man anywhere who would have just gone to sleep in that bed like a little child."

She went on, "I'm going to start all over again—be reborn again. And you're going to help me. Even though we're supposed to be married, we're not going to—you know what I mean. I want to let a decent amount of time pass after Red's death before we—I want to be— What's the word, Boz, I want to be?"

I did not know. As it had occurred to me before, I wished that hotels would provide their guests with dictionaries instead of Bibles. It turned out that she wanted to be chaste, not *chased:* to be pure in thought and act, free from all taint of what is lewd or salacious. My grim report on the precise nature of chastity enchanted her. To be both hung over and locked in a hotel room with such a gorgeous but chaste woman seemed unjust punishment for any crimes I had committed. So the old Boz was not dead altogether.

Rosemarie was perfectly serious about it. Something extraordinary was happening to her. Rosemarie had hit on the quaint notion of chastity to make her feel loyal to Red's memory, even though she had not been loyal when he was alive. At the same time, I suppose she thought it made her relationship with me more interesting.

If I had been a knight and Rosemarie anything like a lady, the trial of honor that began that very day would truly have made history.

Plover assembled his heroes in the afternoon—me, accompanied by Rosemarie, and a seaman named Slattery, all that he had been able to dredge up from the Pacific—and led us aboard a C-54 which winged into the darkness toward San Francisco. Slattery, unlike me, was an authentic hero who had done something insane like wrestling a live torpedo away from his ship off New Guinea and justly earned the Congressional. He was a dumpy little guy with a sad face who sat and looked at Rosemarie all the time but was too shy to mumble even a word or two to her.

Rosemarie had obtained WAC slacks and shirt which were so tight-fitting that they seemed to have been sewn on her. She sat in a bucket seat between Plover and me. Plover rested a hand on her thigh whenever he wanted to speak to her—which was all of the time. Tired of being handled, she removed Plover's hand and rested her palm on my thigh in the cordial, proprietary manner of the happily married cou-

ple. Having her unhand him troubled Plover, but how did he think I
felt about her other-handing me?

"Please," I finally told her while the row of servicemen in bucket
seats opposite stared at us.

"I'm sorry," she said, taking her hand away. "I forgot."

"You forgot what?" asked Plover, grasping her leg to attract her
attention.

"That we're married," Rosemarie said, removing his hand again.

"What an odd thing to say," said Plover, folding his hands on his
paunch, while Slattery, on my other side, gave a sudden loud moan,
the only sound he uttered all the way to San Francisco.

The plan, as Plover never tired of informing us, was that all the
heroes—two from the Pacific and two from the Mediterranean—
would "rendezvous" in Los Angeles for a bond rally and then "sortie
out" on a four-week tour of twenty American cities.

After we landed at Hamilton Field from Hawaii, Rosemarie and I
were given a room near Plover's at the Officers' Guest House. Slattery was forbidden admittance because he was an enlisted man. (He
was agreeably understanding about it, and Plover made sure that he
got a lower bunk in a barracks.) After Rosemarie and I went to our
room to catch some sleep, we got into a regular marital spat.

She complained that I had winked at the pretty club receptionist
when she smiled at me. I replied that it was not easy being married to
a frigid virgin. For some reason she took that as a great compliment
and said she was only being faithful to Red's memory. I said he was
dead, and she asked, "What has that got to do with it?"

Obviously I'd lost an argument with my wife, who undressed in the
bathroom and had me do the same. Then we lay on our separate beds,
wakeful in bright daylight, and Rosemarie said maybe it would put us
to sleep if she talked about Red. Her voice piping childlike, she went
away back to their first meeting and discussed things he, too, had
described to me. From her viewpoint, some incidents sounded quite
different from the way I'd heard them from Red, although neither had
lied.

Far from putting me to sleep, Rosemarie's recital kept me wakeful
and sad. Why couldn't any of us remain loyal to one another instead
of being ruled by selfish instincts and desires?

When Rosemarie spoke of the last time she saw Red and hit him
with a golf club, her voice broke and she said, "It's like I myself sent
him to his death just because I got so mad at him breaking in that

way." I tried to reassure her that she was not guilty of any wrong, but she said, "Oh, yes, I am. It's all the wrong boiling around inside me most of the time that does the damage. It's so hard to forget and start again."

She wept silently. I felt an almost physical ache of sympathy for her. I went over to her bed, kissed her on the forehead and stroked her arm trying to comfort her. She raised her face and our lips met. "Oh, please, no," she said, but both her hands reached up and caressed my neck and head.

"Stop it," she said, and then responded to my kiss with her tongue. I still intended to stop, but found myself gently rubbing her nipples between thumb and forefinger. "Oh don't, dear," she whispered. "My God, it feels divine." She slipped the top of her nightgown off and raised her breasts toward me. I had some vague thought of revenge for her teasing me most of the way from Hawaii as I rolled her erect pink nipples and continued to kiss her deeply.

Turning her head abruptly, she gasped and said, "It's sensational, just tongue and tits, I never knew this before." She began moving her pelvis up and down. "I want to hump like I never did. Aren't you going to ball me now?" I said something about there not being any rush, and she said, "Yes, let's make it last forever."

22

After Red swam away from the hospital ship he found the still water of the lagoon pleasantly warm. Picking a fire on the distant beach as his destination, he swam toward it leisurely. Suddenly he heard the throb of a ship's engine and a shadow blotted out the fire on shore. In panic that the vessel would run him down, he began to thrash the water and yell loudly in order to attract attention.

It seemed that the darkened vessel would miss him by only a few feet. But then he was not sure. A voice bellowed on a deck above, and when something hit the water, he grabbed it—a life preserver attached to a line. He clung to the preserver, and was lifted out of the water.

"Where am I?" he demanded when he was hauled to the deck of the slowly moving vessel.

"Who are you?" was the reply.

"Sergeant Jack—Army. I was taking a swim." He was led into a lighted wardroom where a boatswain's mate looked at him suspiciously and asked. "Since when does an Army sergeant go swimming 'way out here?"

"If you want the truth," Red said, "I know a nurse on the hospital ship and went out to see her. We got caught, and I had to dive overboard."

The boatswain's mate grinned. "I can believe it. You're on the fleet tug *Athene*. We do double duty as a minesweeper. I'll take you to the bridge so the skipper can figure out what the hell to do with you.''

Lieutenant Commander Shimp, skipper of the *Athene*, was a dour forty-five-year-old who had spent his life in ocean salvage and was not fond of his present Navy employment. He had volunteered to serve as a salvage officer, but had spent most of the past two years laying useless mines in senseless places. He had just brought the *Athene* halfway round the world from the Mediterranean, only to sit in the lagoon of The Atoll to no good purpose. Shortly before Red was hauled aboard, Shimp had received orders that finally dispatched the *Athene* on a useful mission: to take under tow a torpedoed cruiser in the Coral Sea, fifteen hundred miles to the southwest, and bring her to Pearl Harbor.

"If you think," Shimp growled to Red, "I'm wasting time from a vital mission where every minute counts to put you on another ship, you're crazy. I think you're crazy anyway. I don't believe your story."

By that time they had passed out of the lagoon into the open sea. Astern the hospital ship, the only lighted vessel in the vicinity, was a fading glow.

"Sir, what kind of story would you believe?" Red asked.

"The true story." Shimp's face was reminiscent of a bulldog's; gazing at Red in the faint binnacle glow on the darkened bridge, he looked ferocious. "Any time you tell me the true story of what you were up to in that lagoon, I'll recognize it and believe it."

Red, though wet and cold, told him the true story at once.

"I believe you." Shimp questioned him at length about the invasion. "I'll radio a message about you, serial number and outfit and all, and ask my headquarters to put it through to your command. There's no counting on that the way the traffic is just now, but I'll try. We'll find ways to keep you busy the next few weeks till we put you ashore at Pearl."

Red hoped that the message went through. Otherwise, Goldman and Boz would think he had drowned in the lagoon. After all the three of them had been through, he felt it was very important to keep in touch. The friendship reminded him of Basset. What had become of him? Surely he was dead; otherwise, Red firmly believed, he would have tracked down his missing friends. And what had become of that recommendation to flight school which Basset had sent? Possibly Red had been accepted, and even now the acceptance was bobbing from command to command around the Pacific trying to catch up with him.

The crewmen were amused by the story Red had made up when Shimp wouldn't believe the *true* story about his being caught with a nurse. They relished the nurse story and never tired of Red's embellishments of it.

"Shimp is a pretty good guy," one said. "Completely fair and very able. He has only one weakness. He's religious. Southern Baptist. He doesn't drink or cuss or gamble or whore or lie or any of that. His trouble is he doesn't want to admit such things go on all the time. You just have to be tolerant of his weakness and shade the truth a little to suit him."

Although it was far from being pilot training school, Red tried to enjoy his new life. He stood a machinist's watch after Shimp recognized his skill, and absorbed himself in the specialized equipment of the big tug. The relatively shallow draft of the *Athene* made her a wallower, yet she showed dignity too as she ploughed along through azure seas at a steady twenty knots toward rendezvous with the cruiser.

There was plenty of work for machinists on the afterdeck, which looked like a mechanical wilderness to the uninitiated. Shimp began superintending a structural change there that had kept him arguing futilely with his superiors for more than a year.

Astride two tracks of mine-laying rails on the aft deck, forward of two rectangular scuppers in the stern coaming, stood two large depth-charge catapults. To no avail Shimp had been pointing out to his superiors that these catapults would restrict the free play of a hawser over the afterdeck, thereby making the *Athene* incapable of towing. The superiors replied: No dice; she had no towing mission anyway. Yes, Shimp said, *but isn't her primary mission towing?* Answer: The catapults are standard operating procedure. Shimp did his best to retain his Christian temper: *Yes, but not once have we been ordered to depth-charge, and furthermore we have no training with the catapults.* Answer: Get with it, Shimp, because the order will come some day.

Returning from his last official interview on the subject, Shimp had told the mess he had maintained control of his temper perfectly. To emphasize that point, he had brought his huge, powerful fist down so heavily that dishes crashed to the floor.

Now necessity had at last vindicated Shimp and let him take matters into his own hands. As the dismantling of the catapults proceeded, he went about whistling hymns and smiling to himself. All thirty-four members of the crew took pleasure in the project and felt it gave meaning to the tedious watches to know that even far out there aboard an obscure vessel on an empty ocean they could strike a blow for common sense against the foolish posturings of authority.

In two days the job was done and the dismantled catapults stowed below for future painting with red lead, but the job had been such a pleasure that all hands wished it might have taken longer.

However, the Navy weather station at Fanafuti reported that a tropical storm was moving southwestward from the Ellice Islands. Its erratic course behind the *Athene* was contrary to prevailing winds that Shimp predicted would turn it away. The next day, an Australia-bound convoy two hundred miles to the east reported being struck by a hurricane with winds of 130 knots. Shimp thought the wind velocity a transmission error; when his radioman requested confirmation, however, he could not raise a reply.

The chief engineer organized an elaborate betting pool from which he was the only one certain to profit since he charged all participants a dollar entry fee. The grand winner was the one to come closest to picking the hour they would reach a precise longitude beyond the New Hebrides, reputed to be shunned by tropical storms. The chief engineer's pool was the central feature of so many complicated side bets that Shimp complained his vessel was being turned into a floating casino. Nevertheless, he too must have believed that there was safety west of the Hebrides, for he stayed on the bridge most of the night coaxing the utmost speed from the *Athene.*

An hour before dawn they were less than one hundred miles from their passage through the islands—a favorite with mariners because it offered open water forty miles in width between Runda Island on the north and Baka to the south. Dawn fizzled, its light dying almost as soon as it was born. In the night the wind had lapsed to dead calm, but by morning it was reborn as a gale from the northeast.

Red, standing the eight o'clock watch, saw ghostly shadows flitting in the feeble light. He sniffed something different from anything he had known in the Pacific: a fresh odor like rain over an inland American lake rather than the stark salt smell of rain at sea. The ocean churned like a whirlpool, and when he went toward the ladder to the bridge he felt like an infant learning to walk.

His machinist's duty on that watch was in the large wheelhouse of the wide bridge where Shimp had decided he wanted all pipelines doubly insulated. But by the time Red was ready to start on the job the sea was running as he had never imagined it could. Mountainous dark waves rose like a wall, crashing against the bow and drowning out all other sounds with its thunder. Insulation work was out of the question in that tumult, but the officers in the wheelhouse were too preoccupied to tell Red to knock off and go below. Wedging himself out of the way in a corner, he watched with fear and fascination.

Shimp reduced speed and took the big wheel himself. Ocean and sky gradually merged into a solid gray, and the *Athene*'s sturdy bow disappeared in a white explosion; water boiled across the foredeck and spray struck the wheelhouse glass like birdshot. The anemometer showed wind rising toward a hundred knots and they ran west before it in the hope that the rolling sea would not swamp them.

Slowly the claustrophobic darkness began to lighten, but the wind continued to buffet the *Athene*. Above, the sky turned blue, with frantic white clouds scudding just overhead. The sun cast an eerie light that glittered like ice on the huge walls of black water that seemed to hang perpetually over their stern. Gradually, the *Athene* became almost weightless, as light and buoyant as a racing yacht, and then she began to surf crazily across the frenzied sea.

Shimp, giving up the wheel, tried to make calculations. They were hurtling at passenger-train speed toward the channel forty miles wide which would take them into the Coral Sea. But any radical change in their wind-driven course would destroy them on the rugged shores of one of the islands. Shimp's calculations as he studied the chart could not be much better than guesswork. He closed his eyes, as if deep in thought, but when Red saw his lips moving, he realized that the Captain was praying. When he opened his eyes, his expression had become serene.

Red longed for some religious faith himself. But even then, though badly frightened and fervently wanting to believe in a merciful God, he could not imagine the existence of a benign, supernatural intelligence.

Shimp shouted to the radar man above the sound of the storm that he figured a land mass should appear on the scope. The radar man cried, "Nothing shows! Absolutely nothing!"

Shimp chose to ignore the probability that the radar had failed. "Well, I guess that's good. It's when that thing shows a windward shore that I get worried."

Half an hour later the anemometer dropped suddenly. All watched in amazement as it plunged to the zero of dead calm. It took everyone, even Shimp, a moment to realize that the hurricane had not abated but had torn away the recording equipment from the roof of the wheelhouse. To Red the wind sounded like a perpetual shrieking cry: *Mo—ther . . . Ma—ma . . .*

Beneath the thrumming of shrouds and guys, the *Athene* replied with notes of deeper protest, a resonance compounded of all the outrages committed by wind and sea against decks, bulkheads, superstructures, walls. Far below, the engine at low speed throbbed like an unfailing heart.

Suddenly the deck officer uttered a cry and pointed to starboard. Through a rent in the opaque sky, they saw treacherously near, a jungle-clad mountain soaring high above them. The view lasted not five seconds before the wind fiercely stitched together the rip in the overcast.

At first Red felt a sudden joy: there was dry land somewhere after all. They were among the coral-fringed islands of splendid volcanoes which he had seen long ago with the coastwatcher on his flight toward Guadalcanal. But his pleasure was soon dispelled by the stricken faces of the seamen. The radar man became hysterical. They had just seen a mountain, yet the wonderful invention in his charge showed not a trace of land.

Shimp kept calm. He ordered all hands aboard the vessel to don life vests and prepare to abandon ship. He asked for increased speed, then he and the deck officer and the enlisted helmsman began to struggle with the big wheel, as if brute strength could wrench them away from disaster.

They were at the mercy of chance—or God. For they could not tell if they were skimming safely through the passage or charging to destruction on the coral of a windward coast. In trying to deflect the *Athene* from her willy-nilly gallop, Shimp might be taking them to their deaths.

The radar man shouted that no mountain such as they had seen showed on either the chart or the screen. Shimp said he knew that. He calmly explained that the sketched land masses on either side of the charted passage were merely impressionistic, and lacked precise geographical detail.

Midday passed unnoticed. In the eighth hour of battling the storm, Shimp gave a yell. He did not release the wheel, but bobbed his head at a blinding glare of sunlight that suddenly flashed above their bow. In the glare they made out a soaring mountain, perhaps the same they'd seen before, perhaps another. The hole in the clouds closed as suddenly as it had opened, and in that instant a gigantic wave lifted the *Athene* like a chip and spun her half around. For what seemed a breathless eternity, they hung on the crest of a steep mountain of water and peered, horrified, down to what looked like the coral bottom of the ocean. Then, yawing and bucking, the *Athene* pitched down the greasy-looking slant at roller-coaster speed.

Red had strange glimpses of incomprehensible fragments of events. The tug's longboat was not wrenched from its davits; it simply sailed into the air, davits and all, snatched away by superhuman strength. Then something else disappeared by weird magic. A big crate of paint had been lashed securely to the deck; mistakenly consigned to the *Athene* as red lead, it had turned out to be bright vermilion. Shimp had kept it anyhow, maintaining it could be put to good use eventually. Now it was gone, as mysteriously as the longboat.

Suddenly the radar man shrieked, flung open the starboard door and disappeared. Perhaps he had seen something that Red had not, perhaps there had been an order to abandon that Red had not heard. Somehow, Red followed him. He never knew if the wind plucked him up and flung him as it had the longboat and crate of paint. He could not tell. The *Athene* disappeared in one direction, he went in another.

Wearing his inflated life vest, he found himself on a canyon bottom between towering, quaking walls of water. Propelled upward with projectile force, he spun on the crest of a wave. Ahead and below he glimpsed straining palm trees bending and snapping before the savage wind as the huge wave sped him toward shore.

He struggled to keep his head above water, but it was useless, and the mighty sea mauled him, sucked him under and popped him into the air like a wet seed, then tumbled him onward. Vaguely he remembered hearing it was not the forward rush of water but its backwash that was the most dangerous. But his attempts to keep up with the wave were futile. He could not hold his head above water, and knew this was the end.

He had the illusion of flying while buffeted by matters large and small—water, wind, land, growing things. There was a loud sucking sound, as if an enormous tub had been drained suddenly.

In what seemed like a very long time, his eyes opened. The place where he lay, while not dry land, was at least muddy. His life vest was gone, his dog tags were gone, his clothing had disappeared mysteriously. With a supreme effort he picked up his bruised, aching body and made himself push, drag, and scramble up a slant of land through a deadfall of brush and trees beyond the reach of waves. When no wave pursued him, he finally sank down and surrendered again to the comfort of unconsciousness.

Next he knew the sun was shining brightly in a blue, windless sky. Only the fallen and crushed trees indicated that there had been a hurricane.

He found that he was not totally naked; he still wore his socks and rubber-soled work shoes. Everything was strange, and weirdest of all was the dead silence. There was no sound of bird or insect, of wind or the sea, as if the world was pausing for a moment of rest before it began again to bring about life.

He got to his feet, testing the parts of his body and finding everything so painful that he wished he could depart from it and wander on as simple spirit. His thirst was excruciating and made worse by a glimpse of the flashing, turquoise, salty sea through the deadfall. Stumbling amid the fallen palms, he found a coconut broken out of its husk and then a loose chunk of coral. By dint of repeated blows he smashed open the coconut on the coral and drank its liquid, but the white meat scarcely yielded to his gnawing. He wandered toward the sea because it was the easiest way to go, perplexed: how had Tarzan happened to possess such essentials as a sharp knife? Burroughs must have explained it, but now Red could not remember the explanation. Was he going mad?

Thinking that a human voice would be reassuring, he tried his own. All that came was a distant, faint croaking. Something else strange: the waves made no sound as they struck the shore. He had become deaf!

As he picked his way along a narrow beach he looked for the wreckage of the *Athene,* but saw not a trace of her. Could the wreckage be somewhere behind him? Was he creeping toward aid—or away from it? The sea was as empty of life as the land. His pleasure at being alive gave way to growing fear as the sky clouded in a rising wind and he no longer could make out the peak of the mountain around whose lower reaches he crawled like an ant around a pyramid.

He was becoming chilled. He thought about finding shelter for the night and cracking a supper of coconuts when he saw what looked like wreckage in the tidemarks ahead. Hurrying on, he made out a large, damaged crate. His imagination ran riot over what it might contain: a dry feather bed, jars of caviar complete with opener, twelve dozen bottles of Coca-Cola. Maybe it contained his acceptance to flight school.

Wading into the shallows, he tugged at the crate. It was so heavy he could not understand how it had floated ashore. Since it lacked markings, there was no way of knowing if it had come off the *Athene*. He tried to wrench off a broken panel. He could see that the crate contained cans. Thinking now of beef stew, apricots, pounds of cookies, and of the ingenuity necessary to break into a can when lacking an opener, he used a piece of coral to pry the loosened panel. His fingers closed around the end of a can, and he began to make mute sounds of idiotic joy.

Tugging frantically, he brought out a quart of Sherwin-Williams commercial paint. Red. Apparently he and it were the only survivors of the *Athene*.

Stupefied, he lifted up quart after quart of the paint. Among the cans were brushes of various sizes, all wet from the sea but usable. Tears of despair were stinging his eyes when he suddenly realized he was not alone.

A tall, strongly muscled black man carrying a spear and wearing only a breechcloth stood staring at him about fifty yards down the beach. His magnificent bush of kinky hair and the white lime patches across his cheekbones made him appear the wildest of savages.

Fear turned Red's body to ice and left him speechless. Nevertheless, he tried to speak. Making a wide and, he hoped, friendly gesture, he piped, ''Well, hi there, pardner.''

The savage remained motionless, his gaze smoldering with hostility.

Red, more frightened, decided to act boldly. Tilting back his head, he drummed his fists on his chest, then flung his arms wide toward the setting sun and uttered the finest Tarzan cry of his life.

The effort sent water running from his ears and restored his hearing as the savage leaped into the air and disappeared.

It was no hallucination. A man *had* been there and no doubt would return soon with others to capture and kill him. Cannibalism was still a way of life for remote peoples in the Pacific. Red had wanted to believe it when he'd read about it, but now he hoped the report had been mistaken.

Frightened so badly that he was shaking, he waded from the crate. He picked up a couple of coconuts on the shore, and lifted his head to see a dozen black men advancing toward him, slowly, spears ready. The one leading them was old, gray, unarmed. When he halted, the others bunched up behind him. He made a gesture Red could not have duplicated—part like a Catholic crossing himself, part like a courtier's bow, and all accomplished with great dignity.

His tone, when he spoke, had dignity too, though the words—in the Bêche de Mer, or pidgin, of Melanesia—sounded a mix of Uncle Tom and a grotesquerie of how movie-makers imagined savages should talk to the mass audience:

"Massa come a fella from a big a wind?"

His gestures made the words intelligible to Red. Yes, he replied, trying to speak in pidgin, he had been cast up by the storm. One of the young men spoke to the elder in their own tongue, and then the elder said something that Red did not comprehend. But on a second attempt he understood they wanted to hear his Tarzan cry.

He did it even more dramatically than before, and they were deeply impressed. Instead of being simply entertained, they found it highly significant somehow, for all bowed low to him and their latent hostility turned to respect.

The elder asked if he was hungry; and when he replied yes, he was handed something wrapped in banana leaves: a piece of cold taro, a starchy root vegetable with a pleasing flavor which was a staple of the Melanesian diet. After thanking them and eating some, Red recalled he had read that basic good manners among so-called savage people involved an exchange of gifts. Yet he had nothing to offer— then recalled the crate of paint. Gesturing to the men like an orchestra leader bringing his musicians to attention, he waded to the crate and took out a can and small brush.

They squatted round him in a semicircle, watching raptly as he shook the can to homogenize the paint, took a machete from one of them, and pried off the lid. Their murmur of delight burst into a babble. One pointed from the paint to Red's hair. Another dipped a finger and licked it clean before Red could stop him; he pronounced the paint delicious by rubbing his stomach and rolling his eyes. Red was not sure he got across his point that it was poisonous. However, the elder seemed to grasp the nature of Red's gift when he dipped the brush in the can and daubed it through his hair.

Almost pandemonium ensued. Red thought the men's thick, black, frizzy hair handsome, but obviously they wanted it to look different, for all except the elder had tried to whiten theirs with wood ashes while the elder had smeared some kind of blacking on his gray—the very color that the younger seemed to be dying to emulate. The desire of these people to change their natural looks made them seem wholly human to Red.

As the men lugged the crate along the shore they made him understand that of course it was his and they meant only to preserve the valuable possession for him—rather like bankers entrusted with his money. They trudged on long after darkness fell, the men helping Red whenever he stumbled, until they came to a small fire which they built into a big blaze. It had been set in front of a low, thatched bamboo hut. Red made out a large fish net drying on the coral and saw that what he had thought at first were warriors' weapons were fishing spears; from these and the smell, it was apparent that fishing was the business of these people.

He made them understand that he wanted something to cover his nakedness, and they found a bit of coarse cloth which he wrapped around his loins. The elder introduced himself as Tata, and Red enunciated his own name carefully. The men kept repeating his name with fascination: "Red Jock! Red Joke! Red Jack!" They served him warm taro and delicious baked fish which he washed down with good cold water brought him in a gourd, then all lay down around the dying fire and fell asleep.

Red had been cast up on Runda, an island of the New Hebrides about forty miles long and twelve to fifteen wide. He had been found by the people of Paguli, southernmost of the dozen villages on the island. The village consisted of about four hundred inhabitants living on a three-mile coastline in a series of hamlets between the Coral Sea and the towering, inactive volcano around which Red had been trudging.

Eventually he learned that Runda had several of what anthropologists called main linguistic units, which meant that people living only a dozen miles apart did not understand each other. There being no tribal, political or other social relationships among these various groups, life was somewhat like that of tenth-century Europe on a much reduced geographical scale. Even villages that shared the same language did not act together: they had no common chief; their inter-village life was confined to important ritual occasions. The villages —even those that spoke the same tongue—had a tradition of warring with one another. But war had become forbidden by two of the most warring nations of all time: Britain and France, which quarrelsomely ruled the New Hebrides in what was called a condominium government—or, in pidgin—two fella massa.

No Briton or Frenchman ever had come to Paguli; they ruled by rumor at a safe distance. Apparently Tata was the only Pagulian who had ever seen a white person, and he took pains not to let Red know where this had occurred. Tata, like everyone else, enjoyed the isolation. There were no roads, no boats larger than the outrigger canoes used in fishing close to shore. There was a network of trails on the island that offered a means of communication if one had the nerve to leave his village and trust his life to the suspicious neighbors. But there was little incentive to travel far from home. Everything important was within hailing distance of the dooryard: relatives, friends, wood, water, fish, pigs, edible growing things, social occasions. The weather was so mild it was not necessary to wear clothing, but men wore breechcloths and the women short aprons or kilts.

Since Captain Cook visited the New Hebrides in 1774, life had passed from the stone age into that of iron. On a remote island like Runda, there was some exchange in cloth, tobacco and shell currency for the smoke-dried fruit of the coconut known as copra, but even that had died since the advent of war in the Pacific. However, no one in Paguli had heard of the war. The airplanes which flew overhead occasionally had become accepted as some eccentricity of the two fella massa, and the prevailing opinion was that there were no humans inside them. Personal matters were more interesting than anything that happened at a distance. There was much magic and ritual for entertainment. There was kava, a narcotic root extract, to drink until one enjoyed hallucinations. There was plenty of black twist, the pungent local tobacco, which everyone—including children—smoked heavily. There was much sexual gratification.

On Red's first morning in Paguli he awakened on the black sand beach to a burst of birdsong. Brightly plumed birds flitted and circled among delicate bamboo trees and nodding areca palms. The village proper had not been damaged by the hurricane. Most of its thatched houses were almost smothered in lush foliage giving off sensuous scents from bright flowers of which Red recognized only the South Sea hibiscus.

Tata had gone, but there were many men and boys strolling about the beach. They were not as black as Red had thought them to be on first meeting; they were, rather, a chocolate brown, and their features suggested an exotic mix of races. A handsome young man, Senga, who had learned pidgin from Tata, assumed the role of friend and explained that the building on the beach was known as the men's house where boys, the unmarried, and men whose wives were in advanced pregnancy or nursing infants usually slept. All were intensely curious about Red, but none—except several naked children

—acted rude by staring at him. Senga guided him to the men's latrine, which was out of sight behind a hummock of coral. They took a refreshing swim, and when they returned to the beach Senga offered him a couple of bananas and a piece of cold taro.

It was the custom of the young men to eat breakfast while strolling about the beach and chatting with friends. Pidgin was a very difficult dialect, and Red and Senga did not understand each other well. Red did learn that Senga was the *luluai,* or chief, of Paguli, but it was an inherited position that didn't carry much weight. The real power in Paguli was Tata himself, the village shaman or "taboo-man."

Young women joined the promenading on the beach. Red found many of them attractive, and most were notable for the beauty of their bare breasts. They cast him sidelong glances and giggled among themselves, like schoolgirls at home when a new boy joined the class. Senga, disapproving their lack of dignity, led Red off to Tata's house. Behind them came four men carrying the crate of paint slung on long poles.

Tata's house was larger than his neighbors'. It had a porch of carefully swept earth where Tata sat in a high-backed wooden chair smoking a clay pipe. He greeted Red ceremoniously and insisted on his taking the chair while he sat on a three-legged stool, Senga squatted on the earth, and the four bearers stood solemnly at a distance around the crate. Tata gave Red a pipe of strong tobacco, lighted it for him with a coal, and they began to palaver.

Red's first concern was to get in touch with the nearest white authorities so that he could be returned to military service. It took him a while to understand that white authority was so distant from Paguli as to be unimaginable, and then he began to see that Tata had no inclination to help him leave. In fact, Tata was determined that he stay. Tata, the most powerful person in Paguli, possessed a private cache of rocks, each related to a specific everyday purpose: for healing of illness, to assure a good yam harvest, to bring good fishing for sea turtles, and the like. Over the years he had used his magic rocks sparingly and wisely to benefit the people of his village. In their appreciation they trusted him, honored him, and gave him all the comforts of life. In short, Red thought, Tata was the smartest politician in town.

Like Senga, Tata asked where he had come from. He pretended to have heard of America, though likely he had not. But he did not believe Red's explanation of having been swept off the *Athene* in the storm. Like everyone, he believed only what he wanted to. There was no sign of a ship having been wrecked anywhere along the coast, he said, but Red could keep his secret if he wished. The point was he was *here,* as Tata himself had foretold at the last *Nekowiar* ceremony: a stranger would come into their midst who would bring Paguli a new prosperity and free the people from their unending toil. Now Tata brought out his precious rocks and studied them briefly before pronouncing Red the deliverer of Paguli who thenceforth would be called the King of America: in pidgin, "King Mel-a-ca."

Red was as willing as anyone to be mistaken for a messiah, but he wanted it to be for only a brief time before the burdens of office became too heavy. Was Tata positive he had found the right person?

Absolutely, Tata insisted. It was revealed both at *Nekowiar* and in the rocks themselves that the savior would come swimming out of the sea and bearing a great gift, as Red had; he would not arrive as man-bust-off-launch, so Red could not possibly have been swept off a ship. First Tata, and then Senga, rose and bowed to King Mel-a-ca, and the four bearers in the yard bowed too. Tata seemed too intelligent to believe what he was saying, but he must—like the creator of anything, even a tall story—have some purpose in his creation.

Red asked what he was expected to do as the King of America. Tata replied that all would be revealed in time. That is, he was the boss and Red simply the candidate who would do his bidding. Meanwhile he would be Tata's permanent guest and live in the house on the left of his compound. Tata explained that he had two wives—an old and a new—and that the old lived in the small house on the right.

Now, Tata made him understand, there must be a ceremony celebrating the fact the King of America had arrived in Paguli and been recognized by the civic leaders—himself and Senga. Maybe he was testing Red's ingenuity when he asked what the ceremony should be. If so, he had picked the right messiah to help him act out his curious fantasy.

First Red stood up and uttered his Tarzan cry, complete with breast-beating. As if in answer to it, the comeliest young woman he had seen in Paguli darted around the corner of the house and stared at him with astonishment. Her face was animated, her body remarkably well formed, with breasts so tautly beautiful that they took Red's mind off the ceremony he was performing. Tata snapped his fingers at the interruption, and the young woman sank abjectly to the ground. Tata looked expectantly at Red, who realized he must offer more than his Tarzan cry.

Mimicking the ceremonial high stomp of British grenadiers, he marched to the crate, took out a brush and can, opened it with the machete of one of the guards, and stomped back to Tata, all the time beaming at the beautiful woman kneeling on the ground who was gazing at him with ardent wonder.

"In the name of Franklin Delano Roosevelt," he proclaimed, "I, as the King of America, dub thee a member of my clan." Then he painted on Tata's chest in bold red letters: USA. Turning to Senga, he did the same.

Tata, trying to look at his own chest and Senga's at the same time, shouted to the young woman, who dashed into his house and ran out with a small hand mirror stolen, Red learned later, during one of the Paguli's infrequent raids on nearby Paova. Tata, snatching it from her, studied the reflection of his chest with joy.

Red turned to honor the young woman similarly, but Tata stopped him. He started toward the guards of the crate with his brush and paintpot, but again Tata stopped him and gradually made Red understand that the decoration was something other citizens of Paguli would have to *earn*. Red presumed that they must pay Tata a fee of some kind to join the order of honor.

Red gestured to the young woman, who did not try to hide her fascination with him, and asked Tata if she were his new wife. Good heavens no, Tata replied in effect, she was one of his daughters by the old wife. Her name was Bak, and when her father introduced her, she became suddenly overwhelmed with shyness and ran into the house.

Tata said she had just divorced her husband Sisto. As in America, divorce was common in Runda. But infidelity was not good cause for divorce there because nearly all husbands and wives were forever having love affairs with others; sex was a great pleasure, and the only taboo was incest. In Runda, Red learned, divorce occurred for what seemed perfectly sound reasons such as a man's sloth at making a living or a woman's carelessness in raising children. Bak, finding Sisto incorrigibly lazy, ate a root guaranteed to prevent a woman's becoming pregnant, since she did not want to bear the child of a slothful man, then finally divorced him. Tata hastened to add that she was a good, hard-working woman capable of bearing healthy children once she found the right man to father them.

Red said he would like to go into the house and spend some time with Bak so that he could decide if he wanted to marry her.

Tata's eyes measured Red. Not yet, he indicated. Maybe later. They would negotiate. Bak might be a part of a larger trade bargain.

He began giving proprietary directions to the guardians of the crate, as if it were *his* paint.

Red was at last weary with always following instead of leading, with forever being told what to do, with having his talent used by others as if it were *their* talent. Was he Tarzan or was he a mouse that hid in the jungle grass?

"Stop!" he cried. "Halt! Avast!" His voice became deep, stentorian, and all grew still, staring at him. "*I* am the god here—not you, Tata! I may not have been the King of America, but I'm sure as hell going to be King Shit of Paguli!"

What a pleasure to deliver a public address to a mesmerized audience even though they did not understand a word he said. But they did understand by his tone that he had taken charge there, that they had incurred the displeasure of the new god, for they began to look uneasy, fearful.

He gave his Tarzan cry and beat his chest in order to rivet their attention. "My great and good friend the Warden, the late Colonel Basset, wouldn't have let you steamroller him in this situation, and you can't steamroller me either. *I* Tarzan! *I* King Mel-a-ca! *I* am pilot who shoot down forty planes. I King Shit of Paguli! *I* Warden! Bow down and repeat after me: *Warden, Warden, Warden!*"

Incredibly, he made them understand. First the members of the guard, then Senga, and finally Tata knelt and began to chant: "Tazan! King Mel-a-ca! King Shlit da Paguli! *Warden, Warden, Warden!*"

"Very good," Red said. "The Warden would be very pleased with you if he was still alive." He pointed at Tata. "Rise, Mr. Prime Minister, and do my bidding." Tata, who suffered from rheumatism, might not have made it to his feet if Red had not helped him.

"Go now," Red said, "and you too, Senga, stroll through the highways and byways of Paguli and show the citizens your decorations. Then they can be inspired to join the legion of honor that I'm forming. Scram! But the paint stays here with me."

With gestures and the force of his words he made them understand. As they hurried away, Bak came out of the house, studying her reflection in the hand mirror. She had just surrounded her left eye with a large circle of yellow berry stain—and to extraordinary effect. The circle made her grin appear quite wicked.

"Ah-ha!" Red said.

"Ah-ha!" Bak echoed mischievously.

"What pretty teeth you have." It was fun to speak to a woman who could not answer him back. "I'm going to do something for you."

Dipping his brush in the paint pot, he carefully drew four large letters across her stomach below her breasts while she shrieked with laughter and indicated that the brush tickled unbearably: M I N E He stepped back, head cocked, a Rembrandt fearlessly critical of his own work. "Period," he said, and placed one after the E.

Bak, holding the mirror so that she could see the letters, was ecstatic. She jabbered endlessly; women had showed less gratitude for diamonds than she for the gift of his handiwork.

"You are entirely welcome, my dear." His tone conveyed an English majesty. "It's a pleasure to do things for such a lovely, grateful lady."

Dipping his brush again, he painted her nipples bright vermilion. It was too much for her. And then it became too much for him to see her nipples harden under the ministrations of his brush.

She ran. He pursued. They went all the way around Tata's house, he taking care not to spill a drop of the precious paint he carried in his left hand. Then she raced into the house. There he caught her. And there she passionately caught him up in an extraordinary experience.

23

After Basset was named managing director of the Project that day in the summer of 1942, he returned to the Willard Hotel and told Helen, "I can't tell you what I'm involved in. Sounds silly considering the big secret you do know—about my identity—but that's the way it has to be."

She asked if he believed he could handle the job, and he replied, "I have confidence. They think they want an engineer, but what they really need is a well-organized person with strong nerves who's capable of running things. My headquarters will be here in Washington, but I'll be traveling a lot of the time. Tomorrow morning I have to fly to Boston. For a man who used to be scared to fly, I'm sure doing a lot of it."

"Pete, may I ask just one question? I suppose this project involves some kind of weapon."

"I suppose so."

"Do they really know what they're doing?"

"That's the second question you've asked. No, I don't think they really know what they're doing. Does anybody really ever? I wonder if the entire universe may be destroyed someday by a high school kid fooling with a chemistry set. The one thing all people seem to have in common is the urge to experiment—to fool around. Let's go to dinner —and I don't want to dance."

They went next door to the Occidental Restaurant, where he struggled against growing depression. She, realizing it, asked, "Are you sure you want to go through with this thing?"

"Show me how I have any alternative. If I tried to disappear now, knowing what I was told today, they'd pursue me to the ends of the earth and then do God knows what."

Helen said, "I'm afraid of things like a—weapon. Of course I know nothing about weapons and always disliked the Army. The people who brought me up taught me that a weapon can be as dangerous to the one who shoots it as to the one shot at."

"Nonsense." He made his tone brusque in the way he was expected to sound thenceforth. "The object is to win this war. The sooner we do, the more lives can be saved. I know some I'd like to save—Red, Goldman, Boswick. But now that I've had time to think it over, I don't dare do anything about them. Goldman and Boswick know I'm Fiddler. As a matter of fact, they started this whole crazy thing. Anyway, I can't take the risk of contacting anybody from the past."

"You always mentioned Red in your letters," Helen said. "He sounded devoted to you. Can you help him?"

Basset winced, for he was still deeply fond of Red. Red had no idea he ever had been Fiddler. But if he helped Red, he'd have to help Goldman and Boswick, too. Yes, he was failing Red by not trying to get in touch with him. But, he told himself, it was safer not to.

Probably he should not contact Vera either. But then he thought it would be more dangerous if he did not: she might become angry, jealous, and blab about him if he broke his promise to stay in touch.

Indeed, he must also take care not to antagonize Helen, another who knew his real identity. Although he did not feel any particular passion for her, he nevertheless decided to try to muster some. He sensed she had been hurt by his ignoring her the night before.

After dinner when they returned to the hotel room, he tried—how he tried! She was receptive to him, but that did not help at all. For the first time he suffered a sexual failure that alarmed and humiliated him.

It humiliated Helen too, but she did not show it. She was sympathetic and carried on about the tremendous psychological pressure he'd been under in recent days.

Next morning she said she must go back to New Jersey. They would keep in touch, both vowed. Basset promises to send her three hundred dollars a month from his pay, and then they kissed goodbye tenderly. After they had parted, he felt relief that his marriage did not seem uncomfortably binding. He would remain a free soul after all.

When Basset began to organize the Army staff to oversee the Project, he realized he needed a good security officer. Who could be better than the loathsome Swisher?

Swisher's superior said of him, "He's cracked up, Colonel. His investigative work was brilliant till he got the idea you're somebody else. He's in a psycho ward at Walter Reed on his way to a Section 8 discharge."

When Basset went to see him at the Army hospital, Swisher hid under his bed. Basset got down on all fours and tried to talk to him, but Swisher wept and wouldn't listen. At last Basset coaxed him to sit up on his bed like a good little boy, then managed to hypnotize him.

"You recognize me, don't you, Swisher? Colonel C. P. Basset, soon to be promoted to brigadier general."

"Oh, yes, sir."

"Why did you ever think I was anybody else?"

"I'm terribly sorry about that, Colonel. It's been my downfall. Now they say I've had a nervous breakdown and they're going to discharge me. It'll be a blot on my record for life." Swisher started to cry again, and Basset told him to stop. Abruptly Swisher resumed talking in a normal tone: "You just didn't look like your pictures to me. And then I stumbled across the trail of Dr. Fiddler, who wasn't really a doctor and looked like you. You remember, sir, the coincidence of your being in the plane crash when he died? That was the point where my logical mind went illogical. I was carried away by a false clue. From there on it was downhill all the way for me." His eyes moistened. "Colonel Basset, I want to apologize to you and Mrs. Basset for any inconvenience I may have caused you."

"I forgive you, Swisher. My wife forgives you. Tell me your honest opinion of me," Basset requested gently.

"Admiration amounting to esteem. A most patriotic and loyal American. When I think of your patience with me after all I put you through, and then your kindness in coming to see me here in this— this ignominious state . . ."

It took the psychiatrists at Walter Reed another day to agree with Basset that Swisher had recovered miraculously from his emotional breakdown and should be restored to active duty. Then Basset had him promoted to major and put in charge of security for the project.

Swisher's gratitude took the form of slavishness to Basset's slightest whim, though in all other respects he was a superior security officer. Sometimes they traveled together, occasionally in uniform, but usually in mufti.

Soon after Swisher joined the staff the two were wearing civilian clothing on a mission to New York when, on 42nd Street near Lexington Avenue, Basset said he thought they were being followed by a portly man wearing a black fedora. Telling Swisher to keep an eye on the suspect, Basset ducked into the Bowery Savings Bank where, as Fiddler, he withdrew savings of over ten thousand dollars, which he took in hundred dollar bills. (Swisher, in the meantime, followed the suspect all the way to the Metropolitan Museum where the man was employed as a guard.) Basset's cash, kept in a safe deposit in the Munsey Trust Company in Washington, he planned to use when he escaped to become Fiddler again.

Swisher's faith in him gave Basset a sense of complete security, for no counterintelligence agent would risk incurring Swisher's wrath by stalking his beloved commander. Thus Basset would go to the post office occasionally to see if there was any mail for Fiddler from Vera without fear of being apprehended.

Basset easily grasped the theory of an atomic bomb involving uranium-235, but the practical matter of building one seemed impossible ever to achieve. In various places around the country groups of scientists were involved with the problem of manufacturing U-235; in other places engineers worked on the means and components of manufacture. Under the general plan of extreme secrecy about the Project, most did not know what the others were doing. But in the main, engineers had trouble getting along with scientists, whom they referred to as "longhairs;" scientists detested engineers for seeming dull and impertinent; the scientists themselves were divided into dozens of factions in conflict over theories or personalities; and absolutely everyone seemed to resent the Army control under which they labored.

Basset, in his endless travels, found trains generally more reliable than airplanes. He took a train to Chicago to see a new atom-smashing cyclotron.

The scientist in charge of the laboratory proudly began showing

Basset how his cyclotron worked while a group of his graduate students listened, enchanted by their professor.

"Well," Basset finally asked him, "how much U-235 have you separated?"

The scientist spoke with pride. "Last month, General, this lab produced three samples of 75 micrograms each." Basset grew depressed as the scientist went on, "Furthermore, each sample contained thirty percent of U-235." A microgram is a speck invisible to the eye. And the production of a few micrograms was the result of round-the-clock work by a dozen scientists!

An engineer groaned loudly and asked the ceiling, "How did a respectable engineering firm like ours ever get involved with these crazy longhairs?"

Turning to the professor, Basset said, "This cyclotron you've invented is a work of genius, sir. The Project commends you in the highest terms."

Then he turned to the group of engineers and said, "All of us—the professor here included—understand that an atom bomb needs *pounds* of U-235. But let us be grateful for small blessings. We'll build hundreds of cyclotrons. We'll make micrograms grow into pounds. Have faith! *We shall overcome all problems!*"

His voice rose with such conviction that all believed him—at least for the moment. They dispersed like an excited but timid mob before a battalion of infantry, to get back to work.

Back in Washington, Basset's engineers pointed out, however, that the cyclotron building process would be tremendously complicated.

Maybe it was the Fiddler rather than the Basset eloquence needed to fire his fellow workers with enthusiasm and convince them—for a while at least—that these huge problems could be overcome.

"We must stop meditating and get off our asses!" he liked to declaim. "We shall conquer this thing, my good people! We'll start with the biggest plant ever built, a plant larger than a large city and yet more than a city. We are inventing a new industry such as humankind never has dreamed of before. This industry will develop new sciences, new technologies, new metals, new tools. Just over the horizon I see gigantic industrial complexes, armies of specially trained scientists and technicians, arsenals of new tools and instruments. We aren't just producing a little old atom bomb. We are introducing a new form of energy that means a new and better way of life to the entire world. . . ."

Basset tried to turn the general antagonism to Army control into a unifying force that might heal the divisiveness of scientists jealous of colleagues or frustrated by both a lack of recognition and by inadequate research facilities. His friend Doc was pleased to find him willing to serve as the common butt and to hear him remark drily, "There's unity in hating a tyrant—at least temporarily." So, instead of blaming one another when things went wrong, researchers and engineers began to blame Basset. In order to cultivate that feeling he adopted a blunt, insensitive manner that deflated egos and stirred the slow to action.

Finding that the War Production Board had given the Project only an AA-3 priority in its quest for materiel, Basset drafted a letter to himself to be signed by the Chairman of the WPB giving the Project top AAA priority. Then he took the letter to the chairman, who threw up his hands and said it was impossible, there were too many other important war projects frantically striving for higher priorities, such as radar improvement and the proximity fuse program.

"All right, goddam it!" Basset gave the Warden's snarl. "My next stop is the White House, where I'm recommending to my friend Mr. Roosevelt that he abandon this program that's so close to his heart. I'm going to tell him it must be abandoned because the Chairman of the WPB won't cooperate with his wishes."

When he left the chairman's office, the Project had a triple-A priority rating.

He went to Tennessee with two engineering aides and they drove into a lovely green countryside bright with dogwood blossoms. In the valleys between the Great Smokies to the east and the Cumberland Mountains to the west Basset became Fiddler, who had loved to explore new terrains. For a few precious private minutes he forgot the war and was carried away into a better, quieter, greener America that had almost disappeared. The air was filled with birdsong and there was a fragrance of something he could not name. An otter emerged from a creek; far ahead a deer trotted across the gravel road.

And then, on a height of land, the engineer riding beside him told the driver, "Stop here."

"Beautiful!" Fiddler exclaimed. "It makes me feel good to know there's still such lovely country."

The engineer glanced at him curiously. "Yeah, but what I see is the perfect site for future atomic plants. It's an isolated area where few people live. There's plenty of electric power, an abundant water supply. The mild climate permits outdoor work the year around. . . ."

Fiddler had sometimes managed to imagine the unimagined. But Basset went to great pains never to try.

Basset believed—indeed, he *knew*—he possessed a miraculous weapon that could end the war in victory with a single devastating detonation. On second thought, however, he always had to admit he did not yet actually possess the mighty bomb; all that he and the United States possessed was the *capacity* to possess it. One of the most horrifying aspects of the muddle was that military intelligence indicated the Germans had a similar capacity and were straining their utmost to be the first to produce a workable atomic bomb. Whichever nation won this race would win the war. It was that simple.

Basset became so obsessed by the Project that he sometimes felt the many problems in producing an atomic bomb were his alone. As Fiddler, he had been innovative in solving problems, but nothing in his experience compared to what he faced in the Project: having to translate a postulate of physics into an instrument of destruction.

Basset's way of life became entirely different from what Fiddler's had been. Fiddler had lived openly; Basset's existence was as protected as a dictator's. His office in the new Pentagon Building was under perpetual guard, and all papers had to be locked up every night in safes to which only he and two others knew the combinations. Swisher made sure that his small apartment on N Street in northwest Washington also was closely watched. Apart from seeing associates in the Project, he was a recluse.

About once a week he telephoned Helen in New Jersey. At first he called because he did not want her to become antagonistic toward him—the same reason he sent her money. Gradually, however, he found that he enjoyed talking with her and looked forward to their conversations. She was always a cheerful voice in a gloom-filled world. Roger, who came home to be with her nearly every weekend, was doing better at school. Although her new financial allotment helped Helen greatly, she did not want to give up her teaching job.

He tried talking to Roger on the phone only once. After the boy piped, "Gee whiz, you don't even sound like my old man!" he and Helen agreed that phone conversations with Roger were risky.

The memory of his sexual failure with Helen nagged him. She seemed to understand that was why he never visited her in New Jersey or invited her to Washington. Once she asked on the phone if he wished to wait till the war was over before they were divorced.

"Yes, by all means," he replied brusquely.

"You sound just like Basset the First," she said without malice.

He often wished he could fall in love with her: she had everything one could want in a wife. But his obsession with Rosemarie was unremitting. It was one of the reasons why he kept up correspondence with Vera, whose letters were boring and concerned chiefly with real estate. Besides his feeling that he must placate Vera to keep the secret of his identity, he hung on her occasional references to Rosemarie. It was a sick existence; Fiddler would have known that, but Basset refused to admit it.

About a month after his promotion to major general, Basset flew with Swisher to Los Angeles. His purpose was to approve for use a testing site far out in the bleak southwest deserts if, in fact, a bomb ever was created. The consensus of most in the Project was that it was progressing faster than anticipated; Basset himself, ever more consumed by anxiety over it, had stopped forecasting success. After he and Lieutenant Colonel Swisher (who received a promotion each time the Boss did) returned from the desert to Los Angeles, they had dinner at the home of a prominent physicist, whose wife insisted they come along to a war bond rally.

24

Rosemarie and I and the rest of our brave little band flew from Hamilton Field to Los Angeles. There we were greeted at the airport by Mr. Rumplemeyer, two famous actors, two beautiful actresses and a lot of other people. Mr. Rumplemeyer, a renowned movie-maker who had loaned himself to the cause of selling war bonds, looked at Rosemarie and asked Plover, "Who's that?"

After introductions, we traveled by motorcade to Mr. Rumplemeyer's mansion in Beverly Hills. Like everyone of our generation, Rosemarie and I had been so heavily exposed to pictures of Hollywood mansions that we felt instantly at ease in Mr. Rumplemeyer's marbled castle. He kept insisting that we must make ourselves at home. I was pleased that Slattery was admitted too, though his room was nowhere near as grand as the suite to which Rosemarie and I were conducted.

She took one look at the enormous bed and said, "You know, honey, even before I knew what it was all about, I think I wanted to fuck on a bed like that."

"Well," I replied, "you are about to realize the dream of a lifetime."

But she was not; before I could even loosen my tie, Mr. Rumplemeyer was there. He said he was going to personally take Rosemarie on a tour of his castle while I worked on my speech for the evening rally with a couple of script writers and Plover.

Rosemarie and I had stopped talking about Red. We had, in fact, almost stopped talking altogether since we had started living like man and wife at Hamilton. The way Rosemarie had put it to me was this: "Let's not talk anymore, but just make love till things get better." And now that we were guests in a Beverly Hills mansion, it appeared that things were much better indeed.

In Mr. Rumplemeyer's library a couple of script writers, a pretty secretary and Plover were working with Slattery on his speech. A servant brought me a Scotch and I wandered around looking at the books.

This looked like such a good life that I wondered if I'd like to settle in Hollywood instead of handling photographic assignments in places like Paris. Since I was pretty good with a still camera, might I learn to be even better with a motion picture one? If I could be a good movie cameraman, why wouldn't I make a good movie director? Then I'd live in a palace like this and be rich as well as famous. Maybe Mr. Rumplemeyer would help me launch this new career.

My reverie on future glory was interrupted by Plover, who explained that my remarks at the rally would be in the form of answers to questions put by the master of ceremonies, a famous comedian.

"Brevity is the most important thing," one of the writers said. "Did you know that the average attention span for spoken words is less than twenty seconds?"

"The M.C. will keep it light and as funny as possible," the other writer said. "People don't want to hear how bad war is. If you use that angle, you won't sell many bonds."

After they had shaped me up, we had a drink together and they apologized for what they had to do. They were the first noted writers I'd met; I'd thought that writers did as they pleased, but to my surprise these two, like Army draftees, hated everything. They hated Hollywood, all actors, and most directors and producers and the studio where they were employed and, by inference, Mr. Rumplemeyer. They especially hated the comedian who was going to be the master of ceremonies. But they explained that they had to earn a living, even as I'd heard draftees explain that they had to win the war.

The pretty secretary, whose name was Gwendolyn, agreed with absolutely everything everybody said. She was attractive enough to make me think of Rosemarie and recall my promise to help her realize the dream of a lifetime. When, however, I remarked that I wanted to see Rosemarie, Gwendolyn said that Mr. Rumplemeyer had finished showing her his mansion and now had taken her to see his movie studio.

"And after that," one of the writers said, "he'll want to show her his yacht."

"And after that," the other writer said, "he'll want to show her his ranch."

"There isn't time," Gwendolyn said. "Not before this evening's rally there isn't time to do those things."

"Do you think," I asked, "that Mr. Rumplemeyer would be interested in helping me start a career as a cameraman?"

"I think," Gwendolyn said, "he'd be more interested in helping your wife start a career as an actress."

"Two movie careers in the same family is bad," one of the writers said. "That's why there are so many divorces in Hollywood."

The rally seemed to me an anticlimax.

While the rally sponsors' main purpose was to sell government bonds to defray the huge costs of war, they also tried to promote several entertainers who were supposed to amuse the audience. As a nimble girl was tap-dancing and we on the platform applauded her, Rosemarie, who had been finding it difficult to look me in the eye since her afternoon with Mr. Rumplemeyer, spoke in my ear:

"Mr. Rumplemeyer thinks I have great acting talent—just never till now had a chance to use it."

I looked at her gravely.

"I have to look out for my future," Rosemarie whispered.

"Of course you do," I said. "If you don't, who else will?"

She clutched my right hand in her damp left. "Boz, you're so understanding, you put things so well. After the rally Mr. Rumplemeyer is taking me to the studio for screen tests. Do you mind? I mean, don't wait up for me because I may get in real late."

I patted her knee reassuringly. "Good luck, Rosemarie. Hope you become a star. Just do the old lieutenant one favor. Don't ever let on to anybody, least of all Rumplemeyer, that you're carrying around a certified check for more than thirty-five thousand bucks. Promise?"

"I promise, Boz. Thanks for understanding."

Plover leaned toward us tensely and said, "Wake up, Boswick, you're on next."

As I got to my feet and started toward the microphone to greet the comedian, I saw a uniformed officer in the front row of the audience who was staring at Rosemarie and me incredulously. He was Charles

Peter Basset, born Morton Fiddler, and he wore the two stars of a major general.

When Basset saw Rosemarie on the stage with me, he grew visibly paler. He looked as though he wanted to run before I recognized him, but was somehow physically incapable of stirring. He gazed, transfixed, at Rosemarie.

The comedian master of ceremonies made a pun about an atoll, called out my name, and said, "Now, here's a guy who took one almost singlehanded!"

Though stunned to see Basset, I managed not to forget my lines with the comedian. I spoke every one of them to Basset while he stared inscrutably back at me.

"But what's a fighting guy without his gal?" the comedian asked the audience. "What's a shoelace without a shoe? While our guy was out there fighting for us, offering his life to keep this the great democratic nation that it is, his thoughts were always on his gal—his wife —his *Rosemarie!*"

He gestured to her, and she came up to me at the microphone in the swinging, sort of slinky way she had learned to move. The applause for her was thunderous, the whistling shrill, as—like the actors we had become—we put an arm around each other and—as we had been directed to do before the show—bowed and waved to the audience. The crowd cared little about me, but it could not bear to let Rosemarie go as it cheered and clapped.

Then she did something unrehearsed. She took the microphone from the comedian, and, so great was the rapport of the audience with her, it almost instantly grew still.

In a husky voice brimming with emotion, she said, "It's so good to have mah man back with me. It's so good of you all to come out this evenin' and join us. Remember the war, all you folks! Buy bonds to support it!"

As we backed away together to applause that sounded louder than ever, I saw that Basset was weeping and Swisher staring at him in astonishment.

I did not try to seek out Basset. I did not hate him because he had failed to rescue Red, Goldman and me from hard times, but I thought of him as a former friend who had betrayed me, did feel betrayed, and decided to avoid him.

After Rosemarie's impromptu remarks at the microphone, when it became apparent to everyone how well she projected herself to a large audience, our relationship changed. It became a kind of business association, devoid of sentiment over Red or the past, but marked by candor and a willingness to help each other in order to help oneself. She was, I decided, mainly ambitious for money.

She told me in her forthright way that her enthusiastic reception at the rally had convinced Mr. Rumplemeyer she had the capacity for "an entertainment career," that he would help her toward that goal, and that, of course, she must do favors for him in return. He signed her to a studio contract before Plover pulled his road show out of Los Angeles and took us to Washington; she signed the contract as Rosemarie Jack, which she claimed was her maiden name. Mr. Rumplemeyer felt that the bond tour of American cities would, as he put it, "advance Rosemarie's eventual career by exposing her name and personality to a large mass audience." She told me that he would join the tour occasionally along the way in order to spend some time with her. And she said he insisted that she cease all sexual activities with me or anyone else: "He just won't stand for me cheating on him with my husband." So loyal was she to her business agreements that she and I cheated on him only once in a while.

It was quite an act we took on the road. Looking back, it seemed a rather mean little carnival advertising the greatest show on earth—that calamity which would cause the deaths of about forty million combatants and civilians in history's most devastating war. We played before hundreds of thousands of Americans who turned out to gaze upon Hollywood stars and four uniformed prisoners of the general hysteria beseeching them to put out hard-earned money for bonds which would help promote the worldwide lunacy.

Plover was ecstatic over Rosemarie's performances. She was the hit of the show in every city, receiving far more attention than either the authentic heroes or the phony one—me. She had taught herself a sinuous way of moving and wore a long red gown which clung to her gorgeous body. She was the golden girl of adolescent wet dreams. The movement of her hands directed attention to the sexiest parts of her body. Sometimes a theater filled with men actually echoed with moans when she rested a hand on a curving hip and with the fingers of her other hand indicated a pert breast without actually touching herself. Her actions were primitive, but then I guess those were primitive times. When Rosemarie, speaking in cultivatedly husky tones, begged people to buy bonds, good ole boys literally howled with lust. And they bought bonds. Rosemarie always got results. I was merely a prop to her act: how could she be a war hero's wife without a husband in tow?

Of course she was having the time of her life. When I thought about her, I always had trouble sorting out her motives. After I'd decide she wanted a lot of money, I'd see that she was equally anxious for fame or even simple notoriety. When I'd think that sex was meaningless to her except as a means to an end, it would suddenly appear as if she cared for nothing but sexual gratification itself. I guess that Rosemarie wanted *everything*—every pleasure and satisfaction that life could offer; she even enjoyed her private sadness over Red. For Rosemarie wished to have an emotional life as well-rounded as her lovely legs.

While playing the South, I shook out my accent to show I was one of the good ole boys. When we were in Memphis, my father brought his current wife up from Biloxi to see us, and I learned that my grandmother in Chicago had died at last without leaving the fortune everyone in the family had anticipated. At a Memphis reception I was miserable for almost an hour in the presence of my father, who gawked at Rosemarie and said, "Praise God I got you a good military education. Look at you now—a hero with a fine Army career."

My personal ambition was simple: I wanted to be some kind of photographer, eventually, but for now to avoid further risk to my life. My wish to survive was deeply shared by the three real heroes in our troupe, though our public line expressed our eagerness to get back to dear old combat. So I became depressed one day when Plover brought me orders assigning me, after my bond tour, to an Infantry combat outfit in the Southwest Pacific. Plover was almost as distressed as I and said he'd see what he could do about it. I suspected Mr. Rumplemeyer of arranging it in order to remove the inconvenience of Rosemarie's husband hanging around, but he pleaded innocence and volunteered to use influence in Washington to have me assigned to a safe camp so far back in the swamps of Georgia that Rosemarie would never be able to find me. I told him to skip it, I preferred the Pacific.

Wherever we went on our tour I began to notice something odd: someone was following us. At the time I did not know who he was, but I recognized him as the officer who had sat next to Basset at the Los Angeles rally. A few times when I tried to accost him, he showed a knack for evaporating.

While we were in New York I almost caught the man. I had been frustrated in my efforts to contact Red's sister in Glenwood, but I did get a telephone call through to Goldman's mother in Brooklyn from our Manhattan hotel suite. We had a long, pleasant conversation in which I obtained Ira's new APO address, and she read me a letter from him, a charming bit of fiction about his idyllic life on a tropic isle. I had just hung up the phone when I saw the door open a couple of inches and the man's dark glasses peer in at me.

With a shout, I chased him down the corridor and might have caught him if a man who claimed to be a hotel guest, but obviously was a confederate, had not bumped into me and sent me sprawling.

Our tour ended in Chicago. Weary though I was of the whole charade, I did not look forward to my next assignment in the far Pacific. Of course Mr. Rumplemeyer was there for the last show. When we came on stage that evening, I was astonished to see Basset sitting in the front row with the man who had been following me. Both were in uniform. Just as in Los Angeles, I could not take my eyes off him throughout the performance while he never stopped gazing at Rosemarie.

After the show I decided to try to speak to him, but before I could, this man intervened and said, "Lieutenant Boswick, General Basset wants to see you at the Palmer House in half an hour. You cannot bring your wife."

"She's otherwise engaged anyway," I said.

"I suppose with Rumplemeyer," the man said.

"Who are you, and why are you poking into other people's business?" I asked, thoroughly annoyed.

"My name is Swisher, and it's how I serve my country. I know all about you, Boswick, You're not married to Rosemarie and your Silver and Bronze Stars are phony."

Once I discovered that silence aggravated him, I wouldn't say a word while we were being driven to Basset's hotel. When he ushered me in, Basset told him, "Wait outside, Eugene, I want to talk to Boswick privately."

"That's quite a German shepherd you've got trained there," I said, after he left.

"The best." Basset's smile made him look like Fiddler. "How are you, Boz?" He extended his hand, and I took it reluctantly. "I suppose you're upset with me for not getting you guys out of trouble." I shrugged. "Believe me or not, Boz, I couldn't do anything about it. I learned that Red is dead, and I'm deeply sorry. I liked him."

"Suppose I opened the door and told Swisher you're Fiddler?"

"I used to worry about things like that. Swisher protects me completely—almost completely—from the past. He carries a .32 in a shoulder holster. At a nod from me, he'd pull it out, put the muzzle between your eyes and press the trigger. He'd get away with it, too. He'd produce evidence you are a German spy. He can produce evidence for anything I want proved. He is full of quirks. The man is mad. Certifiably insane. Perfect security officer. But I didn't have you come here to discuss Swisher. Sit down, sit down. I want to talk about Rosemarie." He leaned back in his chair and eyed me steadily. "I'm in love with her. I want her, must have her, I'm obsessed by her."

It occurred to me that Basset was the one insane.

"Maybe that sounds odd to you," he went on. "I don't love my wife. An admirable woman, but I just inherited her and she does nothing for me. I think it's her morality. I've discovered morality is something that makes me very uneasy. What I like about Vera and far more about Rosemarie is that they're as immoral as alley cats. Do I puzzle you, Boz?"

"Sometimes your ambivalence does. I can't make up my mind about you."

"Don't try," he said. "I gave up long ago. So I find it more comfortable to live in someone else's clothes rather than to try to find my own. Nature is filled with examples of this sort of behavior: call me a hermit crab if you like."

I thought that Basset had analyzed himself better than anyone else could have. He was utterly lacking in character and a complete opportunist. In that respect he was the ideal military man: his principles would never stand in the way of opportunities.

"Do you love Rosemarie?" he asked.

"No. I like her, but love—no."

The fact that I found his opportunism distasteful made me wonder if I had perhaps judged myself a bit harshly. Maybe I was not altogether weak and cowardly.

"How can you say you love Rosemarie," I asked, "when you've seen her only once?"

"I don't know. There are so many things like that I don't understand. It's what makes my passion for her so intriguing. She takes my mind off my work once in a while."

"What is your work?"

"That's none of your business. You don't need to know. And by the way, how did you know I've only seen Rosemarie once?"

"Vera told me. She told me all about your visit and your correspondence."

He became reflective. "I shouldn't have trusted her. But what
alternative did I have? In her last letter she told me that you and
Rosemarie ran off together. She's very angry at you both. How did
you get that medal? You're not brave enough to win one. But you are
clever and I have always admired cleverness. Can you deliver Rosemarie to me?"

"Deliver? You mean as in pimping? No, I will not. Besides, I don't
possess her. Mr. Rumplemeyer does."

"I know all about that. But he's being eliminated."

I gaped at him. "My God, Basset, have you gone crazy? You'd kill
a man just because—"

"No, not kill. Just 'neutralize.' Rumplemeyer is a Russian Jew—
or was before he became a citizen. Swisher hates Russians and Jews
more than anyone except Negroes. I have convinced Swisher that
Rumplemeyer has a connection with a Russian spy ring. Tomorrow
morning he and a couple of his men are going to Rumplemeyer, tell
him that his connection has been discovered, and say that for unspec-
ified reasons he must abandon Rosemarie."

"Basset, what a shit you have become!"

He shrugged. "That's what everybody says, but I get things done.
I'm taking neither life nor property from Mr. Rumplemeyer. I'm just
giving him a little fear and taking Rosemarie. He'd abandon her soon
for somebody else anyway. He has a history of it."

"You say you're 'taking' Rosemarie. Suppose she doesn't want to
be 'took' by you?"

"I have absolute faith in my ability to take her. Are you going to
try to prevent it?"

"Of course not. It's her life, and I'm nothing to her but a good
friend. Besides, I won't be here. I'm on orders back to the Pacific."

"Are you scared?"

I pondered. "I don't think so really. Just resigned to it. Hope they
let me use a camera."

"You're going to the 416th Regimental Combat Team" Basset said.
"Within a couple of months it will be engaged in a messy fight that
may result in fifty percent casualties. Are you scared?"

"You son of a bitch, you're the one put me on those orders."

Basset smiled. "Yes. And now I've decided to take you off those
orders. You're coming to work for me in Washington."

Suddenly suspicious, I wondered if the 416th was preferable. "But not in order to deliver Rosemarie to you."

"We just agreed you can't do that. Only *I* can. I'm offering both of you a job. One thing I definitely do not want is for her to monopolize my attention and divert it from far more important things. Only occasionally, and *I* will monopolize *her*." He paused. "Why don't you thank me for this great gift of life I'm giving you?"

"Thanks—I guess." Then I thought of something. "I'd ask you to bring Red back, but he's dead. However, you can bring back Goldman. In your job, whatever it is, you must be able to use a good engineering officer. I'll go ahead with this provided you bring Goldman back from the Pacific and give him a Stateside job too."

The Warden frowned at me darkly and growled, "You conniving son of a bitch! Goldman is a Jew, and Swisher tries to crucify every Jew who has to be cleared. I don't want to get involved with him any more."

"Then no deal," I said. "I'm tired of being bought. I want to go back to the Pacific. And before I go I think I'll warn Rosemarie that you have incurable syphilis."

He cut loose a string of loud Warden obscenities that caused Swisher to open the door and ask if everything was all right.

"Yeah, I guess as all right as anything ever can be." Then he almost smiled at me as he told Swisher, "Boswick knows an officer I want brought back from the Pacific and cleared. His name is Ira Goldman."

Swisher wrinkled up his smooth, pink face and said, "Boss, that's a Jewish name."

"I know!" Basset roared, and Swisher wilted. Then Basset told him, "Have a brief interview with Boswick and start to clear him."

Swisher looked at me with aversion. "Frankly, Boss, there's something about this man I don't trust."

"Good start," Basset said. "Carry on. Confess something, Boz."

I confessed that I drank too much when booze was available and lusted for women even when they were beyond reach. I confessed I had often cheated in examinations and lied to my father and just about everybody I knew. I confessed to cowardice in battle and shirking all tasks I did not like.

Basset smiled and said, "See how pleasant confession is?"

I had to admit it was indeed delightful.

"Have you ever stolen anything?" Swisher asked.

"No. Wait a minute, I must have." Then I was able to develop for him a pattern of thievery from institutions, but not from individuals. I recalled that at a tender age I had stolen candy from Woolworth's, but never from a small shop merchant. I stole property from all the military schools where my father had incarcerated me, but never a penny from a fellow student. I had filched prodigious amounts of photographic equipment from the Army, but I'd pay back even a dime borrowed from a friend.

"A sort of Robin Hood complex," Basset suggested.

"Well, Boss," Swisher admitted, "he does have a certain dim, primal integrity."

There was no doubt about it, all this confessing was very satisfying, I thought, as Swisher asked me, "Do you believe in God?"

"No sir, I'm sorry to say I do not."

"Do you believe in the United States of America and its democratic, small d, institutions?"

I was about to confess my great skepticism of some of our democratic, small d, institutions when Basset gave me a quick, surreptitious nod.

"Oh, yes, sir!" I exclaimed to Swisher. "Now, there is something I *do* believe in. My country! My country right or wrong, but by God, *my country!* I never get up in the morning that I don't think, God bless America! Right?"

"Right!" Swisher looked close to tears as he said to Basset, "Boss, this man is the very soul of integrity. He has just passed his three-way check."

"Thank you, Eugene. Now go out in the hall and guard the door again."

When Swisher, hastening as fast as he could, returned to the hall, I asked Basset, "He goes through all this stuff so you can procure Rosemarie? What does he think of her?"

"Just what I have him think. He thinks she has something to do with Rodrigo Romanelli."

"Who's he?"

"A Romanian physicist I want for my program, a genius who doesn't want to join it. Or so I tell Eugene. Actually, the man does not exist. I made him up. Whenever Swisher gets in my hair, I send him looking for Romanelli. Drives him crazy that he can't find him from all my false clues. Right now I'm trying to throw Eu-gene off the trail of my lust for Rosemarie. One thing Swisher disapproves of more than anything is lust."

25

There was a forgetfulness about the Pagulians that Red found endearing. In America people were always remembering what you'd done wrong yesterday, whereas in Paguli people tended to forget yesterday itself. In the easy rhythm of village life they quickly forgot that Red had arrived as a god. Tata seemed to forget too. Or he was too absentminded and disorganized to be the effective manager of a god; he'd start one thing, turn to something else, then pause to think about yet a third.

Red did not try to remind the Pagulians of his status as a deity. After his initial firmness with Tata about the paint, which he continued to keep in his possession, he did not try to exert influence over the villagers. He could not sustain the vanity to be a popular god or the ambition to be a capable dictator. And Tata, whenever he did remember that he had a god on his hands, did not encourage him because Tata was used to being the most influential man in the village himself.

Red, knowing he was cast up by the sea on July 12, 1943, immediately began to keep a crude calendar by making knife marks on the soft bole of a silky tree, a demonstration of his wish to return to civilization. But when he found there was no ready passage out of Paguli, he was content to live like a Melanesian, at least for a while.

The day began at dawn when people stepped out of their homes, lovers from the bush, and the singles from the men's and women's houses. No one seemed to have any feeling of impending pressure or dread of what the day might bring. One felt no anxiety about having to do something unpleasant because there was nothing unpleasant to do—no organization of labor to involve one—no factory, no school, no army or police force. They tilled the fertile soil and fished the fecund waters for enough to eat, they strengthened the thatch of the houses, did something extra to trade for necessary garment cloth, and that was the end of essential effort.

Although Red lived in Tata's household and he and Bak were lovers, he would not marry her. He felt that entering into a formal Pagulian marriage would be bigamy, since he already was married to Rosemarie. If he married Bak, he might mislead her into thinking it was a permanent arrangement. Red was determined to escape from Paguli as soon as possible, and he did not want to be tempted to take her with him.

Imagine Bak as a G.I.'s wife! More crazy yet, imagine her after the war as Mrs. Jack, wife of the noted airline pilot Red Jack. What would he do when she wanted to make love in the aisle of a supermarket? How could he get her to wear a bra? Was it remotely possible he could teach her to drive a car? However, it might be worth it just to see his sister's expression when he brought her home to Glenwood and introduced her as his wife.

During his first days in Paguli, Red was content to be a private citizen and Bak's lover. He let his hair grow as long as Tarzan's, shaved once a week with a dull razor borrowed from Tata, and took interest in everyday events. Dinner was a communal evening meal which Red and Bak shared with Tata's large family. The women scraped and prepared the taro while Tata and Red arranged the pile of hot stones, called the *liga,* in which the leaf-wrapped taro was baked. Red, soon tiring of the monotonous diet, varied his own meal with fruit the others did not want and tried to catch fish for dinner nearly every day. (The only meat, pig, was reserved for ritual feasts.) Regardless of the food, he enjoyed dinners as relaxed occasions when he learned more about the character and customs of Tata's family.

Some things about life in Paguli he would never forget. The dawns, when at low tide exotic stalagmites of the sea raised their heads above the coral gardens in a profusion of brilliant colors. Light rain falling in the green afternoons while mist slowly crept up the slender trunks of coconut palms to form dreamlike temples among their coxcomb crowns; pungent woodsmoke that smelled like incense drifting from the fires after dark. But one thing he could never adjust to: the frequent tremors of the earth that made him feel that he was passing through an ephemeral land.

Gradually, though, he began to miss most powerfully the exchange of thoughts with someone—anyone—in conversation. Hard as he worked at learning pidgin, it was an awkward, difficult language devoid of subtleties; as for the local Paguli dialect, he could make no headway with it at all. He soon missed the printed word. If he'd had a number of books printed in English, he would not have grown restless as soon as he did. Eventually, he missed mechanical things, to tinker with and entertain himself. But, most of all, he was depressed by the realization that his dream of becoming a pilot now was slipping further from him.

By early September he felt imprisoned. Bak sensed it. Though she could not offer the sustained conversation he wanted, she was perceptive and they communicated easily about basic things. He did not *love* Bak, as he once thought he had loved Rosemarie, but he had tender regard for her. He was kind to her because she was very good to him. They satisfied each other sexually, but he missed the exchange of words that could lift lovemaking from child's play to exquisite experience. He knew that, given the chance, he would leave Bak with some regret but without the despair he'd felt at separation from Rosemarie.

A question began to nag at him: How long could he stay away from the Army without being branded a deserter? He fretted over the loss of his dog tags. Though realizing it was silly, he felt he somehow had lost his identity along with his tags.

When an airplane flew overhead occasionally, everyone rushed to the beach and waved—none more frantically than Red, until he realized the flights were too high, the missions too purposeful for crews to pay attention to natives on a remote beach. By the time he had been in Paguli two months, he wondered if he ever would find a means of leaving. He was not yet in a panic about it; it was, rather, a slowly growing anxiety. All his efforts to learn if another white lived on the island were unavailing. Once in a while he suggested a voyage up the coast by outrigger so that he could make inquiries of others, but no one in Paguli—not even Bak—would go with him, and he could not manage an outrigger by himself for any appreciable distance.

An idea struck him one morning, and he wondered how he could have been so stupid as not to think of it before. Ignoring his usual tasks, he began laying out a huge S O S of white coral bits and shells on the black sand beach. Children, thinking it a game of some kind, joined in helping him, and the job was finished next day. Everyone came and marveled at the magic he had wrought, but since he did not offer an explanation, all were too courteous to ask its significance. Bak, the first to come and look at the letters, seemed to understand they had something to do with his wish to leave Paguli. Wrinkling up her face, she spoke in pidgin:

"Go-to-launch-flies-like-bird?"

Her eyes were very wide, her face somber. She wanted to know why he wished to leave her. He did not want to, he said, but he had duties he must return to. Then he told her one of man's oldest lies: that he would come back to her later and they would live happily ever after. When she indicated she did not believe him, he thought her strangely sophisticated.

Suddenly people remembered that Red had come to the village as a god. It happened at the great feast known as *Nekowiar,* which was held high above the village on the rim of the extinct volcano where for two days there were ceremonial dances and the pigs were slaughtered and feasted on.

Everyone was incredulous when Red refused to eat the succulent meat. In truth he did not eat it because it was tough and undercooked and he feared trichinosis. However, the people, having no fears about their diet, believed no mortal could resist such delicious meat, and they recalled suddenly that he had come to Paguli as a god.

He wondered if it would help pass monotonous time if he tried to play god. He was pondering this as he trudged down the volcano with the others after *Nekowiar*—and then an opportunity became obvious when they reached Paguli.

In the two-day absence of all but a few of the old and very sick, a raiding party had swept down from Parva, the village to the north, whose inhabitants for generations had been arch-enemies for reasons no one on either side could remember. A dozen houses, including Tata's and Red's, had been burned, fishing nets destroyed, an old man and his ill wife stabbed to death. Red shared the wrath of the Pagulians at the senseless act, then realized with surprise that neither Tata, Senga nor anyone else had the nerve to march against Parva in retaliation.

As everyone milled about, babbling, Red threw back his head, gave his Tarzan cry, and beat his chest. Telling Bak to break out his store of paint, he began to lecture his fellow villagers in English at the top of his voice. They didn't understand a word he said, but his tone and the way he pranced about whipped them into a vengeful fury. When he began to paint U S A on the chests of all able-bodied men, it seemed there was no holding them back. Tata said he wanted to go too, but realized he was too old.

They marched at dawn next morning, about forty men, armed with fishing spears, machetes, bows and arrows, torches. At their head Red carried a club because he didn't like the idea of stabbing even enemies. Behind the armed men trotted a couple of dozen boys beating drums and blasting on conch-shells.

As Red had anticipated, their din alerted the Parvans. And, as he had hoped, it gave the people of the village ample time to flee the wrathful armed host of their enemies. As the Pagulians swarmed into the southern limits of Parva behind Red, he shook his club menacingly at a last aged man hopping away hastily to the north. At Red's order they did not kill anyone, but they burned sixteen houses, stole a large mirror and nine pigs, and carried away all of the enemy's fishing nets to replace their own.

When they returned triumphantly to Paguli, Red thought up a new ceremony to decorate the victorious warriors. Upon all who bore U S A on their chests, he painted a U S A on their backs. This so delighted the soldiers that for weeks they slept on their sides in order to preserve their decorations.

Red, the heroic military genius of Paguli who had restored the lost morale of its fighting forces, was once again acclaimed as a god. The villagers rebuilt his house in a single day, but Tata had to wait two more days for his own. Tata, though eclipsed by Red politically, offered him sound advice by suggesting that the U S A cult be expanded to include women and adolescents. Like most military conquerors, Red was quickly bored with peace; so he allowed all who wished to join the cult and worship him, thus providing some entertainment.

One day several youths caught a Parvan spy hiding in the Paguli underbrush and dragged him before Red. The wretched man, expecting execution, was incredulous at being released and sent back to Parva with a message for the authorities there from the white god: Each new moon they must pay Paguli a peace tax of six pigs and a manload of dried fish; otherwise, the fierce Pagulians would wipe them out. The Parvans, trembling with fear, acquiesced without question.

"Are there any more villages around here to conquer?" Red asked.

Tata said he would look into it.

After Red again refused Bak's plea to marry her, she became quarrelsome and derisive of his status as a god. To his relief, she was not pregnant; maybe she could not bear a child. Following another angry quarrel, Red moved the captured mirror into a small, separate hut; over its doorway he lettered on a flat piece of driftwood: GOD'S OFFICE.

Now that he had become a deity, he no longer tilled the soil and fished the sea; subjects were glad to perform such chores for him. He complained that his mistress didn't understand him as she used to and began to visit the bushes with a variety of nubile young Paguli women. He took to sleeping in the men's hut on the beach, and he spent more and more time at the office.

When hanging around the office became a bore, he decided to overhaul his army. So he taught his troops close-order drill and cadence marching until they were as rhythmic and perfect as the Radio City Rockettes.

Red's Paguli cult members were as fond of decorating themselves as citizens of New York, London, Paris, and every other place. Never had they found decorative material of the quality Red introduced. It would have warmed the hearts of Sherwin-Williams Paints officials to see how durably their product survived on damp human skin in the tropics. Yet even Sherwin-Williams could not last indefinitely when long subjected to human sweat and heavenly rain. One of Red's chief occupations in the rainy season became repairing faded lettering while the citizens preened themselves in front of the large mirror captured in Parva.

The joyful and generous sexuality of the island women made for such fun that Red overcame his notion that sex with someone other than his wife was somehow evil. After an especially exciting romp with a maiden in the office one afternoon, it occurred to him it was not really so surprising that Rosemarie had changed and given way to passion so frequently. He was changing too. As he gradually lost count of the island women with whom he made love, he understood Rosemarie a little better and no longer thought of her as promiscuous.

Suddenly he believed that Rosemarie and he could reach a new understanding. He yearned to be reunited with her as never before. Their past misunderstandings washed out of his mind as having been the acts of anxious, frightened children who had not yet acquired insight and experience. He knew he could not have Rosemarie as he wanted her to be, and just wanted her as she was—provided that she accepted him as openly. He even mused that she could work as a hooker while he was away piloting a plane, if only she would greet him with eager warmth when he returned.

Red's new thoughts about Rosemarie made him more determined than ever to escape from Paguli. History was passing him by, the way distant ships and airplanes passed without heeding his signals. He so wanted to stop being a god and become a mortal participant in history again that he would take the toughest job the Army could offer. Yet deliverance failed to come.

His urgent wish to leave began to take the form of intense anxiety over his health. He might die before anyone found him. There was malaria in Paguli, and he believed he was contracting it. He wondered if he had caught syphilis. Was the catch in his side a sign of appendicitis? Why did his left leg sometimes feel numb? When Tata said that some jealous doctor in Parva might be making medicine against him, he did not reply that there was no such thing as witchcraft; he now believed that anything could happen.

By chance he was on the beach when hope of deliverance came suddenly and shatteringly one morning. The date, if he had kept his crude calendar accurately, was March 4, 1944. The sound of the airplane was not faint and high overhead, but low and close to the sea: a labored roaring of engines. A B-17 Fortress was flying near the island and not more than one hundred feet above the sea. Both the inboard of its four engines were in flames. Suddenly it dropped into the sparkling waters with a muffled, hissing sound. Red, feeling paralyzed, waited for it to bounce up again, but it was gone.

He was in the first outrigger which put out from the beach with a half-dozen men paddling furiously. A piece of the B-17's wing or tail floated to the surface, then an empty life vest and a black rubber bag. The outriggers hovered, with all eyes searching below. In bright morning light the water was transparent, the details of the coral bottom clear more than twenty feet below. Someone cried out and pointed down, and then Red saw the unruptured fuselage, wings and engines of the big airplane immobilized on the bottom as lifeless as a butterfly preserved under glass.

Red dove with the Pagulians. He swam down fast, found a hold on the conning of an enclosed gun station and peered through its glass at the broken, vacant-eyed face of a dead gunner. Then he had to let go and return to the surface. Twice more he made it down to the plane before he was overcome with fatigue. There was nothing he could do: all of its occupants were dead.

He hoped that within a few hours search planes sent out to look for the crashed B-17 might see his S O S on the beach and start a rescue operation. But nothing happened, and by afternoon he felt lethargic as he waited on the beach with hot coals to start a signal bonfire.

Despite his effort to stay awake in the afternoon heat, he dozed off. He awakened in a panic that he had slept through the flight of a search plane and saw a group of excited villagers pawing over flotsam which had washed ashore from the wreckage. Feeling dizzy, he made his way to the high-tide mark where people quarreled over bits and pieces of fabric and a life raft. One man was trying to put on the torn, stained sleeve and shoulder patch of a uniform from which someone else had ripped a second lieutenant's gold-colored bar. Senga held up a chain of dog tags, probably meaning only to show them to him. Snatching them away, Red hung them around his neck. He was halfway home when he was overcome by an attack of diarrhea that sent him running into the brush. When he returned to the road he looked at the dog tags:

JAMES COGSWELL
45036790

The symbols showed that Cogswell, whoever he might have been, had had blood type A, like Red's, and had claimed to be of the Protestant faith.

He barely made it home. Bak found him lying on his pallet, drenched with sweat. She brought him a piece of hot taro, which he vomited back. The vomiting made him feel that someone was kicking his ribs. Bak brought Tata, who carried an oddly shaped stone over which he intoned a long abracadabra. Red passed out. When he came to, Bak was trying to force him to drink a hot, bitter brew. He vomited it back, and she brought Tata's small hand mirror so that he could see how ill he was; then, she reasoned, he would hold down the awful vetch and get well. When he swallowed more, however, he fainted again.

After that he had no clear notion of the passage of time or what was happening to him. Once he thought he heard Americans talking. Maybe he was dying, or maybe he had died and was flying like the angel he never had expected to be.

26

Basset still relished confession. Night turned into morning while he talked to me in his room at the Palmer House. Swisher, jealous of our private conversation, scratched at the door every once in a while until Basset ordered him to bed, and a substitute counterintelligence man was brought in to stand guard.

Basset told me all that had happened since he'd been separated from us at Espíritu Santo—everything, that is, except the nature of the Project. His ego, never small, had ballooned. He was not much interested in my experiences, nor in hearing about Red or Goldman, as he once would have been. He dwelt on his loathing of Swisher and the clever ways he outwitted him, but his favorite subject was Rosemarie. Most of all he enjoyed contemplating aloud his fixation about her—why he could not find another woman as substitute.

"I understand this much about the way I feel," he said. "I'm working very hard and I've got to have something to take my mind off the job from time to time. But I admit that why it has to be *her* is puzzling."

When I asked what I would do next, he said that early in the afternoon I'd receive orders at my hotel sending me to Washington. "Rosemarie will go with you. Tell her, as Swisher will too, that she'll get an interesting job in Washington, and Swisher will confirm it. We'll get you two a nice little apartment near mine on N Street. Your railroad tickets are being delivered. I'm flying to California this morning. I'll see Rosemarie and you for a drink after I come back.''

It was 4 A.M. when I returned to my hotel. Rosemarie was not there; after the rally she'd gone to the private club where Mr. Rumplemeyer was staying. I lay awake and wondered what would happen, for scripts such as the one Basset had written for me had a way of being disastrous flops in my experience. Finally I dozed off and was awakened around 10 A.M. by Rosemarie, who burst in yelling, ''Boz! Boz!'' She shook me. ''The most terrible thing just happened! Mr. Rumplemeyer is an enemy spy!''

''My God!'' I said. ''I knew he was awful, but not that terrible!''

''It was so''—She was angry rather than grieved—''em-bar-rassing! The Federal agents busted in on Mr. Rumplemeyer and me. He fainted dead away. Mr. Rumplemeyer, I mean. Then this nice man in charge of the raid—Lieutenant Colonel Swisher is his name—''

''He's a nice man?'' I asked.

''Very,'' answered Rosemarie with conviction. ''Mr. Rumplemeyer came to and began hollering for his lawyer, and Colonel Swisher said he had no civil rights left. Then the Colonel took me into the bathroom and told me about Mr. Rumplemeyer being an enemy spy for the Russians.''

''But the Russians are our allies in this war,'' I said.

''Not the way Colonel Swisher told it, Boz.''

''Does it occur to you, honey, that Swisher could be mistaken?''

''Never!'' She shook her head vehemently. ''There's something about that man makes me know he's *never* mistaken. But do you know the worst thing he told me about Rumplemeyer? That nasty old man had *no intention* of helping me in a movie career. Imagine! And the way I was putting out for him! Colonel Swisher says he has *documents* to prove it.'' She lowered her voice almost to a whisper. ''The Colonel said Rumplemeyer planned to recruit me as a *spy* in his underground network. Oh, my God! I told Colonel Swisher I'd never *think* of such a thing and how much I love our country.''

''I'll bet he liked that.''

''Oh, he did, Boz. He patted me on the head and said, 'God bless America, and God bless patriotic Americans like you.' Isn't that sweet? And he said he's going to see about getting me a job in Washington. Isn't that wonderful? I've always wanted to go to Washington. All of a sudden I'd like a career in government.''

''I thought you practically had one. Rosemarie, I'm going to Washington too. We'll go together. In fact, I understand Swisher is delivering our rail tickets."

"Oh, how nice you're not going back to the Pacific." She gave me a kiss. "Boz, Colonel Swisher asked me what I know about Rodrigo Romanelli. I don't remember anybody by that name. Am I supposed to know him?"

"Yes, honey, apparently so. We'll think up something for you to tell Colonel Swisher about him."

When I got dressed I threw all my decorations into a wastebasket except for the honest ones—the Purple Heart and the Pacific ribbon with three battle stars for Pearl Harbor, Guadalcanal and The Atoll. The gesture made me feel I'd resurrected a bit of integrity.

When we arrived in Washington we were met by Master Sergeant Tully from Basset's office, who conducted us to a small apartment on N Street where we would live. He told me where to report in the Pentagon next day and told Rosemarie it would be a few days before she was to begin work there. I still had no idea what my job would be, but hoped that it would involve photography.

Next day at the Pentagon I found that until I was officially cleared, I had to sit in a little room and kill time as best I could. The only people I had contact with were Tully and Basset's secretary, a plain, fortyish woman named Schermerhorn who had been a geometry teacher before she became a WAC lieutenant. My first day of hanging around the office was long and the second day seemed longer.

In the afternoon Schermerhorn said that General Basset was phoning from the West Coast and wanted to speak to me.

"Boz, how's Rosemarie?" I told him she liked the apartment and looked forward to starting work. "I'll take care of that when I get back," he said, "and I'll have Swisher hurry up your clearance. Meanwhile I've got an assignment for you. It's of a personal nature and has nothing to do with what your official work will be later. But it's an order—top secret. You can't tell Rosemarie about it."

He had telephoned Helen last night and learned that Roger had fallen into serious trouble at the military school, which was about to expel him; she was deeply concerned because he had been doing well scholastically and expulsion would cause him to lose an entire year of academic credit. "Boz, as I remember, you went to military schools."

"I was practically born in one. It's why I've had such a splendid military career."

Basset's thought was that I should intervene with the school authorities and try to patch things up—an effort he could not make himself. "I feel guilty about the way I've treated Helen," he said. I was to phone her and work out the details; Schermerhorn would provide me with travel orders and money.

I liked the sound of Helen Basset's voice: restrained, yet cheerful. She appreciated Pete's thought, but doubted I could help.

"What did Roger do?" I asked her.

"Well—" She sounded bemused. "He climbed up in a tree, and when the head mistress was passing below, he urinated on her."

"What a perfectly marvelous idea," I said. "I thought up many creative ideas in various military schools, but I never thought of that one. Mrs. Basset, your son has an interesting future."

She started to laugh, then turned serious. "It's his present I'm worried about. I can't put him in a decent public school because there are none nearby and—oh, it's too complicated to explain, Lieutenant Boswick. Kind of you, but there's really nothing you can do. I've found somebody to fill in for me at the job tomorrow and I'm going to Roger's school and evaluate the situation."

"I hate to move in," I told her, "but I'm under orders. And if you know General Basset like I know General Basset, you'll understand I have to appear there."

"I understand," she said quickly. "I remember Pete mentioning you in letters from the Pacific. You're—um, yes. Congratulations on making it to Washington—I guess."

"I guess so, Mrs. Basset, but I'm not sure."

We arranged that she would pick me up next day at a railroad station not far from Roger's school. Schermerhorn got me money and orders for indefinite temporary duty in New Jersey, as Basset had prescribed.

Helen was waiting when I got off a local train from Philadelphia early the next afternoon. Her looks took me completely by surprise. For some reason I had expected an older and plainer-looking woman from Basset's description of her during our long talk in Chicago. But she was small, lively, lovely, and looked much too young to be the mother of Roger, now twelve.

"Um," she said, looking up at me quizzically. "You *are* Lieutenant Boswick?"

"Yes. I'm the one who inducted Fiddler into the Army."

"Well," she said, "I bet you could tell me more interesting things than I could tell you, but right now let's concentrate on Roger."

As she drove us toward the school she explained, "The headmaster there now is actually a headmistress. All the faculty men with warm bodies went off to get into the war. The only male left on the faculty is a very nice man who had the foresight to be a homosexual and so he was spared service. He's the instructor in military tactics and the one I find easiest to deal with in problems involving Roger. The headmistress—I can never remember her name—is a very masculine person. His—her girl friend is the blonde who teaches English. Actually, when Roger climbed up in the tree and did that strange thing, he missed the headmistress and hit the blonde. That seems to be what made the headmistress angriest. Or so what's-his-name told me on the phone."

"Poor marksmanship, eh?" I said.

She had kept glancing at me as she drove and talked; and suddenly she said, "I feel it would be best, Lieutenant Boswick, if you sat in the car while I deal with the—uh—authorities. I'll tell Pete how helpful you were. But this thing seems to be out of your experience."

I explained that actually it was right up my alley, that I also had been incarcerated in military school at age ten.

"My God, you too!" Helen exclaimed. "What did it do to you?"

"Horrible things. I'm an absolute mess. You really should get the child out of there."

"I want to!" She spoke with asperity. "I'm going to do it as fast as I can. But where am I to put him for the rest of the school year? The place where I teach is eight miles from the nearest public school and . . ."

We finally agreed that while she dealt with the authorities I would confer with Roger, who had been "confined to quarters." Helen introduced me to him and then went off to see the instructor in military tactics. Roger was a handsome little smartass; within minutes of our meeting I knew him thoroughly because he was just the way I had been at his age. We hit it off at once. I was entertaining him with lies about the war in the Pacific when Helen and the military tactics instructor appeared.

They had negotiated for Roger to stay in school if he apologized to the headmistress—something he had absolutely refused to do. Then I, hoping to help Helen, began to negotiate that point from his side of the bargaining table. I agreed with Roger that apology was ridiculous and that the awful headmistress probably deserved it. "But," I added, "what the heck, Roger, you might as well go along and do it; it's no worse than going to bed when you don't want to."

He accepted reality with reluctant good grace. After he extended his career in that wretched school a bit longer by apologizing, Helen and I drove him and a couple of his pals to the local confectionary where they stuffed themselves with all manner of sweet things.

When we left them at the school, Roger expressed the wish that I would be at his house when he came home to spend the weekend.

"That is an accolade," Helen said after we drove away. "How did you do it?"

"With guile and lying. Roger appreciated my lack of sincerity and moral cant. Basset could have done the same thing easily."

"No," Helen said, "Fiddler could have, but Basset would have blustered and stonewalled the headmistress until she expelled Roger on the spot."

We talked about that strange man Fiddler/Basset. While Helen expressed gratitude for the generous allotment he sent her, she said she had become disenchanted with him.

"I've heard it said a woman can be more moved by protective instinct for a man than by physical passion for him. Certainly I felt protective the day I saw him sitting there looking so vulnerable in the old War Department Building. From his letters and the way he talked at first I could have fallen in love with him. But he did not fall for me, and so—" She shrugged. "Now I'm just waiting till the end of the war to divorce him."

I asked her plans then.

"By that time I'll qualify for public school teaching. I hope to get a job in some decent community where Roger can get a good education and live at home with me."

She accepted my invitation to dinner before I would take a train back to Philadelphia and thence another to Washington. We found a country inn where the food was passable and the warmth of an open fire comforting. Never had I enjoyed talking with anyone as much as Helen; her conversation made Rosemarie seem infantile by comparison.

I asked how she had happened to marry Basset the First.

"Youthful naiveté. Maybe a hunt for a father figure, since I had been orphaned early. Good heavens, I was only seventeen when I met him quite by accident. Seventeen! The headmaster of my girl's school had the quaint idea that if Quaker girls could meet West Point cadets they could promote pacifism and stem the tide toward militarism.

"Every Saturday a chartered bus drove from our school to a rooming house approved by the military in Highland Falls. It was an austere last stop before West Point. Small, stark rooms accommodating any number from two to five girls. A bathroom down the hall to share. One ironing board and a faulty iron to squabble over while we pressed our dresses for our destination. That was Cullum Hall on the reservation where we were dancing partners of cadets who lacked dates for the weekly Saturday night hop. A girl had to be seventeen—and the very day I reached that august age, I applied to go to the next Saturday night dance at the Point.

"Well, I found myself in Cullum Hall without an escort—there was a shortage of one cadet. I tried to remain calm. With my blank dance program dangling from a wrist, I glanced everywhere but toward the dance floor. I was alone, awash in a sea of uniforms. Then a tall uniform with two silver bars on each shoulder spoke to me. It was Pete. He said, 'I see you don't like to dance either.'

"I had so looked forward to dancing, but I lied that I didn't like it. He was years older than I, a captain back for a few weeks of temporary duty at the Point. He said, 'Let's take a walk and I'll show you around.' As we went down the few steps from Cullum Hall, I tripped. One of my too high heels had broken and somehow torn the long dress I'd borrowed. I began to laugh. What else could I do? But Pete was very upset by the accident. He'd found someone young and vulnerable to look out for and organize.

"We were married six weeks later in the Academy chapel. On my wedding night I lost my virginity and became pregnant. A real Victorian experience. I never went back to school until Pete and I separated a couple of years ago."

It was such a sad story. But within minutes Helen had me laughing over something that had happened to her recently in a supermarket.

I was undergoing an unbelievable experience for the first time. I was falling in love. Maybe the hardest things in the world to explain are emotions. In those moments nothing I'd ever heard or read about love seemed true; the only truth was my sudden, stunning perception that one in love cannot bear to be separated even for an instant from the one beloved.

Helen and I lingered talking too long at the inn, and I missed the last train to Philadelphia. She offered to drive me there, but I would not hear of it: she had enough trouble making her gasoline ration stamps last as long as possible.

"Well," she said, "I can't just leave you standing on a railroad platform at ten in the evening with no trains till morning. My place is about thirty miles down the road. You can stay there and try again tomorrow."

When her old Dodge had brought us almost to her house, she said, "I guess I'm being too hard on Basset the Second. It *was* kind of him to send you to help me out."

"He has some ulterior motive," I said.

"Are you sure about that? What could it be?"

I believed that he wanted to keep me away from Rosemarie for as long as possible while he enjoyed her company on N Street. Since I had not yet been cleared for the Project, I doubted that I ever would be and that he planned to send me to combat instead. Yet I would not try to explain this to Helen, for I did not want her to know Rosemarie even existed. My theory of love was involved: I did not miss Rosemarie at all, but dreaded being separated from Helen.

My belief that Basset wanted to keep me away from Washington was borne out when we arrived at Helen's house. There was a telegram under the door sent to me from Washington in her care.

PENDING FURTHER ORDERS FRIDAY YOU WILL
REMAIN HELPFUL TO MRS. BASSET AND ROGER.
BASSET VIA SCHERMERHORN

"This is Wednesday," Helen said. "He *does* have a motive in sending you here. What could it be?"

"Beats me, Helen." We had long since stopped calling each other Lieutenant Boswick and Mrs. Basset. I wanted to stay up longer with her and talk more, but she said she had to go to work early in the morning and showed me to her small spare room. It seemed to me I lay awake all night thinking about her.

I was up early and looking out a window at the bleak, wintry flatlands of New Jersey when she came downstairs. The gray brick buildings of the school, the leafless trees which sounded like skeletons rattling in the winter wind, made me think of a prison.

"Welcome to Siberia," Helen said. "And you thought the tropical Pacific was bad? Thanks for making coffee."

"Just how," I asked her, "do you explain my presence to friends and neighbors?"

"There are no friends, Boz, only a couple of neighbors. I've given up trying to explain anything to anybody around here."

Most of the day, while Helen was at work, I read her books, then bought groceries at the general store nearby and had dinner almost cooked when she came home.

After dinner we played chess and turned on the radio. We had not made a dozen moves on the board, however, when a woman on the radio began to sing "You, You're Driving Me Crazy" in a voice rich as butter. Suddenly, for the first time since my return, I knew I truly was home again in America and immensely happy to be there. I asked Helen to dance, and instantly realized she was the best. The living room was small, but I held her close enough that we could have danced happily in a telephone booth. I bent to kiss her. She responded. I asked her to come to bed with me, but she refused. In the middle of the night, however, she changed her mind. She was wonderful in a shy and gentle way that Rosemarie was not and never could be. I was more in love than ever.

I said, "I love you."

"Don't use loose language," she said. "Go to sleep."

Later I said, "I love you."

"Shut up," she replied.

Next morning I told her I had to talk with her, but she said she had to get to work. Hoping that my fever would subside soon, I vacuumed her cottage twice, read books, and in the afternoon thumbed a ride to a town where I bought a good steak from a friendly butcher without having to use ration stamps. When Helen came home, my feverish condition had not passed.

I told her, "I have to talk with you."

"What is it?" She sounded weary, impatient.

"I love you."

"When's the last time you said that to anyone?"

"Never before like I say it now."

"How old are you?"

"Twenty-five."

"Hello, twenty-five. I'm thirty."

"So what? What has that got to do with the price of eggs?"

"Not much, I will agree, Boz. What is there to talk about?"

"About my being in love with you. It's such a wonderful feeling that I want to tell you all about it. Do you in any way feel the same, Helen?"

"I don't dare let myself. Consider my situation. I've been married twice and flubbed it twice. The name was the same, but the men were not. I just want to take care of my child and work at a good job. I can't take time for men."

There was something frantic about our love-making that night.

In the morning Schermerhorn phoned. She had a flat middle-western voice that sounded incapable of ever conveying a sense of crisis—which could be a good thing. I always think of those flat-toned pioneer women as a calming force when they announced, "The Indians are coming," as if it were, "Twenty more for dinner." Anyhow, Schermerhorn said that the General sent his best to Mrs. Basset and Roger, but could not talk to them because he was tied up in conference. I was to report to the Camp Dix Air Base transportation office at 1700 next afternoon. Hard as I wheedled Schermerhorn, she would only tell me that I was bound for the West Coast.

"Well," I said to Helen, "I appear to have flunked the course. Welcome, Pacific."

The thought of returning to the Pacific made me remember Red and the fact that I never had reached his sister. Her husband answered the phone that evening and put on Jenny, who had a flat, tired voice like Schermerhorn's. I explained that I had no fresh news but simply wanted her to know what a fine soldier Red had been. She started to cry, then stopped when I asked about Red's father.

"I guess," she said, "you know from Red what a difficult man he was—is. I let him know when Red was missing and now he writes angry letters to the War Department every week about him. But Bill and I never see him anymore. He remarried—frankly, Lieutenant Boswick, beneath this family. Now, there's something I'd like to ask you. It's about Red's G.I. insurance. Do you know who's the beneficiary? Who . . ."

Helen drove me to Dix in her venerable Dodge, wept some, kissed me goodbye tenderly, and at the last minute said, "I love you, Boz, I always will."

27

When the C-54 from Dix landed at Hamilton Field, an intelligence officer told me to check into the bachelor officers' quarters. "There's another officer there waiting word from Colonel Swisher—a Major Goldman—"

My reunion with Ira was downright affectionate. It took several drinks at the club bar for us to start to catch up on all that had happened.

"Saw Vera on my way through Honolulu," Goldman told me. "She's going to own the whole damn island of Oahu before long. She's mad at you for kidnapping Rosemarie. Where is Rosemarie, by the way?"

I tried to explain, then admitted, "I have few hard facts about anything anymore. I live in a fantasy of theories."

He had survived the invasion of another atoll and was grateful for my trying to rescue him from unpleasant situations. While accepting my theory of why I apparently was being sent to the far Pacific, he could not figure why Basset had agreed to bring him back to the States.

Swisher arrived at Hamilton, barking and snarling, before Goldman and I had digested breakfast next morning. He took instant dislike to Goldman, saying, "Major, the investigation of you has become heavy. You're headed for Rockpile."

"Sounds like Leavenworth," Goldman said amiably.

"It's worse. You'll stay there till we clear up allegations you're a Soviet spy."

Goldman thought he was kidding. "Would it save time if I confess now?"

"Don't get snotty with me," Swisher said. "You're in serious trouble, Major. It starts with the fact both your parents are Russian Jews. Do you deny it?"

"I gladly affirm it." Goldman stayed cool. "I don't know a better heredity. My people like to cut the balls off Cossacks like you, you son of a bitch."

Swisher made a wrathful sound, and Goldman said, "I don't want to work with you, you bastard. I'm going to phone my friend Basset and tell him I can't work at anything where you're involved." He got to his feet. "Send me back to the Pacific!"

Swisher, uttering whinnying sounds, trotted off. I asked Goldman if he really meant it, and he said he did.

"See you in combat," I said, but it turned out to my intense joy that I was headed instead to the Stateside post code-named Rockpile with Goldman.

We climbed aboard a C-46 laden with freight and flew southeast as the only passengers. In flight Swisher told us that we were being considered, though had not yet been accepted, for a top-secret military project. Just before sunset we passed over a city which Swisher identified reluctantly as Reno. It was after dark when we landed at a small, lighted air base.

Next morning a staff car took us through low rocky hills into a desert where the temperature was above 100. At last the driver stopped and Swisher said, "This is Rockpile."

At first we could not see anything through heat waves and blown sand. Then, in the glare, we made out a tin-roofed building and a few tents. A wasted-looking officer ambled out of a tent and Swisher introduced him as Major Bishop.

"This is Lieutenant Boswick, who may become useful in public relations. This is Major Goldman, a trained engineer. Brief them, Bishop, under Paragraph C, meaning they do not yet have the need to know anything important. Tomorrow we'll move you to Greenturf. So long, Boswick—Goldman. Maybe see you around." A couple of minutes later his car disappeared in a cloud of dust.

"That Swisher is a very sick man," Bishop said. "I don't know why he's mad at you both, but he sent word to Phelps to keep an eye on you, you're suspected of being spies. Phelps arrived here eight days ago to run the enlisted men's guest house.''

"Where is that?" I asked.

"It hasn't been built yet. In fact, we've not yet received our enlisted complement. I wonder where Greenturf is. Phelps is our only WAC, a captain from Washington. In her words, she 'incurred Swisher's wrath.' She lives by herself in that tent over there and cries all night long. I wonder where Greenturf is.''

Goldman asked, "Is it safe for a woman away out here all by herself?"

"Phelps would be safe anywhere," Bishop said. "Wait till you see her. I wish Greenturf would be in some place like Maryland. I know a girl in Baltimore. Do you happen to know if the winters are severe there?"

"I haven't the vaguest idea," Goldman said. "Go ahead and brief us, Bishop."

"There's not much to brief about. Everything is based on something called the need to know. You, Goldman, will be in charge of constructing a weapons range. And you, Boswick, as Public Relations Officer, will be in charge of preventing anybody from knowing anything about it."

"What does the table of organization of this place require a public relations officer to be?" I asked.

"You have no need to know," Bishop said.

"What kind of weapons are we going to test here?" Goldman asked.

"No need to know. First you'll construct an electrified fence twelve miles square."

"Starting where?"

"You have no need to know now. Somebody will tell you later. After you've built the fence, you'll raise a one-hundred-foot steel tower in the exact center of the fenced area."

"What for?"

"Don't ask stupid questions. I wouldn't even mind if Greenturf was in Massachusetts."

I said, "I really have a need to know what rank the public relations officer of this place should have."

"If you can establish that need," Bishop said, "an explanation may be forthcoming. It goes on and on like that. I'm glad I was a lawyer in civilian life. It prepared me to cope with such things as this. At present there are seven officers and three enlisted cooks and bakers here. As a result, no manual labor gets performed. I took over this post three months ago, but I have not yet established my need to know where to start building the fence. It would be pleasant if Green-turf were in Florida.''

Goldman asked, "What have you accomplished in your three months here, Major?"

"Well, let's see. I hired Indians to dig latrines. I think I showed great foresight in having a women's as well as a men's latrine dug at a time when we had no woman here. Otherwise there would have been no place for Phelps to go to the toilet. Oh, yes, and I've established the water supply. They say you can dig down eight miles in this desert and find nothing but brimstone. So I didn't try. You know what I did? I arranged to have water brought in every day by tanker truck from the air base.''

Goldman stared at him. "That was very clever of you."

Bishop smiled wanly. "Thanks, I think so too."

"I feel a need to know where Rosemarie is," I told Basset when he came to Rockpile a month later.

"In Washington," he said. "She's our office receptionist—a civilian, uncleared, and never will be. She enchants everybody but Schermerhorn—even Swisher is enchanted. He has her sex appeal confused with patriotism. I said I might see you on this trip, Boz, and she sent her love."

"How," asked Goldman, "can she be an efficient receptionist if she doesn't know what's going on?"

"I've discovered they make the best," Basset said. "The important thing is that she *thinks* she knows what's going on. She thinks we're running a huge underground spy apparatus and she may become chief Mata Hari in time. The work thrills her to death. There's something else you should know, Boswick. I haven't laid a finger on your wife. Just as the work thrills Rosemarie, I'm constantly thrilled by being within a finger-length of her and not laying it on her."

"She's not my wife," I said. "At this time, General, I'd like to request a promotion."

He wrinkled up his brow. "Why are you always so aggressive, Boswick? I've done everything for you, but still you wheedle for more. I saved you from certain death in combat. I got you a nice cushy Stateside job here. I found an apartment for your wife and gave her a job and have not laid a finger on her. I brought your crony Goldman out of combat and gave him this nice safe spot where you both can sit and play tiddlywinks. When is enough enough? When does enough become too much? Have you no shame? Look at it this way: in this war where practically everybody becomes at least a major and many are generals, it's a distinction to be a second lieutenant. My boy, you should get down on your knees and thank God for what you have instead of always supplicating for more.''

I did not even try to top that.

"The point is," Goldman said, "that it's all so pointless. We're here, but we have nothing important to do. Everything has become downright silly."

"Nonsense," Basset replied. "Now I'll brief you."

Goldman and I, listening intently, sat sweating on cots in our tent while the sun beat down and the hot wind blew sand under the canvas.

"I bring you into this program," Basset said, "because there are jobs you are qualified to perform. Life won't be the same to you after this. It will turn serious and frantic and you'll work like slaves. It won't seem silly to you any more. From now on it will be hard for you to climb topside of those black clouds."

He described the race to build a nuclear bomb, saying that so far it was one of the most extraordinarily well kept secrets of all time because more than one hundred thousand people on the Allied side were involved in it and the enemy did not appear to have an inkling of what we were up to. Apart from a few like Basset himself, most did not know the entire secret—only bits or pieces involving "the need to know" their particular tasks. However, he wanted us to have a view of the entire situation, not because we were old friends, but because he felt we had a sense of history, and we might be used in many helpful ways.

Naturally Goldman and I were amazed and fascinated by the purpose and size of the Project.

Basset told us about that first meeting with top officials in Washington and explained how he had found it best to unify efforts and drive the Project forward until we understood why he had found it necessary to be more like the Warden than even the original Basset himself had been. And yet, hard as he and others strived at the task, it was impossible for him to say or even guess at when the goal would be achieved—if, indeed, it ever were. The many variables of the project resulted inevitably in uncertainty as to its eventual success and led to suspicions and recriminations.

"Now, let me tell you something about anxiety. At present the chances of our working out more than a stalemate in this war are very dim. Everything is in a mess. In the Pacific we can't do better than hop from island to island with the eventual prospect of becoming bogged down in stupid land war against the Japanese in Asia. We cannot attack the Japanese home islands without such fearful casualties that the American people will demand a halt to the effort. In Europe we're way behind the Germans. It's essential to open a new front there, but if that's planned, I have no need to know about it.

"In every respect the Germans are ahead of us. Their navy has developed the schnorkel, which enables a submarine to recharge its batteries without coming to the surface and thus threatens to put our whole antisubmarine campaign out of business. The Luftwaffe has developed jet aircraft that are faster than anything the Allies possess. German scientists have developed long-range rockets that can turn the whole south of England into a desert. In Italy our armies are completely bogged down. In—oh, the hell with it, it's too depressing to think about."

Basset went on to announce that Goldman's first job in the Project would be to direct the construction of a range there in the desert where the bomb could be tested. Even though a bomb had not yet been built, it was a part of Basset's planning to have everything going forward at once so that there would be no hitches or delays later. Actually, he said, *three* bombs must be built. The first must be tested at Rockpile before the others could be counted on to explode. The second would be one to scare the shit out of the enemy. And the third would be the one to make them think we had forty more equally as powerful. The truth was, of course, that it would take at least another year, a few billion dollars and all the resources of the nation to build only those three.

"I have a question," Goldman said. "Is this really a good idea?"

The Warden, looking apoplectic, roared, "You son of a bitch, if Swisher was here I'd have him put his .32 to your head and press the trigger! Get this—and get it straight! *There is no alternative to what we're doing!*" He poured some tepid water into a canteen cup from the Lister bag hanging on the tent pole, took a sip, grimaced, and spat it out. Then, sounding like a dejected Fiddler: "What alternative is there, Ira?"

"Conventional warfare. Stalemate, maybe. The compromises of exhaustion. Why open Pandora's Box? Think of fifty or sixty countries splattering these crazy things around the world."

"We'll keep our secret to ourselves," Basset said firmly.

"You can't keep such secrets. Did anybody keep the secret of gunpowder? What are the effects of such detonations on the atmosphere—on the general health of humans and animals?"

"We don't know yet. It's a risk we have to take."

"Not *have* to take," Goldman said. "You mean a risk you're *going* to take."

The Warden spoke, self-confidence recovered: "You bet we are! We're going to save a million lives with the bomb—including yours. Do you have the courage of your convictions, Goldman? Do you want to back out of the Project? If so, I'll debrief you this minute and send you to some neutral purgatory to spend the rest of the war."

"I don't have convictions," Goldman said. "Only doubts. The sort of doubts I've had all along about some of the ways this war is being fought. But that doesn't mean I'll stop fighting it. The Nazis are mad dogs who must be obliterated. The same applies to the Japanese war party. I'm in this with you till the end and will keep all doubts about *how* things are being done to myself."

"Good! One with doubts about the efficacy of a program usually does the most to improve it. Now I'll tell you what I want done here and what resources I'm providing you. I give you two months to finish the job, not that we'll be able to use it by that time but because I want to use you in another place."

He launched into a quick technical discussion of the testing range requirements, then turned to me.

"Your only talent, Boswick, seems to be with a camera. That and a genial nature that makes people trust you. If your various organs and glands can withstand the punishment you give them I forecast you'll have a successful peacetime career as a confidence man. Meantime I cast you in an unlikely role. Abysmally ignorant though you are of world events and the tides of history, you have some small intuitive instinct for understanding how people act and react. So I'm naming you a historian of the Project. Not, heaven forbid, that you'll ever be allowed to write a sentence about it. You're not literate enough. We have technical experts to do that. Your work will be done with the cameras and film I brought along. I want a picture record of what we're doing, all classified top secret until some future time when the world can see and hear what a miracle we wrought."

As he said "miracle" his voice fell and he gazed into the distance as if he had finally hypnotized himself. Goldman and I glanced at each other, realizing that to all his other desires Basset had added the wish for history to view him favorably.

Bringing me into focus again, he said, "Here at Rockpile, for instance, you should take some pictures of this desert as it is now—"

"I understand," I said. "And later, as it is after Goldman has made the desert bloom, so to speak."

"So to speak." Basset looked at me with intense skepticism. "And certainly you'll be here on that great testing day to record our triumph on film."

Basset planned for Sergeant Tully to be sent from Washington to serve as my assistant since Tully had much training in photography. He would accompany me to the many places around the country where various components of the Project were under development, serving as liaison between Basset and me, and carrying photos and negatives back to Washington for safekeeping.

"The idea being that I personally do not come to Washington?" I asked Basset.

"That being the idea," he said, "until I order it."

When Goldman and I walked to the car which would take Basset back to the air base, I asked him one more question: "What do you hear from Vera?"

He gave me a somewhat startled look. "Nothing. She became obsessed by real estate—so much so that I wonder if she's quit her previous business. Her letters became only talk about mortgages, taxes, the future of property in Waikiki. We stopped corresponding. I think she understands Fiddler is dead."

Life as Basset's traveling photographic historian was not as easy as I'd expected it would be. There were too many so-called geniuses in the Project, each with his own notion of what was important, most displaying resentments that were not readily fathomable to the itinerant historian. Gradually, however, I began to realize that Basset was employing this picture-taking of mine as a subtle form of flattery to the participants which insured their cooperation. I had to admire him for trying to weave together so many disparate strands into one fabric.

As the weeks passed, I became a kind of Flying Dutchman without a haven. I continued to write Helen and telephone her from time to time while Goldman forwarded her letters to me as long as he was at Rockpile. After he finished the range there, he was sent to Boston, next Chicago, and then Tennessee. My affection for Helen never wavered: I was in love with her, I intended to keep it that way, and nothing showed it more than the fact I had no interest in other women. Twice, while on assigned duties in the New York area, I managed to spend a day and night with her. Most important of all, she made me feel she loved me increasingly as well.

I never communicated with Rosemarie and did not care whether I saw her again. So I was jolted, one day early in September while Tully and I were in Dallas, to receive a phone call from Basset, sounding harsh and tired:

"Boswick, get here to Washington fast as you can! It's time you're reunited with Rosemarie."

"But—"

"Get here fast!" The Warden made a barking sound and hung up.

I arrived the following night and went to the N Street apartment where Rosemarie was waiting. She flung herself upon me like a parachutist leaving a burning plane. "Boz! Oh Boz, I've missed you so! Why didn't you ever write me?"

"Well, why didn't you write me?"

"Pete—General Basset, I mean—said you were on an underground mission but didn't dare tell me where. I thought maybe like Berlin, but I remembered you don't speak German."

She wore one of her see-through negligees, looked great, smelled good too. Putting a chair between us in the little living room, I thought hard about Helen.

"Pete—the General—said you were coming in tonight. He'll be away for a couple of days and said I don't even have to go to the office. Boz, I couldn't *wait* for you to get here."

Since my defense always was weak, I decided on offensive action. Sitting down and folding my arms primly, I spoke with severity: "Rosemarie, I've been shocked to hear in the underground that you've been—carrying on with Basset."

"That's not so!" But her gaze bounced away from mine like rain off steel. "I admit I think—thought—he's attractive. Don't you think so too? What's sexier than a certain kind of mustache?"

"I can think of a thousand things."

"But you're not a girl. Anyhow, I love my job, and working with Pete is divine. He never once made a pass at me, but his eyes were always laying hands on me."

"And what were your eyes doing all that while, Rosemarie?"

"Laying hands on him. I admit it. You were gone away and—well, do you realize that a reception desk can be the loneliest outpost in the world? I mean Pete is like the father I never had."

"Are you saying you always wanted an incestuous father?"

"I don't understand what you mean, Boz."

"Skip it. So we have fatherly old General Basset laying hands on you with his eyes only. Then what happened?"

"Friday night I stayed late at the office to study my telephone numbers."

"Your what?"

"My telephone numbers. See, the apparatus has various underground cells with code names. For instance, there's one named Rockpile. Don't ever repeat that because it's top secret—I mean top top secret. Pete wanted me to memorize the numbers and not keep them written down where some German spy might find them. That witchy bitchy Schermerhorn knows them all, and— well—If Pete says to me, 'Get me Rockpile,' I should be able to pick up the phone and— zip, zip, zip, hello Rockpile. See? So I was studying my numbers late at the office because I had nothing else to do—as you know, all of us in the system are forbidden to date anybody. Anyway, Pete comes out of his office and just stands there—"

"His eyes no doubt laying hands on you."

"Frankly, yes. And all of a sudden he goes, 'Rosemarie, would you like me to test you on your telephone numbers?' I was thrilled to death, and when he says, 'Let's have dinner,' I nearly passed out. I mean he never even bought me a cup of coffee before. But then, instead of going to the Mayflower like I thought, he had the driver bring us to his place on N Street—it's in the next block, I guess you've been there."

"No, Rosemarie, I've never been so honored. Then what?"

"We sat down in his living room. Did you know he has a nice little kitchen where he cooks things? I was wearing that green print summer dress I got in Los Angeles, you know the one I mean?"

"The one you can see through that has practically no top?"

"That's the one. I sat on the divan and he sat in a chair and held the list while I did the numbers. He said I was very bright, and then he goes, 'Why are you always flirting with me?' And I said I didn't know I was, I just admired him as about the greatest general our country has. I said, 'What has Ike got that you don't?' and he goes, 'A big army. If you're going to call Eisenhower Ike, you must call Basset Pete.' By that time he's come around the divan I'm sitting on —he has one of those divans you can walk behind—and he leans over looking down at me and I'm looking up at him and start to tingle all over. Would you believe it?"

"Yes, Rosemarie, I would believe it."

"Well, I shouldn't go on."

"Please do if you'd like to. There's little in this life I haven't heard."

"Well, honey, you never heard of anything like this. He gives me a soul kiss. I never had anybody soul kiss me from the top down before. Wow, what a tickling sensation! It's like when you're having your teeth cleaned at the dentist's and the whirling brush slips. There must be a sensitive place in the gums. Want to try it and see what I mean?"

"No, no, no! I just dropped by to say hello. Have to get to a secret underground meeting."

"They meet after *midnight?*" I explained we worked the wildest hours, and she went on about the way Basset played with her nipples while continuing to clean her teeth with his tongue. "I swear they got five inches long, my nipples I mean."

"Okay, okay. So Basset aroused you and then you had intercourse. Now I've got to—"

"Wait!" Rosemarie said. "It didn't happen that way—the way I expected. He had me so horny I thought I'd have to play with myself if he didn't, and then he just walked back to that chair across from me and goes, 'I want to sit here for a while and admire your exquisite beauty.' I thought maybe he couldn't do it. I've found that lots of times generals can't get it up—admirals neither. But Pete didn't have that problem. I mean I could *see* he didn't. He asked me to undress for him slowly. Well, there's nothing new about that. What was new was the way he sat there and admired me so hard, saying the most exciting things about me until I suddenly found myself standing on his coffee table in my birthday suit. And my high heels. I understand about some men and high heel shoes too, but the way he said, 'Those gorgeous long legs of yours demand high heels.' Nobody ever said it to me just like that before. And then he says, 'Come into the kitchen, Rosemarie, and we'll fix some canapés and uncork some champagne.' Well! Boz, have you ever fixed canapés in your birthday suit?"

"Not while I was wearing high heels," I said. "I'm already late for the underground meeting."

"Wait! You haven't heard anything yet."

As she explained events, I indeed had not. Basset had her spread paté on toast cut to precisely silver dollar size, all the time admiring but never touching her. How wonderfully he instructed her in many arts: like, when serving iced champagne, turn the bottle and hold the cork firmly to prevent the pop that always frightened her. He led her

on from there through various courses of food, seminudity and sex
—the most exciting sex she'd ever had, she said, using words to
describe it that Basset must have taught her.

Suddenly I wanted to laugh. Sex can be very funny.

"By that time," Rosemarie said, "it was getting light. All of a
sudden it was Saturday morning."

"Hi, ho," I said, "off to sleep you go. Hope you both enjoyed a
well-deserved rest."

"Until late afternoon. Then it began all over again."

"Oh my! What about Sunday?"

"He came here to my place."

"So then Monday you both went back to the office just as if nothing
had ever happened."

"No, I called in sick and he called in to say he was flying to
Minneapolis. Colonel Swisher volunteered to fly with him, but Pete
said no. Colonel Swisher thought Pete was in his apartment all the
time and not answering the phone because he was so busy with office
papers. Pete bribed the guards with promises of promotion to say he
was hard at work. So on Monday I went back to his place."

"It must have been exhausting—all that running back and forth
between apartments, I mean."

"No, I felt great. I never got so high on sex before—not even with
you because you never had us doing real different things like me
making hors d'oeuvres in my birthday suit. Anyway, the guard
winked at me when he let me in to see Pete, who said I was there to
take dictation. All of a sudden there I am, us both naked on his sofa,
him sitting and me lying face down and ass up across his lap so he
could do anything he wanted—and, oh boy, did he? Oh boy oh boy
oh boy! When I came it was like thunder booming all through me."

"Rosemarie," I finally interrupted, "why are you peddling me all
this pornographic propaganda?"

"Because I think you can do the same for me, Boz, if you'll only
let yourself go the way you used to. I'm just putting you in the
mood."

But for some reason she was not, and I thought the best thing was
to kid her out of it. I said, "I don't think I could ever manage the part
booming through your body like thunder. Where's Basset now?"

"In Minneapolis, I guess. Around noon on Monday his face began
to get all purple like and he complained of chest pains and said he had
to get to Minneapolis."

"When did you go back to work?"

She grinned. "I still have a bad cold. You ought to hear it when I call in to old Schermerhorn. It doesn't matter if she's suspicious because I'm really under Colonel Swisher's charge and he knows I'm above suspicion and Schermerhorn is scared to death of him. So Pete left—and look how nice I've cleaned up our apartment."

Muttering about getting to that meeting, I bolted out of there. It must have been the first time in my life I displayed a trace of integrity and did not yield to temptation. I kept thinking how much I loved Helen.

I ran through the early morning darkness to Scott Circle and then down Sixteenth Street and across Lafayette Square in front of the blacked-out White House. In times past, had I been able to resist Rosemarie, I would have been running in search of a drink to help me try to forget her; but for two months I'd been on the wagon, and I thought it smart to stay there. Was I maybe running in search of maturity? Regardless, I finally came to a port of night drifters—Bassin's, a deli on E Street. There I ate cheesecake and drank coffee until it closed at 4 A.M., when I went across the street to a pigeon-splattered bench in a little park and thought about Helen.

Early morning found me at the Project office in the Pentagon, yet early as it was, Schermerhorn had arrived before me. Looking at me with aversion, she said, "General Basset wants to see you. I called your wife—does she really have a cold?—and she said you'd gone to a meeting—is she really as dense as she sometimes sounds?—but I suppose you've been out drinking all night."

"I suppose so. Is Basset in already?"

"Haven't you heard?" she exclaimed. "He's at Walter Reed."

"Well, I would think so," I said. "Is he in intensive care?"

She looked at me strangely. "It's simply a case of exhaustion."

"Well, I would think so, Lieutenant Schermerhorn."

"He's been working terribly hard and he finally overdid it."

"Well I would think so—"

"Stop saying that! Colonel Swisher is with him. You look awfully seedy and need a shave. Spruce up before you go see the General."

He had a private room which Swisher seemed to want to share by the officious way he hovered at bedside. Stepping in, I said, "You want to see me, General? Gee whiz, you look terrible." He really did. "So gray and wasted."

Swisher let out a scream. "Boss, I'm going to throw him down the stairs right now. You're really looking so much better—"

But Basset, smiling wanly, said, "Let the wretched child stay. He's

too young to have good hospital manners. Now, Eugene, I want you
to do me a favor. Go down to the coffee shop and bring me a chocolate popsicle.''

"Why not have Boswick do it?" countered Swisher.

"Too important. He'd foul up and bring the wrong flavor." As
Swisher trotted out on his mission, Basset said to me, "Let's not
waste any time. Rosemarie has to be removed. I mean it's not even
safe for her to be on the same continent with me. I'd gladly give up
my life for such bliss, but the Project can't afford the loss. My hours
of happiness have got to end. Do you know that because of what I
did the Project was set back five days?"

"At least that's longer bliss than merely a lost weekend. What do
you have in mind?"

"I have it all figured out. Listen, do you know Rosemarie is a
nyphomaniac?"

"Now she is, and you made her that way."

"No I did not! *You* did, Boswick."

While we were quarreling over who had turned Rosemarie into a
nymphomaniac, Swisher hurried in with a chocolate popsicle. Basset
let out a Warden's roar and said he had ordered vanilla. Swisher,
chagrined, trotted out again to fetch the right flavor.

"Quickly now," Basset said. "Rosemarie is never to be cleared
under any circumstance. She's only to *think* she has been. Listen to
the clever way I've thought up to eliminate her."

28

Red, having died, began to live again in a heaven of clean sheets and comfortable pillows. His life ebbed and flowed for a while, and then one day he awakened to the extraordinary fact that a woman's brown eyes were gazing closely into his while her hands ran through his hair. Her skin, unlike Bak's, was white, and he asked who she was.

"Captain Graf, Women's Army Corps. Sergeant Cogswell, you have the most beautiful head of hair I've ever seen on a man."

"I'm not Cogswell, I'm Sergeant Jack. Where am I?"

"Moritanai Army Base Hospital, Sergeant Cogswell. I'm the assistant administrator, and see what a nice private room I've arranged for you to have. Are you homosexual?"

"No, I'm the other kind. My hair's so long because Paguli, the place where I was, didn't have any scissors. Please stop pulling it, Captain Graf."

"It's funny you can remember my name but not your own. I'm not pulling it, Sergeant, I'm stroking it." Graf, neither young nor pretty, tried to compensate for her looks with an air of self-importance. "I've come here this afternoon to cut off your hair. Orders of the administrator, Lieutenant Colonel Jakes. It's nonregulation, being so long. I cut all the hair in the hospital east wing. I save and package the best. I'll save yours and let you look at it whenever you want to. I guess I have a half ton of servicemen's hair by this time, all packaged and catalogued by color and texture. I'm going to sell it when we get to Japan. I hear there's a great market there for hair.''

Red felt badly frightened. At first he was afraid he was merely imagining what was happening, and then he was afraid he was not just imagining. Under Graf's scissors his hair fell away in long shards; she carefully collected every bit, put it in a paper bag, and let him look in a mirror.

''Thank you, Captain,'' he said. ''You did a very good job. Bet you were a hairdresser in civilian life.''

''I certainly was, and a good one. I closed up my shop and joined the Army because there was a shortage of hospital administrators.''

Red's fright grew. Was he the one crazy in this perfectly sane hospital? He said, ''There's just one thing, Captain Graf. I want it straightened out who I am. I'm Staff Sergeant Andrew Jackson Jack, serial number 42003183.''

Graf's expression saddened as she stared at him. ''Sergeant, tell me what day this is.''

He grimaced. ''Frankly, I don't know. See—''

''Sergeant, hold up those dog tags hanging around your neck and read me what it says.''

''I can explain that,'' Red said. ''See—''

Graf, shaking her head, left the room while he began yelling for a doctor. He started out of bed, but was so weak that he had to fall back into it. No doctor appeared that afternoon because Jakes had ordered the entire staff to attend a turkey raffle in the hospital west wing. A refrigerator ship had put into Moritanai with an excess of frozen turkeys and sent several to the hospital; though it was nowhere near Thanksgiving, Jakes had decided it would be good for morale to pretend it was and hold a turkey raffle.

Next day in answer to Red's vociferous demands, Jakes assembled four other physicians at his bedside and began, ''This is Master Sergeant James Cogswell of the Air Corps—'' Red started to shout and was silenced only by Jakes' threat to bind and gag him.

''As I was saying, gentlemen, Cogswell here, serial number 45036790, as those dog tags around his neck do attest, is a gunner with the 419th, which was based here on Moritanai. His B-17 was on a routine mission when it crashed off the island of Runda on—what day was that, Sergeant Cogswell?''

''I'm not quite sure,'' Red said.

''I'm not quite sure, *sir,*'' chided a major.

"Cogswell was the only survivor," Jakes went on. "Not long after he was rescued from a native village down there by a Navy PBY search and rescue plane and transferred here. He was suffering from malaria, amebic dysentery and what I diagnose as brain fever. Young Captain Wilson here is skeptical there's such a thing as brain fever, but I assure you, Wilson, that there is and Cogswell had it. He was left with amnesia, didn't know where he was when he came here, doesn't know what day it is."

"Disoriented," nodded the major.

"Check," said Jakes.

"Could he be malingering?" asked the major.

"Double-check," said Jakes. "I've wondered." Leaning toward Red, he asked loudly, "Cogswell, be honest now, are you malingering?"

"No, sir. Look, this confusion can be cleared up easily. Bring anybody here from the 419th who knew Cogswell and ask 'em am I him."

"We can't do that," Jakes said. "The squadron has been transferred to New Guinea. Can't have men flying all over the place to identify other men. Best we can do is to send for your records, Cogswell, and that has been done."

Captain Wilson spoke up. "Colonel Jakes, would it be a good idea to have this man tell his version of what happened?"

Red explained as briefly as possible.

"Utter fantasy," said the major.

"It is a fantastic tale," Jakes said. "But let's be scrupulously fair about it. I'll put an urgent message through all the way to Hawaii and get the record in case there really is such a person as this Sergeant Jack."

Court was adjourned and all filed out except Wilson, who told Red, "I believe you, friend. It's bound to be cleared up—if not before, then when they send you back to the 419th. I'm supposed to be a doctor, not a lawyer. But a word of advice, and I'd appreciate your keeping it confidential. Just as soon as you can, file a statement on what you said here with the Judge Advocate General's Office. After this, I don't know why you should believe in American medicine, but let's try to believe in American jurisprudence."

Red asked to speak with a representative of the J.A.G., but none came. Two days later Graf asked in her friendliest manner, "Sergeant Cogswell, would you like to look at some of my hair collection?" He replied that all he wanted to look at was a J.A.G. officer.

"Well, I'll tell you frankly," Graf said. "I got this straight from Colonel Jakes, he's tired of you malingering like this. We don't know how you got hold of the name, but the man you claim to be is dead. Come on, Cogswell. . . ."

He spent an entire day writing identical, painstaking letters to Goldman and Boswick at the old company APO address, describing briefly what had happened and giving past details of their associations so that they would know it was indeed Red who was writing. He urged both: *Please get somebody to understand I'm me and still alive.* His letter to Boswick was short-stopped by the hospital censor, who exceeded his authority and returned it to him with the curt admonition to stop writing such insanity. His letter to Goldman got out of Moritanai, but was returned ten days later stamped: ADDRESSEE UNKNOWN.

He longed for Paguli, where he had been accepted as who he wanted to be. What had possessed him to want to return to this institution for the insane called the Army? He yearned for Bak and the others. But most of all he wanted to see Rosemarie and try to set everything straight between them.

Gradually, since he appeared to have no choice, he decided to pretend he was Cogswell until he was returned to the squadron where friends of the dead man could swear that indeed he was not their buddy, the one everybody insisted he was. What was the advantage in being Red Jack anyway? He had never made it to flight school. He felt totally alienated from his family, cut off from all friends, never wanted to return to the horrors of Infantry combat—or, for that matter, to the tedium of garage mechanic in Glenwood. He did not know what had become of Goldman and Boswick or how to get in touch with them. And it seemed impossible that he would ever contact Rosemarie.

Some advantages to being Cogswell began to emerge when his records arrived at the hospital and Red studied them. Jakes and Graf, priding themselves on being good administrators, fumed over the records. "Incomplete, incomplete, incomplete!" Graf grumbled. "It happens all the time. Why don't we get *complete* records?"

Cogswell's looked complete enough to Red; he would have liked to show the records to Wilson, but the captain had been removed from the staff and sent to a field hospital—a real comedown, Graf said. Cogswell had been born the same year as Red in Sandusky, Ohio, and had been a steamfitter in Akron when he entered service. His IQ was lower than Red's, but he had been rated superior in air gunnery school. He listed his next of kin as his grandmother in Marietta, but he sent no allotments to her or anyone else from his pay. Altogether, he seemed to have fared better than Red in service: Air Force gunner, master sergeant. "Son of a gun!" There was no one present to hear Red's words of astonishment. Maybe if he pretended to be Cogswell he could get into pilot training school!

Shortly afterwards, two enlisted men came to the rec room where Red was playing Ping-Pong and took his fingerprints. At the time of his induction as an early draftee, the Army had not fingerprinted its enlisted men unless they were put on special confidential duty, so he was glad to have his on the record when the time came for him to prove he was Jack. For, tempting though it sounded in some ways to be Cogswell, he *was* Red Jack, and he did not want to be anybody else.

When fully recovered and about to be discharged from the hospital, he went to the post Judge Advocate General's office and told a second lieutenant he wished to make a sworn deposition. The Lieutenant, an earnest young man, wrote down every word Red told him about his odd experience; it would take a day to have the statement typed in triplicate, the Lieutenant said, and meanwhile he must be finger-printed. Red said he already had been, but the Lieutenant replied, "Let's do it once more, Sarge."

Upon Red's return the next day, the Lieutenant said, "Tough shit, Sarge, it didn't work. Don't blame you for wanting out of combat and we won't press perjury charges against you. But your fingerprints prove beyond a doubt you are Sergeant James Cogswell."

In panic Red ran half the way to Graf's office, where she patiently explained that the chief thing missing from his records had been his fingerprints. "But now," she said, "we have that all straightened out."

He was sent to the Air Force enlisted men's pool on Moritanai and waited restlessly to be returned to the 419th, where all would be resolved. However, it proved to be not that simple. In August 1944, he went, instead, to Guam, which had been largely secured from the Japanese. Again he found himself in an enlisted men's pool, this time close to a flatland where bulldozers rumbled day and night construct-ing the longest airstrip he had ever seen.

The food was good, the beer plentiful, the duty negligible. Half the night the men played bridge, poker, or blackjack; during most of every day they assembled under large tents by specialists' ratings, carrying their records and whiling away the monotony by talking, smoking, and reading paperback books. Red was in the gunner's tent. By then he had stopped saying he was anyone except Master Sergeant James Cogswell, though acquaintances still usually called him Red.

The men listened to orientation lectures that began, ''You're now in the Twenty-first Bomber Command of the Twentieth Air Force, the best and toughest outfit anywhere in the world. . . .'' In the gunners' section, as among all other specialists, everyone longed to get through his quota of missions—whatever number the Air Force currently made the rotation number on its ever-changing schedules. Then they would be sent back to the bomber training command, the Second Air Force, to safety as a gunnery instructor till the war was over.

Cogswell had flown sixteen combat missions, and so Red had more than thirty to go. He decided to bide his time in applying for pilot training and he took pains never to show fellow enlisted men how eager he was for air combat. It would be the realization of an old and long-frustrated ambition. Until then his military career seemed to him to have been one long fuck-up for reasons beyond his control. But if he completed the prescribed combat missions as a gunner, he'd feel it all had been worthwhile—it would be like Tarzan's longest leap to the farthest tree. However, Red knew he would be unpopular among his fellow soldiers if he appeared gung ho about fighting. For, in this war, the gunners waiting on Guam displayed among themselves a distaste for combat rather different from that of other wars. They often remarked that an air gunner fought in such a cramped position it was a very foul life if you farted a lot—which every good gunner was said to do.

The aft ball turret on a B-29 was a lonely dome equipped with two 50-caliber machine guns where a gunner tracked and tried to shoot down enemy aircraft. His trigger sticks also moved the turret, a metal sphere with a glass porthole, and revolved the gunner with it. Because of the cramped space, it helped if a gunner were small. But above all he must have strong nerves, for in his lonely position he was, of all the crew, the most exposed to enemy antiaircraft fire, attacking planes, and the worst situated in crash landings. There was no good reason for a man to want to be a ball turret gunner, yet thousands did. Some even lived to tell of their frightening experiences.

Red knew he had little chance of realizing his ambition. He was large for a job in which a small man was desirable. And after he explained he had never fired a gun from an airplane—which he must explain since so many lives depended on him—no commander in his right mind would want him.

After the first long strip was completed on Guam, big B-29 Superfortresses began to arrive from the Indo-China Theater and the casuals were taken on conducted tours of the planes and shown their wonders. Plane commanders interviewed casuals to add to their crews or to form new crews. Most commanders wanted to read men's records first, but a few simply came into the tent and looked over the bodies like men buying livestock.

"You!" A tall, thin, dark captain beckoned Red on the very first day of interviews and they sat down facing each other at a small table. "They call you Red? I think redheads bring luck. Do you believe in God?"

Again Red thought that no commander in his right mind would sign him on, so maybe one out of his mind would accept him. "Yes sir, I believe in God," he lied.

"Mmmph. My name is Maybury. Red, do you want a gunner's job or are you here just because you have to be?"

"I want a job, Captain Maybury. I want to be a gunner, but I've got a problem. You won't believe this, sir, but I've never fired a machine gun from an airplane."

"You say you're a Christian." Maybury's hard, gray gaze probed him. "What church?"

"Baptist."

"Mmmph. I presume you know that your Redeemer liveth?" Red thought he might be kidding, but he was not. "I want a crew of good Christian boys, Red. We pray before every takeoff and we pray after every landing. We know we're fighting infidels, and that's all there is to it. How does that strike you?"

"It strikes me fine, Captain Maybury," Red said. "I pray all the time anyway."

"Now what's this about your never firing a machine gun?"

"I'm expert with a 50-caliber on the ground, sir." At last he uttered truth. "But I've never fired one in the air, if you'll please believe me."

"I'll believe whatever a good Christian says. Go ahead and tell me how it happened. I've got days with nothing to do but pick a tail gunner."

Almost an hour later Maybury said, "I believe you, Red. Let's get a Jeep and go to the range."

On the stationary range Maybury pronounced him perfect; on the moving-target range he showed Red how to lead his target.

"The point is, Red, do you want to be Jack or Cogswell? It would be safer for you now to be Jack. If you go back to the J.A.G. often enough you'll eventually find somebody like me who believes every word you say. There are legal beagles in that department who love to fight administrative foul-ups and try to set all sorts of matters straight. Of course it might take the rest of the war, and if you sign on with me you stand a good chance of dying. Our mission here is perfectly obvious. We're going to bomb Japan into little pieces. We're going to kill a lot of people and a lot of us are going to get killed in the process. The plan is to strip down the armaments of the B-29 so we can carry a bigger payload in bombs. The only gunner will be the man in the tail. He's got to be a good man, and if you spend a week on the moving-target range you'll be the best. Pray about it, and let me know in the morning."

Thus it happened that Sergeant James Cogswell became Captain Matthew Maybury's tail gunner. Maybury had named his B-20 *Sword of the Lord,* notable in a command populated with Flying Fortresses bearing such names as *Hot Lips* and *Nellie Mae Not* and *Muff Diver.* Before Maybury had felt a patriotic urge to serve his country, he'd been a Campbellite preacher in Tennessee.

Late in October 1944, *Sword of the Lord* made its first bombing run in a squadron performing a high-altitude attack on Osaka. War at 30,000 feet was, obviously, quite different from combat at sea level. From his turret aft in the heavy-bodied Fortress Red felt as secure as an angel with an unhindered view of eternity. Far below, the northern Pacific blue faded into slate gray seas which died against a dun coastline. Japanese fighters could not rise to such a height and try to intercept the B-29s; Red watched them fluttering as harmlessly as sparrows and did not fire his guns after his initial clearing of them. Osaka looked precisely like the map of it, which somehow seemed surprising. They dropped their bombs and learned later that the attack inflicted scarcely any damage on the big port city.

29

Basset's plan to "eliminate" Rosemarie was novel.

"As we cooks say," he told me, "we want to keep this goody warm by putting it on a back burner. *Reserve,* as we say in our recipes. You will return her to Vera's clinic and have her kept there for me till the war is over."

"That's easy for you to say," I replied, "but suppose she doesn't want to go or stay there?"

"She'll go because it's an order. This is her first underground assignment. At last she will make like Mata Hari. She will go to Vera's after we explain that her job is to keep on the lookout there for the nonexistent Romanian scientist Rodrigo Romanelli. We'll supply her with a full description of the man. I think she'll like the assignment because it will put her back in the old professional grind."

"So all I'm to do is accompany her back and set her up again with Vera?"

"No, you'll just drop her on the way to something else. Your mission is to collect classified information for me on the capabilities of B-29s and airstrips in the Marianas. If all works out, we're going to fly two bombs from one of those fields against Japan."

The Project could have obtained the same information through the Pentagon, but my trip was the excuse Basset used to have me transport Rosemarie back to Hawaii.

Vera was delighted to have Rosemarie return and was no longer angry at me. After she embraced us both as old friends, I spoke privately with her: "I return the child to the orphanage, so to speak. She's just too difficult to keep."

"Too hot to handle?" Vera replied. "She's welcome back. I don't pay as much attention to the practice as I used to, but we're busier than ever. I won't ask how Fiddler is. His letters gradually sounded less like himself till it came over me he no longer exists. I quit writing. So did he. And I won't ask how Basset is because I just don't care. Boz, this real estate dealing I'm into is really fascinating. . . ."

It was what now obsessed her. Ruth had become the managing director, if that is the proper term of the clinic. She'd had a brief but happy reunion with her husband, who had been exonerated of blame in the collision of his ship and had gone back to sea blissfully unaware of his wife's profession. Orvie Snook had been sent back to the mainland where he planned to keep an eye on his unfaithful wife. Lulu, still not admitted to Radcliffe, had not given up hope.

"Spend a last night with Rosemarie if you want to," Vera told me.

"No thanks. She and I stopped being playmates some time ago. I've fallen in love with somebody else and like the idea of being faithful to her."

"Oh?" Vera did not ask whom I loved, and, if she had, I would not have told her. "How odd, Boz, for someone with your tendencies."

Following Basset's orders, I did not mention his obsession with Rosemarie. Secretly I believed he was finished with her and did not intend to see her again; this was merely his way of getting rid of her as easily as possible. I could not imagine what would eventually become of Rosemarie. Many members of her profession turned to some other vice, like Vera to Hawaiian real estate. For the rest, after youth faded, I supposed that many took up a conventional marriage in a conventional suburb. But I wondered if Rosemarie's youth would ever fade.

When I said goodbye, her smile looked wistful. "Boz, I'm sorry things didn't last better for you and me. Finally I understand I am like I am and don't expect to be much different. But I feel like a big disappointment to you."

"No, Rosemarie, you're the best."

"What else am I supposed to do here for the apparatus besides look for Rodrigo Romanelli?"

"That's all. Just keep looking for Rodrigo."

I thought it sad that she should stay there looking for someone who did not exist. Would anything ever seem funny again? It was in this somber mood, as if carrying the weight of the Project on my shoulders, that I arrived at Guam. It seemed to me the war had been going on forever and I could not wait another day for it to be over.

My first morning on Guam, as I left the tent area where transient officers were billeted, I came face to face with Red. My first feeling was of terror, so convinced had I become that he was dead. His own wish at first was to avoid me, so determined was he to fulfill the role of Cogswell. But our pleasure at the reunion overcame our first reactions!

"Red!"

"Boz!"

We hugged each other, laughing, and hugged each other again.

All air traffic had just been grounded for twenty-four hours because a typhoon threatened the Marianas, so Red and I had the whole day and evening to talk. I had a hard decision to make when he asked:

"Did you ever look up Rosemarie? Did she really become a prostitute? It doesn't matter, Boz. I don't care if she is whoring. I still love her and want to see her again."

"I looked her up," I said slowly. "She is a prostitute, Red. She's a very beautiful young woman. Remember that she—like all of us—thinks you're dead. She talks about you with sadness."

Tears came to his eyes. "How will she feel when she hears I'm alive?"

"Very happy. I'm sure of that. If you want to, I think she might be glad to get back together with you. Or give it a try. Now, let me try to help start straightening out this mess about who you are. Let's go to the J.A.G. office together and—"

"No." He shook his head firmly. "Thanks but no thanks, old buddy. I'm making it as Cogswell like I never did in the Army as Jack. I feel a debt—a loyalty—to that kooky preacher who pilots *Sword of the Lord*. He's a good guy. Maybe a little nutty about some things, but aren't we all? The rest of the members of our crew are good guys too. I'm finally among friends again. I don't want to give that up till I've completed my missions."

I argued with him. I'd send a message to Basset, who had the connections to straighten things out; Basset had not tried to help him before, I said, because we'd been informed he was dead. Basset would get him into pilot training school and thus he would realize his long-standing ambition.

Still Red shook his head. "Maybe later, okay. But not now, Boz.

I'm finally doing something important, a thing I like. I'm going to stay with the kooks and complete my missions." He thought for a time. "But there's one favor you can do me. Take a picture of me with that camera you're carrying. I'll get you the use of a darkroom and then I'll autograph a picture for you to give to Rosemarie."

After viewing my prints and selecting one, he said, "I'll sign it 'To Jane from Tarzan.' " But then, hesitating: "That's pretty sappy. I can't spend the rest of my life acting sappy. Boz, do you ever feel you're getting awful *old* while this war goes on? Tarzan is finally dead. I killed him off in Paguli."

He signed the photo of himself which he liked best:

To Rosemarie—
Love always,
Red

By nightfall the typhoon no longer threatened the Marianas. Next morning, while it still was dark, I was up to see *Sword of the Lord* roar down a runway on another attack against the Japanese home islands.

As soon as I landed in Hawaii on my way back to the States, I phoned Rosemarie.

"Honey," she said, "are you sure there's a scientist named Rodrigo Romanelli drifting around somewhere in the Pacific? I've been asking everybody, but nobody ever heard of him. Pete wouldn't kid me about this, would he?"

"Does he ever kid anybody, Rosemarie?"

Eager to see me, she asked me to late breakfast with Vera and her next morning.

When I told them that Red was alive and I'd talked with him, Rosemarie started to weep and Vera asked crossly, "Boz, is it your main purpose in life to make Rosemarie unhappy?"

"But he hasn't," Rosemarie sobbed. "I'm just so damn happy Red's alive!"

At first his picture, with his message, made her ecstatic. Yet then, tearful again: "He wouldn't have written 'Love' if he knew what I— I—how I make a living."

"I let him know, Rosemarie. And he wrote that word on his picture after he knew. He looks forward to seeing you more than anything else in this world."

A while later she said, "I'm going right on making my living, but you can't know how much I want him to come back to me."

When I returned to Washington and told Basset what had happened, he said, "The kid is crazy."

"No, the kid is patriotic—in spite of the fact he has generally fared worse at the hands of friends than from the enemy. He'll let me know when he's completed his missions. Then we can get him back here and straighten out his identity problem."

"You said you told Rosemarie he's alive. How did she take it?"

"Like she does everything—emotionally."

"Damn you for telling her, Boswick. You're always complicating things between her and me. Dammit, I love her more all the time. So much that I must keep her far away in Hawaii."

I did not believe him.

I was tempted to tell him I loved Helen, but that might lead to trouble. Hoping to spend the weekend with her, I said I'd like a few days off.

"No," Basset said. "I'm giving you a nasty assignment. While you were gone, there was a dangerous leak. . . ."

A foreign-born scientist working in the Project had developed humane misgivings about dropping a nuclear bomb on the Japanese or anyone else and confided his worry to Ivory Spence, the noted pacifist whose yacht had been anchored in Pearl Harbor on the day of the attack. Then the scientist, remorseful over his breach of security, had confessed all to Basset. Swisher, having made sure that neither the scientist nor Spence had mentioned the secret program to anyone else, proposed to solve the problem by having both assassinated.

"You dumb bastard," Basset told him, "nobody gives a damn about an atomic physicist, but you can't assassinate a leading pacifist without questions being asked."

"We'll make it look like a car accident," Swisher said.

"Murderer. Spence's death under such circumstances would raise questions that would be carried all the way to Congress. And if there's one place we can't let know about the Project, it's the flannel-mouthed Congress."

Usually pacifists thrived in wartime, but passions for the current war had been kindled so universally among Americans that a proponent of peace could rarely find a convert. Because pacifism was at an all-time ebb and ocean racing had been abandoned for the duration,

Spence had found little to do during the years since Pearl Harbor except make more money—an effort that had caused *Fortune* magazine to rate him currently as the third richest person in the world. Now that Ivory Spence had learned about the atomic bomb project, however, he could visualize a resurgence of pacifism. No matter how few wanted to listen, he was determined to be heard.

Basset, realizing that Ivory must be dealt with, invited him to Washington for discussion. He sat for two hours while Spence berated him and the government for trying to make a bomb which could kill scores of thousands at a single blast.

"This is where you enter the picture," Basset told me. "Spence will be back this afternoon to kill more of my precious time. He has promised not to tell anybody what Bigmouth, the mad scientist, told him about the bomb. Says he's too patriotic an American to squeal about the secret—and I believe him. What he's determined to do is criticize what we're doing—to us, nobody else. Since you're such a good listener and everybody always seems to enjoy pouring it into your ear, I appoint you liaison officer with Ivory Spence."

"This is ridiculous," I said.

"You've said that before," Basset replied. "How often must I point out that this is war."

When Spence appeared, I was surprised at how much he looked like Fiddler in the days when he wore spectacles. Which meant, of course, that he looked like Basset. Their mustaches and a stubbornness around the jaw were so similar that I became bemused at how a fierce atomic warrior and an ardent pacifist could pass as identical twins if they were dressed alike.

Basset, who seemed oblivious to their resemblance, introduced me as his assistant. "Boswick was studying for the Baptist ministry before he entered service."

"Interesting." Spence studied me carefully. "Where were you studying?"

I could not think of a seminary. "Mostly correspondence courses at home, sir."

"Boswick is a vegetarian," Basset said.

"Interesting," Spence said. "Why?"

Basset answered for me: "Meat makes him constipated and gives him pimples. But the most fascinating thing of all about Boswick is that he's a pacifist."

"Then why," asked Spence, "aren't you in a conscientious objectors' camp? Why are you wearing the uniform?"

"You have to put on the uniform," I said, "to learn how bad war really is."

"Furthermore," Basset said, "I've declared him essential, so he can't get out. His protest has taken an interesting form. Do you know, Mr. Spence, that Boswick could sit here a colonel today, but refuses all promotions? It's his way of protesting war to insist on remaining a permanent second lieutenant."

"Remarkable," Spence said. "I admire you, Lieutenant Boswick. You're my kind of man."

"I think so too," Basset said. "That's why I've appointed Boswick here as permanent liaison officer with you. I want you to phrase your protests and criticisms of our program to him and then he in turn will feed them to us and we'll try to do something about them. If that's agreeable with you, sir."

"It's most agreeable. But must this liaison work be done in Washington? Couldn't Boswick come home with me and then communicate my thoughts on how you should change your program?" Basset said that was all right provided communications were classified top secret and carried by courier to Washington. "I have my own airplane," Spence went on. "The government, knowing my sentiments, made some protests about my using fuel, but I fooled 'em. I get my fuel from my private refinery. I have a home in Every, Oklahoma, and one on the coast near San Diego and—well, it doesn't matter. At present I think it would be a nice idea if Boswick and I fly home to Every. . . .

I barely had time to call Helen in New Jersey and tell her I was off on another secret assignment before we were airborne in Spence's large, sumptuously appointed plane. Its stewards were young men studying for the Baptist ministry who served us a vegetable dinner with fruit for dessert.

Although Every, Oklahoma, was the buckle on the Bible Belt, Ivory's home itself was a mansion in a fertile oasis beyond the outskirts of town. In Every, women's underwear could not be displayed in store windows and even a motion picture theater was forbidden. The people who served Ivory on what he called "the ranch" shared most of his repressions, although many ate meat and were not pacifists. All attended services in the chapel Ivory had built, and every Sunday they listened to him preach about the evil of hatred and the need to love others.

For all his preaching about love, Ivory did not show much himself. He explained to me once that he was finished forever with that stupid thing, sexual love: what a bore it was! Although he'd been married three times, he hated women; or maybe he hated women because he'd been married to three of them. Anyway, he did not like to have women around; even the maid work in his houses was performed by young male Seventh Day Adventists who were opposed to the draft. Probably if Ivory had known there was such a thing as homosexuality as well as heterosexuality, he would not have allowed *anyone* around him, but he seemed to be totally uninformed about that.

The sort of love other than sexual, the spiritual kind he preached about, had not taken much hold of him either. There was a remoteness about his manner that held the whole world at bay. His secretaries and business aides never looked him in the eye because he always acted as if they didn't exist, and so they, in turn, liked to pretend he wasn't there. None of this bothered me because our relationship was temporary. I liked him and found him highly intelligent. He understood, for example, the scientific theories and manufacturing problems involved in a nuclear bomb far better than I. The one thing he did not understand was why anyone should want to create such a horrible weapon. Quickly seeing that Basset's description of me as pacifist, Baptist and the like was "rhetoric," as he called it, he required me to take the position of bomb advocate. Then he went to work on my stance, scribbling his thoughts on pads and forming a rambling essay on the dangers of releasing atomic energy.

"Look, Boz," he said at one point, "I don't expect to change life very much, I just want to Ralph Waldo Emerson it." Emerson was his favorite writer, and he always referred to him as if he were a contemporary living down the road in Every. Another time he said, "Just because some people call me eccentric, it doesn't mean that my ideas are."

Once he'd written down his thoughts and organized them to his satisfaction, he was ready to call it quits with me and the Project. It took him about two weeks to complete his arguments and have me type a single copy after which we burned all his notes. I stamped his essay TOP SECRET, put it in a pouch chained to my left wrist, and carried it to Washington aboard his private plane. He was satisfied by this opportunity to express his views; the secret was as safe with him as with Swisher or Basset himself.

I expected that Basset would file the essay in a top-secret drawer and then forget it, but one evening I came upon him in his office carefully reading Ivory's arguments word for word.

After returning from Oklahoma I got a weekend off and went to see Helen. She had moved to Philadelphia, where she had a better job while she continued to take courses toward a degree. She had salvaged Roger from military school forever; he was doing well in public school and was very happy to live at home with Helen. Roger and I had become fast friends. Like many of the young, he intuitively understood matters that his elders never thought to explain to him. He understood that his parents were separated, that Basset's telephone calls were mere formalities, and he approved of my affair with his mother.

Helen's home was the best haven I ever had known. She liked to collect books and trinkets; so did I, but I couldn't collect much in footlockers and barracks bags, which had been the coffers of my estate for several years. After we started a blaze in her small fireplace and opened a bottle of California Burgundy, she asked, "How's my husband?"

"I feel fine."

"I mean my previous husband, what's-his-name."

"As time drags on in its way," I said, "I grow less kindly disposed to General Basset. It's not just that he drives himself and everybody harder and harder. It's not just the glee he displays over refusing to promote me. It's his egomania. He seems to be incapable of one simple kindness, and he isn't interested in anything outside his project."

"How's that mysterious thing going?" Helen asked.

"Well, obviously, I can't say."

"Sorry. I guess what I mean is—are you having any fun in your job?"

"Not the least any more. I've no enthusiasm left. When there are photos to be made, I take them. When a courier is needed, I'm usually the one. When pencils require sharpening, here is Boswick. Enough of that." I turned to her. "I don't think I've told you my future plans. I intend to become a good photographer and marry you."

She sipped her wine and said, "You're already a very good photographer, but you're too impetuous to be a husband. We'd better just stay friends."

"Divorce Basset," I said, "and marry me."

"That's what I mean, my dear Boz. You're too impetuous. I can't divorce that man until the war is over. If I filed now, I'd only cause trouble for him and for myself and—I don't know, maybe for the war effort. It's funny—I still have some fondness for a man I didn't marry —a rogue named Fiddler. But having been married to *two* Bassets is two too many."

"Suppose," I said, "that Basset disappeared and Fiddler came back. Would you make a pitch for him?"

"Oh no, never again. My love life has become so complicated. You see, I've become infatuated with this young chap Boswick. . . ."

In such a happy vein, Helen and I never found our time together long enough.

We weren't alone in resentment toward Basset. Goldman felt the same, he told me when he came to Washington for a conference.

"But he gets things done," Goldman said, "sometimes mainly because so many resent him. Thanks chiefly to his efforts, a major breakthrough in production is imminent. I should be happy about it, but I'm uneasy. The way things are going now both in the Pacific and in Europe, I hope we never need to use the damn thing. But you know how people seem to think it necessary to use something just because it exists. I'm afraid that if we do complete the bomb, it'll be used just because it's *there*. And no thought is being given to the effects of an explosion—except the idea of victory. We simply don't know what the results of an atomic bomb explosion will be."

I agreed with him. "Basset has become totally obsessed with winning the war, and winning it *his* way. It's true of everybody else who's spent years at the Project. It's understandable, but that doesn't make it right."

Basset, in his obsession with his weapon, was increasingly harsh in his criticism of Allied plans and leaders employing conventional warfare. He called them inept or slow—or both. When, for instance, the Germans launched their counteroffensive through the Ardennes in December, 1944, Basset sounded as if Allied defeat in Europe was imminent; after their breakout was contained, he refused to see that Allied victory in Europe was inevitable. The only certain victory, in his opinion, would be gained by using *his* weapon.

His angriest diatribes, however, were against American efforts in the Pacific. He hated the Hero who had lost the Philippines and fled, then returned and was regaining ground there. The day he read in a top-secret report that the Hero and his arch-enemy Cominch for once shared the same opinion and favored attacking Formosa next, Basset galloped angrily about the office like a drunken Cossack seeking a

Jew to slaughter. He found one in Goldman, who happened to be in town for another of those conferences.

"Why?" Basset demanded, thrusting a forefinger at Goldman's surprised face. "Why must we attack Formosa?"

"But we must not," Goldman replied.

"Right!" cried Basset. "Right, right, *right!* Damn, Goldman, if one of these days I don't promote you. They want to take Formosa and use it as a base to invade China."

"Why invade China?" Goldman asked. "That's as dumb as Hitler invading Russia."

"Right! But they say we have to invade China because that's where most of the Japanese Army is and we have to defeat it. They say Chiang Kai-shek has a million troops there to help us. What do you say to that, young Goldman?"

"Bull, sir. Chiang Kai-shek is a corrupt old war lord who won't try to help anything but his own Swiss bank accounts. His army isn't much good, and what there is of it he wants to use against his enemies the Communists."

"Ah yes, but Goldman, the Hero promises to lead an army of five million against the Asiatic hordes of the Japanese Army. What do you say to that?"

"The Asiatic mainland is a military graveyard, sir, reserved for the glorious dreams of tired old Western soldiers. That goes for Formosa too. Next we must invade Okinawa."

"Oh, Goldman, Goldman"—Basset beamed at him—"you're practically a lieutenant colonel already. Why must we go to Okinawa?"

"It will put us on the enemy's interior lines of communication and give us two main advantages. First, it offers better bases than the Marianas for the bombing of Japan. Second, it gives us strategic control of the East China Sea. We have to have that if we're going to do what I want—blockade Japan into surrender while its armies wither on the Asiatic mainland. No ground force invasion of Japan. Absolutely not. Because the Japanese are going to fight for their homes the way I'd die for Flatbush Avenue in Brooklyn."

"Right!" Basset said. "But you're forgetting that neither blockade nor invasion will be necessary once we drop our thing."

Meanwhile, American military leaders saw that high-altitude bombing of Japanese cities was not achieving the necessary results. New tactics were required, and so a new, tough commander was brought in to lead the Twenty-first in low-level area bombing of the cities where Japanese industry was concentrated. He instituted night attacks at such low levels that wind could not be an important factor in scattering light incendiary bombs.

On the night of March 9, 1945, more than three hundred B-29s, taking off from bases on Guam and Tinian, throbbed over Tokyo at altitudes between 4,900 and 9,200 feet and dropped tons of incendiaries and napalm containers. In long hours of horror, nearly a quarter of the buildings in Tokyo were burned to ashes. Japanese records, not made public until after the war, showed that 83,793 persons were killed, 40,918 injured, 1,008,005 made homeless.

Among the Fortresses participating in the giant raid was *Sword of the Lord,* with Red in the tail gunner's slot. A week previously he had written me: "Only three more missions and I'll be ready to have you fix me up with General Basset for a cushy job Stateside. Do you still think I can go to flight school? I'm sure grateful to our former colonel for remembering me. I want to surprise Rosemarie in Hawaii on my way there. I keep wondering what she will say. But first I'd better figure out what *I* am going to say. Maybe just love. No letters ever come to Cogswell. But then old Sgt Jack didn't use to get many letters either. I keep thinking about writing Rosemarie, but every time I sit down to do it I don't know what to say. I thought to change Cogswell's next of kin to her name, but decided not to. Instead I made it you and your Washington address as next of kin, Cousin Boz. . . ."

On March 21 I received notice, as next of kin, that Sergeant James Cogswell was missing in action on March 9. Checking with an officer I knew in Air Force public relations, I heard bad news: "That would have been in the big Tokyo fire raid. We're scrubbing all crews missing in that as dead. After what happened there, we're sure the Japanese didn't take any prisoners."

I was contemplating the news in my cubicle of an office with teary eyes when Basset happened to look in. He demanded to know what was wrong, and I told him. The planes of his face broke, and then he reformed them into a Warden-like expression of anger.

"It needn't have happened to him! If only we could get on with our job faster . . ."

I wrote Rosemarie that Red was missing and that this time we had to be positive he was dead. She wrote back a moving, simple letter that ended:

"I'll never believe Red is dead till I never see him again."

Never had I thought of Rosemarie as prophetic, but on April 1 I received notice that Sergeant James Cogswell was a prisoner of war in Japan. Hotfooting it to my friend in Air Force public relations, I learned that the Japanese had supplied the International Red Cross with a fresh list of prisoners and that Red was indeed among them, along with a few other airmen who must have parachuted safely to the ground in the big Tokyo raid and been captured rather than killed.

Elatedly I danced into Basset's office with the news. His expression turned grave and he said, "Remember, this still is the Army, and today is April Fool's Day."

His reminder made me curb elation, but I still believed that Red, a cat with nine lives in this crazy war, had managed to survive again. He was still in my thoughts next day when I went to see Helen for the weekend. Usually she picked me up from the train in Philadelphia, but that Friday, since she had teaching business in Newark, she met me at Pennsylvania Station there. First off I told her about Red immediately.

"How wonderful!" Helen was as happy as I. "Have you ever told his family he's alive under a different name?"

"I should have, but I didn't. I figure they've already spent Red's insurance money. He told me on Guam that a long time ago he made his folks the beneficiaries after Rosemarie ran out on him."

"Why don't you call his father if you know where he is?"

That, I thought, was a great idea. In the Essex County telephone directory Helen and I found Noah Jack listed and I called.

"This is Noah Jack," a ready voice answered. I started to explain who I was, but he interrupted: "Oh yes, Lieutenant, I suppose you're calling from the War Department. So you people have finally decided to answer my letters about my son." It was impossible to turn him off as he went on angrily: "The trouble with you people—one of the troubles—is that you don't keep the families of servicemen properly informed. That was my first point in my first letter. . . ." It took almost the full time of my nickel before I could wedge in that Red was a prisoner of war.

"Oh?" He paused, digesting the news. "How can you be sure about that?"

Suddenly I was not sure of anything and barked like the Warden: "Well, so we have cause to think, Mr. Jack!"

"All right, all right," he said, "no need to get huffy with me about it. It's terrible the way you military people like to shove us civilians around."

As Helen and I drove toward Philadelphia I felt depressed. "Sometimes," I said, "it seems all I do is try to build bridges between places that no longer exist.'' I reached out to her, and she released a hand from the wheel and took mine. ''Helen, let's always be strong and reasonable enough not to let anything ever pull us apart.''

She squeezed my hand hard and said, ''Nothing ever will.''

30

Basset broke the news with a Warden-like growl on July 1, 1945. Summoning Goldman and other experts along with Swisher and me into his Pentagon office, he announced:

"We now have completed the manufacture of three bombs—a test one and two others far more powerful. It's impossible for us to produce more for some time. If we're going to end the war as quickly as possible, we have to act now with these three. Any questions?"

His manner was so fierce that no one would speak, even if he had a hundred questions.

"In two hours," Basset continued, "everybody here is leaving for Rockpile for the experimental testing of the first bomb. I have such faith it will work that I've already sent the other two on the way to the Marianas by swift cruiser. I've had the pleasure of code-naming those two bombs myself. The first is Little Boy, and the second—even more lethal—is Fat Man. Any questions?"

There was silence.

"As I said, we're leaving in two hours for Rockpile. A plane is waiting for us. If it's possible that any of you monkeys have any loved ones, tell 'em you're going away for a couple of months. After the test at Rockpile, all of you will be going on to the Marianas base we choose for dropping the big ones on Japan. I'll be coming back here. I'd love to go with you, but the Secretary of War wants me to come back to Washington after the test and report to him personally while you're dropping the first big one on Japan. Everybody report back here with travel gear in two hours.''

As we started out, he called me back. "Boswick, I know I'm interrupting your dash for the phone. Know you have a cutie-pie hidden away somewhere you rush off to see at every chance. Who is she?''

"That's none of your goddam business, General Basset.''

He grinned. "Spoken like the good soldier you've never been. I've wondered who she is for some time. Could have had you trailed, your phone conversations tapped—but never did. In case I don't have the chance to talk with you privately at Rockpile, hear and remember this. When you pass through Hawaii on your way to the Marianas, *do not contact Rosemarie*. Tell Goldman the same. Now go make your phone call.''

A new anxiety began to crowd out my other worries. My main concern was no longer just wanting to survive until peace. Now what I wanted above all was that Helen's love for me endure. There was no question about mine lasting for her.

The time we spent together had become the most important thing in my life, and I knew that she felt the same. Separation seemed more cruel to me with each day that passed—and now I had to go back to the Pacific for at least two months more!

After I told her on the telephone, her voice became unsteady. "Take care of yourself, my darling.''

"And you do too. I love you.'' I was close to weeping. "S'long!'' I hung up.

When our group arrived at Rockpile, there were technical problems that drove everyone frantic, and the test of the first atomic bomb was postponed until July 16. My job, with the help of a couple of assistants, was to photograph the testing—not an easy task.

At last the test day arrived. Goldman, Swisher and I waited at our observation post miles off. The bomb exploded with a tremendous bang that stunned, deafened and half-blinded everybody. Swisher began to dance around like a child who had set off the world's biggest firecracker. "Gosh oh golly, Boss!'' It was his new, tiresome oath. "If such a little thing can do *that*,'' he said, surveying the enormous mushroom, "think what we're going to do to Japan!''

Goldman, Swisher, I and the others flew immediately to Tinian in the Marianas while Basset returned to Washington. When we changed planes in Hawaii, I followed Basset's orders and did not call Rosemarie or Vera.

On Tinian Island Little Boy was made ready for the drop. There had been much discussion about the target, in which the dead President's successor, Harry S. Truman, took an active interest, although the Joint Chiefs of Staff were not even consulted. Basset's only stipulation about the target was that it be a city where no American prisoners of war were held. Hiroshima, passed over by the Air Force in its bombings, was favored. Then, after our team arrived on Tinian, intelligence officers informed us that there were, in fact, American prisoners in Hiroshima—at least a dozen, maybe more.

"As far as we can tell," an intelligence colonel said, "there's no major target left in Japan that doesn't have prisoners. They've spread 'em around in every important city. They've made it clear in the messages our communications listeners have picked up that's what has happened. They hope we'll stop bombing all their cities for fear of killing our own men. Of course we've gone right ahead. But an atomic bomb of the force you describe is entirely different. So what do you do?"

Swisher looked guardedly around the conference table. "The Boss has been very specific about this. And gosh oh golly, nobody has been more loyal to him than I, but— well, all we have to do is swear there are no American prisoners in Hiroshima."

"How can you swear to that?" somebody asked.

"Because," Swisher said, "we're involved in a war that threatens the future of civilization. So it's morally responsible to swear to anything that will help win the war."

"But," said the intelligence colonel, "there are documents to prove there are American prisoners in Hiroshima."

"Then call 'em in right now!" Swisher snapped. "Make sure you get every last damn copy. Reclassify them. Give them a special top-secret classification. Bury them so deep in the files that they won't be dug out for generations. Then I can swear to the Boss there are no Americans in Hiroshima."

Thus Hiroshima became the primary target for Little Boy, with Kokura and Nagasaki as alternative targets in the event of unfavorable weather or unanticipated interception. On August 6 the B-29 which carried Little Boy was blessed by a Roman Catholic priest before it took off from Tinian. I, riding in a follow-up B-29, was among the photographers of the enormous mushroom that rose from the bomb's fireball and ascended to 50,000 feet.

"Gosh oh golly," Swisher said after he saw our pictures, "if Little Boy can do that to Hiroshima, think what Fat Man can do to the next target if they don't surrender right away."

There was no surrender immediately after the destruction of Hiroshima, and so, on August 9, the 10,000-pound hydrogen bomb Fat Man, last available weapon in the Project's arsenal, was put aboard a B-29 and sent toward Kokura. The weather was so overcast there, however, that the pilot turned to his alternative target, Nagasaki. I took photos of that explosion, too, from an accompanying plane.

Estimates of the human toll at Hiroshima and Nagasaki varied widely and have not been fully agreed upon to this day. Japanese sources say that about 240,000 persons died from the atomic bombing of the two cities. American estimates of the dead were that 66,000 to 78,000 perished at Hiroshima and 39,000 at Nagasaki.

In Swisher's words: "Gosh oh golly, no matter how many it was, a lot of folks died in those cities, and this should end the war."

And so it did.

"Now," Swisher said, "we've got to get ready to take on the Russians."

We waited on Tinian until we could go to Japan and assess the damage to the destroyed cities. Goldman headed an intelligence team that went to Nagasaki; I was the photographer on the team led by Swisher that went to Hiroshima. I did not want to go—all I wanted to do was return to Helen—but I had no choice. Basset, meantime, stayed in the States and defended the use of the bomb against vociferous critics like Ivory Spence.

Swisher's team arrived at a Military Police camp on the outskirts of Hiroshima on the night of September 12. Next morning all but Swisher began to interview survivors of the blast through interpreters. Swisher did not want to interview anyone for fear that what he heard might disarrange his opinion of what had happened.

I rode by Jeep with Swisher and a Japanese interpreter to the edge of the city. I was left speechless with horror while Swisher became garrulous with awe over what the Project had wrought.

A four-square mile reddish brown scar was all that remained of Hiroshima. Here and there a shell of building or broken wall raised itself above the level of rubble. Many streets were still filled with twisted remnants of autos and bicycles, as they had been left after the great flash of August 6. But the weirdest sight was the rampant growth of weeds and flowers from the ashes. Somehow the bomb had stimulated bluets, morning glories, day lilies to flourish among the ruins and almost hide them in a verdant intertwining.

Our interpreter, a bright young man named Hachiya, said, "If you like, I show you where your G.I.s died."

Swisher jerked up his head and exclaimed, "You're wrong about that! There were no American servicemen in Hiroshima."

Hachiya smiled. "I show you." He gave the driver directions. "There were fourteen American prisoners of war kept in an old Army barracks."

At last we got out of the Jeep and walked down through a jungle of weeds and flowers toward a riverbank. The quiet seemed oppressive as Hachiya led the way.

Pausing, he turned to us and said, "Barracks was here, where you now stand. That is piece of one wall. Nobody knows what happen to bodies. They just disappear like so many Japanese disappear in explosion. One didn't die right away. He had paint, he put his name on wall. I show you."

"No!" Swisher cried. *"This was plotted! There were no American soldiers here!* The Project has enemies who object to our winning a great victory."

Hachiya shrugged and pointed to the broken wall where there was some kind of lettering I could not make out at a distance.

As I stepped closer, Swisher shouted, "Stay here! I'm going to get a bulldozer and have that thing destroyed!" He trotted toward the Jeep and called back to me, *"Boswick, do not take any pictures!"*

The lettering might have been made in red paint that had aged and faded until it was the color of dried blood—almost black. The hand that formed the letters had been tremulous and must have paused often to rest.

S/SGT ANDREW JACKSON JACK
42003183
RED WAS HERE

I visualized him taking a rest to admire his shaky handiwork, then try again since there was plenty of space left on the wall.

Hachiya said to me accusingly, "I thought you wanted to learn the truth here."

"I do," I replied. Then, dashing away my tears, I began to take careful photographs of Red's lettering from different angles.

ME TARZAN!
KING OF AMERICA
GLENWOOD NJ USA

He must have been pleased with his handiwork and rested again. Then:

ROSEMARIE
LOVE

There still was room on the wall for more. I imagined him thinking *Wish I could leave 'em something to remember me by.* Probably he felt that time was running out, so he scrawled hastily:

FRIENDS D
                I
                D
                I
                T

Soon Swisher scurried back with a couple of Japanese workmen, followed by a bulldozer which knocked down the wall and obliterated all trace of its lettering.

"You can never be too careful about a forgery like that," Swisher said. "Now we'll get on with our survey."

31

We came to Hawaii from Japan.

I wanted to hurry on to Helen, but Goldman, Swisher and I had received radioed orders to report to Basset at Fort Derussy. He had been promoted to three stars for his distinguished work with the atomic bomb and had come to Hawaii for a long-postponed vacation. For that purpose the Army had provided him with a sumptuous bungalow amid palm trees at Derussy overlooking the Pacific.

When we filed into his quarters, we found a remarkably changed man. He wore dirty ducks and sneakers and a touristlike sport shirt that revealed his comfortable girth; he was unshaven and his hair was as disorderly as a haystack. But most interesting was how grimly unhappy he looked for one who had just been promoted to lieutenant general.

"Boss, you look great!" Swisher cried. Basset stared at him sourly, and Swisher, with his eye for strange detail, said, "You're not wearing your Academy ring! Did you lose it?"

"No, I just decided not to wear the goddam thing any more." His voice had changed subtly too. "The war's over and there's nothing left to a military career."

"Oh Boss, Boss," Swisher remonstrated, "there's everything to live for. There's the Russians, for one thing. We've got to make more bombs and get ready for the Russians."

"Ah, fuck the Russians," Basset said. "Fuck the bomb, fuck the Army, fuck everything."

Swisher looked close to tears as he turned to Goldman and me: "That's what Alexander the Great said when there seemed no more worlds to conquer. But, Boss, there *are* more worlds for you to conquer and—"

"Eu-gene," Basset said, "I want you to fetch me a chocolate popsicle. They have 'em at the PX. It's about a half mile down the beach. It's a hot day, so don't run. Just take your time."

After Swisher had left, protesting, Basset said, "How are you guys? Help yourselves to Scotch—" He waved his own half-emptied glass. "Boz, I've put you in for first lieutenant. Sorry I took so long about it. Goldman, I put you in for lieutenant colonel."

We thanked him, and I asked how Rosemarie was.

"Haven't seen her yet. I'm sort of building up to her. Sort of husbanding my strength, you might say. Know what I've been doing?"

Suddenly I knew. He sounded like Fiddler!

"I've been swimming and playing checkers with Ivory Spence. He's an interesting creep. Under different circumstances he and I might have gone into the oil business together. His biggest yacht is anchored at the basin. He's on his way to Japan to mourn its atomic bombing. For two cents I'd go with him, that yacht is so damn comfortable. The only trouble he keeps it dry as a bone—nothing but Coke at the bar. Tell me what's new. Tell me what you can't say in front of Swisher."

I told him about Red and showed him the pictures I'd taken.

He got to his feet and walked the full length of the long room. When he returned to us he was weeping. Then he cursed. At last he said, "Tell you what I'm going to do. I'm going to build the greatest war memorial to Red Jack the world has ever seen. Wonder what he'd think of that?"

"He'd be impressed," Goldman said.

"What form should it take?" Basset asked.

"One time," I said, "when Red and I were in the hospital after Guadalcanal, we somehow got to talking about public buildings. He said the greatest building project the government could undertake would be public toilets in every city, town and hamlet."

"That's a good idea," Basset said. "Did you ever have to take a piss in New York? Chicago is worse."

"Boston's worse than either of 'em," Goldman said.

We were projecting a national chain of public toilets as a memorial to Red when Swisher came in with a half-melted chocolate popsicle.

"I ordered vanilla," Basset said. Swisher looked like he was going to cry, but Basset was ruthless. "Go back to the PX, Eugene. Go! Go! Go!" After he'd gone, Basset said to us, "Now let's get off our asses. You can't have a chain of anything as a public memorial. It's got to be a single great big thing like the Lincoln Memorial or the Statue of Liberty."

"I still like Boz's idea of a toilet," Goldman said. "It's so essential —down to earth—and bound to be patronized by tourists. Let's build the biggest, snazziest public toilet in the world with one side for men and the other for women."

"But that will just be the base of the memorial," I said. "It'll be like the pedestal of the Statue of Liberty. On top of it there will be a huge statue of Red wearing Tarzan garb."

"Very good," Basset said. "But we can't have Red just *standing* there. Let's have him riding astride a huge sculpted fighter plane, taking off into the wild blue yonder."

All agreed it was a wonderful idea. But then we began to quarrel over where the statue should be raised. Goldman favored Glenwood, Basset insisted on Washington, while I held out for a beach at Waikiki. In the midst of our arguing Swisher came in and stood, popsicle dripping all over him, and listened to us with the frightened look of one thrown into a den of maddened lions. In his nervousness he gulped down what was left of Basset's popsicle.

Suddenly Goldman thought of something: "Where are we going to get the money for this memorial?"

"That's easy," Basset said. "My good friend Ivory Spence will pay for it. It's the kind of project would appeal to him. I'll bring it up to him today when we go swimming together. What we want now is an architect. Eu-gene, don't just stand there, fetch me an architect!"

"Wh—what did you say, Boss?"

"Get me an *architect!* You bastard, you just ate up my popsicle!"

Swisher, tears streaming down his cheeks, collapsed on a sofa, and Basset said, "I just remembered something else." He shouted, "Orderly!" and grinned at us. "This post provides about six orderlies for a three-star." A sergeant bounded in, and Basset directed him to bring the mail.

"Scarcely a fistful," he said as he took a single envelope from the sergeant. "Eugene, you get none—what's the matter, no friends? I get none, no friends. Goldman, why doesn't your dear old mother in Brooklyn ever write you? Ah ha! Here is a letter for a Lieutenant Bos-vick. It was forwarded from Washington and arrived the same day I did. I've been studying it ever since. Didn't open it, Lieutenant, just *studied* it from the outside. The mysterious thing is that it looks like my wife's handwriting. And it looks like her return address. But it surely cannot be from my dear Helen.''

Swisher said, ''Let me see it, Boss. If Boswick has in any way—''

''Keep your nose out of this, Eu-gene.'' Basset held the letter away from him. ''You want me to send you back for another popsicle?'' Beaming, he handed me the letter. ''Boz, I hope you both will be very happy.''

''You son of a bitch, you've been reading my mail!''

''Boss! I'll—''

''That's it, Eu-gene! Back you go for another popsicle. Vanilla. And run all the way. Go, go, go!'' Swisher went, and Basset said to me, ''Honest, Boz, I never opened that letter. But I never dreamed that you and Helen— She's the finest. Somebody should warn her about you. If I were even slightly worthy of her, I'd make a play, but —well, dammit, I love Rosemarie. Tonight I'm going to call her. But first let's all go down to Ivory's yacht and have a swim. Let's beat it out of here while Eu-gene is gone.''

While he went to get his swim trunks, I opened Helen's letter, written two weeks previously. She reported that she and Roger were well and that she had made plans to divorce Pete so she could marry me. She had told him of her plans and believed the divorce would be amicable. ''Wherever you are, I'm thinking of you. . . . All my love always. . . .''

When Basset returned, I handed him the letter. He read it through and gave it back to me solemnly.

''Thanks, Boz, I've already received the news from her. No problems between Helen and me. You gentlemen might not believe this, but I want to marry Rosemarie. Think it's the only way to tame her. Ring, parson, the works. Does anybody object?''

Goldman and I said that we certainly did not.

Basset went on, ''I won't take you to Ivory's yacht till tomorrow. I'm going down there by myself this afternoon and talk to him about the memorial to Red while you both perform one last mission for me. Go to Rosemarie, both of you, and tell her about Red's death. Show her the pictures. Let the poor girl get it over with—he was dead, not dead—dead, not dead. Enough to drive her out of her mind. Tell her I'm arriving tomorrow. Damn it, here comes Swisher before I can get away to Ivory's.''

Swisher, holding two popsicles, was panting after his run from the

PX. "Here you go, Boss. One vanilla and one chocolate, in case you change your mind."

"Thank you, Eu-gene. That was both thoughtful and intelligent of you." Basset leaned toward him, and gradually a dazed look came over Swisher's face. "Repeat after me, 'I'm so glad the Boss is holding consultations with Ivory Spence.' " Swisher repeated the words, and Basset said, "Now sit down and eat the popsicles before you go to sleep."

As we stepped outside, Goldman said, "I didn't know you could do that any more."

"Neither did I," Basset replied. "Apparently all I have to do is try."

He was driven away in a sedan to the yacht basin and we drove to Vera's.

"He is no longer Basset," Goldman said. "He's become Fiddler again."

I agreed: "I'm just wondering when everybody else will notice it."

We were greeted by a comely young woman we had never seen before, and then Vera appeared.

"Hey," Goldman exclaimed, "you're prettier than ever!" She did look good, but not great enough in my opinion for him to throw his arms around her and start smooching like a high school freshman.

Vera was highly pleased. "You don't look so bad yourself, Ira." She squeezed him hard, looking him over so searchingly that she barely said hello to me. "So lean and tanned—sort of a Semitic Gary Cooper. My goodness, my first client! Hey, Ira, wanna buy a duck?"

"Yes!" And then he said something surprising: "Could I be your last client?"

"That's the nicest thing anybody ever said to me." I thought she was going to cry as, still holding her arms about his waist, she leaned back and continued to gaze at him searchingly. "Not even Fiddler ever said anything so nice. Ira, would you like to design and engineer a model community for me here on Oahu?"

"Yes!" he exclaimed. "I'd give my right arm for something creative to do after all—this nonsense I've been into. A civil engineer can do *anything*. The civil engineer can . . ."

"Oh my God," I said to the receptionist, "is there a young lady named Rosemarie works here?"

"Yes," the receptionist said, "but she's all booked up."

"I want to build this model community on the last parcel of land I bought a couple of days ago," Vera was telling Goldman. "Frankly,

Ira, I have enough money now that I can begin to think of others. Among all the hotels and houses for millionaires I'm going to have built, I want this model low-cost housing project. I've taken so much from the public that I feel it's time I gave something back.''

"Vera, you're offering me the dream and opportunity of a life-time," Goldman said. "Rarely does a civil engineer like me have the chance to . . ."

"Oh my God," I groaned to the receptionist, "when will Rose-marie be free?"

"Why are you men always so impatient?" she replied.

"I like your enthusiasm," Vera was saying to Goldman. "Come on up to my office and let's discuss things in greater detail."

As she and Goldman started up the stairs, she called back to the receptionist to cancel her appointments for the rest of the day.

While waiting for Rosemarie I learned from the receptionist that Ruth had returned with her husband to their home town in the States where, she informed Vera by postcard, she had opened a clinic of her own. Lulu had actually been accepted at Radcliffe under the name of Louella Hale, and had written back that to her great relief she found herself the most experienced, best trained freshman in Cambridge.

When Rosemarie scampered downstairs and flung her arms around me I was, as always, incredulous at how sweet she smelled and how youthfully radiant she looked.

"Have you come to debrief me?" she asked.

"No," I said a trifle sadly, "pleasant though that would be, it will be done by more responsible hands than mine. General Basset is arriving tomorrow and he'll take care of it."

She let out a squeal. "The General is coming *here? Tomorrow?*"

"Yes. He's a three-star general now."

"Oh how *wonderful,* Boz! I've never been so excited in my life! I'll cancel all appointments for the next week. I'm sorry I never found Rodrigo Romanelli before the war was over. I tried, but—'' Her voice trailed off and she looked at me guardedly. "What are you doing here?"

"I have bad news."

"It's about Red?" Her tone was hushed.

"Yes."

"He's dead?"

"Yes. Finally. Irrevocably. I have some pictures. It's not pleasant news, but, well—''

We went to her apartment. She stared for a long time at the photos, and began to weep silently. At last she asked, "Where's the picture of his grave? Where was he buried?"

"Apparently he wasn't, Rosemarie. Or probably it was in a mass grave. I didn't see a single individual grave in Hiroshima."

She stopped crying suddenly. "I thought you had a picture of his grave for you to be so positive about him being dead. I'll tell you something. No grave—no death. Red isn't dead. I know it! He's *alive!* And if we just wait long enough, he'll turn up again."

32

When Basset returned to his quarters from Ivory's *Dove of Peace,* he asked me how Rosemarie had taken the news of Red's death.

"Perfectly. At least that's the way I look at it. She's convinced he's still alive. What better way is there to accept death? No grave —no body. No body—no death. He lives!"

Basset meditated a while. "That's a smarter woman than anybody gives her credit for. I'd like to believe that what she says is absolutely true. And I'd like to believe it as much as she does. Ivory adores the idea of a huge memorial to Red. All I have to do is sell him on its public toilet aspects. Where's Goldman?"

"Designing a model low-cost housing community for Vera."

"What an odd time to start that." I asked what had become of Swisher, and Basset said, "I had an orderly give him his supper and then I sent him to his crib. Want to play chess?"

Next morning he said, "Where *is* that Goldman?"

"I guess he hasn't yet finished designing the model low-cost housing community for Vera."

Basset decided that he and I should go to the *Dove of Peace* for a morning swim; for many days the surf had been so rough that there was satisfactory swimming only in deep water.

"Then I'm going to rest this afternoon," he said. "I want you to bring Rosemarie here about four o'clock. I've had orders cut for you, Goldman and Swisher to leave on a seven o'clock flight back to

Washington. I'll stay here another month while I try to figure out some new employment."

Before we could get away to the yacht basin, Swisher joined us and insisted on going too. "I know you must be right, Boss, to hold consultations with that filthy pacifist Ivory Spence, but it seems to me you ought to be getting more rest." He begged to remain with him in Hawaii, but Basset said absolutely not.

The *Dove of Peace,* with its crew of clean-limbed, white, young Christians, was still a thing of beauty. Ivory greeted me warmly and said "the people" would provide me with trunks if I wanted to swim. Swisher said he did not want to swim because it was too deep there to touch bottom.

I put on trunks and went toward the bow of the big yacht. In the glare of morning sun reflected off the Pacific I saw what appeared to be two Bassets—or was it two Spences? I knew, of course, that they looked very much alike, but both, wearing purple swimming trunks, appeared to be identical twins. In fact, the only way to tell them apart was that Spence wore glasses. In order to swim, however, he had taken off his glasses and put them on a hatch.

Swisher, taking one of the twins by an elbow, said, "Please be careful, Boss—"

"That's Spence," the other twin said. "Basset is over here, Eugeney. You're even cloudier than usual today." Balancing himself precariously on the rail, he yelled. "Last one in is a rotten egg!" and took a belly-flop dive.

Ivory smiled grimly. "By Jove, haven't heard that challenge since I was ten." He held his nose and jumped.

Swisher and I looked over the rail as one of them surfaced. "Boss!" Swisher cried in relief.

"I'm not your boss, Colonel Swisher. Where is General Basset?"

Swisher screamed as I dived. I finally found the body with a foot caught in the anchor chain; most of the crew had also dived in, and several of us got the body to the surface and to the deck. A couple of experts at artificial respiration went to work on Basset while Swisher wrung his hands and wailed.

Turning suddenly, I came face to face—not with Spence, not with Basset, but with a very live Morton Fiddler, who was bellowing, "Oh, try to save my good friend General Basset!"

"Why would you want to try a thing like this again?" I demanded.

"Where are my glasses?" he howled. "I can't find my glasses!"

"Here they are, Mr. Spence." A crewman handed them to him.

In the confusion, Fiddler and I could speak freely. "What are you going to do if they bring Spence to life?" I asked him.

"Say I was only kidding. Boz, I'm doing this because I want to look at things from a different angle. A few billion dollars helps you look at things from a different angle. And besides that, I think I can get away with it." He shoved at Swisher, who was jumping up and down in agony over the failure to revive the Boss. "Save my friend the General!" he cried. "*Save* him!"

But the body lying on the deck could not be revived. General Basset was dead. Morton Fiddler survived in the guise of Ivory Spence. I, feeling numbed, and a grief-stricken Swisher identified the body as that of Lieutenant General Charles Peter Basset. Ivory's personal secretary, remarking how much the two had looked alike, said that if one had to die, thank God it had not been the noble Mr. Spence.

"Yes, yes, yes," agreed the new Ivory Spence. "Break out the Bibles. Find appropriate scriptural quotations, young men. Let us hold prayers for the late General Basset!"

Swisher took charge of arrangements zealously. The body was placed under a military guard of honor in a Honolulu mortuary while newsreel cameras whirred and servicemen, under the threat of severe reprimand if they failed to obey, were herded past the catafalque in dutiful mourning.

The new Spence asked me in one of his frequent asides, "How can we tell Rosemarie? The dear girl may slit her wrists in her grief over my—I mean his—passing. What has become of Goldman? Couldn't he be useful at a time like this?"

I summoned Goldman from his work with Vera on the housing project. He acted dazed, and Vera was indignant over the interruption to their planning operations. I decided it was not safe to tell them the true story about Fiddler/Basset/Spence after Goldman, sounding totally unlike the keen mind that had forecast the attack on Pearl Harbor, chirped to me, "It's surprising how much Spence looks like Basset."

However, I took a chance on Rosemarie, who became hysterical upon learning that her beloved commander had died. "General Basset has risen again," I told her.

She quieted down at once. "Like in the Second Coming?"

"Just about. I mean even more miraculously. I must swear you to secrecy."

She swore, and late that night I brought her together with Spence under a palm tree at Derussy. They kissed, and Spence said, "Come underground with me, honey. I'm sorry about this, but at least we'll go as billionaires."

"That's all right," Rosemarie said. "There's nothing I won't do for my country. We can float around on his—your—yacht till Red shows up again."

Shortly before Swisher, Goldman and I left to accompany Basset's body back to Washington, Ivory Spence's devout secretary was shocked to learn that his employer intended to take a beautiful young war widow named Rosemarie Jack on a cruise all the way around the Hawaiian Islands before sailing on to Japan. But then the secretary was appeased by the fact that he, as an ordained clergyman, was asked to join Mrs. Jack and Mr. Spence in holy matrimony on board the *Dove of Peace*. Fiddler/Spence had persuaded Rosemarie that his vast fortune would keep her clear of bigamy charges the next time Red showed up.

Goldman, once he shook off the mentally numbing effects of working with Vera on her low-cost housing project, divined what had happened—and I confirmed the secret. He and I delayed departure of the body long enough to attend the marriage ceremony and toast the bride in an excellent champagne which rendered Rosemarie so forgetful she had become the wife of one of the world's richest men that she kept calling him Pete.

Helen and Roger were waiting in Washington when we arrived. Immediately I got her aside and explained what had happened. Curbing her amusement, she said, "I'll always maintain Fiddler was—is —a kind and thoughtful man. Look how he's just saved me the inconvenience and expense of divorce proceedings. I'll have to try awful hard not to giggle during the funeral."

"Be sad for Ivory Spence," I suggested. "He was a sweet guy who had the misfortune to get a foot caught in an anchor chain. And I wish you'd speak to Roger. He's been going around grinning ever since his father's body arrived in Washington."

No pacifist was ever laid to rest in Arlington National Cemetery with such military pomp. Afterwards, no widow was ever more thoroughly consoled than Helen.

Goldman was eager to be discharged and hasten back to Hawaii to finish plans for the low-cost housing project. It was built, and to this day remains a model of the ideal that all people should, regardless of income, lead a decent life. Then Goldman went on to plan and direct the construction of dozens of hotels and apartment houses on Oahu property which was owned by his wealthy wife Vera. The story circulated was that Vera had inherited her wealth, and all agreed that the new buildings were making her even richer.

Naturally the activities of the billionaire pacifist and his beautiful wife Rosemarie enchanted the world. Every major newspaper and radio station covered their efforts in the creation of a memorial to her first husband, universally described as one of the great heroes of World War II. That the memorial was a huge public toilet caused intense opposition among a people that generally hated to admit the necessity of elimination. However, the architectural planners of Washington, D.C., rejected the memorial on other grounds: the planners scorned the projected figure of Red dressed as Tarzan astride an airplane as poor taste. The town fathers of Glenwood, on the other hand, liked the symbolic art proposed yet spurned the toilets.

Ivory finally had to offer to buy land and build his memorial wherever it would be accepted. After his idea was disdained everywhere else, he turned to the remote island of Runda in the far-off New Hebrides. Encouraged by the delight of people in a village called Paguli, Ivory hired craftsmen and brought them in by boat to raise the controversial memorial to Red Jack.

Helen and I read about the event in a newspaper almost eight months after the birth of our first son. We had lost touch with our wealthy and famous friends, though we always enjoyed hearing about them. Both Helen and I were busy and happy, she as a teacher and I as a photographer—at first for a newspaper and then with a national magazine.

The very day we read about Red's memorial on Runda, an event far more exciting to us occurred at home. We had named our son Andrew Jack Boswick and gradually strange things began to happen. Andy Jack's eyes turned green. The fuzz on his head became red hair. His crying sounded like an infant Tarzan. But the strangest thing happened on the day we read about completion of the memorial to Red on Runda.

That afternoon I brought home one of Andy Jack's first toys, a little rubber airplane. The instant he saw it, his green eyes lighted, he let out a Tarzan yell, grabbed the airplane from me, and uttered his first word: "Zooom!"